W9-CXO-091

withdrawn

East Berlin Library
East Berlin, Conn.

MIRROR,
MIRROR

NOEL B. GERSON

MIRROR, MIRROR

William Morrow and Company, Inc. New York

19 70

Copyright © 1970 by Noel B. Gerson

All rights reserved. No part of this book may be reproduced or utilized in any form or by any means, electronic or mechanical, including photocopying, recording or by any information storage and retrieval system, without permission in writing from the Publisher. Inquiries should be addressed to William Morrow and Company, Inc., 105 Madison Ave., New York, N.Y. 10016.

Printed in the United States of America.

Library of Congress Catalog Card Number 75–96300

For Edwin J. Harragan

To believe that beauty is its own raison d'être is to be guilty
of a corrupt and corrupting hedonism that, insofar as it indulges
vanity, warps integrity and destroys initiative. He who claims he
holds, with Michelangelo, that beauty is a catharsis of superfluities,
fails to recognize the artist's insistence that this purgation is a
dynamism dependent upon the purity of thought and purpose that
create, develop and shape the metamorphosis of the mundane
into the beauty that frees the soul. Since truth alone is the essence
of beauty, it becomes self-evident that beauty cannot exist without
freedom of conscience, freely expressed.

————William Godwin, 1830

PART
ONE

"That girl is perfect. A real beauty." Ian MacDonald, who rarely raised his voice, had to shout in order to make himself heard above the uproar in the dressing room closed off at the end of the Better Dresses department of Schwartzman-Burns, one of the few New York department stores with a genuine elite standing.

Paul Howell glanced at him, lifted an eyebrow and said nothing. All of the eight girls who, in varying stages of undress, were making up, trying on costumes or frantically searching for the right shoes and accessories, were on the roster of the Howell Model Agency, and Paul instinctively dealt cautiously with a client as important as MacDonald, the owner of a large chain of mass-market department stores.

But the truth of the matter was that he disliked MacDonald. The man had no connection with Schwartzman-Burns, yet he had insinuated himself into the dressing room with the quiet authority of one who owned the place. It wasn't genteel brashness, however, that Paul found offensive; the man was downright ugly— which wasn't his fault and in all fairness shouldn't have been held against him. But Paul rationalized his feelings: himself a highly successful model before and since he had opened his agency twelve years earlier, he had reached the top in a highly competitive business because of his ability to recognize, appreciate and develop beauty as a commodity. MacDonald was endowed with the colossal self-confidence of the very short, middle-aged man who had made himself wealthy and powerful. His nose was a hooked caricature Goebbels would have loved, his pale eyes were piercing behind thick, steel-rimmed glasses and his hair, what was left of it, was the carrot shade of red that even the most patriotic of Scotsmen ridiculed in their fellow-countrymen.

"Look at her, Howell! She's lovely." MacDonald gestured imperiously with a sinewy, manicured hand.

Obeying the order, Paul decided that what he really hated about the man was his arrogance, but had to admit that MacDonald showed good taste. Marni Kendall had been in ever-increasing demand since she had come to him two years ago, at the age of twenty-one, and he hoped he soon could raise her fee from the standard sixty dollars an hour paid to first-class models to the one hundred and up that the handful of stars commanded. He felt guilty about Marni, he knew. Mutual friends had insisted she visit his office when she finished her junior year at Wellesley, and immediately he had seen her as something more than another pretty honey blond with green eyes and a slender figure. It wouldn't be long before his judgment and guidance paid enormous dividends; but he knew it grieved her that she hadn't finished school, and he blamed himself, which was absurd. No one had forced her to become one of the highest paid young women of her generation in all the world.

"She's very attractive, Mr. MacDonald," he said politely.

Marni, oblivious of their interest or the commotion around her, finished applying lashes to her eyelids with professional speed and competence, and, rising from her rickety gilt chair, backed off to observe the effect in a lighted mirror. Though clad only in a skimpy bra, panties and a very short half-slip, she, like her colleagues, felt no self-consciousness because of her near-nudity. She collided with a dress designer's nervous assistant, gently pushed aside a chattering young man who was trying to decide which shoulder bag another model should carry with a camel's-hair pantsuit and studied her reflection intently.

"She looks as though her beauty might have some depth," MacDonald said. "I can't help wondering if she has character behind that exquisite face."

Paul stiffened and bit back an angry retort. It was against every unwritten rule of the industry employing models to comment, in personal terms, on a girl's appearance. She was expected to be very tall and almost painfully thin, so she could show off clothes to good advantage before the cameras, which added weight. And it was taken for granted that she was well-proportioned. Under no circumstances was she the legitimate object of nonprofessional discussion by those with whom she did business. "I know nothing about her character," Paul said.

MacDonald darted a glance at him, and it wasn't necessary to speak. His look indicated the strong suspicion that the head of the Howell Agency, although tall, rugged and masculine, was a homosexual.

"Marni!" A young woman in thigh-high boots and a matching cape and microskirted dress that looked as though they had been made from a patchwork quilt dashed into the dressing room. She was breathless, her short-cut hair was windblown and she was brandishing, in triumph, a flimsy contraption of black nylon that Paul immediately identified as a backless bra. "I searched all over the apartment for it!"

Marni snatched the garment. "Where was it, Rosalie?"

"You'll kill me for this, but I'd put it on my dummy."

"Rosalie, you're impossible!" Marni turned to another model, who was removing her own bra at the insistence of an overdressed man in Edwardian attire who was telling her that his creations were intended to be worn without undergarments. "Beth, did you hear that? Never take an apartment with a kooky designer. They'll rob you blind."

The Edwardian sniffed audibly.

Paul's smile was caused more by the interruption than his appreciation of the scene. "It's wild in here. Let's get out to the showroom." He took MacDonald's arm and started to guide him past a brunette model with a waist-long fall who was struggling into some glitter pantyhose.

"I'd like to meet her," MacDonald protested, blemishes appearing on his face as the color rose in his cheeks.

"Not now," Paul replied vaguely. "Louis Burns is a nut for punctuality, and the show is scheduled to start in ten minutes." He half-pulled his companion into the spacious ivory and gold opulence of the Better Dresses showroom.

Here the atmosphere was animated but genteel. Four hundred invited guests, the overwhelming majority of them women, were crowded into the room for the quarterly after-hours fashion show that was one of the most successful standard events at Schwartzman-Burns. Gilt chairs were arranged on both sides of a carpeted runway that had been erected down the length of the room, and the front rows were already filled with stylishly dressed ladies— from girls in their late teens to equally trim grandmothers with white hair, all equipped with order pads and pencils thoughtfully provided by the management.

Most guests had not yet taken seats, however, preferring to stand in clusters, the women drinking martinis, Scotch or sherry and nibbling low-calorie snacks as they chattered with the well-bred enthusiasm of those who were born wealthy, or the elegant imitation achieved by the beautiful people who were social climbing. The husbands, whatever their class, were morose, in the main, and concentrated on Schwartzman-Burns liquor.

There was a healthy sprinkling of business rivals, too. Buyers from the more expensive departments of Saks Fifth Avenue, Bergdorf-Goodman and Bonwit Teller were on hand, as were a few designers whose products were not represented in the show, chic women and even more elegantly attired men, all of them at home with the social as well as financial equals whose love of changing styles gave them a living unparalleled in the history of dressmaking.

Paul tried to estimate how much money was represented in the clothing and grooming of the guests, but quickly abandoned the attempt. New governments had been launched on less than the furs, short-skirted dresses and pantsuits of the ladies had cost, and even the men, in their tailor-made suits, shirts and shoes, their razor-cut hair and imported colognes, had poured vast sums into the maintenance of an appearance for its own sake.

Ian MacDonald, Paul noted, did not feel at home in this gathering of the elite, real and self-styled. The president of Clothco, a corporation that owned and operated thirty-two profitable department stores in every major American city, New York excepted, was unrecognized and ignored. Nor would anyone in this crowd who learned his identity be impressed, a fact he apparently realized. Hostility seemed to ooze from him, Paul thought, but he probably didn't know his suit was a trifle too sharply tailored, his haircut almost too precise, his shirt a shade too elegant, making him anathema to people who worshiped at the cult of the casual.

Someone leaning against a post at the far side of the room was waving, however, and Paul saw Louis Burns talking to a woman who was hidden by the post. It infuriated him that the urbane, silver-haired Louis, a third-generation Fifth Avenue merchant with an international business reputation and a list of friends that included most of the *Social Register* and the inhabitants of the beautiful people's newest discotheques, should be going out of his way to welcome someone as gross as MacDonald. He supposed it did

7 :

Louis no harm, and it certainly cost him nothing, to exert himself a bit for someone who was a power in the same business.

"I think Louis wants to say hello," he said.

MacDonald waved to Burns, then glanced briefly at Paul, who realized the man seemed incapable of looking at anyone for more than an instant before averting his gaze. "You know him pretty well, Howell?"

"My wife is related to him." Paul had no intention of elaborating.

At that moment he saw that the woman with Louis was Barbara, and caught his breath, but she seemed under control. When she was sober, her makeup still looked professional, and she was able to arrange her platinum-blond hair in a neat, high-swept style. Her mink coat, although not as new as some in the room, was in the same class. She still followed her custom of wearing only black to events like this, and he had to admit that her legs beneath her miniskirt and what could be seen of her body beneath a semitransparent blouse looked good. At thirty-five, when she was on the beam, Barb could still hold her own with anybody.

Burns called an effusive greeting to MacDonald, then said, "Ian, there's someone here who says she's never met you. Mrs. Howell, my colleague, Ian MacDonald."

Barbara extended her hand and gave him her warmest smile.

"I'd know this lady anywhere. You did the Exotique perfume ad with Howell here."

"Imagine anyone remembering that, after all these years," Barbara murmured.

"It doesn't take much imagination," MacDonald replied with a laugh that sounded unintentionally unpleasant. "They still use it in all their posters, everything, and we sell it at the counters in every one of my stores."

"Well, it was a long time ago, and seems longer." She had not acknowledged her husband's presence.

Paul saw that Louis was embarrassed, and for his sake made an effort. "I didn't expect you to turn up, Barb." There was nothing in his attitude to indicate they hadn't spoken in almost a week.

Her manner was calmly domestic, too. "Mama dropped over this afternoon, and I persuaded her to stay with the kids, so I didn't have to get a sitter. She'll stay all evening, if we like."

Paul told himself he should have known: she always dropped her grievances, real or imagined, when she wanted a night on the town.

MacDonald intervened swiftly. "Maybe we could all have dinner together."

"Another night, thanks." Aware that MacDonald was thinking of Marni, Paul cut in before Barbara could accept. "I'm afraid we have something planned for tonight."

His wife's blue eyes widened, but she had the sense to remain silent, and it was a relief that she didn't contradict him.

MacDonald handled the rebuff with greater finesse than Paul had given him credit for possessing. "I'm crushed, but since your husband is probably going backstage again, maybe you'll ease my disappointment by sitting through the show with me."

"I'd love to," Barbara Howell said, and looked as though she meant it.

"Louis?"

"As the nominal impresario of this extravaganza, I'm too restless to sit, Ian. What will you drink before we start? We stop serving when the show starts."

"I don't drink, thanks. One of my lesser vices."

Paul noticed that MacDonald, in addition to his other defects, had yellowing teeth. The man gave him the creeps, and he wondered how Barbara could be polite to him. They were chatting like old friends as they wandered toward seats near the runway.

Watching her, Paul had to concede that she had not only kept her figure, but was still beautiful. She was 120, up only 10 pounds after a decade of retirement and the birth of two children, which was pretty good.

"Relax," Louis Burns told him softly, steering him toward the dressing room. "Barbara is always okay when she comes into the store."

"Sure. She has to play the great lady. Can't forget she owns a chunk of stock in the place."

"It's her pride, Paul. It may feel like a long time to her, but it wasn't so long ago she was killing them up on that runway, and you'd be surprised how many of the customers remember her."

"I'm familiar with the situation," Paul said dryly. "Every top model faces it when she retires from the business, even those who have inner resources to fall back on. The all-American princesses. Our only royalty, now that the film actresses have had it. And then, overnight, the strobe lights start flashing on somebody else. It's very touching, and I think I might cry."

They were circling around the edge of the big room, away from the crowd, and Burns put a hand on his arm. "What's eating you, Paul?"

"Sorry, Louis. I didn't mean to take it out on you. Damned inconsiderate of me, with all you have riding on this show."

"This week we'll have lunch together, just the two of us. To talk about you and Barbara."

"What's there to talk about? Besides, it isn't Barb who's bugging me particularly. That MacDonald character gets under my fingernails."

"There's no corporation in the business more influential than Clothco. Last year they did a gross—"

"Spare me, Louis. As far as I'm concerned they could run the finest stores in the country, which they don't. It wouldn't make MacDonald less of a slime. You heard that attempt to set up something for dinner tonight. He's slobbering over one of my girls."

"How long have you been running your agency now? Ten years—"

"Twelve."

"You should be used to it. He isn't the first to be drawn to a pretty girl whose business it is to look attractive. And he won't be the last."

"He makes me feel like a pimp, and I don't know why. It must be a clash of chromosomes or something, but my flesh starts to crawl whenever that guy gets within ten feet." Paul paused at the dressing room entrance. "Coming in?"

"No, we start in three minutes, and I've got to check on a few things out here."

Paul nodded and pushed his way inside. The dressing room bedlam was quieter now, but more intense, and the tension was thick. The models, dressed in their opening outfits; stood in line, almost immobile except for the cigarettes they were smoking, while designers' assistants and the Schwartzman-Burns fashion show corps fussed over them. Shoulder bags, bracelets and gloves were being adjusted, last-second repairs were being made to lipstick, mascara and eye shadow, and one red-faced helper whose gestures marked him as a homosexual was kneeling beside one of the girls, tugging up her stockings in an attempt to smooth them. Everyone but the models themselves was talking.

Paul looked down the line with a critical professional eye and saw that everything was in order. Then, automatically counting, he realized there were only seven girls in the line, and glanced toward the back of the room. There, clad only in panties and pantyhose, was the exceptionally tall, remarkably angular red-haired model who was billed only as Katya. Her disdain icy, she completed her makeup without undue haste, then donned a body shirt and matching slacks, refusing help from the frantic crew crowded around her.

One of the few girls in the business who not only refused to work for less than one hundred and fifty dollars an hour, but was in such demand that the Howell Agency had to assign one operator to handle nothing but her calls, Katya was the star of the show and knew it. At any moment her notorious Hungarian temper would explode, and Paul wanted no scene. Two of the girls were relatively new to modeling, and might be upset by a Katya tantrum just prior to facing an audience.

"Katya has never been late yet," he called. "Get off her back, why don't you, and everything will be just fine."

His number one model rewarded him with a fleeting smile before devoting her attention to a seashell belt with a tricky clasp.

Paul made his way down the line, speaking a few words of encouragement to each girl. It was an old habit, dating back to his earliest days in the agency business, and he rarely indulged in it these days, having become too busy to make an appearance at such routine events as a regularly scheduled fashion show. But a Schwartzman-Burns show was different; no matter how insignificant, he always came around.

"Good luck, Melanie," he told a brown-haired girl. "I see they've got you wearing falsies, so make sure they don't slip."

"Falsies?" The tall model simulated indignation. "This is me, you crud! All of it!"

He grinned at her. "I'll have to start raising your fee, honey." Why did Schwartzman-Burns hold such a special place in his affections? His feeling, in fact, his relationship with the store, was odd.

"Keep that damn dyke off my back, will you, Paul," a very tall, painfully thin blond muttered, gesturing in the direction of a designer in slacks who was lounging against the far wall of the dressing room, smoking.

"I'll do what I can, honey, but you can take care of yourself." Karen was a nuisance, he thought, always becoming involved with Lesbians, but always protesting. Apparently she was unaware of her own tendencies in that direction. "Inge," he told another blond, "you're gorgeous today."

"Oh, yes," she replied with the matter-of-fact attitude of the Scandinavian who accepted her attractiveness as a commodity that needed no discussion. "They let me buy this dress for half-price, one hundred and seventy-five dollars. Is good?"

"That depends on how much you need or want a pleated sports outfit, honey. On you a burlap sack would look spectacular."

He had always told himself that Barbara was the tie that bound him to the store, and to an extent, of course, that was true. Louis Burns was her uncle, and her ownership of stock in Schwartzman-Burns gave him the best of reasons for feeling close to the place. But there was more to it than that. Louis Burns had done business with him because the Howell Agency was good, not because its head was a relative-by-marriage, and Paul had a soft spot for the store because Louis had been his first account, back in the days when Barbara had still been modeling. If there was such a thing as a home base, the store was it.

"All your fans are out there, Cleo," he said to a lanky Negro model. "They'll start chanting 'Black is beautiful!' the minute you hit the runway."

"They better. Or they're wasting money on the integration bit." The girl could afford to laugh without rancor. She had come into the business at a time when every magazine, every fashion show, every glossy advertisement wanted at least one black model, and Paul was getting a fee of one hundred an hour for her services these days, with a higher top very much within reach.

"Paul!" Katya gestured imperiously, the star demanding her due.

Had she been anyone else, he would have ignored the summons, but there was nothing to be lost by humoring her.

"Are these pants too loose in the seat?"

The crew gathered around the redhead assured her the fit was perfect, but she silenced them with a sharp wave.

Paul studied her critically as she turned for his inspection. Her request had not been made for the purpose of satisfying her vanity, he knew, but had been the serious demand of a perfectionist who relied on more than her natural assets to maintain her place as the leading model in the business. "Okay, honey," he said at last. "Snug, but not skin-tight."

"They feel loose." Katya twisted to peer at her rear in the nearest mirror.

The designer's assistant, a fussy little woman with heavy glasses, sighed, then cursed under her breath. The pants had been made for Katya and therefore were a precise fit.

"You're okay," Paul told her.

The girl's fleeting smile indicated that she accepted his opinion as much as she did that of any man, but still had reservations. "What you think, Marni?"

Marni Kendall, who stood directly in front of Katya in the line, had been busily observing the fit herself. "They're just right, Katya," she said.

The star nodded, and the group around her relaxed.

"Marni," Paul said, lowering his voice, "you've got a personal fan out front. He wanted to set up a dinner date for tonight, but I ducked for you. He can spell trouble."

"Thanks, Paul." Marni's smile, as photographers were discovering, was dazzling. "As it happens, I have a date already, and he's out front to watch the show. Who's the fan?"

"Ian MacDonald." Paul felt a twinge of uneasiness as he saw the light of interest in the girl's eyes. He felt responsible for Marni, having built her career from scratch, and felt that her ambition sometimes clouded her judgment. "I don't really know how much of a help to you he could be, but he'd make you pay for it."

"I can take care of myself, thanks." Her smile softened her words. "Anyway, David would love the excuse to look after me."

"David?"

"My date."

Her attitude was frivolous, but this wasn't the moment to tell her that, in his opinion and from what he'd heard, MacDonald always played for keeps, always for high stakes. For the moment his preliminary warning would have to suffice, so he patted her shoulder, wished her well and left the dressing room.

The commentator, a Broadway musical star whose standing was due, at least in part, to her love of clothes and the consequent attention paid her by the fashion magazines and women's pages of the newspapers, was making her preliminary remarks as Paul emerged into the showroom. He made his way around the side and joined Louis Burns, who was standing at the rear with several of his departmental buyers.

Then the spotlights blazed, Melanie appeared on the runway and the show began.

Paul concentrated on the girls and was indifferent to their costumes. No outsider would have recognized differences in the semi-glide, semistrut that was known as the model's walk, but Paul was alert to every nuance and filed away his observations for later comment, Melanie moved a shade too rapidly, Inge executed her pirouettes sloppily, Katya looked a trifle too bored. Cleo, who pretended she wasn't color-conscious, was a little too stiff and dignified in the presence of what was virtually an all-white audience, and Freddie, the young brunette who was just breaking in, would have to learn not to jiggle when appearing without a bra. The purpose of her march down the runway was to show off clothes, not her own charms.

Marni was good, Paul thought, as accomplished as Barb had been in the old days, smooth and professional, carefully projecting only enough of her own personality to enhance the outfits she was wearing, never allowing herself to dominate her clothes. The star quality couldn't be taught; a girl was born with it or developed it instinctively, and Marni was making rapid progress. She had the drive, too, and Paul's feeling about her future was confirmed. Barring the unexpected, she would be his next to hit the top. Provided, of course, she didn't make too many mistakes and mess herself up.

It was part of his job to see that those errors were avoided, and sometimes he was tempted to feel sorry for himself. It was only natural that a very young woman, idolized and pampered and petted because of her glamour and beauty, should develop a violently inflamed ego and become incapable of viewing herself and her career objectively. She could earn thousands in a week; she saw her photographs everywhere, and men, particularly those whose own egos demanded that they be seen with the reigning beauties of the day, besieged her with social and personal offers.

It was a rare model who remembered that even if she reached the pinnacle, her time in the sun was limited. Only under the most extraordinary circumstances could the very best count on more than five years of high income and glory. And it was even more unusual for one to parlay a modeling career into something more substantial. Paul could count on the fingers of both hands those who had become fashion or beauty consultants, opened successful models' agencies or gone to work for the magazines as editors. Scores had sought careers as actresses, but only one had become a real motion picture and stage star. And he couldn't even count the one who had become a best-selling author; her talents as a writer had been irrelevant to her career as a model.

In fairness to the hundreds of young women he had represented through the years, only a handful had wanted continuing careers, just as relatively few had been willing to fight their way to the summit as models. The majority had been content, some while still working as models, to accept marriage and motherhood, to be satisfied with the title Former Model.

None—at least, none Paul had ever known—had been able to achieve simultaneous vocational and domestic triumphs. Barbara had wanted both, to be sure, and her greed— Paul brought himself up short and refused to let his thoughts dwell on Barb. It was enough that he could see her sitting beside MacDonald, her face lifted to study the girls moving up the runway. Leaving well enough alone meant putting Barbara out of his mind, and before the show ended he'd call home to find out from her mother how the children were doing. Ann Burns could handle them, if anyone could, but in view of all that had happened, he never knew what he'd find at home.

Katya, he told himself, wrenching himself back to the present, needed a no-gloves lecture. Arrogance was part of her stock in trade, to be sure, but she was going too far too often; and if she didn't tamp down a bit, there would be a sudden slackening in the demand for her services. After spending more than three years as the queen, Katya was vulnerable, but he expected her to cause no problems. The mere hint that her income might drop would mend her attitude, since Katya, of all his girls, was the complete pro.

"Well, darling. Watching your chickadees?"

A scent of strong, musky perfume swept over Paul, and he felt a supple hand slip through his arm. Didi Martin, the omnipotent fashion editor of *Chic*, was too clever to let anyone gain the impression that she was even aware of the power she exercised through the pages of her magazine, and instead of bullying, she snuggled. But looking into the gray eyes only a few inches from his, he saw their complete lack of expression and knew the act had become meaningless. No matter what he thought of Didi, however, he could snub her only at his peril, and slipped into one of his own conventional poses, favoring her with the strong, masculine half-smile that had been his biggest selling point in his own modeling days.

"What a nice surprise," he murmured. "I thought you hated fashion shows."

"I do, but we've featured half the numbers Lou Burns is showing today, so I had to make sure he's doing them justice." She took a single, backward step so he could admire her.

She was such a cold fish that the gesture was mechanical, but Paul nevertheless inspected her with the interest of a man who made his living judging attractive women. And he had to give Didi credit: she was thirty-five, certainly, but didn't look it in her usual "black nothing" dress, which made it unnecessary for her to stay ahead of the styles, as her position otherwise would have demanded. As always, too, her hair was cut like a little boy's, enabling her to circumvent trends. This was typically clever, but harmful, since it stressed her neuter quality; and although Paul was no advocate of falsies, he thought that Didi, of all women, should wear them, inasmuch as they probably had been first devised for totally flat-chested women of her sort.

"Honey," he said, still scrutinizing her, his half-smile unchanged, "you look marvelous."

Due homage having been paid her femininity, she dropped her pose. "I want to know something."

"Anything I can tell you."

"We're working on a special beauty issue, and I keep hearing that divine creature of yours was the first to use different liner

17 :

shades in a circle around the eyes." She gestured toward the runway. "What do you know about it?"

Paul knew literally nothing, but would not willingly admit it to someone in Didi Martin's position. Catching a glimpse of Katya awaiting her turn at the end of the runway, he nodded. "That Hungarian always invents new rules for the game," he said, sensing a possible feature article on Katya.

Didi's gray eyes became scornful.

He looked again and saw Marni on the runway, executing a classical pirouette, a leather cape dragging artfully on the carpet behind her. He was caught, but had the grace to admit it. "I'll have to find out for you," he said, shrugging an apology.

"I'll do my own finding out," Didi snapped. "Tell Kendall to call me for an appointment."

Paul did not glance in her direction again as she moved away, and felt sorry for any man on the *Chic* staff who was subordinate to her. Didi lived, breathed and originated fashion trends, but she probably acquired her fragile strength by eating males alive.

Sustained applause greeted Marni Kendall as she swept down the runway in a bare-midriff evening dress of pleated chiffon, and Paul watched her appreciatively as she whirled lightly, the pleats in her full skirt fanning out in a circle. All models experimented with makeup, so it wouldn't be unusual if Marni had done something-or-other to her eyes and the trend caught on. Most changes in make-up were started by models.

But, if Marni was responsible, now was the time to take advantage of the good luck she had enjoyed. He'd sit her down in the immediate future for a serious talk and, if she was ambitious and determined, as he believed, the agency could start its concentrated drive to push her to the top. She'd forget, once she became the new glamour queen, that Paul Howell had been responsible for her success, but he'd know. And, aside from the increased revenue he'd enjoy, that would be compensation enough for a man who earned his very lucrative living in a highly unusual business.

Or would he be satisfied? Lately nothing had made him happy, and he couldn't put all the blame on Barb. Something was happening to his own aims and ambitions, and he couldn't understand the change that was taking place within him. Soon, when he had an opportunity to sit back and do a little intensive thinking about Paul Howell, he'd have to figure out just what was happening to his internal chemistry, or whatever it was that was making him so damned restless.

Of all the Manhattan restaurants frequented by professional athletes, Rusty's probably was the least pretentious. The brick walls, once red, had been blackened by smoke over the decades, and although both local and visiting figures from the sports world were in attendance, the only picture gracing the establishment was a large color photograph of a horse, the champion of champions, Man-o-War. The sawdust on the floor helped give the place a homelike atmosphere, as did the blue-and-white checked tablecloths and napkins; the waiters were unimpressed by celebrities from any walk of life, and the food, moderately expensive, was plain and hearty.

Marni Kendall, dressed in a simple, light-blue turtleneck sweater and matching suede miniskirt but still wearing full model's make-up, sipped her vodka gimlet on-the-rocks and sighed.

David Bernstein looked across the table with a sympathy that seemed at odds with his broken nose, his six feet four inches of height and his two hundred and forty pounds of bulk. "That fashion show wore you down, did it?"

"Well, I'm a little tired," Marni admitted. "But the show at Schwartzman-Burns was just the finishing touch, Dave. I had two sessions with photographers today, and I spent hours at fittings. I loathe fittings."

"I know what you mean, I think. I always hated training camp, but once the exhibition games began, it was different." He removed his heavy, horn-rimmed glasses and polished them.

Marni cocked her head and considered the question, her green eyes reflective. "I love everything about my work except the fittings. There's no challenge to them."

Her companion grinned. "Exactly. Just like training camp. Anyone who wants to get somewhere in the world is bored by routines. Believe it or not, I find the attitude in my brighter students. When I deliver a lecture that follows the course syllabus, they sit doodling in their notebooks and yawning. When I digress to tell them— well, a quick example—how Napoleon Bonaparte's private life influenced the development of his policies, the foot-shuffling stops, and you hear nothing in the room but the scratching of pens."

A young couple approached the table hesitantly, the girl staring at Marni while pretending not to look at her, the man devoting his full attention to the bulky figure opposite her. "You're Dave Bernstein, aren't you?"

David concealed his annoyance and managed a smile. "Guilty."

"I wonder if you'd autograph—"

"Sure." David reached for the pen and paper.

Watching him, Marni knew his sense of ease was no pose. Eleven years as an all-pro linebacker had given him a poise that couldn't be shaken and made him completely at home in the limelight. Oddly, she didn't think of David as a retired football player, which would have made him seem old; instead he was a young associate professor of history at New York University, and most of the time he sounded like one.

The girl standing beside the table summoned the courage to speak, while continuing to stare at Marni's eyelashes and elaborate makeup. "Are you—somebody, too?"

Marni shook her head. "Nobody."

"Don't you believe it, miss," David said emphatically. "Ever read *Chic*, the magazine? Look at this month's issue. She's on the cover."

The young man promptly thrust the pen and paper at Marni.

She signed her name, flushing slightly and feeling a trifle embarrassed.

Once the couple had gone, David's smile vanished. "I'm sorry," he said. "I honestly didn't realize that would get to you."

"Oh, I'm just not used to it, I guess," Marni replied. "I'm in—an anonymous profession, you could call it. Oh, people see us. On the air, and in magazines, and wherever. But hardly anyone outside the business ever knows our names, and we rarely have direct contact with the public."

"You had an audience of several hundred people at the fashion show I just sat through."

She smiled as she recalled how uncomfortable he had looked in a gilt chair that barely supported his weight. "Even the biggest shows attract only a tiny segment of the public, and half the people who come to them are either in the business or they're good customers, repeaters, who go to all the big shows. So, I'd guess, there are only a few thousand people at most who know a model, and most of them don't know our names."

David ran a hand through his short, crisp hair. "I can't believe," he said, "that a girl who appears on the cover of *Chic* is anonymous. If you really think that way, you're blind to your own celebrity."

Laughing to cover her embarrassment, Marni tugged at her metal belt. "All right, *anonymous* is too strong a word. People may know us, but they don't know *who* we are. When I'm on Fifth Avenue, or Madison—anywhere, really—I find people gaping at me with that expression that says, 'I've met you somewhere, I think.' That's because they recognize me, vaguely, from a magazine picture or a TV commercial."

"Is that enough to satisfy your ego?"

"Haven't you heard?" she retorted, tossing her long blond hair. "Models are narcissists. We're never satisfied, no matter how much we're recognized."

He started to order their meal.

21 :

"No soup for me," Marni said, interrupting. "Just a shrimp cocktail, a steak about half the size everybody else in this place is being served, and a salad."

"You work at your career, don't you?"

"Do you know anybody who doesn't? Anybody who makes the scene, I mean. If I gain five pounds, the camera will register it as fifteen or twenty, and that's the end of me, just as I'm about to start hitting the big money."

"Ah, then it's the money you're after," David said, teasing her.

"I find it useful, but it's basically the ego gratification I crave. You can see what happens to a girl who took a couple of psychology courses before dropping out at the end of her junior year."

"Where?"

"Wellesley."

"A fellow Ivy Leaguer. I might have known. I'm the only Brown graduate of my generation who went into pro football, and I was the freak of the NFL for a while, according to the press. There were plenty of us who used words of more than one or two syllables occasionally, and more are getting into the game every year. But you wouldn't have thought it from the stories they printed about me."

"Did you mind, David?"

"I was earning more than any other linebacker in the league, and the fans knew me, which was unusual for a lineman a few years ago. You see, *I'm* a narcissist, too."

"You're no such thing." Marni spoke slowly, careful to say only what she meant. "Instead of starving as a grad student, you were socking away money in a career that gave you all sorts of things while you were preparing for your lifework. The combination was a little unusual, which is what caused the stir. Nobody would have given you or your problem another thought if you'd worked as a lifeguard, say, or taught physical education somewhere."

"For a professional glamour bird," he replied, starting to spoon up his thick vegetable soup, "you're very astute."

"I don't think I am. Or maybe I'm wrong. Most of the girls in the business, at least the ones I've met, haven't had much education. Being pretty was a cushion they could lean on, so they didn't study very hard in high school, and most of them never went on with school after that."

"Why did you?" He made no excuse for his curiosity.

Marni expected and wanted no apologies. For the first time in months a man was interested in her beyond her beauty, and she was flattered. "Oh, I was saved, almost, because I didn't become photogenic until late in life."

"If you'll permit a compendious observation, that's a lie."

"I swear it, David. I had braces and acne, everything."

"Is that why you've acquired a sense of proportion, of balance?"

"I'm not sure I have." She put her fork on the side of her plate after eating two shrimp.

"I work with kids only a little younger than you, and I'm telling you, you have it. Also," he admitted, "I've known a few other models in my day, and their minds don't function on the beam that yours does."

Marni felt a quick stab of disappointment. Every successful model knew men who wanted to be seen with someone in her profession, but David Bernstein hadn't seemed that sort.

"What's wrong?" he asked, sensitive to her change in mood.

Marni smiled blandly. "Nothing."

David was silent as he emptied his soup dish, and then leaned back in the oversized chair that Rusty's provided for its oversized patrons. "I've made an informal study over the years. A private hobby, you might call it. I've noted that professional athletes always tend to marry beautiful women. It's a way of demonstrably proving our masculinity, which you, as a psychologist, ought to know. My private curse is that I've never found beauty enough to satisfy me. Beauty for its own sake becomes a palliative, and I need more. Character, intellect, call it what you will." He broke off abruptly. "I'm talking too much."

"You're not." Marni was soothed, and had to admit she found him interesting, but reserved judgment. This was just their second date, and she wanted to see whether he continued to treat her as someone with a mind and inner stature of her own. So far he appeared to respect her, but she had known others who had put on the same front before turning into lungers and grabbers.

"There's a wonderful saying attributed to Otto von Bismarck, who never uttered any such words: '*Schein vergeht, Warheit besteht.*' You don't know German? 'Appearances pass away, truth abides.' Or remains. I'm getting too old to cover for my true feelings. Or it may be my odd mixture of vocations. Football taught me to strip everything down to fundamentals, and history teaches me the uselessness of deceit. Put them together, and I talk too much to a girl who doesn't care what I want in life, and why should she?"

Marni tried to interrupt.

But David gave her no opportunity. "What do *you* want?"

His ferocious glower, she thought, must have put dread into the hearts of his football opponents. "I haven't thought that much about marriage," she said faintly.

"I didn't ask you about marriage. You're barely out of your teens—"

"I'm twenty-three."

"—so you have the right of youth to dream about the future. What-do-you-want?"

"Before I do anything else, I want to be as prominent a model as Katya. Or as Jean Shrimpton was. Or Suzy Parker before her." She sensed his next question, and anticipated it. "It's much more than money. I want to be the very best."

"I know the feeling," David said.

Their steaks came, and she knew she could not eat more than a small fraction of the food set before her. "I couldn't cop out," she said. "Eventually I'll get tired of modeling, and I hope it happens before the business gets tired of me."

"Then you'll be ready for marriage and children?"

"Of course I'll want a husband, and I suppose I'll want children, too. At least, I've always assumed I will, although I haven't thought about it much. But I'll still want another dimension in my life, and I haven't the faintest idea right now what it will be."

The expense-account crowd had made The Golden Urn more than a success; they had convinced the management it could charge outrageous prices and still fill every table at both lunch and dinner. The decor, dark and sumptuous, was in keeping with the right side of the menu, and some of the table captains were becoming financially comfortable on the investments made with their accumulated tips. It was said, with a certain measure of justice, that anyone concerned about prices had no business going to The Golden Urn.

The temperature was maintained at an even seventy-four degrees, warm enough for ladies in low-cut, sleeveless dresses, but Barbara Howell kept her mink coat thrown over her shoulders, a sure sign that she was sulking. "If I'd known we were coming here," she said, "I'd have had my hair done this afternoon, and I'd have worn something dressier."

Paul tried to catch their table captain's eye so he could signal for their first course. Barb was attacking her third martini, and he had no idea how many she had consumed at the fashion show, so she was reaching the danger point, and needed food. It would be useless to remind her that she recently had complained at length that he never took her to The Golden Urn anymore and that he had arranged the evening exclusively for her sake. Experience had taught him the kind of scene that remark would create. First, she would insist she had made no such demand, and then, if he refused to back down, she would announce in a voice loud enough to be heard at neighboring tables that she considered an appearance at the place helpful to his business and came here for no other reason.

A minor theme was best, Paul decided. "Anything dressier

would have been wrong for the fashion show, and that was more important."

Her sniff told him he had won the round.

"Why don't you like Ian MacDonald?" she asked suddenly.

He glanced at the nearest table to make certain she had not been overheard. People who frequented a place like this undoubtedly knew MacDonald and might be his friends. "Who says I don't?" he countered.

"I could feel you bristling, and you weren't exactly subtle, the way you chopped him off when he suggested we go out to dinner together."

"I had a previous engagement." He had no intention of discussing the head of Clothco in a public place. "A private date with my wife."

"Did you have some private reason for trying to put a fence around the model he wanted to date?"

Paul's models were responsible for his living, just as he secured theirs, and until recently Barbara had retained her perspective. She, of all people, should have understood the business, and certainly she knew he would destroy the agency's reputation if he became involved with one of his girls. Nevertheless, of late she had been displaying distinct signs of jealousy, and idiotic thinking of that sort had to be nipped quickly. "What private reason could I possibly have?"

Barbara heard the chill in his quiet tone and retreated. To the best of her almost positive knowledge, Paul had never played around with any of his models. He appreciated, actually needed, beauty; her own charms were fading, and the knowledge that she was at least partly to blame increased her ever-present sense of guilt. One day, she felt, it was inevitable that he would turn elsewhere, and the humiliation would be too much for her to bear.

"When I look at myself and then see someone like that Marni Kendall, I just shrivel," she said. "I've got everything she's got, and more, but that was a long time ago."

Paul was uncertain where his love for her ended and an overwhelming sense of pity began. It wasn't unusual to see former models growing panicky as middle age approached, and Barbara was making it painfully evident that she didn't know how to utilize her inner resources. "At forty-one," he said, "I don't get yens for kids half my age. In a few years Ann will be grown up—"

"What *do* you think of Marni Kendall, Paul?"

He was married to a woman with a stubborn, one-track mind. "She has a fine potential."

"Better than mine was?"

"Different, Barb. Your projection was unique."

"But hers isn't?" Barbara relished the idea.

Paul shrugged. "She's got all the bookings she can handle at sixty an hour, but we won't know whether she can climb any higher until we try."

Her sense of pleasure faded. "Are you grooming her for it?"

"I haven't decided yet." That wasn't quite true but it kept the peace. He would take Marni all the way, if she were willing and would follow instructions, but, in a sense, he was telling Barbara the truth. Nothing would be determined until he had his talk with Marni.

"I don't like her."

He couldn't tell whether her criticism was personal or professional.

Barbara didn't really know her own mind, but realized her views would be tolerated only if she voiced them in professional terms. "She's getting too old for the ingenue approach. And you know better than I that nobody will pay a hundred unless a girl has that ultimate gloss. What they once told me at V*ogue* was a sophistication so great that you have a patina of untouchability. I've never forgotten it."

There was no need for him to reply, since she frequently enjoyed quoting the phrase.

"It's a quality I had."

The point was debatable, but she didn't want candor, and he had no desire to increase the inner turmoil that any objectivity on his part almost inevitably produced. If he lied just for the sake of agreeing with her, however, she would pursue the matter and would trap him.

"I could have done everything Katya does," Barbara continued, lost in her own thoughts. "We even look alike in profile."

"So you do." The observation was accurate, but had never occurred to him.

"But she's got to tamp down. God, the way she looked at the audience during the show tonight, you'd have thought she was Catherine the Great walking over the bodies of peasants. Then I ran into Didi Martin as we were leaving—did you know she was there?—and she practically hissed when I mentioned Katya's name. That crazy Hungarian has had her last sixteen-page color spread in *Chic*, I can tell you!"

"Maybe not." Didi could be handled, and Andrew Reilly, the publisher of *Chic*, was still a Katya admirer.

"It makes me furious," Barbara said, taking a large swallow of her champagne, which had just arrived, "when somebody like Katya starts thinking she's so wonderful."

There was nobody Barbara liked, Paul thought, and she despised herself more than anyone else. That was her problem, and she was infecting him, as well as their children, with its virus.

When Ian MacDonald dined alone in New York he could indulge a whim forbidden him in any of the thirty-two cities where Clothco stores were located. At Hillebrand-Morris in Baltimore and Houston, at Myers in Chicago and at all the rest, thousands of employees either knew or instantly recognized him. So, even when unaccompanied, he felt his position demanded that he appear only in the best restaurants.

But New York was different. There were fewer than three hundred persons on the headquarters staff, most of them living in such godforsaken places as Forest Hills or Jackson Heights. What was more, Manhattan's greatest luxury was the anonymity it afforded, enabling a man to do what he pleased, when and where and how he pleased to do it.

So Ian MacDonald ate his solitary meal in a small, pseudo-French restaurant in the west 50s, where a complete dinner was served for only $2.50. It was difficult to break the habits of the years of struggle, and he saw no reason to break them. The food was palatable, the service was both rapid and impersonal, which gave him time to think, and he was within walking distance of his Park Avenue apartment. Inasmuch as he had not touched liquor in more years than he cared to recall, dining alone was a necessity that he saw no reason to prolong. His meal finished, he paid his bill, told the matronly cashier he would return before the end of the week and went out into the night.

As usual, a majority of the pedestrians walking in the opposite direction stared at him, and, as usual, MacDonald ignored them. Long experience had taught him that people gaped at someone who was ugly just as intently as they did at the beautiful, and he had taught himself to pay no attention to the curiosity of strangers. Sometimes it amused him when he saw people staring with the identical expression he had so often noted when they looked at a great beauty, but tonight he was in no mood for irony.

He tried to pretend he had become inured to the stir he created, but he knew better and resorted to the only methods he had developed to ward off the painful hypersensitivity that made him so uncomfortable. First, he tried to close his mind to the people around him and pretend they did not exist. When that ploy proved ineffective, he made an attempt to become interested in something he knew would make him forget himself.

It was odd, but he lost his self-consciousness when dealing with professional prostitutes, and even the fear of impotence that was his curse in his relations with other women no longer plagued him. Perhaps it was because he knew the prostitute was beneath him.

Whatever the reason, he could forget his accursed appearance.

The black whores were out in force, and MacDonald amused himself by walking a couple of blocks down Sixth Avenue before turning east. He inspected the girls critically, from a distance, but his eyes glazed whenever he passed one of them, and he turned a deaf ear to the repeatedly suggested, "Want a party?"

Some of them, he had to admit, were jazzy tricks, but experience had taught him these streetwalkers were not for him. He couldn't take one of them back to his apartment, where the building's hired help and his neighbors would have been scandalized, and he refused to accompany a professional whore to one of the riding academy hotels of the area. In one of those dumps he could be rolled, knifed or otherwise mistreated and would be defenseless. Had one of the girls been willing to accompany him to a hotel of his choice, it might have been different. But he had been rebuffed whenever he had made the offer. He assumed they thought he was a plainclothes detective trying to trap them and therefore were leery.

A tall, rather buxom whore wearing the shortest skirt he had ever seen, her black legs encased in net stockings, the platinum hair of her wig cascading down her back, came toward him, and MacDonald's resolve almost weakened. But he increased his pace, looked past the girl and kept walking. The game had lost its savor, so he quickly left Sixth Avenue and headed homeward.

But his appetite had been whetted, so he paused at a corner telephone booth to make a couple of quick calls. Then, although there was no need to hurry, he resumed his walk, moving still more rapidly. That blond model in the Howell stable was the cause of his restlessness, he reflected and damned Paul Howell for refusing to set up a date. It would have been easy enough to arrange, and he had learned from Barbara Howell that she and her husband had made no special plans for the evening.

Perhaps they had wanted to spend the evening by themselves, but MacDonald was inclined to doubt it and suspected that Howell, for whatever his reasons, had been sidestepping him. Certainly

Barbara had given him the impression that she would have preferred going off with him to meeting her husband. He had toyed with the idea but hadn't given it serious consideration. For one thing, there would have been complications and repercussions. Under the best of circumstances MacDonald avoided involvement with a married woman, and at all times he was cautious.

Barbara Howell, of all people, was someone to handle with care. She was attractive, and he enjoyed women in their thirties, but even had she been divorced he would have refrained from taking her out. She was related to Lou Burns, he had learned, and that was more than ample reason to treat her with caution. He was beginning to have interesting thoughts regarding Burns, and although they hadn't jelled yet, he wanted to let nothing interfere with them. He hadn't built his company from nothing by allowing anything whatever to stand in the way of business, and he had no intention of starting now, when his ultimate goals were almost within reach.

"Nice evening, Mr. MacDonald," the apartment-house doorman said, touching his uniform cap.

"I'm expecting some friends," MacDonald told him. "They've been here before, so you'll recognize them. Send them right on up."

He repeated the instructions to the elevator man before unlocking his front door and then halted for a moment in the entrance after switching on some lights.

The impressive apartment afforded him one of his few abiding pleasures. The large entrance foyer was lined with prints of famous churches, bridges and buildings in all parts of the world, souvenirs of his travels and constant reminders of the financial status that enabled him to go anywhere he pleased, and in style. The enormous sunken living room, done in Scandinavian modern by a high-priced decorator in teak and other expensive woods, was an even more emphatic symbol of his affluence, and he stood for a few moments, gazing out of the floor-to-ceiling windows at the lights of the city. Thirty-two other towns were his, and although he had not yet conquered New York, the largest and wealthiest of all was next on his list.

It never failed to gratify and even awe MacDonald that he had come so far, completely on his own initiative and merit. He wished, as he often did, that his parents had survived long enough to see him living in a splendor far removed from the cold-water flat off Fulton Street on the lower East Side, where he had spent his boyhood. Not that they would have cared. His father, who had spent his life in the fish market, cleaning and scaling the day's catch, and his mother, who had augmented the family income by taking in sewing, had made it plain from his earliest childhood that they had considered their lone, ugly son a nuisance and an expense. They had been relieved when, lying about his age, he had obtained his first job at thirteen, wrapping mail order packages at Schwartz-man-Burns.

Memories of his parents rankled, so MacDonald put them out of his mind. Unless he closed the door on that compartment of his past, a ruthlessly self-disciplined faculty he had long enjoyed, his evening would be ruined. Carefully putting away his new cashmere coat and the hat that had been made for him on his last trip to London, he closed the heavy living room drapes, then went around the room, carefully lighting just enough lamps to dispel deep shadows in every part of the chamber.

Fran Black was the first to arrive, and while MacDonald put away her shaggy fur coat in the foyer closet, she sauntered into the living room, the heels of her boots clicking on the hardwood steps. Completely at home, she helped herself to a cigarette from an inlaid teak and ivory box on a coffee table, and MacDonald, pausing at the top of the steps, inspected her with cautious pleasure.

Fran was stacked, knew it and was not bashful about revealing her charms, but did it with circumspection, which was one of her major assets. At first glance her blue-black hair, tumbling freely down her back, was ordinary, but when it picked up lights the sheen it reflected made it come alive. She was wearing a demurely high-necked, long-sleeved dress of paisley-printed wool in blue and green, but it was a soft, clinging material, and the skirt was short enough to reveal generous expanses of her shapely thighs. When she straightened, her very large but very firm breasts jiggled beneath her dress, and MacDonald suspected that, as was her sometimes custom, she was wearing no undergarments.

She glanced at him, and when her mascara-fringed, violet eyes met his, MacDonald couldn't help wondering whether she was older than she claimed. No twenty-five-year-old he had ever known had such wise, cynical eyes, capable of probing deep inside a man as she fathomed his desires—and his needs.

"I haven't seen you for a long time, Fran," he said. "How's the world treating you?"

"Oh, nothing ever changes." Her skirt rode still higher as she sat in a low-slung easy chair and, with seeming carelessness, crossed her legs.

"What you need is a drink." He headed toward the well-stocked bar at the opposite side of the room.

Fran's hesitation was almost imperceptible. "Is this a big party, or just us?"

"Neither." MacDonald grinned, but his ugliness made it resemble a grimace. "Carlo Bennett from my office is dropping in too. I think you may have met him."

"Yeah." Again she paused, then spoke firmly. "Make it a fairly stiff Scotch. You know how I like it."

"Of course." He put several ice cubes in a glass and poured several inches of Scotch over them.

Fran accepted the drink with a faint smile. "How's the tycoon business?"

"So-so." MacDonald never revealed details of his affairs to anyone.

"When will you have a job for me?"

"Take your pick right now. Thirty-two towns. Just say the word, and you'll be chief lingerie model in any one of my stores."

It wasn't the first time he had made the seemingly generous

offer, and she shook her head. "You know I won't leave New York for the sticks. This is where it's all happening, lover, and I had to scratch too hard to get where the action is. I wouldn't go back to Ohio if you made me president of one of your goddam stores there." She took a large swallow of her drink.

Her inconsistency amused him. "Well, if you hate your present job so much . . ." His voice dwindled away.

"Oh, it really isn't that bad. I spend eight hours a day traipsing around the showrooms for out-of-town buyers in nighties and bra-and-panties sets. They ogle me, they try to make dates and I turn them down. At the end of the week I collect my hundred and fifty, and I go home. It could be worse." The violet eyes seemed to look through him. "Except that the place is starting to get shabby, kind of. My sofa is wearing out."

"Maybe you give it too much use."

She did not join his laugh. "I bought it years ago, when I couldn't afford anything good, and now it's falling apart."

MacDonald took a small notebook from the inner pocket of his jacket and scribbled something with a gold pen.

Fran raised a smoothly plucked and painted eyebrow.

"You're in luck, baby," he told her. "Our furniture department got a great buy recently on the inventory of a factory that's closing out. I'll have a sofa, one of the best, sent to you from our Jersey City warehouse."

"That'll be just fab, Ian. How much will I owe you?"

He waved a hand, a surprisingly large hand attached to a slender, small-boned arm. "My pleasure."

"You're a darling. I appreciate it."

"Friends," he said, "always come through for each other."

"Sure," Fran said, and took more of her drink.

The door chimes sounded, and MacDonald admitted Carlo Bennett. A dapper, clothes-dummy-handsome man in his early forties, the balding, dark-haired Bennett was known as the "mystery man" of Clothco. His official title was assistant to the president, and no one quite knew his precise duties or authority. He spent much of his time traveling to the company's stores, and, since the discharges of executives sometimes followed closely on the heels of a Bennett visit, he was believed to be MacDonald's hatchet man. But the close-mouthed Bennett had no intimates other than his superior, and, since neither was willing to discuss the subject, even the vice-presidents, of whom there were six, were as much in the dark as the junior executives and general staff.

Certainly the man was at home in his employer's apartment. He greeted Fran with friendly reserve, then went straight to the bar to mix himself a gin and tonic. "While I'm over here," he called politely, "can I get you another?"

"Why not?" Fran made no attempt to join him, but handed her glass to MacDonald, who carried it to the bar.

Bennett sniffed, poured in a quantity of Scotch and added ice. Taking it to her himself, he bowed slightly as he handed her the glass, a gesture that would have looked absurd in a man less graceful.

Their eyes met for an instant, and a communication of some sort passed between them, MacDonald saw. Both remained impassive, however, and he wondered if they were laughing at him, but it was too early in the evening to judge. "I'm glad you could drop by, Carlo," he said. "I'd thought you were going to the theater tonight."

"I was, but I exchanged my tickets when my date stood me up," Bennett said.

"Too bad I didn't know." Fran glanced up at him as he leaned against the divan to which she had moved.

"It's been so long since we last saw each other up here—the better part of a year, isn't it?—that I didn't think of you. But I won't forget next time. Fran Black likes the theater."

"Musicals, especially."

Bennett lowered himself onto the divan. "With your figure, you could get a job in any musical, if you're a real theater nut."

She brushed back a long lock of hair. "No thanks. I can't sing, dance or act, and I'm damned if I'd parade around as a showgirl, half-naked in front of an audience."

Both men laughed, and MacDonald said, "You wear less in that lingerie manufacturer's showroom."

"That's different," she said seriously. "The buyers are there to see the nighties, or whatever. Not me."

"I understand what you mean." Bennett patted her sympathetically on the thigh and let his hand linger there.

Fran made no attempt to remove it. "It's like this, Ian," she said to MacDonald, who was still chuckling. "In the theater I'd be paid for showing myself off. This way, it's my company's products. I just happen to be a necessary prop."

Bennett illustrated her point by telling a long, involved story about some people he knew in show business.

Both glasses were empty by the time he had reached the climax of his tale, and MacDonald, unbidden, went off to refill them.

When he returned, Bennett's arm was stretched out across the back of the divan, behind Fran.

Bennett's story reminded Fran of an anecdote about a friend who had been a showgirl, and she told it slowly, with frequent digressions.

As she spoke, Bennett absently toyed with a lock of her hair, then let his arm fall across her shoulders.

She gave no sign that she was aware of his touch, but soon took another gulp of her fresh drink.

MacDonald made no attempt to join in the conversation now, but sat back in his chair, listening and watching.

Bennett was reminded of a joke, and as he told it he shifted his position slightly, an arm dropping forward around Fran's neck, a hand closing over one of her breasts.

She stiffened and sat rigidly beside him, but continued to make no protest.

Bennett, sipping his drink, which he held in his free hand, casually fondled her, his manner that of a man who was unaware of what he was doing.

Fran made the effort to match his mood, saying she was reminded of a joke, but her effort was painful, hampered by pauses that grew longer before she lamely finished speaking.

By now she was responding to his ministrations, and the outlines of the nipple, which was stiffening, could be seen through the fabric of her dress.

MacDonald hurried back to the bar to replenish the glasses. His eyes shining, he wanted to miss no part of the scene being enacted before him, but by the time he found the bottles and peered across the room, Fran and Bennett were locked in an embrace, kissing. The man's hand landed on the girl's thigh again, remained there briefly, and then moved swiftly upward, disappearing beneath her skirt.

Fran shuddered, her legs parting.

MacDonald spilled some gin on the surface of the bar.

The couple on the divan pressed closer together, straining, and Bennett, still caressing the girl, began to breathe heavily.

Fran's hand crept across his lap toward his zipper.

MacDonald, carrying both glasses, walked quietly across the room and placed them on the coffee table. His precautions were unnecessary, however; both seemed totally unconscious of his presence.

Suddenly Bennett rose and, still kissing Fran, carried her from the room. He knew the apartment and headed straight for the nearest bedroom, a short distance down a broad corridor.

MacDonald, moving more rapidly, was only a few paces behind them.

Displaying the finesse of long experience, Bennett unfastened the zipper of Fran's dress, and, as he lowered her to the bed, managed to remove it.

As MacDonald had guessed, she had worn no underclothes, and was nude. Peering at her, he moistened his lips.

Looking up at Bennett, who loomed above her, the girl wriggled as she raised her arms to him.

He undressed quickly, then joined her and their embrace was explosive.

MacDonald hastily turned on another light so he would miss no detail, his rasping breathing almost as labored as that of the couple on the bed. Slowly he raised a hand to his ugly face, shielding it, and his nails dug into his cheek, drawing blood; but he did not know it.

The brandy had been a mistake. Barbara had been unaffected by the champagne and had eaten most of her dinner, but had demanded a cognac, then a second, and before Paul had paid his bill she had lapsed into a remote silence. He had intended to take her dancing but knew that the longer they stayed out, the greater became the possibility that she would create a scene. The risk would increase, since she was no longer able to judge her capacities, and she would continue to drink, so he felt he no longer had an alternative.

She made no comment when he gave the taxi driver their address on the upper East Side, but huddled at her end of the seat, staring out of the window. She did not speak until they pulled away from a stoplight on Park Avenue. "You can be a real bastard."

Too many fights had started that way, and Paul made no reply.

"If you thought I was drunk, you could have said so, and I'd have proved you were wrong. There was no need to sneak me home, like a criminal."

"We're not sneaking anywhere. I'm tired, and I have a long morning ahead tomorrow. I've got to sit in on an advertising agency casting session for a thirty-nine-week series."

Barbara muttered under her breath before averting her face again.

The rest of the ride passed without incident, and at last they reached the apartment house, an older building with large, high-ceilinged rooms that charged relatively reasonable rentals because it long had been subject to controls.

Barbara wrenched herself free when her husband tried to help her alight. "I can still walk by myself, thanks!" she said angrily.

The taxi driver looked at Paul with a hint of sympathy in his grizzled face.

Ann Burns, who was reading in the living room, looked up from her book when the couple entered the apartment. Almost as tall as her daughter, with hair only a shade darker, she had a poise that, her late husband had sworn, could not be shaken. "Well," she called cheerfully, "you're home early. Have a nice time?"

Paul started to reply, but Barbara cut him off.

"My company bored him, so he couldn't wait to bring me home." Barbara marched off, and a door slammed at the end of a hallway.

Ann exchanged a quick glance with her son-in-law. "Is it bad?"

Paul shook his head. "She was in pretty good shape until she had a couple of cognacs after dinner."

"Couldn't you stop her from taking them?" She carefully placed a marker in her book.

"By then she'd had too much for me to try. The in-between stage is always the trickiest, and I knew at least a half-dozen people at The Golden Urn, including an advertising guy I've got to meet in the morning. If I'd been firm there would have been an explosion." He sighed and slumped into a chair opposite her. "I'm damned if I know how to handle her when she gets this way."

"Sometimes I think you're too patient." Ann accepted a cigarette.

"Only when there's no choice. Tonight I really wanted to belt her."

"I wish you had." She sighed, too.

"How'd it go with the kids?"

"Just fine. Annie was an angel—you know how she always tries to impress Grandma. Phil came out for a glass of water a couple of times, to test me, but he stayed in bed when I told him not to get up again. I have no trouble with either of them, and I just wish I'd been as firm with my own daughter."

"You can't blame yourself, Ann."

"It isn't your fault, either." She listened for sounds from the master bedroom, but heard none.

"Can I fix you a drink?" Paul asked, breaking a heavy silence. "Or a cup of coffee?"

"I should be getting home."

"Stick around. It really is early, and I'll put you into a taxi a little later." He, too, glanced down the hallway. "I want your advice, Ann."

"My record would indicate that any I might give would be bad."

"Rubbish. Barb was fine for the better part of her life. This thing has been creeping up on her gradually, in recent years, and I still don't know for sure how far along she is."

"It's my understanding there's no difference between a problem drinker and an alcoholic."

"She's been under control for at least a month. When she starts to let loose, I've tried to urge her to look into A.A., Christian Science, anything. But for weeks—until tonight—she's been handling her liquor without any trouble. You know, one or two before dinner, and that's been it for the night. Fine with the kids, okay with me."

"What set her off tonight?"

"I wish to God I knew." Paul laced and unlaced his hands. "It may have been an invitation from that rear end of a horse, Ian MacDonald." He explained briefly.

His mother-in-law shook her head. "If I know her, people like MacDonald don't impress her." She half-turned in her chair. "Did I hear—"

: 40

"Not a peep. By now Barb is in bed, and in another five minutes she'll be out for the night. Another drink or two, and she'd have been tearing down walls, but I got her home in time. If it wasn't MacDonald, what—"

"In my opinion, it was going to that fashion show." Ann rose and went to a small bar in the corner, where she poured herself a glass of soda.

Paul was on his feet at once. "Why didn't you let me do that for you?"

"Even at my age," she said, "a woman sometimes wants to do some things for herself."

"Is that supposed to be a remark weighted with significance?"

"I'm not sure," she confessed, returning to her seat.

"At least let me give you some ice and some brown stuff in it."

Ann smiled wryly. "We're not a drinking family. And it would keep me awake. As I was saying. This is purely a theory, and I can't prove it, but it seems to me that Barbara's drinking is almost always sparked by exposure to models, especially Paul Howell models."

"Why— Hell, I guess it does make sense. Having the kids cut her off from her career."

"You oversimplify, my dear. The roots are much deeper. Growing up in a department store family didn't help, and being very beautiful was an even worse handicap. Her father and I tried to insist that she go to college, but she wouldn't listen to us. Arthur had let her do a few shows for the store when she was still in high school, remember, and from that time on, she wanted to be a model."

"What you're trying to tell me is something I've thought about many times." Paul mixed himself a weak bourbon and water. "She resents me—and my business—because I took her away from the work she loved."

"She resents you, and the children, and me, and her Uncle Louis and everybody else. She imagines she lost her career." Ann was crisp. "But let's face it, my dear. She was never that good a model.

If it hadn't been for Schwartzman-Burns at the start and, later on, you, her career would have given her up years earlier. She was never as prominent as she likes to remember."

"Barb did pretty well," Paul said.

"She started at eighteen, she was married to you at twenty-two and she worked for almost three more years before Annie was born. You pushed her after you started the agency—"

"Not very hard. I didn't have to."

"You get the medal, Paul. Loyal husband of the month. Don't you see? The loss of her modeling career is just Barbara's excuse. She was always too beautiful, and her father's spoiling didn't help. She's one of those girls who can't tolerate the prospect of growing older, of becoming middle-aged."

"I keep trying to hound her into seeing a doctor, but she refuses."

"What she needs is a psychiatrist. But her father hated them, and I'm afraid she'll have to go much further downhill before she agrees to see one."

"Do you suppose it would help," Paul asked, speaking very slowly, "if I went into another business?"

"Not just because of Barbara's drinking problem, I hope!" Ann was startled.

"Primarily for my own sake. I do fine at the agency, but I've built it to its limit. I've had a number of offers—advertising agencies, publishers, one of the big dress manufacturers who wants me as a merchandising vice-president."

"Have you discussed this with Barbara?"

"Not yet. I'd like to have a clearer picture in my own mind first. All I know is that if I'm ever going to become more than I am now—and I want to be a great deal more—this is the right time of life for me to make a major move."

"I always wanted to be the wife of a very ambitious man. How I wish you were twenty years older—and single." Ann took another cigarette. "Barbara doesn't know how lucky she is, and never will. Would it shock you if I said that I believe she takes you for granted, as she has everything else that's been good in her life?"

"I'm hard to shock." Paul's smile was stiff.

She wanted to ask whether his sex relations with Barbara were as unsatisfactory as she imagined, but that would be presumptuous, even though she and her son-in-law were close.

"I know what you're thinking," he said.

Ann hoped she didn't appear startled.

"Sure, I've been tempted to clear out. Often. But a man can't do it when he has—three kids."

"And the youngest of them is Barbara." Ann brought her own recent thinking into the open. "If you're planning a career change, you can't be distracted by this problem. Would it help if I moved in, at least for a while? I'm not saying I can handle Barbara, but I might be able to help."

"Thanks, Ann, you're terrific," Paul said. "But I know how much you value your independence, and I can't ask you to make the sacrifice. We're not that desperate. Yet."

Audrey Burns was one of a very few women who could wear an elaborate peignoir from her husband's lingerie department without self-consciousness. "Why should I be awed by what Louis sells?" she asked her friends. "After all, I was buying every stitch I wear from the store long before I married him, and I swear to you, the only reason I gave in to him was because I could start getting all my clothes at cost."

Louis, moving in and out of his dressing room as he prepared for the night, looked admiringly at the gray-haired woman stretched out imperiously on the chaise, drinking tea. For thirty years he had told himself he was fortunate to be married to such a natural patrician, and only when they had quarreled violently had he momentarily changed his mind. One of the town's more celebrated hostesses, the loving mother of three splendid children, a level-headed business advisor, and, when the mood struck her, a surprisingly tempestuous mistress—he couldn't ask for more.

"Why," Audrey demanded with asperity, "must I ruin a perfectly balanced dinner party by asking Ian MacDonald?"

"Now sweetheart." Louis reappeared in the door, one sock in hand, both feet bare.

"Put on your slippers before you catch cold," she snapped, "and answer me."

"Ian isn't all that bad."

"He's the most repulsive-looking man I've ever seen." Audrey sipped her tea. "Do you remember what the Third said when he was home for Christmas vacation and we ran into your Mr. MacDonald as we were coming out of the store? 'He looks like a gargoyle.'"

Louis rarely appreciated the humor of Louis III, and when he was on the domestic defensive his son's wit left him cold. "Ian might not win any prizes as a male model," he conceded, "but he's bright, very successful and he knows which fork to use. So he won't embarrass you in front of your society friends."

Audrey glanced up from her tea and saw that her husband had disappeared again. "They're your friends, too," she called.

"Okay, okay. Let's not start that again."

"You still haven't answered me. Why is it so necessary to have him?"

Louis returned, buttoning the jacket of his silk pajamas, the most expensive in Men's Sleepwear. "It isn't necessary," he said patiently. "I just happen to think it's a good idea."

"I don't." Audrey yawned, and her attitude indicated the subject was closed.

"I told you he went out of his way to hang around, talking to me tonight, after the fashion show."

"Perhaps he was lonely."

"Ian MacDonald never does anything without a purpose. He wants something."

"What?"

Louis shrugged.

"The store?" his wife asked facetiously.

"He'd get it over my dead body." Louis's voice and manner suddenly hardened.

"I can't imagine anything else you have that might interest him."

"That shows how little you know about the business. Ian has been trying to upgrade the more expensive departments in his stores, and I wouldn't be surprised if he's had a hard time getting merchandise from some of the snootier designers and manufacturers. The Clothco stores aren't Schwartzman-Burns or Bergdorf, you know."

"I've never set foot in one of his stores, and undoubtedly never will, so I'll take your word for it." Another yawn briefly distorted Audrey's chiseled features. "But I don't see what all this has to do with you."

"I could get the designers to accept Clothco."

"Why should you?"

"Because," he said, his own irritation showing, "Ian doesn't compete with us in New York. With all of his stores buying the same merchandise, we'd get a far lower price from the manufacturers."

"I wish you'd said so in the first place." Audrey discovered he had vanished again. "Can't you stay in one place when we're talking, Louis?"

He returned, struggling into a brocaded dressing gown that hadn't sold because it had been priced too high, forcing him to buy it—at cost—for himself. "So you'll oblige me, sweetheart, by inviting Ian." His tone indicated that he would not tolerate either dissent or further discussion.

"This means finding an extra woman." Audrey spoke with resignation.

Her husband started toward his humidor, but knew he would be banished from the room if he lit a cigar. "I remember somebody asking a hostess who was complaining about finding an extra man whether it was for dining or mating."

"You didn't hear it. You read it. The remark was written by Dorothy Parker, and you never met her."

"But she had a charge account at the store." His dignity salvaged, Louis felt free to press his point. "Why do you have to get somebody?"

"I don't tell you how to run the store. I'll balance a dinner party in my own way. Name someone suitable, I dare you."

He searched his mind. "There's always Ann."

"Ann who?"

"Burns, dummy."

"I suppose so."

"All right, what have you got against Ann?" Louis demanded.

"Nothing, dear." Audrey was wide-eyed. "If anything, I've envied her for years. She was so self-reliant from the time Arthur died, and she leads such an independent life. It's wonderful."

"I could make you happy by dropping dead, so you could copy her. But I'd like to stick around for a while, if you don't mind."

"Oh, I don't." Audrey's smile faded. "Seriously, the one thing I don't like about Ann is the way she gets one or the other of us aside to talk about Barbara's damned problems."

"She'd hardly do it at a dinner party."

"I dare say she wouldn't. Still, I don't think I'll invite her." That settled the matter, but her thoughts lingered on her husband's niece. "Is Barbara really turning into a lush?"

Louis shrugged. "She came to the show today, and she looked fine."

"Then it's Ann's imagination?"

"She's too sensible. No, the problem is real, I'm afraid."

"Then why doesn't Barbara's husband take care of it? What's wrong with Paul Howell?"

"Nothing, except that he's too decent, maybe. But don't you put a cut rate on him. He's sharp. Ambitious. Watch him, sweetheart,

: 46

and you'll see somebody who is going places. I wish the Third was more like him."

"Don't start that again. You can't expect a junior at—"

"Why can't I? I went to college, too, even if it wasn't Princeton. And every vacation, every spare minute I had, I worked at the store. Not because my father made me do it, but because I wanted to." Louis paused for breath. "By the time I was ready for a full-time job, I'd worked in every department, and I really knew what put the store together. Am I so rich that my boy can't get his hands dirty?"

"Your son's future," Audrey replied wearily, "was decided the day he was born. He won't disappoint you—or all those ancestors looking down at him from the Valhalla of Scottish merchants, wherever that is." She hated the store, the always-dominant factor in their lives, but knew it was the essence of her husband's being. It would be a waste of breath to persuade him to take a less active interest in Schwartzman-Burns, much less retire, although he had enough money to spend the rest of his life in travel and at their Palm Beach winter place. Like it or not, and she loathed it, the store meant more to him than his wife, his children and his fortune, and without it he'd have no reason for living.

Rosalie James, wrapped in an old, ankle-length flannel robe, her one concession to fashion an elastic band that held her auburn hair in place, sat cross-legged at the foot of her bed, watching her roommate at the dressing table. "Who's the fairest flower of all?" she asked, waving a half-consumed bottle of Coke. "The James electoral college unanimously elects you."

Marni Kendall stripped off her false eyelashes and vigorously applied cold cream to her face. "You've got to be kidding."

"Look at you."

"If I do, I'll get cold cream in my eyes. Besides, I know what I look like. A greasy mess."

"There are none so blind," Rosalie intoned, striking another pose, "as those who will not see. I think I got that old saying right. Did I?"

"Close enough." Marni expertly worked the cream into her skin.

"Take that sexy outfit you're wearing. Semitransparent baby-doll nightie and matching coat. Reveals the figure that thousands of palpitating males thirst after—"

"Stop it, Rosie. You know this was a present from a manufacturer trying to persuade me to do lingerie photography. And as long as I've got it, what'll I do with it? Let it rot in the box?"

"Well," Rosalie replied judiciously, taking a swig of her Coke, "you might give it to the indigent poor. Me."

"Do you want it?" Marni, eyes closed, reached toward the box of tissues at one side of the table and began to wipe off the grease.

"A thousand times no! With my scarecrow body, I'd look like Little Emily dressing up in Mommy's clothes. Strong men would weep—except they'd never catch me alive in it."

"They won't catch me in it, either," Marni assured her.

"Then you've got to do some fast sprinting, sister. It seems the whole pack is chasing you."

"That," Marnie replied, "is a gross exaggeration. In fact, it's just plain gross. Anyway, I've had some practice as a sprinter."

"You've never had Dave Bernstein after you. He's sudden death. Like he's a gorilla. I used to go out to Yankee Stadium with my brother, and freeze watching men playing boys' games. Except they played for keeps. And that Bernstein. When he'd blitz a quarterback, he'd swarm all over the poor fellow. Something awful. Sometimes they didn't get up again."

Marni finished cleaning her face and applied a thin coating of night cream. "David is not only a very gentle man, but he's building a career as a distinguished historian."

"He's all man, a quarter of a ton of him."

"Rosie, he hasn't once tried to make out with me. I swear it!"

"Hans Christian Andersen and the brothers Grimm could have taken lessons from you, Marni."

"It's true. No hand-holding, no goodnight kiss, nothing. Just talk. Deep talk."

Rosalie emitted a long, low whistle. "That does it. Girl, you're in trouble." She finished her Coke, and, leaving the bedroom, went off to the refrigerator for another.

Marni was brushing her hair with long, vigorous strokes by the time her roommate returned. "Why am I in trouble?"

"I tell you, I saw him doing his thing every Sunday when he was with the Giants. He's an animal. And when an animal turns on the intellect to impress you, he's twice as dangerous."

"I like him," Marni said flatly.

"I'll start designing a wedding dress tomorrow."

"You jump to conclusions as fast as my parents. I've seen him twice, and I scarcely know him. Liking him doesn't mean—"

"What *would* your parents say?" Rosalie demanded sardonically. "He's Jewish."

Marni flushed. "My mother and father," she said, "are convinced that no man on earth is good enough for their darling little beauty. But, at the same time, they worry. Lately they've been turning white-haired because I earn almost a thousand a week, and they say that'll scare away any man who has pride in himself."

"They may have something there." Rosalie started on her new Coke.

Marni let her arm drop for a moment before resuming her brushing. "If that's going to make me a spinster, the odds will get even higher. If I have anything to say about it. I hope to make maybe half again as much. Maybe double."

"Sheer greed. You pay the government more in income tax than I earn, and I'm a creative artist with a soul as well as a talent."

"Of all people, Rosie, you ought to know better." Marni glared at her friend in the mirror. "I'm good for a maximum of three to four more years."

"With your bone structure, you can model forever."

"But the market won't want me. And by then I'll be very tired of modeling. I get tired now sometimes."

"Cashing all those checks would exhaust me. Endorsing them, standing in line at the bank—oh, it would beat me to my knees."

"I like the money, naturally. It's all the rest. The glamour bit."

"Marni, I know you better than you know yourself. You'll always dress to the teeth. You not only can wear clothes, you love them."

"In other words, the narcissist."

"Don't start that again! There's a narcissistic streak in every woman, and you know it as well as I do. The clothing industry feeds on it. Up to ten billion dollars a year. The cosmetics people. Another two billion. And so on. What's more, anybody who looks like you has the right to be a little more narcissistic than most. So you don't have to hang a sign around your neck and walk through the streets ringing a bell while you wail, 'Unclean.' "

Marni laughed, then became thoughtful as she let her arm fall again. "I've got to admit that I like the way jazzy clothes look and feel. It's neat."

"Bless you. Tomorrow's leading designer hopes you'll encourage that attitude in all red-blooded American females. Don't just buy clothes. Confine yourselves to Rosalie James originals and really live it up!"

Marni laughed again, then dropped the brush onto the table. "That's enough for one night. Besides, you've been talking so much I've lost count."

"Don't blame me if you lose your pzazz. As if you could."

"Oh, I will. I'm fighting the calendar, and I don't ever forget it. That's why I've got to grab every opportunity that comes my way. And *that* reminds me. Ian MacDonald of Clothco is interested in me."

"In your lily-white body or as a model?"

"Paul Howell has his own thoughts on that. He told me to stay clear."

"If the head of Clothco would let me design an exclusive line for his stores," Rosalie said fervently, "I'd let him seduce me in the show windows of every one of his stores. We could tour the country together, showing the line and putting on free exhibitions for the customers in the windows."

"I don't care what Paul says, Ian MacDonald is too big a man in the business for me to give him the brush." Marni stood, looking fiercely determined.

Rosalie sobered. "What can he do for you, Marn?"

"I don't know, but after I talk to Paul, I intend to find out."

Her roommate stared at her. "You know, I sometimes think I can read you inside out, and then, all of a sudden, I realize I don't dig you at all."

"What is there to dig?" Marni applied lotion to her hands, arms and legs, the last of her night's beauty preparations, and then wandered around the simply furnished bedroom while the liquid dried.

"According to the standards of ordinary mortals like me, you've got everything. You're so beautiful that—well, if I were you, I wouldn't do anything. I'd just loll around, letting people look at me."

"I had nothing to do with making my face and body the way they are. I guess that's why I've got to prove I can *be* somebody."

"Lord, girl, you are. Four pages of ads in the last *Vogue*, four in *Chic* and two editorial pages in *Bazaar*. Not counting all the automobile and refrigerator and God-knows-what-all ads in a jillion other magazines. Not to mention one out of every three glamour commercials on TV. You have brains. And you could marry any one of a dozen sterling fellows. From that investment banker with the cute little dollar bills showing—to Dave Bernstein."

"David and I scarcely know each other, so I wish you'd stop—"

"Consider my tongue cut out, and let's start all over again. Everybody I know and nearly everybody you know would change places with you at the drop of a hemline."

"I suppose I ought to be satisfied, but I'm not." Marni clenched her fists, her long nails digging into the palms of her hands. "And even if I could change the way I feel, I wouldn't. No matter what happens, I'm in this crazy business all the way!"

The morning started badly. Barbara was ashamed of her previous night's conduct and, avoiding Paul, tried to ease the guilt-created tension by screaming at the children. Her attack was baseless, Paul came to their defense at the breakfast table and they quarreled bitterly before he left the apartment, putting him in a sour mood.

His advertising agency meeting lasted the better part of the morning, an hour and a half longer than he had anticipated, making a hash of his appointment schedule and increasing his frustration. But there were compensations, he thought, as he finally hurried on to his own office in a taxi. He had sold six models for the commercials that would be made for the thirty-nine-week series, and although Katya had not been available, it hadn't been difficult for him to replace her with Marni Kendall.

His offices were located on the forty-fourth floor of a new skyscraper tower, and Paul eased himself in through the telephone room, the heart of his operations. There four operators, under the direction of a supervisor, accepted booking calls and worked them into the hour-by-hour, day-by-day schedules of the girls. Unauthorized visitors, including the agency's clients, were not permitted to visit the telephone room, and doors through which they might enter were kept locked. The calls were coordinated by the supervisor, who made the actual job assignments, and notations—on green paper for fashion shows and other personal appearances, yellow for photography work and a bright orange for television—were posted in the so-called models' room, a lounge restricted to the use of clients. There the models congregated between jobs to gossip, await calls and, if they wished, drink coffee made by a mammoth machine that Paul had purchased when a large restaurant had gone bankrupt.

An air of greater formality pervaded the front office. One section was occupied by the chief accountant and his assistants; bills were sent to those who had utilized the services of models, checks were received and pay checks were made out. According to house rules, a model was paid only on Mondays; but many of the girls were perennially short of cash, and Paul conveniently looked the other way when he saw a line at the accounting window on other days.

In the executive suite were the so-called assistant directors, their associates and secretaries. Here could be found four interlocking departments, all concerned with sales. One, headed by a man, handled television appearances, and the others, run by women, busied themselves with fashion shows, advertising and high fashion photography. All models under the Howell banner paid regular visits to these department heads, who sold to the more important accounts and were responsible, in the main, for building the careers of promising newcomers.

Special events, the hiring of models for ceremonies and other occasions not covered by the principal departments, were the concern of Paul's assistant, Harriet Allen, herself a former model. The seemingly bland Harriet appeared to be the least important cog in the agency's machinery, but every girl who worked through Howell knew better. It was she who held primary responsibility for finding new talent, and there was a constant parade of both experienced and of hopeful, would-be models through her office. She flew to Europe twice each year in her search for new faces and had brought a number of girls to New York from Sweden, Germany and England, as well as a few Eurasians from Paris. It was her firm theory that French, Italian and Dutch girls did not meet the beauty standards of American modeling, and there were none under contract.

Paul, in order to slip unseen by employees or models into his own sanctum, went from the telephone room through Harriet's office, and it was his practice to hurry through the room silently.

But Harriet, a plump woman with sprinkles of gray in her brown, curly hair, halted him.

"There's someone I want you to meet, Paul," she said, and he saw she was conducting an interview. "Miss Black, Mr. Howell."

Fran Black rose from her chair and held out her hand.

He was rushed and noticed only her obviously dyed hair and wise-eyed smile.

"I wish you'd have a little chat with her, Paul," Harriet said. "I think we might have a place for her."

He could have strangled Harriet, who should have known better than to force an interview on him when he was already so far behind in his day's work. But, strictly speaking, he couldn't blame her; she had authority to sign clients herself only when she made her European jaunts, and ordinarily she recommended newcomers for Paul's consideration.

"I hope you don't mind waiting, Miss Black," he said, trying to sound apologetic, "but I've been out all morning, and I've got to sweep a few crises under the rug before I can sit back for a little chat with you." He made his escape quickly, before she could reply.

His own office, although simply furnished with a swivel chair and desk, a few visitors' chairs and a table on which stood a small motion picture projector and equipment for viewing enlargements of photographs, always gave him a sense of pleasurable accomplishment. Lining the walls were scores of color photos of beautiful young women, past and present Howell clients who had made the operation one of the most successful in the history of the business.

Putting his hat and coat in a small closet, he went to his desk and rang for his secretary as he began to look through telephone messages. The door opened and he spoke without looking up. "Morning, Edie. My notes and the binder memo on this morning's meeting are here in my attaché case. Four copies, and make sure television gets two. Tell them to notify the girls who'll be working the series, and make sure they stress that this job is to take priority over everything else. I've made firm commitments, and the sponsor won't accept substitutes."

Edie stood before his desk, calmly scribbling the orders. Tall, half-Chinese, she was mistaken for a model by most visitors, and, in fact, had come to the office eight years earlier hoping to become a client. Fortunately for the agency, she had been unable to lose the necessary weight for the purpose, and instead Paul had acquired the best secretary he had ever known.

"*Two* messages from Didi Martin, Edie? What's eating her?"

"Something about an appointment with Marni Kendall. Miss Martin was—well, insistent. And nobody can be bitchier."

Paul grinned sympathetically. "I'll give you the pleasure of calling her back. Tell her I'm talking to Marni today, and we'll have Marni give her a direct ring this afternoon. She'll demand to talk to me, but tell her I'm still out. Tell her anything, just so you can keep her off my neck, and if you keep promising Marni will call her without fail, you can get her off the line. What's this from Ian MacDonald?"

"He said it was personal, Mr. Howell."

For a moment or two Paul was lost in thought, tapping the telephone message against the edge of his desk. "I'll have to stall him until this afternoon. But this seems to be Marni Kendall's day. Get me her schedule."

Edie went to his telephone, pushed a button on the miniature switchboard, and had a low-voiced conversation with the supervisor. "She's free between one and two-thirty."

"That'll be just right. Cancel my lunch date, get hold of Marni and tell her I've got to see her and then make a reservation for us. Somewhere close, because I'm rushed. And make sure it's quiet. Can you reach Marni?"

"She's on photographic location with Gary Carey, but they're finishing the job at his studio."

"Fine, you can snag her there." He picked up the last of the phone messages that he deemed important, "Do I have to call the mayor's office myself?"

Edie shook her head. "It's about the models for the opening ceremonies of the Beautify Fun City campaign."

"Tell Harriet to handle it. She's making the assignments." He reached for his mail, already sorted into several piles for him, and was picking up the microphone of his dictating machine before the secretary had left the office.

For the next half hour he worked steadily and did not look up until his phone buzzer sounded. "Yes, Edie."

"Somebody in Gary Carey's studio went out to location, and brought back word that Marni will meet you here at one. I'm holding several routine calls that I'll bring in whenever you're free. And there's a girl named Black waiting in the reception room. She says she met you in Harriet's office and you said you'd see her."

He had forgotten the girl, and winced. "Let me have Harriet's poop sheet and then show her in. And Edie—"

"Yes, sir?"

"Ten-minute maximum, and I do mean maximum. If I'm not rid of her by then, the building is on fire."

"Very well, Mr. Howell." The secretary's metallic voice sounded calm.

A moment later she brought in a form, neatly typed by Harriet, who rarely used longhand:

Name: Fran Black   *Age:* ?—Claims 25
Vital Stats: 5'8"; 120 lbs; 38-23-34
Hair: Dark brunette—bad dye job   *Eyes:* violet
Type: lingerie exclusively
Experience: showroom only. 2 yrs. Lovely Lady Co; 2½ yrs.
          (current) American Beauty Lingerie & Foundations Co.
Present Income: $150 wk.
Recommendations: Too *softig* for anything but live presentations.
          We do get plenty of calls for freelance lingerie
          work, and I've found it very difficult to line up
          clients with the right figures for it. We could
          keep her busy. Potential top of about $300 wk.
          (Note: we don't often see those kind of boobs
          around here) H.A.

Paul looked up to see Fran, guided by his secretary, on the threshold. "Sorry I kept you waiting," he said, as Edie disappeared. "I'm afraid it's one of those days."

She was fascinated by the photographs. "They're all Howell

models?" She wandered down the length of the wall, studying them.

Paul had an opportunity to inspect her, which he found to the good. Her shaggy fur coat was open, and he agreed with Harriet that her figure was suited only for show work. On camera she would look far too heavy, and her breasts would be enormous.

"I guess you know I want to join the gallery." Fran shrugged out of her coat as she took a chair opposite the desk.

Paul glanced through Harriet's memo again. "I hope you aren't thinking of photographic work, Miss Black."

"I'm not skinny enough, huh?" She accepted the dictum philosophically. "Of course I could rip off a few pounds—"

"At your height," Paul interrupted, "you'd need to take off fifteen. That's a lot of pounds. However, we get calls for free-lance lingerie models. Occasionally from companies that need extra help during the buying seasons, but usually from the sponsors of fashion shows. You do bathing suits, too, I presume?"

"Anything," Fran said, and smiled her wise smile.

Paul ignored the implications. "I don't know what kind of an income you have in mind—"

"You tell me, Mr. Howell."

"Miss Allen believes you can hit a top of around three hundred a week, and usually she's remarkably accurate. Of course, you understand we offer no guarantees—"

"Sure, no hangups for anybody."

"And I hope you realize it may take us a little time to get organized on your behalf."

"I won't starve. Miss Allen told me, though, that she thought she could start finding work for me right away."

"Did she? In that case, you'll start with a bang. We don't believe in fooling our clients with false promises, and if Harriet Allen says she'll have work for you, she will. Have you looked through our client contract?"

Fran took a folded copy from her shoulder bag. "It looks okay to me. Except there's one paragraph I don't dig."

57 :

"Clause Eleven?" Paul smiled.

She looked briefly at the form. "That's it."

"What it means is that we demand certain standards of appearance. Being a Howell model carries a stature in the business, and we don't want anyone to let us down."

"Is there some way I'm not okay?" Fran stood, and, before he could stop her, unzipped and removed her dress, letting it fall to the floor.

She stood before him in a transparent bra and bikini panties, and even as he hoped that Edie wouldn't walk in, he couldn't help admiring the girl's figure. There was no question about it, she was ripe, and he rarely saw a model with her curves. "That isn't what I meant," he said hastily. "You can put your clothes on."

Fran averted her face so he wouldn't see her expression. She had stripped off her dress for a purpose and felt sure she was one client Paul Howell wouldn't forget in a hurry. She took her time climbing back into the dress.

He waited until she was seated again before resuming. "Let me be specific, although Miss Allen will go into more detail with you later. First of all, there's your hair."

The girl became belligerent. "What's wrong with it?"

Paul left more details of indoctrination to Harriet, but hoped he could convey a basic principle with a simple illustration. "For most purposes, I dare say it's all right," he began.

"I like it, and so do my friends." Fran became sullen.

"I doubt if many of your friends come to the Howell Agency to hire models, and those who do are—like everyone else—seeking a certain type of girl who will conform to an image we've tried to create through the years. Our models make an attempt to convey sex appeal and gentility at the same time."

She felt a little uncertain of herself, and her hostility began to ebb. "I've had two jobs, and I held both of them for a long time and neither company ever said anything about my hair." She reached up to stroke it, smoothing several long strands that had fallen forward.

Paul had dealt with similar problems so often that he knew how to deal with her. "Maybe they were satisfied, but apparently you weren't, or you wouldn't have come to us."

His logic dispelled some of her fears. "What do you think I ought to do?"

"I assume you're a natural brunette?"

Fran's suggestive smile indicated that after seeing her in the near-nude the question was superfluous.

Paul remained impersonal. "Provided that Harriet Allen agrees with me, as I'm fairly certain she will, I'd advise you to remain a brunette. Dark hair goes with your eyes and coloring."

"How'd you know that? I've tried being a blond—several different shades. And I even dyed my hair red once, but it made me look grungy. I don't even feel like I'm me unless I'm a brunette." She was surprised to find a man who could discuss such matters so authoritatively.

"I'm glad we're on the same beam. All I'm suggesting you do is tone it down. Keep it dark, by all means, but don't dye it that blue-black shade. Real hair is seldom that color, and never solidly so. It makes you look artificial—and hard."

"If you keep criticizing me, you'll have me all shook up." Fran was half-joking, and smiled flirtatiously.

"You'll find that Harriet's criticism will be far more intense. She often advises all sorts of makeup changes."

"Tell me the truth, now. Don't you think I look pretty good?" she demanded, fishing for a compliment.

"You're an attractive girl, as you well know."

"Then I don't see why I should change. Don't I turn you on?"

Long practice had made Paul adept at handling this sort of situation with inoffensive indirection. "It's our job to make you even more attractive. We don't make money unless you earn it. If we didn't think you could, we wouldn't take you on, and for our own sake as well as yours, we want you to live up to your full potential."

She moved in her chair, almost imperceptibly, so her skirt inched up to the tops of her thighs. And it gratified her to see that, in spite

59 :

of his high-flown talk, he was finding it difficult to avoid staring at her legs. He might spend his days in a harem filled with other beautiful women, but Fran Black saw she had the power to capture his interest, and she relished the sense of power the realization gave her.

Paul decided to cut the interview short before Edie found it necessary to interrupt. "So whenever you're ready to start, sign the contract and Harriet Allen will go to work with you."

"I'm ready right now." She leaned forward to take a pen from a marble holder on his desk, not bothering to ask permission, but paused when a framed photograph adjacent to it caught her eye. "This one must be somebody special," she said, inspecting the picture with undisguised interest. "One of your big money-makers, huh?"

"Not anymore. That's my wife."

Fran examined the photo even more closely before she signed the contract. The blond Mrs. Howell looked distant and haughty, and wasn't the type of woman he needed. Fran's snap judgments of men were seldom wrong, and she felt that Paul Howell would respond to someone who was warm, sympathetic and ultrafeminine. One never knew when an analysis might prove useful, so she filed it away in her mind.

A stiff, cold wind blew through Manhattan's canyons, seemingly picking up force, and ruffled the waters of the East River, causing a large barge laden with steel products to rock. But the weather had no effect on the small crowd gathered on the railed, asphalt pedestrian walk above the river in the east Seventies. Mothers and maids with small children, some in carriages, a pair of merchant marine sailors, an elderly man and two old women, along with several schoolgirls in their teens, had gathered to watch the free show.

Gary Carey, a slender young man with long hair, who was dressed in a long jacket, trousers and shoes of dark green suede, held his camera up to his face, and, moving backward, clicked the instrument repeatedly as he directed an unending stream of instructions at the model he was photographing. "Keep coming toward me, that's it. Now glance out at the river. Is the barge still there? Good, look at it. Pretend it's a yacht. You love yachts, darling, who doesn't? Look back at me, slowly, and show me how much you love yachts. An adorable expression. Hold it, but don't let it freeze. Marvy, darling!"

The photographer's assistant, a short, squat young woman laden with coats, extra cameras, and a clipboard, called out a sudden warning. "You'd better stop. Her hair is blowing in her face!"

Carey's voice rose a half-octave. "Don't dare stop. And Eleanor, when I want your advice, I'll ask you for it, darling. The way her hair is blowing in her face makes this a lovely summer day, with a sweet little breeze cooling her."

The teenagers in the crowd laughed loudly.

"Keep walking, darling. Now, I want you to turn slowly toward the railing. When you reach it, lean on it and look out across the sea. You don't see Welfare Island, darling. Just the open sea, and your lover, who's out there on a sailboat. Give me the left profile, and look pensive. You wish he'd taken you sailing, instead of leaving you behind for the day. Oh, marvy!"

The model gasped.

"You caught the mood perfectly. Whatever is wrong?" Carey became waspish as he lowered the camera.

Marni Kendall, attired in a sleeveless, low-necked dress of organdy chiffon, stood shivering and rubbing her bare arms as the wind whipped her short, full skirt. "I dare you to look pensive for more than ten seconds when you rest your arms on that rail. It's made of ice, Gary."

"You'll have to be a big, brave girl, Marni. It's what the client wants. Right, Eleanor?" While he waited for the script girl to look through a sheaf of papers on her clipboard, he busied himself with

61 :

Marni's appearance. First he applied an additional coating of pale gloss to her lips, and then, after dabbing at her forehead with a tissue, he took a long comb from his pocket and brushed her hair to one side. "The exotic touch," he said with a grin.

"You're right, Gary. It's one of the musts."

"You'll just have to bear it, darling, but I give you my word, it won't take long. Do it right, and we'll be on our way back to the studio in less than five more minutes."

Marni struck her pose, placing her forearms on the cold iron railing without flinching.

"That girl is going to catch pneumonia," an old lady said indignantly.

Someone, wise in the way of Manhattan street scenes, explained to her that an advertisement or fashion photo of some sort probably would appear in print during the coming summer months.

Marni found it easy to shut out the sounds of the crowd. When she had been breaking in as a free-lance model, it had been torture to be observed by total strangers, but she had been watched by so many such casual audiences by now that she was no longer bothered by either their gaping or comments. They, like the skyscrapers to the southwest and the streams of six-lane traffic on the Franklin D. Roosevelt Drive adjoining the walk, were part of the background to which every model working in New York eventually became accustomed.

"Your lover," Carey said, "has gone pearl diving, and is bringing back a graded necklace for you. That's why you can't wait until you see his sailboat. Marvy, darling! Hold the laugh, but don't freeze it! Think of those matched pearls!" Suddenly he spoke in a deeper, matter-of-fact voice. "And that, my love, is the end of this roll of film."

Marni immediately broke her stance and hurried to the script girl. Twisting a long silk scarf around her throat, she donned a trench coat, then exchanged her pastel pumps for a pair of knee-high boots, which she took from a large canvas tote bag. "If I had mittens," she said, "I'd wear them too."

"Don't crush the dress," Eleanor said.

"Let the client sue me!" Marni retorted. "With my compliments."

Carey was putting away his camera. "Back to the grog shop for an assignation," he announced cheerfully. Like Marni, he ignored the still-lingering little crowd.

"I'm just going to have time to change, Gary," Marni told him. "I hope they don't want any more indoor shots."

The photographer turned to his assistant. "Eleanor?"

The script girl ruffled through the papers on her clipboard. "We got most of the indoor frames before we came out here."

"I have no time for more," Marni declared. "I'm booked solid for the rest of the day." Her teeth were chattering slightly or she would have sounded annoyed.

Carey took her arm, and they headed for the walk over the drive. "As soon as I've made the prints," he said soothingly, "I'll check them against the order. And if we need more, I'll book you for a two-hour minimum, darling."

"I'm busy all day tomorrow, too. I won't have a minute."

"The day *after* tomorrow, then. You're turning into another Katya. A real prima donna."

"Am I?" Marni was contrite. "I'm sorry, Gary."

"Don't be. The more heavily you're booked, the more you can throw your weight around. And the busier everyone knows you are, the more they'll demand that Howell send them you, nobody else. The guaranteed formula for success as a model. Become so popular you can't handle more than half the jobs that are offered to you. Grab the brass ring while you can get it, darling."

"I fully intend to," Marni said.

The executive reception room of Clothco, Incorporated, was impressive in its simplicity. Located on one of the top floors of a new skyscraper, it was furnished in stark decor. There was no reading material on the Scandinavian-modern tables, and the only ornamentation was provided by a photographic montage, filling one entire wall, that displayed all thirty-two of the corporation's department stores.

The office of the president resembled a living room and might have come, intact, from one of the furniture departments in the chain. Chairs and sofas, rugs and drapes and lamps looked as though they belonged in a private home, and the chief executive used a polished oak table rather than a desk. There, however, the illusion ended. A battery of telephones stood at one side of the table and were in constant use as twice-daily reports came in from each store manager. Papers stood in compulsively neat stacks, awaiting disposition; the table was bare at the beginning of each day and would be cleaned off again by night. Everyone in the organization knew that documents moved swiftly across the table, orders scribbled in the margins in a small, neat hand.

"We work in a shirtsleeves business," Ian MacDonald frequently told his vice-presidents, and he acted accordingly. He placed his jacket in a clothes closet when he first arrived each day, and if he thought his trousers were too wrinkled, he changed into another suit before going off to an outside meeting or engagement. His subordinates sometimes joked, privately, that he looked like a clerk who was out of place in the large office, and they wouldn't have been surprised to see him write with a quill pen.

But when he removed his steel-rimmed reading glasses and glowered at someone sitting opposite him, he made it very plain that he was a commander who expected unquestioning obedience to his wishes. He wasted no time in personal conversation, and anyone who expected to hold his place in the hierarchy, much less rise higher, confined himself strictly to the business at hand.

Carlo Bennett was valuable to his superior because he seemed to possess a sixth sense that enabled him to guess, most of the time, why he was being summoned. When the buzzer sounded in his office, calling him to his master's presence, he gathered three files that he had put aside earlier in the day and went at once.

"Good morning, Mr. MacDonald," he said, always careful to address the president formally during business hours.

MacDonald did not glance up from the document on which he was scribbling. "Bring in your confidential financial folder," he said.

"I have it right here."

MacDonald grunted, put down his pen and removed his glasses. Nothing in his hard eyes or coldly precise manner served as a reminder of the previous night's intimacy they had shared with Fran Black. "What have you learned about Schwartzman-Burns? Give me a complete rundown."

Bennett opened two of the manila folders and placed them before him on the table. "It's a privately owned corporation, so a purely arbitrary value has been placed on the stock. The last sale I could trace, about thirty months ago, brought twenty-four thousand dollars per share."

"It's now fifty thousand." MacDonald offered no explanation of his own knowledge.

Not questioning him, Bennett made a notation. "The owners have always kept their basic finances simple. There are only one hundred shares of the stock, but the paper value of fifty thousand doesn't represent their true worth. That would make the store worth only five million, and it would be a steal at that price."

MacDonald made no comment.

"Louis Burns is the single largest shareholder. Until a few years ago he owned thirty shares, but he now has forty, having bought his late brother's stock from his widow, Mrs. Ann Burns. The Schwartzman heirs represent the second largest block, with thirty percent among them—"

"Not any longer," MacDonald interrupted. "Their shares recently were accumulated by outsiders."

Again Bennett made a notation, but it was unnecessary for him to ask the identity of the buyers. When his superior expressed an interest in a property, he took it for granted that Clothco was beginning to acquire its stock. "The other owners are very difficult to trace. There are a couple of shares out in California somewhere, each of them owned by a senior executive who has retired. All the Schwartzman-Burns people seem to go to California when they retire, and there must be six or eight of them floating around out there. I'm not sure which of them got the stock, and if they've died, the shares have been passed along to their heirs, which further complicates the problem."

"Do you know where these people have settled?"

"Mostly in San Diego and Palm Springs."

"How soon can you make a trip out there?" MacDonald's tone indicated he would tolerate no delays.

Bennett hastily revised his personal plans. "I've tentatively penciled in week after next."

MacDonald nodded. "Don't go near our Los Angeles or San Francisco stores. Even though nobody would know the real purpose of your visit, they might start guessing. I'm sometimes amazed at the way word leaks out when something big is in the wind. And we've got to play cozy on this operation. Very cozy."

"Yes, sir," Bennett said, wondering how he could trace retired Schwartzman-Burns executives if he couldn't casually question their possible friends on the Clothco payroll.

"What else?" MacDonald became impatient.

"I've told you all the shares I've been able to locate so far, Mr. MacDonald."

"Then you don't know about Barbara Howell?"

His scorn made Bennett want to cringe. "No, sir."

"I had the very great pleasure of sitting with her late yester-day, at the Schwartzman-Burns fashion show." MacDonald was becoming increasingly contemptuous.

His assistant was trapped, and knew he would only make matters worse if he dissembled. "I'm afraid I don't know who she—"

"The daughter of Mrs. Ann Burns and the late Arthur Burns. The wife of Paul Howell, the models agency man. She was a model herself before she started having kids."

Bennett's faint smile indicated his availability for extracurricular activities, should his services be required.

"She owns five shares." MacDonald spoke succinctly.

His assistant scribbled a few words inside one of the manila folders.

"I'll want to know a great deal more about Mrs. Howell. I believe, as you've indicated, that the rest of the stock is scattered, and I'm inclined to doubt that any one person owns more than a single share. That makes Mrs. Howell's five shares vital to us. We can expect retired executives to show loyalty to Lou Burns."

"Won't his niece be even more loyal, Mr. MacDonald?"

The narrow shoulders rose and fell. "You never know about families. Or about who controls what, inside one. Is Barbara Howell her own boss, or does she do what her husband tells her in business matters?"

Bennett started to write again.

"Don't bother putting any of this down. I'll look into the Howell situation myself."

The assistant looked and felt slighted.

"If you step in, no matter how subtly, Carlo, they'll know the company is involved. But I have an opening, on a purely social basis, so I'll take it from there. The Howells won't know what I'm after, any more than they'd imagine I'd do my own detective work." When MacDonald smiled, he became even uglier.

"If you could buy those five shares—"

"I'd be creeping up on Lou Burns. But I can't move too quickly with the Howells. Burns would be sure to find out I'm trying to gain control of his store, and he'd fight. He has an advantage, and he'd buy out enough of the other shareholders to get a majority interest. I'm going to save Mrs. Howell until I've salted away some other shares, and then I'll use her as the club to beat Lou Burns into selling me the whole store."

"I've heard from a dozen sources," Bennett told him, "that the store means everything to Burns. If he's really determined to hang on, we might have to go into some sort of partnership with him. It's one way to get the place."

"Clothco has never yet made a partnership deal with the owners we buy out, and I have no intention of starting a new precedent now." MacDonald rapped on the table with his knuckles to emphasize his words. "I've waited almost twenty-five years for a New York store, and I won't share it with anyone. New York is the heart of the retail trade, and Clothco won't be recognized as big time, no matter how many outlets we own, if we don't have our own here."

"Do you want me to start investigating some other properties, Mr. MacDonald?"

"I do not. I couldn't get Bergdorf or Saks. Or Bonwit Teller. Bendel is too small, and too specialized an operation. Altman's has too many departments of the kind we can't use. No, Carlo, only Schwartzman-Burns is tailored for us. Treat yourself to a walk through the store, and you'll see what I mean. We can use it as the model to upgrade the whole chain, and there isn't a store in the whole country that fits our specifications more exactly. Burns won't be the first we've squeezed out of control, or the last, and if he won't be reasonable, it'll be his neck, not mine. I need his store, and I'm going to have it!"

The restaurant was convenient to Paul's office and quiet, but those were its only assets. A converted brownstone in a neighborhood where real estate had soared astronomically, it had managed to hold out against huge offers for the property, but it could not survive much longer. The owners were elderly, the quality of the meals they served was declining rapidly and most lunch patrons were middle rank and young executives who went there only because of proximity or the desire for privacy.

Everyone in the place looked at Marni Kendall, but she was accustomed to the stares, as was Paul, of course, and neither paid any attention. The girl refused a drink, settling instead for a glass of tomato juice, and after ordering jellied madrilene, lean lamb chops and a small salad, she sat back in her chair to listen to Paul. It was the first time he had ever taken her to lunch, an honor reserved exclusively for the small handful of Howell Agency stars, and she tried not to show her feeling of excited anticipation.

Paul took a sip of his bourbon-on-the-rocks and came straight to the point. "It won't be long," he said, "before you can stop lugging your portfolio around town every day." He referred to the cumbersome contraption resembling a large thin briefcase in which models carried a sampling of their best photographs, copies of their magazine covers and their most important advertisements to show photographers and advertising agencies.

"It sounds good," Marni said. "I hope you're right."

"It's my business to be right. There's a strong groundswell in your direction, and now is the time to take advantage of it. Your bookings have been climbing, and I'd like to move your rate up to one hundred an hour. Under certain conditions."

She looked calm, but her hand trembled a little as she raised her glass of tomato juice to her lips.

"First," Paul said, "you must be willing to make the sacrifices that your new standing will demand. You've been around long enough to know what I mean, but let me run through them. You'll work like a dog—"

"It can't be much harder. I spend every day racing from one job to the next."

"It'll be worse, because you can't afford to make mistakes. When a client pays that much, he expects perfection. Consistently. If you're leading an active social life, you'll have to cut down. Show up with smudges under the eyes for just one photographer, and that'll be the end."

"I'm pretty careful," Marni said.

Paul studied her, and there was admiration in his voice as he replied, "You look it. Something has given you that extra sheen, that final plus quality."

"I suppose," Marni said thoughtfully, "it's because I want to reach the top."

"Why do you have all this ambition?" He offered her a cigarette, which she refused.

"I'm not sure, but I suppose it's because I can't stand being second best at anything."

"Fair enough." He had tested her attitude and was satisfied. It was a cruel business that required ultrafeminine young women to display a masculine drive if they hoped to reach the pinnacle in their profession. But that quality, in and of itself, was not enough. "How's your weight?"

"I've been one-ten for the past year and haven't varied more than a half-pound in either direction. I have no trouble watching the calories during the week, but after I've been up-tight for days, I sometimes go on an evening's eating binge and gobble everything in sight. I must admit I've been lucky. No matter how much of a pig I am it goes after a night's sleep. If I'm getting a bigger fee, though, I'll have to be even more careful."

"No, when a system is working, don't change it." Paul waited until their glasses were removed and their waiter brought the first course. "Will your love life get in the way?"

"I wouldn't let it. As it happens, there's nobody around I'm serious about."

Paul was not surprised. Not only were most models too busy for romances that consumed their time and sapped their energies, but their beauty and glamour frightened off all but the most determined of suitors. All the same, the assurance relieved him; all too often, when a girl did become immersed in a romantic relationship, the jealousy of her partner hampered her career.

"I've watched Katya," Marni continued, "and I think one soap-opera life is enough for any agency."

Paul returned her smile. Katya was notorious for her affairs, falling in and out of love with agility, and needed constant supervision to prevent untoward lapses in her tight schedule. "So much for love," he said. "Now, there's another angle that's on the rough side. You're fairly friendly with some of the other girls, I believe?"

"Quite a few. We're all one big sorority up at the agency." A huge imitation diamond ring sparkled on her forefinger as she spooned her madrilene.

"That will have to stop."

She was startled.

"I'm not suggesting you cut off any friends. But you'll have to become a little more remote. Not that you have much time as it is to hang around the coffee machine at the office. But stardom has its own mystique. You consciously create a difference between yourself and the herd."

"Now I see what David means," Marni said.

"Who is David, and what has he told you?"

"A friend of mine. He was a football star for years. He says he had to be one of the boys and yet stand apart, all at the same time. I'm not sure I can do it, Paul."

"You can, honey, and you will. Does your makeup embarrass you on the street? Or right at this table, with everybody in the place gaping at you?"

"Oh, no. I'd feel naked without it. Most of the time I forget I'm even wearing as much as I am."

"But you remember how it felt when you were breaking in?" Paul persisted.

Marni giggled. "For weeks I kept tripping over my eyelashes."

"Developing a new mental attitude requires the same techniques. You'll be imitated by millions all over the world, from teenagers to the middle-aged. Your hair styles, your smile, everything about you. By now you've discovered that, in the strict sense, there is no natural glamour. We manufacture it, you, the photographers and I. But the glamour is essential, and even though it may be artificial, it becomes part of you."

"I sometimes wonder."

"My wife hasn't done any modeling for years," Paul said. "But she wouldn't go out of the house without wearing full makeup, not even to do the marketing. She wears a snappy robe and some Turkish harem slippers with bells on them when she's giving our kids their breakfast. And I'm sure she puts on a half-slip covered with lace when she has a doctor's appointment."

"You're sure it isn't a put-on? I'm not questioning Barbara, but I mean—"

"No, she's thought and dressed and lived on a certain level for so long that it has all become second nature to her. Just as stardom must for you. It'll really become necessary to build a wall around yourself. Beauty is more than a natural resource. When a girl reaches the top, it has become a talent, and it must be shielded as well as nourished. Think of yourself as one of the girls, and you'll stay at your present level. Think of yourself as a star, and you'll earn six figures a year."

Marni couldn't finish her madrilene. "I'll try."

"You'll do it." Paul patted her hand. "Is that colored circle you put around your eyes your own innovation?"

"No, my roommate—you've met Rosalie—is a kook, and she encouraged me one night when I was fooling around at the mirror. But a lot of the girls do it."

"Didi Martin of *Chic* thinks it was completely your invention. Don't disillusion her. Now she wants a chat with you. All I know is that she's planning a spread on you."

"Paul, that's neat!"

"Depending on how it's handled, it could be very helpful," he said cautiously. "Don't let Didi browbeat you—"

"She wouldn't. She just oozes charm," Marni said.

"Didi," Paul said, "would burn a model alive at the stake if it would enhance her own reputation. Listen to what she suggests, but don't agree to anything. Tell her I want to see the preliminary sketches and layouts before I'll sign you for the job."

"She'll have kittens, Paul, and will scream about her editorial integrity."

"Or freedom of the press. Sure. I won't make an enemy of Didi, I promise you, not just for you, but because I'll need her as long as I operate an agency. But there are ways to skin a bitch like that, and I can always go quietly over her head—or behind her back—to Andy Reilly, her publisher."

Marni had her own ideas, but thought it would be presumptuous to express them so soon after being offered potential stardom.

"I'll set up an appointment for you with her. But watch your step. When Didi goes mod or psychedelic or arty, she can make a laughingstock of any model."

"I'll be careful," Marni promised, trimming a few bits of fat from her lamb chops.

"That leaves one minor matter to discuss. Ian MacDonald wants to take you out, and I believe you should avoid him."

Marni appreciated Paul's interest, but told herself that her social life was her own responsibility. "Why?"

"Apparently you don't know him when you see him," Paul said dryly. "They manufacture Halloween masks that are his likeness."

"Does it matter how he looks? If he's a nice person—"

"He isn't."

73 :

"There's nobody more important in the retail business, is there?" Marni realized she was being stubborn, but felt there was a principle at stake.

"Well, he and his company aren't nonentities, but MacDonald can't do much for you. Oh, his chain advertises in the fashion magazines, but the photographers and agencies Clothco uses would hire you regardless if they wanted you. You don't need him."

"I've learned to take care of myself with some pretty nasty men," Marni countered.

Paul found her persistence annoying. "You won't have to put him off yourself. I'll take care of the whole thing for you."

"Thanks all the same, but I wish you wouldn't."

Ordinarily he would have let the matter drop, reasoning that a girl who would not heed a serious warning deserved whatever might happen to her. But Marni's determination infuriated him, and he wanted to forbid her to see MacDonald. His common sense told him, however, that he had no right to interfere in her private life, and he wondered why he should care. She was valuable to the agency and would be even more important if he succeeded in establishing her as a star, but she was entitled to date anyone she pleased, or, for that matter, go to bed with anyone.

Was it possible, after all these years of keeping his models at an emotional distance, that he was becoming interested in one of them? Marni was lovely, to be sure, but so were at least a score of others under contract to him. His problems with Barbara were upsetting him, he realized, and he warned himself not to reach out to someone else.

"MacDonald has been trying to reach me today," he said curtly. "Do you want me to give him your number?"

It occurred to Marni that he was manifesting symptoms of jealousy, which delighted her. She knew literally dozens of models who automatically flirted with Paul Howell, and without exception they complained that he refused to spark to them. It was flattering to know, or at least believe, that she had aroused a personal feeling in him. "Perhaps," she said, "you and Barbara could come along to chaperone us."

Paul didn't like the idea, but at least he'd be able to keep an eye on her.

Suddenly, without warning, he wanted to get out of the degrading business of operating a models agency. It was absurd that a man of ambition and talent should spend his entire adult life acting as a nursemaid for young, beautiful women who enjoyed a brief day in the sun before being replaced by others equally glamorous and vapid. Yet, in spite of his self-disgust, he couldn't rid himself of a feeling of responsibility for Marni Kendall. Perhaps, he thought, it was because he had failed Barbara and wanted to expiate his guilt by helping someone who otherwise might make the same mistakes.

Cocktail parties for visiting high priests and priestesses of fashion were identical. The same people invariably were invited to the same hotel suites, where they drank the same drinks, ate the same semidigestible hot canapes and made the same polite, inane remarks to the same wealthy, clothes-conscious women whose sense of competition drove them to spend thousands on their wardrobes each year.

Louis Burns was tired after spending a hard, frustrating day at the store and, retreating to a far corner of the drawing room in the suite he himself sometimes rented for the identical purpose, he sipped a weak Scotch and water and debated whether he could leave quietly enough to cause no hard feelings. Then someone grasped his arm.

Anyone at the party who didn't know that Andrew Reilly was the publisher of *Chic* might have guessed it after one glance at him. Dapper in a superbly tailored suit, with shoes made for him by a famous London bootmaker, he was perpetually suntanned and always looked as though he had just come from the chair of his barber.

"I tried to return your call late this afternoon, Louis," he said, "but you were in a meeting."

Here was an opportunity to delve into something that was bothering him, and Louis Burns seized the chance. "Do you think of this party what I think of it, Andy?"

Reilly waved to the flamboyant Katya and her escort, a wealthy, middle-aged stockbroker who, at her instigation, was investing in a boutique that would bear her name. "It's hideous, but I can't leave. These people are heavy advertisers."

"Nobody will be in the little parlor that comes with this suite." Louis led the other man through a partly opened door into a smaller, ornately furnished room that, as he had predicted, was empty. "Andy," he said, closing the door, "you and I have been friends for a long time."

Freely translated, Reilly thought, that was Louis's way of reminding him that Schwartzman-Burns had advertised in *Chic* for all of the fifty years the magazine had been in business. "Good friends, Louis."

"Because of that friendship, I'll speak freely. More than twenty years ago your father acquired a share of Schwartzman-Burns stock. Ten years ago, when he died and you took over *Chic*, you also became the owner of that stock."

Reilly knew the stock was valuable, but didn't want to admit that he seldom thought about it.

"Something is going on, something I don't like. This morning I had a call from an old associate who also owns a share. He told me he's had an offer for it. When he turned down fifty thousand, these people kept raising the offer until they were willing to pay him seventy-five. He still turned them down."

"Who are these people, Louis?" Reilly was only mildly interested.

"Aha!" Louis Burns offered the younger man a cigar, and when refused, lighted it himself. "That got me to thinking, so I called Henry Schwartzman's granddaughter in St. Paul. She sold her stock a month or more ago. She thought I knew."

The matter assumed a greater significance, and Reilly's boredom vanished. "Who—"

"I wish to God I could find out." Louis chewed on the cigar, puffing hard. "Everything is being done through a dummy front, an investment banking firm. They wouldn't tell me who the principals are. So I have to ask myself, why should people start buying my store's stock and try to hide their identity? I can only come to one conclusion. Somebody wants to gain control and take the store away from me."

"Sounds logical."

Louis looked hard at him. "Has anybody approached you, Andy?"

"I haven't had a nibble."

"That's very strange." Louis frowned, wondering whether to believe him.

"Probably," Reilly said, "it isn't even known that I own it. You've never made a list of your shareholders public, have you?"

"Why should I?"

"Then that explains it," the publisher said. "I'd guess I haven't been approached because the takeover crowd doesn't know I hold the stock."

"In the name of our friendship," Louis said solemnly, "I want to ask a favor of you."

"I'll gladly do whatever I can."

"Don't keep it a secret. Tell a few people you have the share. Let the word out to your staff, even to the free-lance photographers and models. The authors who do articles for you. Everybody. And pretty soon the news will spread, the way everything does in the fashion industry. Then, maybe, the investment bankers will come to you, and you can find out what I can't, who the principals are."

"It's a tall order, Louis, so I won't make you any promises I might not be able to keep. But I'll be glad to do what I can for you." Reilly felt he had nothing to lose.

Ian MacDonald's quick telephone call had done the trick. He had four seats for the opening of a new Broadway musical, and he hoped Paul and Barbara Howell would join him. Perhaps the model he had admired would be free that evening, too.

Paul had recognized the clever ploy, but in view of Marni's intransigence had accepted. It was better, as they had agreed at lunch, that he and Barbara accompany her on a date with MacDonald. And Barbara had been so pleased by the invitation that she hadn't asked him, when he had explained the situation to her, why he felt it necessary to shepherd a model whose private life, after all, was her own business. It was just as well that she hadn't been curious, as he couldn't have answered, even to himself.

The evening got off to a far better start than Paul had anticipated. The women had conferred by telephone and had agreed not to hide shapely legs beneath long evening dresses. Barbara, in a short gown of black bugle beads and her mink, made no attempt to compete with the younger girl but still looked exceptionally attractive. Marni, in a backless, halter-necked dress of white sequins and a sable cape she had borrowed from a furrier whose coats she modeled in his monthly fashion-magazine advertising, was radiant.

The crowd that always gathered in front of a theater for a major opening surged forward when the two women alighted from their taxi, and several teenagers thrust autograph books at them. Barbara, walking beside her husband, smiled but demurred; Marni, at a quick nod from Paul, scribbled her signature in the books. Her name meant nothing, but the two hundred people who were watching the scene realized she was a celebrity of some sort and would recognize her likeness the next time they saw her in an ad or a television commercial.

Necks craned in the sophisticated audience, and there was a quiet murmur as the quartet moved down the aisle to their seats. Marni and Barbara enjoyed being the center of attention, and Paul was surprised to observe that MacDonald seemed unmoved by the experience. Apparently he wasn't a man who felt a need to be seen with a spectacularly attractive girl on his arm, and Paul grudgingly revised his opinion of the man.

The musical was an obvious success from the time the curtain went up, and at intermission Marni and Barbara drew more than a fair share of attention in the milling throng that pressed out to the outer lobby to smoke, see and be seen. Barbara, relishing her return to the limelight, was in high spirits, MacDonald's behavior was impeccable and Marni, as much at ease as though she had spent all her life at theatrical openings, seemed to grow lovelier. Paul cast his misgivings into the back of his mind, relaxed and stopped worrying.

After the performance they went on to a night club in the east Fifties, a crowded establishment dark enough to create an atmosphere of intimacy, yet just light enough so the habitués could see one another. MacDonald, still the gentleman, ordered champagne by the magnum and danced decorously with Marni. No one was hungry, so the host decided to delay ordering supper for a time, and the first cloud appeared on the horizon. Barbara, excited by the evening, was drinking too much, and Paul became concerned. But she was still steady on her feet as he piloted her around the dance floor, so he had no legitimate cause for complaint.

Eventually it was time for an exchange of partners, and a few moments after MacDonald took Barbara to dance, Paul and Marni rose, too. "Miss Kendall, you have an extraordinary back," he said, and it occurred to him that he, too, had been imbibing rather freely.

Marni giggled as she turned and extended her arms to him.

"You always have your mind on business. What a man. I'll bet you tell that to every girl in the shop."

"No, just you." They started to dance, and he caught a glimpse of Barbara clinging to MacDonald; the man's stance made it apparent that he was carefully refraining from taking advantage of her condition.

Marni saw her partner's glance and looked across the floor too. "Admit you were wrong," she said.

"About MacDonald?"

"Yes. He's very decent, and nice. From your description, I expected him to be a pig, but he hasn't groped once."

"So far," Paul admitted cautiously, "I seem to be wrong."

"You stew about everything."

He found the proximity of Marni's lovely face disturbing.

"I know you're upset because Barbara has been drinking—"

"You notice everything." Accustomed to the self-centered attitude of most models, Paul was surprised by Marni's sensitivity.

"Some things. But there's no need for you to be hung up. None of us is exactly sober right now." She giggled, then stumbled slightly.

He tightened his grip, holding her upright.

"Especially me."

"I'm right with you." Whatever the perfume in her hair might be, he thought it right for her.

"I'll take care of things when we get back to the table."

"A sorceress! How will you do that?"

"By telling Ian I'm suddenly starved. The crabmeat pancakes here are guaranteed to sober anyone, and I'll insist that Barbara have some, too. Okay?"

"You're very sweet, Marni."

"This is one of those nights when I think so too. All I need is a few buckets of champagne to get rid of my sense of inadequacy."

The majority of girls who came to the Howell Agency were shy, and Paul had long since learned that beauty was frequently a crutch rather than an asset. A young woman whose appearance was envied often felt herself intellectually or socially inferior and hated her own physical appeal, even when falling back on it because of real or fancied lacks in other realms. But Marni had always seemed better adjusted than many of her colleagues. "I can't imagine why you should feel inadequate," he said.

"For one thing, I'm not very bright—"

"But you are. Talk to as many women as I do, and you'll realize how far above the average you stand."

"There's a time for all things. Ecclesiastes. Right now I don't want to talk about me. I want to dance, and you have no right to be so devastating."

Paul had taken his own appearance for granted over so long a period of years that, discounting his looks in his own mind, he was surprised when someone else reacted to his physical appeal. "I'm almost old enough to be your father."

"I'd never dance with my father like this," Marni murmured, and giggling again, softly, she nestled closer.

He could feel her warm, supple body close to his, but made no attempt to put space between them. MacDonald, whom he had criticized, was more of a gentleman than he was, but at the moment he didn't care. Something stronger than Marni's beauty was a magnet that drew him to her, and he wondered what it might be, even though he realized it might be dangerous to find out.

They drifted slowly across the floor, oblivious of their surroundings and conscious only of each other, their silence deepening the bond they were forming.

Suddenly Marni broke the mood. "Let's sit down."

Paul looked at her, afraid she, too, was troubled by their unexpected intimacy.

"The head of my agency will shred me," she said, "if I show up for work with smudges under my eyes. And I'm booked for a four-hour experimental job with Didi Martin at *Chic* tomorrow at ten."

Following her back to the table, Paul saw that Barbara, who had already returned with MacDonald, had resumed her drinking, and discovered he was relieved rather than apprehensive. By now she

81 :

was too far gone to be aware of his inexplicable interest in someone else, and a feeling of freedom mingled with his oppressive guilt.

The *Chic* photographic studio was a barnlike, rectangular-shaped room located on the top floor of a thirty-six-story building. Once the penthouse office of the publisher, it had been sacrificed by Andrew Reilly because it had north, east and west exposures. What had been the secretary's office had been converted into a completely equipped darkroom and photo-processing room, and the former reception area was now a handsomely furnished dressing room.

There two young assistants from the fashion department were hanging costumes on a rack, checking a list to make sure each item was placed in the proper order. In the studio beyond the closed door Gary Carey was directing the unrolling of several sheets of heavy paper, and his strident voice carried clearly to those inside the dressing room. "Idiots! Start the blue at the ceiling molding, and bring it down to the floor. Then take another sheet and spread it across the floor. When that's done, do the same with the green on the other side of the studio. And be careful of fingerprints on the pastels. Smoothly, you imbeciles! Don't handle a roll eight feet wide like a fallen log!"

Marni, clad in a short, smocklike model's kimono, sat before the lights of the makeup mirror, calmly applying cosmetics to her face and ignoring the bustle.

Didi Martin stood behind her, watching critically. "Gary likes the blue background better than the green, so we'll try it his way first, although I don't think I agree with him."

"A little heavier with the blue shadow, then?" Marni asked.

"Well, try it, darling, and we can always tone it down."

Marni applied a subtle shade of blue to her eyelids.

Didi stopped her when she reached for a dusting puff. "Leave them shiny. I'd like to see how they'll show up."

Fashion editors always had definite ideas, so Marni, who did not care for the effect, did not protest.

"Are you ready to look at your outfits, darling?"

Marni stood and joined her at the rack.

"In this spread on you," Didi said, "I want to show each successive step, working from the outside in, of a model's all-in-one dream wardrobe. We'll start with the coat, then the suit, then the body-blouse and skirt without the jacket. And so on. Eight color pages in all."

Marni inspected each item.

"I thought we'd do a caricature of a striptease," Didi said. "You'll exaggerate each pose, but not so much that it would become grotesque. What I mean is that we'll want pzazz as well as humor."

Marni nodded, already blocking out some of her poses in her mind.

"Of course, what we're doing today is strictly experimental. I'll need Andrew Reilly's approval, and you say Paul Howell wants to horn in, too."

"That's right. He won't let me do the spread without his okay," Marni said.

"He's an ungrateful wretch, but no matter. He'll flip when he sees what we're doing. All these clothes are your size, naturally, but we won't have the final fittings done until we know we're going ahead." She handed a box of clothespins that would be used for adjustments the camera wouldn't see to one of the assistants. "Take these out to the studio. We'll do the pinnings for Gary rather than in here."

Marni, moving down the rack, came to a hanger from which two wisps of nylon were suspended. "What do you call this?"

"The ultimate essential of the all-in-one wardrobe," Didi told her. "They're used as a bra and panties, and they double as a bikini."

"You're not planning to photograph me in them?"

"But, of course, darling! They're made of the new kind of nylon —I forget the name—that dries in less than five minutes. You wear this dear little outfit swimming, and then you keep it on when you dress."

"I don't do lingerie," Marni said quietly. "I'm afraid this disqualifies me for the spread, and I'm sorry. But I thought you knew, Didi."

"You do bathing suits, don't you?"

"Well, yes. Occasionally."

"Then there's no problem. This *is* made for swimming. It's been developed too late for the summer trade, but it'll have a big advertising push for next winter's cruise wear. And you'll kick off the campaign in our spread."

Marni hesitated. "I'm afraid that's just a technicality, Didi. It's so—skimpy."

The fashion editor refused to admit defeat. "Suppose we emphasize the swim-wear angle. We can give you a beach background. Wear shades and we'll smear you with tanning oil."

The suggestions did not alleviate the nakedness of the flimsy costume, but they were reasonable; and Marni didn't want to antagonize one of the most powerful women in the industry. It would be heartbreaking to lose the job, particularly at a time when Paul was trying to create a new star.

"All I ask is that you try it today, darling," Didi urged. "We're just doing roughs, after all."

"No matter how the shots turn out, you won't use them if they look as I'm afraid they will?"

"I have no intention of embarrassing you," Didi replied firmly. "All I'm asking, for now, is that you rely on my taste and judgment."

Marni still felt misgivings, but was forced to accept.

"We'll dress you in one outfit at a time for Gary." Didi smiled soothingly and handed her the ankle-length greatcoat she would wear with high, two-toned boots.

A few minutes later the photographic session began. Gary Carey's helpers were banished to the corner from which they would operate the complex batteries of lights. Didi's assistants tugged and smoothed the greatcoat while the patient Marni stood immobile, and whenever Gary approved, a clothespin was fastened to the coat. Then Didi was dissatisfied with the model's makeup, and one of the assistants went to the dressing room, returning to apply another layer of lip gloss to Marni's mouth.

At last the photographer and the fashion editor were satisfied. Marni and one of the assistants, both in stocking feet, walked across the "carpet" of blue paper to a spot near the far wall, halting when Gary called to them. Then Marni, aided by the assistant, climbed into the high boots, moving as little as possible so she wouldn't unduly disturb the clothespins. In spite of her care, however, one fell to the floor and two others slipped, so adjustments had to be made.

"Do we need the lights while this is going on?" Marni called. "I'll be a pudding by the time we're ready to shoot."

Gary shouted an order, and several banks of hot lights were extinguished.

The fashion assistant fussed for another quarter of an hour, and by that time Didi was dissatisfied with the model's hair. This necessitated a round trip across the blue paper by the assistant, and Marni stood very still while her hair was being combed, brushed and patted into place. Since she was now wearing the boots it was essential that she move as little as possible in order to avoid making footprints on the paper.

"Give me the lights," Gary called. "Set, Marni?"

The girl closed her eyes for a moment in order to make them more luminous when she reopened them, then moistened her lips with the tip of her tongue. "Ready," she replied.

The camera started to click, and the photographer began his monologue. "You've just strutted across the stage, and the baldies out front are shouting, 'Take it off!' That's an angelic pose, Marni, but don't smile. Not yet. Strippers don't smile at the start of an act. That's better. Hold it. Hold it for another. And another. All right, rest."

Marni lowered her arms and shielded her eyes with her hand so she could see the photographer and the editor who hovered near him. "Wouldn't it be more effective if I open one button and start on the next?"

"It's an adorable idea," Didi said, "if it doesn't ruin the lines of the coat. But let's try it."

Gary was attaching a new lens to the camera. "When we do this for real," he said, "why don't we use a mockup of a stage? Something 1910-ish or thereabouts, with huge footlights."

"Adorable!" Didi exclaimed. "I wish we were using it today."

"We might put some burlesque music on the turntable, too, to provide the right atmosphere for our girl," the photographer said.

"Don't you dare," Marni called. "I'd crack up. I couldn't work with that bump-and-grind music pounding away."

The photographic session was resumed.

For more than two hours Marni alternately posed, went off in stocking feet to the dressing room to change, then returned for more photographs in the next of her costumes.

"We'll take a ten-minute break," Didi announced. "Coffee or tea, darling?"

"Something with lots of ice in it, please." Marni sat at the dressing table, propping up her feet on another chair and carefully patting her face with a tissue so she wouldn't streak her makeup.

The soft drink that one of the assistants brought her was of the low-calorie variety, which was automatically served to models.

Marni took a long swallow, then put down the glass while she massaged her calves and ankles. "I feel sorry for the girls who specialize in leg modeling," she said. "Somebody was telling me that after four or five years of it they get varicose veins."

"An occupational disease." Didi looked at her sympathetically. "Are you exhausted?"

"Not as bad as I'll be by tonight. I have a couple of hours of fittings this afternoon and then a washing machine ad."

"I'd like to see you move out of commercial advertising and confine yourself to fashion photography."

"My fee has just gone up, Didi, so I can't be that particular."

"You can be, and sooner than you think." Didi lighted a cigarette and handed it to her. "If this spread works out, as I'm sure it will, I have an idea for another series we'll use the next month, and still another for the month after that."

The prospect was breathtaking. To the best of Marni's knowledge, no major fashion magazine had ever featured spreads on one model in three successive months. "That would be so fantastic I don't think I could live with myself!"

"I intend to tie you up so exclusively that when the industry begins clamoring for you, they'll think you belong to *Chic*." Didi was smugly possessive. "Do you want to use the iron maiden?" She indicated a contraption at the far side of the dressing room, a sheet-covered mattress attached to a plywood base, which stood at a forty-five-degree angle.

It had been created for the purpose of allowing a model to lie down without mussing her hair, but Marni had never found it comfortable. "This is just fine," she said. "I'll be ready to go again in a minute."

"We're almost finished for the day, darling. All that's left to shoot is the bikini, and Gary is setting up some sand and sea effects now."

"Must we do it?" Marni sighed, stood and removed her kimono.

"If I had a body like yours, I'd insist on being photographed in the nude every day." Didi fastened the bra after Marni pulled on the panties.

The girl reddened as she looked at herself in the mirror. "If my mother sees a photograph of me wearing this thing, she'll split! And my father will disown me."

"Try these beach clogs with it, and you can hold a straw cartwheel hat in one hand. How will that be?"

"I'd like to hide behind it, frankly." Marni slipped into the clogs and put on a pair of sunglasses.

Didi laughed as she picked up a bottle of perfumed tanning oil. Marni looked at it dubiously. "That's horribly sticky stuff."

Didi was gentle but firm. "We'll end the session fifteen or twenty minutes early so you can shower. And we won't use any on your face." She began to apply the oil to the girl's shoulders, arms and back.

Marni sighed and allowed herself to be subjected to the other's ministrations.

Didi stroked on the oil, her hands caressing.

The unexpected intimacy of her touch was embarrassing, and when she began to apply the lotion to the girl's thighs, Marni deliberately broke the silence. "I wouldn't mind going to a beach."

"Perhaps I can arrange it, darling. I can think of several companies that would jump at the chance to pay for a cruise-wear feature. I've been dying to fly down to San Andros Island."

Marni looked at her blankly.

"The new in place. It belongs to Colombia, off the coast of Central America."

"It sounds marv, but I'm not sure I can get away."

"We'll talk about it." Didi wiped her hands on a towel, then flipped on the lights that encircled a full-length mirror set against the wall. "Look at yourself—the most adorable beach nymph I've ever seen."

Marni winced as she studied her reflection. "I look like a greased refugee from the pages of an under-the-counter girlie magazine I'm positively 'gusty."

"You're mad. You don't know total glamour when you see it. You not only have the smart consumptive look, you manage sex with it, and that's an achievement."

Marni took a step closer to the mirror. "You can make out the outlines of my nipples through this fabric, Didi. This is worse than doing lingerie."

Didi stood at one side to inspect her and shook her head. Then, moving behind the girl, she said, "Raise your arms."

Marni did as she was bidden.

Reaching around her, Didi lightly ran her hands across the model's breasts, then took the thin fabric between thumbs and forefingers, deftly loosening it. "How's that, better?"

Marni was startled and, unable to determine whether the gesture had been accidental or deliberate, needed a moment to recover. Then she studied her reflection, and doubly reassured herself by looking down at her breasts. "Much better," she said, and told herself the price of stardom might be higher than she was willing to pay for it.

"Show him in," Ian MacDonald said on his intercom, and stood, smiling, as his visitor was ushered into his office. "Thanks for making this at my convenience," he said.

"That's part of my business," Paul told him, shaking hands and, after doffing his coat, taking a proffered seat on a couch.

"Strictly speaking, when I indicated to you the other evening that I'd like a chat with you, I wasn't thinking in terms of your models agency. Not as such."

Paul was surprised, but thought it unlikely that the request was in any way connected with MacDonald's interest in Marni Kendall.

"I'll waste no time. Clothco thinks you're our kind of man, Paul, and we're prepared to make you an offer to join us that I hope you'll find attractive."

Really astonished, Paul's guard rose higher. "I hadn't thought of giving up the agency—"

"You wouldn't have to."

"Well. I'm flattered, Ian, and I'd like to hear more."

"We've made a thorough investigation of your background, and we like everything we've learned. And from what I've seen of you myself, I think you're our man."

"You and I have done no business together."

"True, but if you'll forgive a very personal observation, you showed great tact the other evening when a couple of ladies had a little too much to drink. You handled them—and yourself—with the touch of the expert who knows women. And that isn't easy when one of them is your wife."

Obviously, the man saw a great deal.

"Clothco is a big company, and we're still expanding. We have ambitious plans. We hope to acquire a number of additional department stores. Perhaps it's even more important that we want to start changing our image for the better. In some cities we had to take over second-rate stores in order to get in, and in others we had to dip even lower. We're starting to improve both the quality of the merchandise we sell—and our image. That's where you'd come in."

Paul lighted a cigarette.

"We want better models and better-looking models in all of our stores—"

"You don't need me for that. Start paying higher salaries. I realize there's a limit, but you can't compete with the free-lance market until you raise your wage scale."

"Fair enough. But that's just the beginning, and we do need you. We want to retrain and put a gloss on all our salespeople. Dress, appearance, manners, the whole works. We'd like our customers to feel they're walking into stores like Bergdorf-Goodman or Schwartzman-Burns. You'd run the entire program. I—we—would also put you in charge of a top-to-bottom redecorating job, and with thirty-two stores in the chain—more by the time you'd finish —that would be quite an effort. I know you're no decorator, but you'd supervise the job to make sure we're high-toned enough, but not so fancy we'll scare off our old customers."

Paul saw that MacDonald was watching him closely, but showed no reaction, and merely nodded.

"We'd also give you responsibility for something we've had in mind for a long time: the training, from scratch, of all our employees who deal with the public. Salesclerks, auditing, complaints, personal shoppers, elevator operators. We'd like you to establish a school. Call it a charm, personality and tact school for purposes of discussion. They'd also have to learn something about the business, and you'd work out those courses with other departments. The school would operate on a budget, and our financial people are prepared to hammer out the details with you before you join us, if you'd like, so you'd know where you stand. Are you interested, so far?"

"Of course. I have several questions, as well as some reservations, but I'd rather hold off until you're done," Paul said.

MacDonald liked his response. "You may be wondering why we've come to you. Because you've been highly successful in shaping, managing and selling glamour. And it's glamour we need. You've taken attractive raw material, and you've shaped it and then packaged it."

"I've had offers in the past," Paul said carefully, "that have tried to take advantage of whatever reputation I've built up. They haven't really wanted me, and they weren't willing to give me any authority. They simply wanted the Howell Agency name."

"We've never had a vice-president in charge of all personnel. I'll give you both the title and the job. Does that satisfy you?"

"To an extent, it certainly does. But I hope you realize, Ian, that I'm no labor relations expert."

"You'd have to work closely with the labor relations people, but they have their own setup. Eventually we might incorporate them into your division. That's some years away, though, so there's no sense in worrying about it now. Let's get down to the obvious, which you haven't asked about."

"I knew you'd bring it up." Paul returned MacDonald's smile, and had to admit that when the man put himself out, it was almost possible to forget his ugliness.

"We understand your present earnings average somewhere between thirty-five and forty thousand a year. Closer to forty these past few years."

"That's pretty accurate," Paul admitted.

"Clothco would make the job worth your time, so we're happy to offer you fifty as a starter. With a five-year, nonbreakable contract."

Paul laughed. "That's flattering, too, but any contract that lawyers draw up can also be broken by lawyers."

"What I mean is that if we parted, for whatever the reason, we'd guarantee you the full five years of salary."

"Very generous."

"You have to pay in this world for good men," MacDonald said. "Now, from something you indicated at the start of our conversation, I glean that you're reluctant to give up your agency."

"Very."

"You might not have to. Keep an interest in it, and turn the management over to somebody else. And here's a thought we can examine more closely some other time. Clothco is making acquisitions outside the department store field. We recently bought a dress manufacturing company, although I'll ask you to keep that under your hat, as we've made no announcement yet. And we're looking into a cosmetics company. We might be interested in buying out the Howell Agency and continuing the operation. We'd keep your name on it, and you'd supervise it, but you'd have to put someone else in active charge."

"I'd have no time for day-to-day operations, that's certain," Paul said.

MacDonald brightened, acting as though an idea had just occurred to him. "We might even work out an arrangement that leaves you a rooting interest in the agency."

"I'd like that."

"Good. That's the basic offer, Paul. We can refine the details later, but I'd like your initial reactions."

"I want to think about it and explore the whole thing."

: 92

"Call on anyone here. I believe you'd find chats with several of our vice-presidents useful. All of them are at your disposal, and I'll have someone call you in a day or two to set up a few dates, if you'd find that helpful."

"I would, thanks."

MacDonald remained pleasant, but a slightly harder note crept into his voice. "You indicated there were several things you didn't particularly like?"

"I wouldn't put it that way," Paul said, realizing it would not be easy to work for a man who habitually put others on the defensive. "I'm trying to think of my long-range future—"

"So you should. We can give you the contractual right to invest five thousand of your salary each year in Clothco preferred stock. How does that sound?"

"Good, thanks." Paul hesitated briefly. "I suppose I'd spend quite a lot of my time visiting the company's outlets around the country."

"Like the rest of us, you'd spend one-third or more of your time on the road."

"Don't misunderstand me, Ian, I don't mind travel."

"I expect every executive in the company to pay at least one visit to each store in the chain every twelve months. I do it myself. There are feelings and currents you can pick up only on the ground."

"I've learned that in my own business. What bothers me is a personal quirk. I came straight to New York from college, and fell into modeling almost by accident. In those days I wanted to be a theatrical producer and hoped to work my way up by starting as an actor."

"But there weren't many jobs for actors, and somebody steered you into modeling."

"Your investigators did a good job on me," Paul said. "I'm mentioning the past for only one reason. I've become a New Yorker. There are other parts of the country I'll always love, but this town has become home to me. This is the nerve center of America, and the decisions that are made here influence the rest of the United States."

"It isn't accidental that the Clothco headquarters is located here," MacDonald said, his smile bloodless. "California might argue, but this is where clothes are designed, made and given a start across the country."

"That's my argument," Paul said, "and it's what disturbs me in your operation. You may have your headquarters here, but your stores are everywhere else. Men who sit in an office all day, just don't know what's happening here. Milwaukee, St. Louis, Denver, even the West Coast cities, pick up their trends and tempos from New York. And visits to those towns—or Boston, Atlanta, where will you—aren't going to enlighten you. They're following the trends set in New York, and in the case of the Clothco stores, they're someone else's trends. You get me, I'm sure."

MacDonald's fleeting grin indicated his belief that he was far ahead of his visitor.

"You could set your own styles here, and create your own fads," Paul said. "I'd think that would be almost a necessity, now that the company is moving into manufacturing, too."

"I don't think we're blind to the potentials," MacDonald told him.

"I don't think we're meshing, Ian. What I'm trying to say is that you have no New York outlet, and from what I've heard and read and seen, it's a major weakness. I wouldn't want to make Clothco just another stepping-stone to a still better job. If the potential is here, I'd want to spend the rest of my life with the company, helping it grow. But the lack of a Judas sheep to lead the flock is a positive weakness, in my opinion, and I'd want to know a great deal more about your operations before I can give you a final answer."

"We're in the process of overcoming the deficiency," MacDonald said. "Please consider that information confidential, and I'm sorry I can't tell you any more at present."

: 94

"You're getting a New York store?"

"We've been conscious of our weakness, as you've rightly called it, and we're doing something about the problem. I hope—and expect—it to be solved before the ink on your contract is dry. So, if I were you, I wouldn't give that aspect of the matter too much weight. The New York merchants run an exclusive fraternity, but the door has been battered down occasionally."

"I've been hearing rumors about you for several years, you and several others who supposedly have been shopping for a New York store. May I ask you—off the record, like the rest of this talk— what store you have in mind?"

MacDonald was deliberately vague and misleading, never failing to keep in mind that, if their projected deal didn't jell, he was talking with Louis Burns's nephew-by-marriage. The risk he was taking was great, but there were times when a man had to take chances, and the stake was high. "We're dickering with several. It isn't generally known, but there are three stores here on the market. Two are on the shabby side, and the third isn't much better, but we could pull them up." Now, if he was quoted, Burns might become confused.

"You seem to have every base covered."

"That's our system."

"How soon will you want an answer from me, Ian?"

"I can't expect you to hurry a decision that will be a major influence on your life. On the other hand, we need you now, and if not you, someone with your qualifications."

"That's the one thing I don't understand. It's a great offer, but why make it to me? There must be men better qualified for the position than a guy who runs a models agency, no matter how well he runs it."

"We don't agree," MacDonald said. "In our corporate view, and in my emphatic personal opinion, you have assets that make you just right. Unique. You can be valuable to us in so many ways, including some that you yourself don't even know."

Cleo stood in the center of the little living room, her slender body encased like a mummy's in yard after yard of gleaming ivory satin, with only her black arms free. Rosalie James knelt beside her, a cushion of pins attached to one wrist and other pins in her mouth, and she muttered unintelligibly when the doorbell rang.

"If you leave me standing here," Cleo said, "I'll probably topple over."

Rosalie stood and started toward the door. "I still haven't decided whether to put a slit in the skirt. If I ever finish it. So you'll just have to topple. But don't get that material dirty." She opened the door, and flushed. "Hi, Dave."

"Hello," David Bernstein said, his bulk filling the door frame. "Am I interrupting something?"

"No, come in and watch the world's most artistic, unrecognized designer in the throes of creation. But I'm afraid Marni isn't home." Giving him no chance to reply, she continued quickly, "Cleo, this is Professor David Bernstein. Dave, meet my living dummy."

"I don't dare shake hands, professor," the black model declared. "I'm being held together by a couple of small pins, and under all this drapery I'm not suitable for mixed company."

"I've barged in at the wrong time," David said, and started to edge toward the door.

Rosalie jabbed a long pin through his sleeve, holding him. "We're drinking some very bad wine, and there's no reason you shouldn't help us kill the bottle, even if Marni isn't home. Unless you think we're carriers of some exotic disease."

"Rosalie can't drink," Cleo added, "and she takes my life in her hands with those pins. *And* a scissors. So please save me, professor."

"All right," David said with an apologetic laugh. "I'll stick around for just one glass."

"Tumblers—the only glasses we have—are in the kitchen cupboard. Second shelf. And the bottle is on the table."

David shed his coat, went into the small kitchen for a glass, and, as Rosalie returned to her labors, picked up the bottle from a coffee table. "Did you call this a bad wine? It's probably the most expensive aperitif made in France. It's tremendous."

"She's ignorant," Cleo said. "We put up with Rosie because she sometimes gives us the dresses she designs."

"When nobody else will buy them, and you're an ungrateful bitch. I'm a beer girl myself. I can't help it when men bring wine to the apartment."

It seemed obvious to David that the man responsible for the wine was one of Marni's admirer's, not Rosalie's, and a wealthy one at that. "As I said, I should have phoned. But I just finished a lecture, and I dropped in on impulse."

"I expected Marni home for dinner, but she phoned. A last-minute date."

"A business date," Cleo added diplomatically.

David grinned at her.

"I'm like Heidi, I wouldn't lie," the model said. "It's with Ian MacDonald, who owns more department stores than I have dresses."

Rosalie, kneeling again, jabbed the other girl with a pin to silence her.

David was embarrassed, too, but covered. "I know you," he told Cleo. "You're Julius Jones's girl."

"You read too many gossip columns, professor."

"Not one, from one year to the next. I've met you when you've been with Julius."

The draped satin interfered with her shrug.

But David correctly interpreted the gesture. "I spent half my life behind Julius's position at left defensive tackle."

The girl's mascara-fringed eyes widened. "You're that Bernstein! God, I'm stupid. What's with the 'professor' jazz? Oh, I know. Julius said you were going to be a teacher."

"You see what a small world it is." He poured some wine into the tumbler near her hand.

"Don't give Rosie any more." She warned.

"As a matter of fact, don't," Rosalie added. "It's groovy but I won't be. One is my limit. And you two have met. Small-world department. Or do all football players dig models?"

"Only the smart ones," Cleo said. "And I don't go with Julius anymore."

"I'm sorry," David said politely.

"I'm not. When he started carrying his paranoid rages off the football field, I had it."

"There!" Rosalie exclaimed, standing again and backing off from her creation. "It's done. What do you think?"

"Very pretty," David said blankly, then rallied. "Anyway, Cleo looks great in it."

"I can't see myself in the mirror from here, and I can't move," the model declared.

"Where's the mirror?" David asked.

She gestured in the direction of the adjoining bedroom.

He laughed, and gently picking her up under the arms, carried her to the mirror and deposited her in front of it.

"That's what I call groovy service," she said, and added to Rosalie, who had followed, "It's divine, Rosie. Honestly. And you're in."

"Right now I hate it," the designer said morosely, "but it's the best I can do. I'll have to take out a couple of pins before you climb out of it."

"I'll move on," David said hastily, backing toward the door. "Tell Marni I'm sorry I missed her, and I'll phone first, next time."

He paused at the door. "Come to think of it would you kids like to go somewhere for a bite?"

"Love to," Cleo said.

"I haven't had a real meal in a week," Rosalie said in the same breath, "but this is one night that's out. I've got to put this dress together for real so it'll win me a job tomorrow morning. But you and Cleo go."

David could not persuade her to change her mind and retreated to wait behind the closed door separating the two rooms while Cleo changed into her own clothes. It felt odd to be in Marni's apartment, waiting for someone else, and he felt a strange twinge of guilt, but consoled himself with the thought that the casually arranged meal with Cleo wouldn't be a real date.

"What makes this pantsuit neat," Marni said, "is that the tunic makes a perfect dress for a concert when I take off the pants."

"That's one reason we sell so many of them," Ian MacDonald told her, escorting her through his apartment. "In any case, let me apologize again for getting hold of you so late."

"Please don't! I didn't get the message until I was leaving the photographer's studio. His receptionist had forgotten to send it in to me. I know I'll love the concert, and I appreciate the opportunity to get patched up here for the evening instead of going all the way home. There just wouldn't have been time, not if we're going to eat first, and I'm starved."

"Well, I'm delighted you could make it at the last minute, so there we are." MacDonald paused before the open door of a guest room. "Will this do? There's a bathroom beyond it."

"Sheer luxury," Marni said, admiring the room.

"Is there anything you need?"

"No, thanks." She held up her leather nosebag. "A model can

travel around the world with what she carries in one of these. I won't be long, I promise." She entered the room, and the door closed.

MacDonald started toward his own room but heard the chimes at the front door and went to answer the summons.

Carlo Bennett came into the apartment. "I was just behind you," he said, "but I thought I'd give you a few minutes alone. She's a real doll, this one."

"Obviously, you got my message at the office."

"You bet, Ian." Bennett's quick eyes searched the living room. "Where'd she go?"

MacDonald remained in the foyer. "I want you to go through these tonight," he said, picking up a sheaf of papers from a small table. "Be ready to give a summary at the executive committee meeting in the morning, Carlo."

Bennett absently stuffed the papers into his attaché case and started down the steps into the living room.

His superior put a detaining hand on his arm. "I wanted you to pick up the reports, that's all," he said calmly.

Bennett had known him to be coy when they were dealing with a new girl, and grinned. "You've got great taste, Ian," he said. "I'm raring to go."

MacDonald stared at him for a moment, then reached out and, with surprising force, flicked him across the mouth with the back of an open hand, a ring on his finger cutting a deep gash in Bennett's lip. "You'll keep your distance from this young lady," he said coldly, "now and in the future."

Bennett's eyes grew black, but he curbed his temper, and applying a handkerchief to his bleeding lip, silently left the apartment. Some day, he thought, someone would even the score with Mac-Donald, and he loathed himself for lacking the courage.

Barbara Howell went to the sideboard cabinet for a bottle of brandy and brought it with her to the dinner table. "Want some in your coffee?" she asked, pouring a generous quantity into her own cup.

Paul shook his head. "And that's about all we said, honey. Neither MacDonald nor I mentioned any specific time limit, but he intimated as I was leaving that he'll give me a few weeks to think about the offer. Call it a month, I'd think."

She looked down at her cup as she stirred the brandy into the coffee.

"Well, what do you think?" Paul asked.

Barbara raised her head. "You don't want to seem too eager, I suppose, so you'll have to wait a few days. But who needs a month?"

"I'm not at all sure I'm going to accept," he said.

The spoon clattered as it dropped onto the saucer. "You've got to be joking."

"There are all sorts of angles that need to be explored and weighed," Paul said. "Once I make this move, I can't go back to the agency, so I want to be certain this offer is right before I commit myself."

"What could be wrong about it? Clothco is powerful and rich, and Ian told me the other night that it's the fastest-growing store chain in the country. What more do you want?"

"An impartial analysis of their position, for one thing."

Barbara had considered her question rhetorical, and did not hear his reply. "And I'd think Ian would be a wonderful person to work with."

"You liked him socially, and so did I. But everybody who has ever done business with him says he's a complete bastard."

"Are you going to listen to other people or use your own judgment?"

"Both, if I can help it. The challenge is attractive, and so is the opportunity to grow. For that matter, I like the money, and the chance to keep at least a part of the agency. In fact, that's one of the problems. The whole setup looks too good, Barb. Out of nowhere this offer has come to me, a guy who creates and sells glamour. I'm not even in the retail business. So why come to me?"

"I thought Ian explained that to you." Inhaling the aroma of brandy and coffee, she became scornful. "He thinks you can do the job, you self-effacing jerk."

"I'm sure I can handle it, if the responsibilities are what he outlined to me. Once I've learned something about department stores, that is. What bothers me is that there must be a dozen men in the field already who could do every bit as well."

"Then be glad you've been called to his attention."

"Why are you so anxious to have me accept?"

"For all the obvious reasons. Plus a few of my own."

"Such as?"

"When you're no longer active in the agency, people can't say I'm getting calls because of your influence." Barbara spoke defiantly.

Her husband blinked at her, slowly lighting a cigarette and pouring himself another cup of coffee. "When did you decide to go back to modeling?"

"I've been thinking about it for a long time, and don't look at me like that. I have no intention of competing with twenty-year-olds. But there's a market for someone of my age, and you know it."

"Well, yes," he conceded. "A limited market."

"I'm sure I could pick up layout advertising and TV. And an occasional fashion show. I still know everybody, so I might even do some high fashion photography. Not much—I'm not kidding myself—but enough to prove I still have it. How many women do you know in their midthirties with my face and figure?"

"None." A return to modeling could be her salvation, provided she succeeded, he thought. But, if she failed, she might fall apart at a far faster rate. "Both of us," he said, "have a lot of thinking to do."

"Not me. I know what I want." She saw an opportunity at last to rid herself of the bleak desperation that engulfed her and was prepared to do anything in order to achieve her desires.

"I'm sympathetic, Barb. Certainly I'm not refusing you the right to go back to modeling, if that's what you really want—"

"You couldn't."

"But I've got to decide my own future on the merits of the situation. First off, I want to have a chat with Lou Burns—"

"Oh, no," Barbara wailed.

"For God's sake, why not?" Paul demanded. "He's a relative, he knows the retail business as well as anyone in it, and he'll give me an honest opinion."

"For once, just once, I wish something would be done in this family without having to listen to the oracle of Schwartzman-Burns."

"I thought you liked Lou."

"I do, in a way. But that damn store has been a part of me all my life, and I'd like to be free of it."

Her logic, or the lack of it, was so incredible that he thought it useless to remind her she owned stock in the store worth a quarter of a million dollars, and that the income she derived from Schwartzman-Burns dividends provided her with almost innumerable luxuries. Having known nothing else, she took her very comfortable situation for granted.

"If you want to be stuck for the rest of your life as a models' den father, go ahead. But if you do, I'll still go back to work. I'll sign with another agency."

None of his competitors would take her, of course, but in her present state she wouldn't listen to reason. Paul realized that even though she was deeply involved in his own situation, he would have to work out his problem on a basis of what would be best for him.

Rusty's was crowded, and everyone there sooner or later stared at the stunning black model in the bell-bottomed tweed pants, matching gold-chained vest and sheer, long-sleeved blouse. But Cleo, although conscious of the tribute being paid her, was too absorbed in her conversation to strike poses for her audience. "Why can't I mean it when I say I have no hangup on integration? It's true!"

"If you'll forgive me," David Bernstein replied, "that's horseshit. I'll grant you that you, personally, may have won acceptance in the white world. Or that part of it relating to your immediate life. I'm a Jew who achieved the same kind of standing in football, and when I first went into the pros, there weren't many of us in the game. But that doesn't mean I'm unaware of anti-Semitism in the world—"

"I'm not an ostrich, Dave. I know the obstacles my people face."

"Let me finish." David spoke with the clinical dispassion of the academician. "Anti-Semitism doesn't touch me, right? I made my place in football, and there's very little anti-Semitism in teaching, particularly in my field. However, and this is the crux of my argument, I still resent it, both in the abstract and in the specific."

"Well," Cleo said, sipping her cocktail, "I'm not joining the black-power junkies on the barricades."

"Irrelevant, my dear child. The essence of my claim is that you're trying to escape your blackness—"

"With my skin? I couldn't pass, no matter how much bleach I used!" Her musical laugh attracted additional attention.

David, enjoying the talk too, smiled and then sobered. "But you do straighten your hair."

She raised a tapering, long-fingered hand to her glossy mane. "What does that prove?"

"Only that you work in a white world. You model for magazines that sell to a predominantly white market. The first time I saw you, you appeared in a fashion show before an almost exclusively white audience—"

"Of course," Cleo interrupted. "And I'll go another step. I rarely appear in black publications."

"Then we're agreeing. You try to orient to a white society."

"Lambie," she said, "I'm oriented. When I make out with somebody, it's because we want to, and I don't have any more of a hangup about the color of his skin than he has about mine."

"Let's have another drink," David said, and pretended to leer at her.

Both laughed, but suddenly Cleo stiffened and muttered under her breath.

He followed the direction of her glance and became taut too. Marni Kendall, lovely in a simple, violet-colored tunic of a shiny material that looked as though it had just been dipped in water, was making her way to a table. Following her was the ugliest man David had ever seen, so it was possible that, as Rosalie had indicated, this was a business engagement, but the man's pride and obvious interest in his companion indicated otherwise.

"Just my luck," Cleo said. "She's going to think I've stolen you."

"Hey, I don't belong to anybody," David protested, but his response was feeble. Marni, he observed, carefully refrained from looking in their direction, so he reasoned she had already seen them.

"I'll have to explain to her," Cleo said, still stricken.

"I try to live according to the precepts of Lady Mendl's maxim; 'Never explain, never complain.' Besides, what's to explain? We're both free, twenty-one, and white—or whatever."

105 :

Cleo managed a smile, but the effort showed.

At that moment Marni and Ian MacDonald were placed at a table across the room, directly facing the other couple, and it was impossible to avoid recognition any longer. Marni smiled brightly and waved.

Cleo, her expression identical, returned the gesture.

David, in spite of his bravado, found his face stiff when he tried to grin at Marni.

MacDonald was aware of the exchange. "Friends of yours?" he asked, his tone casual.

"Yes, Cleo and I work together, and we're both with Paul Howell."

The black girl was exceptionally attractive, but MacDonald found himself studying the hulking figure beside her on the banquette and instantly disliked him because of his brawn. "Is that her fellow?"

"David?" Marni failed in her attempt to speak lightly. "No, he isn't. At least, I don't think so."

MacDonald's instinct had been right: she was interested in the man, and his mouth tightened. "He looks like a wrestler."

"He played football for many years." Marni, for the sake of those across the room, simulated a greater interest in MacDonald than she felt. "Now he teaches."

"A nobody." He saw her resentment flare and knew he had erred. Perhaps there was more to the situation than met the eye, so he would play it safe, and step up the pace of his own campaign accordingly.

PART
TWO

The Clothco boardroom was reminiscent of similar chambers in Metro-Goldwyn-Mayer comedies of the 1940s, and, indeed, had been faithfully copied by its designer from that refuge of giddy heroines' stern financier-fathers. Enclosed by panels of heavy oak, it was dominated by a long, gleaming table that reflected the lights of the crystal chandelier above it. Carafes of water and glasses, pads of yellow, legal-sized paper and oversized ashtrays stood at each place, but the high-backed chairs were empty, giving the room a somewhat desolate air.

Ian MacDonald had elected to assume a casual pose on the cushioned seat beneath curved, leaded windows, and he waited until his visitor entered the room before he put aside a sheaf of papers, stood and held out his hand. "I'm sorry I had to see you in here," he said, "but we're taking a break in a directors' meeting, and I'll be swamped with details if I go back to my own office."

"There's no need to apologize," Paul told him. "If you ever want to impress someone, this is the place for it."

MacDonald returned his grin. "You're sharp. I like that. I also like the conscientious approach you've taken to my offer. Five or six people have told me you've asked their advice in the past couple of weeks, so you must have been checking with twice that number."

"At least." It was odd, Paul thought, that the longer he knew MacDonald, the less conscious of the man's ugliness he became. "And I'm not sure it was such a good idea. I've heard so many conflicting opinions that I've had to pay no attention to any of them, and simply make up my own mind."

"You're coming with us?"

"Yes, you've hired yourself a new boy, Ian, if you're willing to meet a few counterconditions."

"I like to think I'm amenable to reason." MacDonald tugged at the cuffs of his new pin-striped suit, which had just arrived from his London tailor.

"I don't want to sell the Howell Agency to Clothco. I prefer to turn it over to my key employees and increase their holdings. I'll continue to be the majority stockholder, although I'll take no active part in the business."

MacDonald's eyes were guarded, giving no indication of his reactions.

"If there's a conflict of interests," Paul said forcibly, "then I'll have to turn you down, regretfully. But I've decided I can't give up my agency after all these years or see it lose its independence. If you insist, I can give you a guarantee of some sort—in writing, if you wish—that I won't deal with the Howell Agency on behalf of the corporation."

"Wouldn't that be foolish?"

"It would, in my opinion." Paul knew this was a time for bluntness and pulled no punches. "If and when I may have reason to use the services of a models agency, I'll want the best. And I know which one is the best."

"If I couldn't rely on your honesty as well as your other attributes, I wouldn't want you here. Any other conditions?"

Paul shook his head. "My lawyer and I have gone over the contract you sent to me, and I've already signed it, after taking out the paragraph on my agency." Paul took several copies of the contract from his attaché case.

MacDonald accepted them from him without comment and went to the directors' table. There, still standing, he initialed the deleted paragraph on each copy, then signed the contracts in a neat, small hand. "Neither of us will regret this," he said.

"If I didn't agree, I wouldn't be here."

MacDonald again shook hands with him. "Can you stick around for about an hour, until I can wind up this meeting? I'll have someone show you around."

"I'd like that."

MacDonald pushed a buzzer on the base of the telephone console beside his place at the table and chatted about inconsequentials for a few minutes until the door of the boardroom opened. "Mr. Howell, Carlo Bennett, my personal assistant. Take him on the grand tour, Carlo, and then fix him a drink in my office if I'm still here."

Paul's first impression of Bennett was that the man was handsome enough to be a model, and the realization that MacDonald would hire such an assistant to compensate for his own ugliness gave him fresh insight into the character of his new employer. "That's quite a suntan," he said as they started down the corridor toward the executive offices. "Vacation?"

"Not exactly," Bennett said. "I was out in California for the company, so I took a long weekend at Acapulco on my way home. I tan fast. Here, let me take your coat and briefcase, and we'll leave them in Mr. MacDonald's office. I'm sure you'll like it here."

Paul was amused. "How did you know I was coming with Clothco?"

"Why else would I be showing you around?" Bennett countered. "I knew we were negotiating with you, so it didn't take a genius to figure out the rest. When are you joining us?"

"I'll have a better idea after I've talked with MacDonald."

"It can't be too soon."

Paul waited for an explanation, but none was forthcoming, and he resisted the temptation to develop the subject. It seemed to him that Bennett had deliberately dropped a leading remark in the hope that he would be drawn out, but it was wiser not to fall into a possible trap. Life here would bear little resemblance to the existence Paul had known at his agency, and it would pay not to become entangled in office politics.

Bennett took him to the offices of several vice-presidents, with whom pleasantries were exchanged, and then Paul found himself in the outer office of an unoccupied suite.

"This is yours," Bennett said. "Your personal staff will work out here."

"I see." Paul noted there were desks for a secretary and three other assistants.

"And this is your own home."

Paul followed him into a large inner office and had to prevent himself from whistling aloud. The upper portions of the walls were expensively papered, and the lower parts were paneled in oak. The corner room had four windows on each side, giving him a breathtaking view of Manhattan. A telephone console sat on an otherwise empty eighteenth-century desk with a leather-tooled top, and the sofa and visitors' chairs were done in matching leather. The ultimate in executive status was the private bathroom, complete with shower, that opened off the inner portion of the office.

Paul was overwhelmed, but saw Bennett watching him closely for his reactions and remained wooden-faced.

"Not bad, is it?" Bennett could keep silent no longer.

"I like it." Paul was forthright, but did not allow himself to enthuse.

"Enjoy the fringe benefits, Mr. Howell."

Aware of the unpleasant undertone, Paul looked at him.

Bennett could not speak freely to a newly appointed vice-president he had just met, but his cynical shrug was open to a variety of interpretations.

Paul resisted the urge to question him, knowing it would be wiser to form his own judgments than to strike up a confidential relationship with an employee who appeared to be disgruntled. However, he promised himself he would remain on guard; although his future with MacDonald appeared bright, perhaps his first, instinctive reaction had been valid. Clothco might not be paradise.

Louis Burns was attending a meeting in the advertising department but hurried back to his own office to take the call and carefully closed the door behind him. "This is mental telepathy, Andrew," he said. "My advance copy of *Chic* arrived just this morning, and I was going to call you. Your coverage of the American collections is masterful, and I've never seen better coordination with retail advertising. We couldn't have come out better, what with our spreads running from Galanos to Gernreich."

"I'm glad you're satisfied, Lou." Andrew Reilly sounded sincerely pleased. "I wish every merchant was as open to our suggestions as you've been."

"Why shouldn't I be?" Burns reached for a cigar in the humidor he kept on his desk. "You're the magazine merchandisers. I'm just the fellow who sells the nuts and bolts in the store."

"Some of the world's most expensive nuts and bolts." Reilly laughed, then sobered. "Lou, do you remember a little cocktail-party chat you and I had a few weeks ago?"

Burns grew tense. "Very well."

"I followed your suggestion. I let the word drop here and there that I own a share of Schwartzman-Burns stock. And I finally hooked our fish."

Burn's hand trembled as he reached for his desk lighter.

"He was cagey, I can tell you. I was approached by a Wall Street investment man who didn't want to tell me his client's name, but I refused to deal with anyone except his principal. And there the matter rested. Until yesterday. I didn't hear another word."

Burns puffed hard on the cigar.

"I finally got a call." Reilly paused. "From Ian MacDonald."

"The son of a bitch," Burns said. "I should have guessed, but he was too clever covering his tracks."

The publisher did not respond to the reaction he had expected. "At Ian's suggestion, I met him for a drink at the new Savoy late in the afternoon. If you haven't seen the men's bar there, I urge you to try it, Lou. They've created an authentic replica of a seventeenth-century English tavern—"

"I'm convinced it's great," Burns interrupted savagely. "And I'll go. So what's with MacDonald?"

"He offered me fifty thousand for my share and indicated he might be willing to double the price. But he kept stressing that he couldn't really pay me in cash what the stock is worth to Clothco."

"Those scavengers would send their mothers into the streets. If you haven't heard how they put the squeeze on the Thalheimer family to get their Atlanta outlet, I'll have to tell you the story some time. It'll chill your blood."

"Clothco isn't noted for its sentimentality, Lou."

"I thank God I have friends and don't operate like a calculating machine. I can count on you to stand with me, Andrew?"

There was a moment's silence at the other end of the line. "I hope it will be possible for me," Reilly said.

: 114

Burns gripped his cigar so hard that it broke, and he threw it into a large, ceramic-tile ashtray without stubbing the burning end. "I'll appreciate it if you don't talk in riddles. Your father and I were always blunt with each other, and I'd be badly hurt if we couldn't have the same kind of—"

"Give me a chance to tell you, Lou. I understand how you must feel, and my sympathies are with you. But I'd like to explain my position."

"Sure." Burns removed his glasses and pressed thumb and forefinger over his closed eyes.

"Clothco is a major factor in the industry and is expanding its influence very rapidly."

"I can't offer you their kind of advertising, Andrew. You know that. One store is in no position to compete, dollar for dollar, with more than thirty."

"Lou, I'm shocked." Reilly sounded aggrieved. "I maintain my position regardless of advertising, and you know it. *Chic* maintains a totally independent position."

"I'm talking about you, not the magazine. If I have to, I'll outbid MacDonald for your share, and for all the others I need to keep control of Schwartzman-Burns."

"You ought to know my share isn't for sale, Lou." Reilly was gently, regretfully chastising.

Burns bit back an angry retort. Although it was probable that he had lost the publisher to his opposition, he could not afford to slam any doors. "Andrew," he said, "I'm going to rely on your loyalty to the close ties that have existed between your family and mine for almost a half-century. You know what's at stake for me, so I won't make any speeches."

"As I've already told you, I feel for and with you, Lou." Reilly's glibness was matched only by his calm in a situation that would have made most men in his position feel distinctly uncomfortable. "And I'm sure everything will work out for the best."

Burns hung up after a brief word of farewell and addressed himself to the humidor. "The best? For Andrew Reilly and *Chic*, which is the same as the best for an advertiser who owns thirty-two stores. Not what's best for Schwartzman-Burns. So we won't be an institution anymore. We'll be just another branch of a push-button chain." He stared hard at the humidor, then pounded the desk. "No, by God!"

"A man needs challenges," Paul told Barbara at breakfast, "and he needs to lick 'em."

He was inundated with problems at Clothco but was solving them, and never had he been more content. Immediately after starting work for the company he had made a two-week flying tour, visiting the major stores in the chain, and his current schedule, to which he was adhering, sent him out for a week each month.

The task of redecorating and modernizing the appearance of the Clothco stores proved to be simpler than he had imagined. He was hiring decorators and designers in each city, then coordinating their efforts with experts, including merchandisers, in the home office. So far his biggest problem was the organization of what he called his "charm school," and after long consultations with the heads of other departments, he decided to send out teams of instructors to each store rather than bring the company's personnel to a central school located in New York.

By establishing four teams, each working on a regional basis, he would be able to give the course to the employees of all stores in less than two years, provided he could set up an eight-week curriculum. At the moment he was hiring instructors, and had found that many with the best qualifications were former models who had worked under his auspices at the Howell Agency.

Assistants screened the candidates, but he interviewed the finalists himself. And, leaving no essential detail to chance, he also supervised the organization of the material that would be taught by the faculty units. The superintendents who were preparing this material had been the first members of his staff whom he had hired, and all five, including three former Howell models, had already proved their worth.

Paul also found himself becoming involved in other phases of Clothco's activities, all of them beyond the original scope of his areas of responsibility. At his suggestion the merchandising department had made drastic changes in the appearance of the show window dummies used in the company's displays, and his advice was sought by the principal buyers of dresses, coats, sportswear and cosmetics.

He had not exaggerated when he had told Barbara that he felt like a surfer riding the crest of a rolling wave that did not break. He had been afraid he would miss the excitement as well as the routines that had made up his life at the Howell Agency for so many years, but he was so busy, so immersed in his new existence that he had no time to spare for the old. Oddly, his sense of exhilaration was constant, no matter how severe the hour-by-hour pressures and day-by-day tensions to which he was subjected.

Now, conducting interviews with candidates for his new faculty, he dictated letters and memos between engagements, speaking in a rapid, steady voice as he held the microphone near his lips. His initial doubts concerning his place at the company had vanished, as had any traces of a lack of self-confidence. He knew what he was doing, he felt certain he was achieving what he had set out to accomplish, and his involvment with Clothco was complete.

A red light appeared on the intercom console, and he flipped the appropriate switch. "Yes, Ian."

"If you can tear yourself away from those gorgeous lady professors who are crowding your waiting room, I'd like to see you for a few minutes."

"I'll be right there." Paul stopped in his outer office long enough to tell his secretary he would return shortly, and then, using a side door to avoid the candidates waiting in his reception room, he hurried down the corridor to his superior's office.

MacDonald was studying a report, which Paul recognized from its green covers as a product of the accounting division of the treasurer's office. "The money people tell me there's no mistake in these figures," the president said without preamble, "but I can't believe it."

Paul made himself comfortable in a leather visitor's chair. "I've found accounting accurate to the penny," he said.

"Not this time. Are they right when they say you've hired eighty percent of your faculty?"

"Closer to ninety percent were on the payroll as of last Friday, if you include the original members of my staff who are training the teachers."

MacDonald scribbled a notation in the margin of the report. "Then I don't see how you can be $120,000 below the budget estimates for your school."

"Not quite that much. I make it about $118,000," Paul said.

"How do you manage it?"

Paul smiled. "I don't believe in throwing money around."

"But you don't want to compromise with quality, either."

"I have no intention of it. I'm hiring the best people available, and I'm not stinting in buying equipment and teaching aids."

"Then this is the second time you've come through. The redecorating in Minneapolis is far enough along now to show an appreciable saving. I had a conference on the phone with the key staff men out there right after lunch, and all of them say the same thing. Howell's ideas will bring them in well under the wire."

"That's because the redecorating estimates made before I took charge were too high."

"The wails of protest that filled this office would have made you think I was suggesting a five-and-ten decor."

"In the short time I've been around," Paul said delicately, "I've noted a tendency on the part of local store managements to push their own interests rather zealously. Which is only natural, of course. The management of any unit is interested solely in protecting and advancing its own store."

: 118

"Now you sound like me. It's what I've been preaching at every vice-presidents' council. I believe the requests of individual stores should be taken with large grains of very coarse salt. Except in special instances, to be sure. I'm speaking in overall terms."

"Until something comes along to convince me otherwise, and it would have to be strong, I'll go along with that approach." Paul couldn't remember what had sparked his initial dislike of MacDonald, but, regardless of the reason, he had never shown worse judgment. The more he saw of the man, the more he respected him.

Evidently the feeling was mutual. "If you keep bringing in successful projects below budget estimates, the directors are going to give you my job."

"I wouldn't worry about it, Ian, and I don't believe you'll have to bolt your chair to the floor. It'll take me twenty-five years to learn no more than a portion of what you know, and by then I'll be ready for retirement."

MacDonald accepted the compliment with a grin that made his resemblance to a gargoyle rather startling. "You're happy here, I take it," he said suddenly.

"Far happier than I had imagined."

"Good. You've won the support of the division chiefs, which justifies my own faith in you, so it would appear the marriage is successful. How are you making out with the divorced bride?"

"My agency? I try to have a brief chat with Harriet Allen, the assistant I put in charge, about once a week. But I'm finding that the problems of the modeling business are becoming more and more remote."

"That's as it should be." MacDonald hesitated for a moment. "Don't think I'm prying into your personal business, but it's important to the company—and to me—that you don't lose your enthusiasm. So I hope you won't mind telling me how Barbara is reacting to your new situation."

"I don't mind in the least. She doesn't say much, as you may have gathered when you've met her, but she seems quite pleased for me, and she listens to every word about the company that I pass along to her."

"That's natural, I dare say, since she grew up in the industry."

"Not as much as you'd think. I've gathered that her father didn't particularly care whether she spent much time at Schwartzman-Burns, and she just drops in now when she wants to buy something at the family discount."

"That must make Lou Burns pretty sad," MacDonald said, probing cautiously. "He's the kind of guy who'd like to see a total family involvement in his precious store."

"I haven't figured Lou," Paul said, somewhat surprised to find himself discussing intimate matters with a superior he had, until recently, been reluctant to trust. "I've been pretty busy since I've been here, but I have tried to reach him a couple of times, and he hasn't returned my calls. Barb says she hasn't seen him or heard from him either."

MacDonald nodded, his expression indicating polite sympathy.

"I can't help wondering whether his nose is out of joint because I've joined Clothco. He has such a fetish about that store of his that he may think I'm a traitor who deserves to be drawn and quartered because I didn't go with him."

"Far be it from me to get mixed up in family affairs, but I've known Lou for a long time, and I'd advise you to sit tight. He'll simmer down one of these days and will forget whatever it is that may be eating him." MacDonald had learned what he wanted to know: Burns was reluctant to discuss his situation with his niece and her husband, believing their loyalties would necessarily be cast on the side of Clothco. At the same time, however, his silence seemed to indicate his confidence that, in the event of an ultimate showdown, he could count on the support of Barbara's five shares of Schwartzman-Burns stock.

"You're probably right," Paul said. "Thanks for the tip."

MacDonald's wave indicated he had done nothing worthy of gratitude.

"I've taken up enough of your time, and I have an office full of people waiting for me." Paul rose and started toward the door.

"Keep going in the direction you're headed," MacDonald said, "and it won't be long before I'm forced to recommend your promotion to an executive vice-presidency." MacDonald sat back in his chair after Paul had departed and stared at the ceiling. Louis Burns's rectitude was an unexpected break, and only an idiot would fail to take advantage of the surprising situation. There had been no more than a remote chance of winning Barbara Howell's support, but the prospects looked much brighter, and, with her husband already in the Clothco camp, it might be possible to win her away from her uncle's camp.

The metamorphosis of San Andros had been sudden and violent. A low-lying island off the coast of Central America at the western end of the Caribbean, it had dozed for decades in the tropical sun, ignored by all outsiders except for a handful of bureaucrats who administered it on behalf of the Republic of Colombia, to whom it belonged. The farmers of lush San Andros were required to work only a few hours each day to grow the crops needed to sustain the local population, and the fishermen, whose catches were traded for mainland supplies, found the blue waters off their shores teeming with fish, and labored no harder than their inland cousins.

In the late 1950s an airstrip was built on the island to accommodate the Colombian officials stationed there, and soon some of the wealthier residents of Bogotá and Baranquilla began to visit the isolated retreat. San Andros's first hotels were built, and, although comfortably air-conditioned, were far from pretentious. Life remained simple, and the beaches were still deserted; a single night club located in a shack near the fishing wharves satisfied demands for entertainment, and the only meat served on the island came from cans packed in Argentina.

Then, as the 1960s drew to a close, an era came to an end. San Andros was "discovered" by the North American tourist, and quickly became the newest mecca of the in people who conducted a ceaseless search for places in the sun found only on unbeaten paths. The vast throngs of vacationers who played follow-the-leader were sure to be close on their heels, and the transformation of San Andros was under way.

Construction work began on several new hotels, and the night club was so popular that several imitators appeared, all of them housed in seedy shacks erected for the purpose. Plans were drawn for the expansion of the island's airport to accommodate the larger jets, and the farmers, the fishermen and their families, finding their services in sudden demand, happily abandoned their old vocations to become bartenders, waiters and maids at salaries higher than they had ever dreamed they might earn.

In spite of the ferment, however, San Andros was not yet spoiled. The water spout that sent geysers shooting high into the air when the tide rolled in remained the primary tourist attraction, and vast sections of beaches covered with a fine, golden sand were still almost completely deserted. It was on one of these, beside a small cluster of coconut palms, that the crew from *Chic* spent a long morning.

The air was moist and hot, heavy with a sultry intensity found only in the tropics, the sun blazed in a cloudless sky, and the palm fronds rustled faintly in a listless breeze. Gary Carey worked in shorts and sandals, the two assistants from the magazine were attired in a minimum of clothing, and only Didi Martin, resplendent in a huge straw hat and white sharkskin spectator sports dress, tried to observe the dictates of fashion.

The two models leaning against either side of a palm tree were the center of the group's intense scrutiny. Cleo, in a transparent white jumpsuit worn over a minimal bikini of the same color, appeared sleepily negligent as she stood with her eyes closed. But Marni Kendall, in black transparent tunic and pants over a somewhat more modest black, single-piece bathing suit, clapped on her sunglasses and shifted her position.

"I'm looking straight into the sun now, Gary," she said, "and I'll have to keep the shades on until a second or two before you shoot. Or my eyes will look like tomato puree."

"I'm reloading as fast as I can, angel, so be patient," Gary muttered.

Didi said something to one of the assistants, who hurried to the tree, patted a trickle of perspiration on Marni's face and repaired the makeup damage with a deftly applied grease stick.

"This is worse than posing under lights," Marni said. "Would you believe that the grease stick was actually hot?"

"I'll feed you a gallon of San Andros rum punches at lunch, darling," Didi called.

"Then I'll sleep all afternoon and won't be able to work. What I want is a swim."

Cleo opened her eyes and shaded them with a hand heavy with rings. "Didi, this adorable jumpsuit was made for the Arctic. The material doesn't breathe, and it feels like one of those rubber reducing outfits."

"It looks smashing," Didi replied firmly.

"I'll take your word for it, but I'm giving Gary no more than five minutes to finish, and then off comes the torture suit. Little Cleo is heading straight into that lovely green water."

"I'm no cooler than you are," Gary snapped, "so shut your rosebud lips."

"I'll find some way to torture you," Cleo retorted. "Like setting up a date for you with a girl."

Didi intervened hastily. "Don't squabble, children. We have a day and a half of shooting ahead of us, and we can't afford nastiness."

"It's bad enough working with that bitch in New York," Gary

told her, "and I wish we'd done this job at home, in my studio, as I begged you to do."

"The authenticity of the background would be missing." Didi sounded self-righteously prim. "We owe our readers a real setting for the clothes they'll be wearing in places like this."

Marni privately agreed with the photographer, but had no intention of taking part in a fruitless discussion. She, too, believed that the results of several days' work would have been equally effective had the job been done in New York. But efficiency, expense and comfort meant nothing to Didi and her colleagues, who delighted in doing fashion photography all over the world. Thanks to the persistence of the Didi Martins, authentic backgrounds had become a status symbol which no fashion magazine could afford to ignore.

"Ready, girls." Gary, who kept his private life to himself, was still smarting and had become grim. "Cleo, don't slouch against the tree. Try to lounge. That's better. All right, half-look at each other. Off with the shades, Marni. For God's sake, you're enjoying yourselves in the carefree Caribbean, girls. Smile! You're having a gorgeous time, and you just love being together!"

Marni went through the routines of the session with mechanical precision, but could hardly wait until the morning's work came to an end. She was not only unbearably hot, but found it almost impossible to share the assignment with Cleo, to whom she had not spoken in several weeks. In fact, she would have refused the job had she known before arriving at the airport that the other girl would be her partner.

Occasionally, when their eyes met, Marni looked through the other girl, almost literally not seeing her.

"Smile, chickadees!" Gary called. "Balance on your right foot, Marni. Haul in your elbow, Cleo. Oh, what a picnic you're having. You'd like to spend a year on San Andros, making pictures with your best friend, Gary. That's it. Natural smiles at last! Hold it, hold it! All right, Didi, we've milked every potential. Come along to the jeep, and we'll scout locations for this afternoon's shooting before I collapse for an hour in that air-conditioned room, where I shall dream of snow."

"Are you finished with us, Gary?" Marni wanted to know.

"Until three this afternoon, angel."

"Then I'm going into the water." Marni began to peel off the tunic and pants. "You said we can keep these bathing suits, Didi?"

"They're yours now, darling. But don't get your hair wet, and try not to burn."

The very idea of avoiding a suntan on a beach where the little clump of palms provided the only protection from the tropical sun was so absurd that Marni laughed as she stuffed her hair under a tight-fitting bathing cap.

"Are you sure you wouldn't prefer that rum punch, darling?"

"Positive, thanks." Marni concealed the irritation that Didi's persistent attentions were causing. Still uncertain whether her suspicions about the fashion editor were correct, she was determined to remain as aloof as possible, a difficult feat to accomplish on an island as remote and isolated as San Andros.

"Do be careful, darling," Didi said as she watched the girl kick off her wooden-soled clogs. "I never believe these natives when they claim there are no sharks in the water. The Caribbean is just teeming with them."

Embarrassed by the tenderness she heard in the other's voice, Marni turned away and ran quickly across the hot sand. She splashed through the shallow water, then plunged in when it was little more than waist-high and was mildly surprised, as she had been when she had taken her first swim the previous afternoon, to find that the water was tepid. She was so hot and sticky, however, that it refreshed her, and she headed away from the beach, swimming with long, lazy strokes.

The water was so clear she could see the bottom, and so smooth that she was able to identify an occasional shellfish. Putting all thoughts of her work out of her mind, she floated on her back,

then swam again, and eventually was at peace. She lost all consciousness of time but remembered that the group's hotel was a
twenty-minute walk down the beach and reluctantly started toward
the shore.

At that moment someone spoke from a distance of no more than
a yard.

"We've got to have us a little chat, baby," Cleo said. "We can't
avoid each other forever on a junket like this."

Marni made no reply.

The black model matched her pace, stroke for stroke. "I learned
to swim at Jones Beach and the Rockaways," she said, "and I can
keep this up all day, if I have to."

Marni reached shallower water, stood, and, as she began to walk,
hauled off her cap, letting her hair fall free.

"Cool it, baby, and listen."

"I'm listening." Marni, staring straight ahead, splashed toward
the shore.

"I didn't steal David from you," Cleo said.

Marni made no reply.

"My first date with him, the night we bumped into you at
Rusty's, was an accident. Ask Rosalie if you don't believe me.
David came around looking for you, and—"

"I know. Rosalie told me." Marni resisted the desire to linger for
a few moments on the wet, hard sand beyond the water.

"What happened the next day was all your own fault, baby.
David called you twice, trying to explain, but you were so shook up
you wouldn't talk to him."

The hot sand burned the soles of Marni's feet, and she broke
into a run as she went to retrieve her clogs and sunglasses, which
she had left beneath the clump of palms.

Cleo doggedly trotted beside her. "You were the one who
snubbed him, not me. So you can't blame anybody but yourself for
putting his nose out of joint."

They reached the shade, where the sand was cooler, and Marni
breathed an inaudible sigh of relief.

Cleo felt better, too, and after easing her feet into her cork sandals, put a hand on the other girl's shoulder. "What good does it do anybody to give me the silent treatment? Grow up, baby!"

Marni was incensed, and shook off her hand. "You knew I was interested in David, but you moved right in."

"It didn't look like interest to him, not when you wouldn't even talk to him or allow him the courtesy of explaining something that was one hundred percent innocent." Cleo tousled her short hair with a towel, daubed on lipstick and removed her sunglasses from her pouchlike shoulder bag, finding nothing incongruous in carrying a bag considerably larger than the tiny bikini she was wearing.

"All right," Marni said. "I goofed. Because I was upset. But David would have called me again—if you hadn't moved in for a kill." She averted her face as she slipped on her own sunglasses, and was glad that the other girl could no longer see the pain in her eyes. Not waiting for a reply, she started down the beach toward the hotel.

"Let's walk down there in the wet sand," Cleo said, falling in beside her. "Otherwise we'll blister our feet, and that Martin bitch is going to have us standing all afternoon."

Marni reluctantly accepted the good advice and removed her clogs when they reached the hard sand.

Cleo kicked off her sandals, then retrieved them.

Studying her surreptitiously, Marni felt hopelessly inadequate. Although Cleo was as slender as any other model, her figure was more feminine, perhaps because her incredibly tiny waist accented her breasts and gave a more rounded line to her hips. She looked spectacularly attractive in her abbreviated bikini, and Marni told herself that she, too, would wear one if she looked as appealing in it.

Aware of her scrutiny, Cleo grinned at her.

Marni quickly averted her gaze and began to walk rapidly.

"Slow it, baby, or we'll have sunstroke. And try to be reasonable. When David called me, he was upset. And all he wanted to do was talk. Would you have stuffed cotton in your ears?"

Marni tried to overcome the hostilities she had been feeling for weeks. "I'm not sure," she admitted. "I've never been in that position, so I'm not able to say how I would have acted."

"Well, I am, and I'm not ashamed of it. When a man has been hurt, he wants soothing. And David is an impressive hunk of man to soothe. Show me a chick who wouldn't be glad to give him a shoulder to cry on, baby."

Marni's jealousy flared anew. "If it stopped at a shoulder, I wouldn't mind."

"You're a big girl, Marni." Cleo became a little annoyed, too. "You don't need an anatomical chart to know that one thing leads to another."

"It wouldn't have if someone came to me for sympathy. That's all I would have given him."

"Come off it. If you have a halo, it's invisible."

Marni flushed beneath her glowing tan. "I didn't mean to sound like a priss, and I can understand that David would be pretty hard to resist."

Cleo softened, too. "For me it was impossible. I've always had a weakness for gorillas, and this one has a brain. I could no more hold out than that little wave out there can help being swallowed up by the big wave coming in behind it."

Marni was silent as she directed her attention to the gentle surf.

"If I'd known you were in love with him," Cleo said, "I would have put up a harder fight. Honest."

"I don't know that I love him," Marni said. "There's somebody else who has come along, and I'm interested in him, too."

Cleo wondered if it was possible that she had sparked to the ugly Ian MacDonald of Clothco, but refrained from asking any questions that would complicate an already delicate situation. "If you don't love him, I don't dig all this."

"I feel cheated, I suppose. David and I were just getting to know each other, and all of a sudden he was gone. Oh, I'm to blame for being standoffish, but he could have tried a little harder to see me."

"None of us knows where to draw that invisible line, I suppose.

That's what comes of the glamour life. We have so many men buzzing around us we become spoiled."

"You do, I'm sure, but I'm not in your league, Cleo."

The black model stopped short and put her hands on her bare hips. "What kind of crap is that? You've become a hundred-an-hour superstar, and I'm still earning sixty. Doesn't that prove the difference between us is balanced the other way?"

"You're talking about business, and even there it doesn't mean a thing. I can drop back any day, and I probably will, seeing I don't know how long I can take the pressures of being on top. And you may shoot ahead tomorrow. But I don't mean modeling, and I'm not using it as a standard. I'm talking about men."

Cleo slowly looked her up and down. "Any man who didn't want you would be insane," she said.

"Then David is insane."

"Who says he doesn't want you?"

"I see no indication of it."

"What do you want to bet that he'll come back to you?"

"I don't want him," Marni said angrily.

"That's just your pride. When I had a thing for Julius, I always took him back, no matter how many romps he had with other gals, including some friends of mine. What the hell, baby, I didn't own him. And your claim to David wasn't even that clearly staked out."

"I've had no claim." Marni couldn't help sounding as sulkily out of sorts as she felt.

"He'll be as good as new. And he's worth it."

"Then you ought to keep him."

A party of swimmers carrying snorkels appeared from behind a sand dune and stared at the two models.

The girls appeared unaware of their existence, but did not resume their conversation until they were out of earshot.

"You're assuming I'll want to keep him, and that's an assumption I can't buy," Cleo said in an unexpectedly metallic voice.

Marni was startled by her bitterness.

"I know of only one sure way to hang onto a man. Marry him.

129 :

Even then you may have only a part of him, but at least you have a legal right. If marriage is your bag. It doesn't happen to be mine."

Marni hadn't actually thought in terms of a marriage between Cleo and David and didn't quite know what to say.

Cleo, however, was ruthless in her self-examination. "I'm not prejudiced, baby. I don't judge my friends by the color of their skin, and that includes you. But I draw the line at marital miscegenation. A marriage to David—or any other white man—is not my hangup."

The embarrassed Marni murmured something under her breath.

Cleo did not hear the interruption. "David is too sensible to want marriage with me, either. He'd run away from it just as hard as I would, and I'm sure the idea hasn't even crossed his mind. My God, baby, a few laughs and a few drinks together doesn't mean you want the Good Housekeeping seal of approval forever after."

"I'm sorry, Cleo." Marni was weary and confused. "I guess I'm so mixed up I don't know what I want. That includes David. And the other fellow who has come into my life. And my career. And just about everything."

Cleo's sympathy drained away all her other feelings. "Baby," she said, slipping an arm around the other's waist, "you've let the tropical heat—and that butch Didi drooling over you—and worrying about that hundred-an-hour tightrope, all get you down."

Marni, grateful for the demonstration of friendship, didn't know whether to giggle or weep, and her bewilderment grew worse.

The hotel, long one of the most distinguished in New York, had maintained its impeccable reputation by observing the highest standards through the years. The Georgian Room, paneled in discreet mahogany, was the sort of cocktail bar in which staid executives entertained their elderly parents and visiting midwestern bankers. A nineteenth-century atmosphere clung to the place, and no man of sensitivity would have chosen it as a rendezvous for an illicit romance.

So Ian MacDonald had selected it with great care for his private meeting with Barbara Howell and was rewarded when he saw she was relaxed, at ease. The mere fact that he had invited her to meet him here had been a signal that adultery was not his goal.

Certainly Barbara looked at home in the staid setting: her worsted suit and blouse were handsomely tailored, her makeup was subtle and she had even worn a small, off-the-face hat for the occasion. "I just love this place," she said. "It's so dignified. I don't know why Paul and I don't come here more often."

"You don't find it too stuffy?"

"Not when I'm in a stuffy mood," she confessed with a laugh, and belied her words by ordering a martini.

MacDonald thought midafternoon no time for hard liquor and asked the waiter to bring him a glass of sherry. Then, his smile fading as he lighted Barbara's cigarette, he looked at her solemnly. "You're wondering why I phoned you, and particularly why I suggested that you tell no one you were meeting me."

"Naturally I'm curious."

He was pleased that she showed no embarrassment. "I make it my policy," he said, "to learn something about the attitudes of the wives of my key people. It's been my experience that a man is efficient and enthusiastic only when he has the support of his wife. Paul has already proved to us that we made the right move when we brought him into the company, and he has a great future with us. *If* he has your complete support."

"Of course he does." Barbara's words and intonation were all that could have been expected; only her tone was a trifle flat.

Their drinks arrived, and MacDonald raised his glass. "To Paul, and to you."

"Thank you. Mmm, they do make good martinis here."

"You do approve of Paul's association with us."

"When he was trying to make up his mind, I kept urging him to take the job."

"I'm delighted, and you won't regret it. Of course, you may have to acclimate to a new life. Some of our wives find it hard to adjust, at first, when their husbands are spending so much time out of town."

"Well, I haven't been bouncing with joy. But I won't have any problems if I go back to work. Modeling."

"I see." MacDonald was careful to express no opinion.

She misinterpreted his caution. "Do you think I'm too old, that I've lost my looks?"

"My dear Barbara, all you need to do is glance at yourself in a mirror to dispel any such foolish notion. It isn't necessary for me to tell you that you're an exceptionally beautiful woman."

She brightened, beaming at him over the rim of her glass. "I have no intention of trying to compete with the kids, you understand. But I'm convinced there's plenty of work available for a good model who doesn't show too many crow's feet yet."

"What does Paul think?" MacDonald wanted to learn more before deciding how to react.

"He doesn't think I could be successful again at my age, and that's why he won't help me. He wouldn't have to do more than make a few phone calls to open every door in town to me." Barbara spoke calmly, without any sign of bitterness, but revealed her feelings by drinking her cocktail too quickly.

MacDonald unobtrusively signaled to the waiter for another.

"Not that I want his help. If I can get where I want without him—and I'm not being ridiculously ambitious. I mean, I know I can't ever compete with girls like Katya or Marni Kendall, but if I can achieve something solid, Paul will have to admit I was right and he was wrong."

MacDonald had felt a glow steal over him when she had mentioned Marni but curbed the temptation to talk about her. It was essential that he concentrate exclusively on Barbara herself. "Will Paul mind if you go ahead without his help?"

"Oh, not in the least. He'll think I'm silly, but he won't object or try to stop me or anything like that. He can't."

Again MacDonald nodded, his eyes revealing nothing.

"Actually," she said, absently accepting her fresh drink and taking a long swallow, "Paul would be very proud if I made it on my own."

MacDonald wondered if her judgment was sound. There was no way he could check direct without creating too many complications, so he would have to rely on her analysis of her husband's feelings. "What makes you so sure?"

"A million things," she said flatly. "I've been married to him for a long time, and I'm willing to bet you that once I'm doing all right in modeling again, he'll brag to everybody about me. Including you and all the other people at your office."

MacDonald weighed his decision swiftly, and realized he had to take a risk. It was urgently necessary that he win Barbara's confidence and gratitude, and he could not afford to miss the opportunity she was giving him to ingratiate himself with her. "I sympathize with your position," he said, "and I find myself torn."

She looked at him without comprehension.

"Paul is very important to me and my company. Your own happiness is important too, partly for Paul's sake, and partly because I like you. I admire your ambition, Barbara. It isn't often that a woman in your position—the wife of a highly successful man and the mother of several children—wants to go back to her old profession and make a second success in it."

"I'm glad you understand how I feel. You're sweet, Ian."

"I might be able to do something concrete for you, although it breaks one of my rules. I don't believe in becoming involved in any domestic controversy—"

"Oh, we aren't fighting—"

"—or situation." He paused at length. "On the other hand, the potential good I can do here more than balances the problems that could arise. That is, if you and I could reach an understanding."

"I know we can." Her smile was dazzling, although forced.

"I'm not exactly unknown in this town, and there are a few strings I can pull. Our stores are major advertisers, so the fashion magazines wouldn't mind doing me the small favor of hiring an experienced and beautiful model at my suggestion. And, since Clothco is a major buyer on Seventh Avenue—and a good customer of some of the big-name designers—I feel sure they'd take the hint if I told a few of my friends there's someone they ought to hire for their fashion shows."

"If we weren't in the Georgian Room," Barbara said ecstatically, "I'd kiss you!"

MacDonald smiled fleetingly. "If I were to go ahead with these suggestions, I'd put myself in a compromising position. Paul might become very angry if he learned of my interference."

"There's no reason he need know, now or ever!"

"That's easy to say, but much harder to live up to. You might let something out when you're quarreling with him, for instance—"

"Never!"

"Obviously, it would hurt your own relationship with him. The reason I'm being so careful should be obvious to you. Paul is worth a great deal to Clothco, and I can't afford to let him turn sour."

"He'll never hear a word from me, I give you my word. Ian, you're marvelous!"

"I'll make a few calls in the morning. Get in touch with me before noon, and you'll be launched on your second career. Would you like another drink, to celebrate?" Not waiting for her reply, he again signaled the waiter.

"This is too good to be true, and I don't know how to thank you."

MacDonald's magnanimous wave made it impossible for her to pursue the subject further. "Regardless of what I might be able to do for you," he said casually, "you'll have a solid base at Schwartz-

: 134

man-Burns. They average more than twenty-five fashion shows a year."

"That's the one place in town I won't find work."

He pretended surprise.

"Uncle Lou would think it was beneath my dignity as a matron. Even if we were on speaking terms."

"I'm sorry to hear there's been difficulty." The twisted homeliness of MacDonald's expression mitigated the unctuousness of his tone.

"If there is, we don't know about it. Uncle Lou is an unpredictable man."

MacDonald clenched a fist under the table but his smile remained bland.

"Sometimes," Barbara said, "I wish he'd retire. He'd be doing my aunt a favor, you know. It's what she's wanted for years.

"Anything is possible."

Barbara shook her head. "About twenty years from now, Uncle Lou will die of a heart attack in a Schwartzman-Burns elevator at the height of a spring clearance sale."

"Not many men know when to retire, but they can be nudged." He appeared to be making polite conversation.

"My aunt would love you."

MacDonald took the plunge. "You could help her cause."

"I could?"

"You own some Schwartzman-Burns stock."

"A few shares." Barbara went to work on her third martini.

"Those shares could be important. A number of corporations would give their souls to buy that store."

"I don't have a say in what happens at the store. I'm not a director or anything like that."

"All the same, the day isn't far off when you'll be able to name your own price for your stock."

"Oh, I couldn't," she said, "unless Uncle Lou gave me his permission."

Her innocent deferral to Louis Burns forced MacDonald to drop the matter for the moment, but he was not discouraged. He had expected Barbara to demonstrate automatic family loyalty, but the narcissistic ambition she had revealed was a crack in her armor, and he intended to exploit the weakness. It was enough for the present that he was placing her in his debt, and in time he would find a way to relieve her of her precious, control-determining shares in Schwartzman-Burns.

"This office is overwhelming! It snows me." Marni, attired in a brown suede jacket, miniskirt and high boots, stood inside the door, her expression childlike as she slowly looked around.

"That tan is pretty sensational, too," Paul told her as he offered her a chair.

Knowing she could not haul down her high-riding skirt when she sat, she did not try. "I've been home almost a week, and it's almost gone."

"I envy your trip, Marni."

"Don't. It was ghastly."

"I heard a bit when Harriet phoned me from the agency this morning."

"I wish she hadn't set up this appointment with you, Paul. You have no idea how guilty I feel. I've been anxious for your advice, but I have no right to come storming in here when you're busy with a million important things. You aren't even active in the agency anymore."

"If Harriet hadn't been in touch with me, I'd have called her, Marni." Paul couldn't remember when he had seen a more radiantly lovely girl and told himself that her worries weren't reflected in her appearance. "I'm offering part-time faculty openings to several of the best Howell models, and you're first on the list. We'll need you for a few days each month to go around the country showing our employees poise, carriage, charm and the like. You'd get your usual fee of five hundred a day and expenses."

"It sounds like fun. Harriet filled me in, and I'd do it for you even if I didn't go for the idea. But I don't think I'm worth five hundred a day, much less a hundred per hour. That's one of the things that's bugging me."

"I can't see why. Harriet says your schedule is filled every day."

"For the moment, maybe." A frown temporarily marred the perfection of Marni's face. "My eyes were bigger than my tummy, and the air doesn't have enough oxygen at the top of the ant heap."

"You look as though you're surviving."

"I'm not sure I can live through the next couple of days, I'm so mortified."

"Harriet briefed me on the Didi Martin business. She's publishing some revealing pictures of you in *Chic*?"

"Experimental shots that were taken just before my fee went up. She promised me they wouldn't be printed, but now she says she doesn't remember making any agreement with me. And she claims it's too late to take them out of the issue." She opened her oversized tote bag and rummaged in it. "I'm ashamed to let you see the color proofs."

Paul took the prints from her and studied them. Although he had seen pictures of many hundreds of girls in the nude and near-nude, he was unprepared for the impact that Marni's photographs had on him. Her flimsy bikini left virtually nothing to the imagination, and his trained eye told him that her figure was as flawless as her face. What surprised and disturbed him was the desire for her that suddenly engulfed him, a response unique in his long experience.

"If you didn't mind, I thought you could help me by calling Andrew Reilly and asking him to eliminate these pages from the magazine. I would have gone to Ian, but he'd want to see these photos, and I don't know him well enough."

Paul knew he had no right to be jealous of MacDonald, with

whom she appeared to have a growing friendship. "As I remember it," he said, unable to tear his gaze from the proofs, "you've never done lingerie modeling?"

"No, and this is worse than any of it. How can I let thousands of people see me this naked? That will be the end of my reputation."

Paul folded the proofs and handed them to her. "Five years ago," he said, "I would have agreed with you. But nudity has become so commonplace in our culture that no stigma is attached to it anymore. Katya would have done this job, and so would every other hundred-an-hour star. I can guarantee that you won't suffer professionally from the appearance of these pictures, Marni. In fact, you'll be in demand for more of the same kind of work."

"Which I won't do." The girl blinked back the tears that began to form in her eyes, aware that she would spoil her makeup if she wept. "Damn Didi Martin!"

"In a sense," Paul said, "I can't blame her for using them. They're so spectacular that any editor would have found them irresistible, Marni."

"That wasn't Didi's reason. She was punishing me, whipping me into line."

Perhaps Harriet had been right, Paul thought, when she had told him that Marni seemed incapable of bearing up under the emotional stress of her new, exalted position.

"I'm convinced she's a dyke, but I don't intend to find out for sure. All I know is that she kept trying to make out with me the whole time we were at San Andros, and I did nothing but run."

"Every model who reaches the top has her share of lesbian as well as heterosexual admirers," Paul said. "You've always been able to handle passes."

"I'm so tired these days. And all mixed up inside."

"Other than these photos, what's bothering you?"

Marni took a deep breath and told him the long story of sending David Bernstein into the arms of Cleo.

Paul made no comment until she had finished with a recital of her own talk with Cleo on the beach at San Andros. "Are they having an affair?"

"Well, Cleo didn't admit it in so many words, but I'm sure they are."

His shrug was eloquent. "It doesn't really matter, of course, since you don't know whether you'd like to get together with him again."

"Cleo told me it's my pride, but that part doesn't go beyond David coming back to me, and giving me the chance to decide what I want. We had something going, but it was cut off before I found out what it was."

She sounded so young and naïve that Paul wanted to take her in his arms and comfort her.

"Then," Marni said, "there's Ian."

Again Paul's jealousy choked him.

"I've seen him a half-dozen times, and Rosalie—my roommate—thinks I've gone crackers. She says the very sight of him makes her want to throw up. But he takes me to the nicest places, he's the most considerate date I've ever known, and he hasn't touched me, not once. That sounds too good to be true, doesn't it? I know you warned me against him, but he treats me—well, like an ancient Greek would treat a goddess."

Paul found it very difficult to admit what, in all justice to MacDonald, had to be said. "I was wrong about him, honey. He's even sharper and more clever than I'd thought, which isn't surprising. But I've yet to see him deal unethically with anyone. You'd know more about him on a social occasion, alone with a girl, but he seems to be a gentleman in every way."

"He's even a little on the Dullsville side, sometimes." Marni was silent for a moment, brooding. "Can I tell you something really kinky? I have no right to make you my confessor—"

"I don't mind." Paul knew he was behind in his appointments and that his waiting room was filling, but didn't care.

"Rosalie says Ian looks like a refugee from a 1940s horror movie, and she's right. That's what I dig. He's so fantastically ugly that he fascinates me."

Her rush of juvenile enthusiasm made Paul laugh. "Beauty and the beast, huh?"

"Don't. That's one of Rosalie's favorite jokes, and she repeats it until I'm ready to die." Marni stood, tugged vaguely at the hem of her skirt and smoothed the suede. "Now you know all. The life story of a mess."

Paul put an arm around her shoulders as he strolled with her toward the door. "For whatever my advice is worth—"

"Everything, to me."

"—don't make a fuss over the photographs *Chic* is going to publish. You can't stop the printing, and you won't suffer. Your nudity was professional, not personal, so look at it that way."

Leaning against him, Marni swallowed hard. "I'll try."

"As to being mixed up, you have several alternatives. First, take a vacation, go home and see your family."

"I can't. I'd be in a big whoop and hassle with my parents a day after I got there."

"Second, quit modeling. I'd be glad to give you a permanent job that would utilize your experience, and it would pay you a good salary, but you'd get only a small fraction of what you're earning now."

"Thank you, Paul. You're the kindest, wisest man there ever was, but I couldn't live with myself if I were a coward."

"Then you have only one other choice." He halted inside the closed door. "Stick it out. If you drop back to your former level, you'll lose all your clients. They'll believe you couldn't make it at the hundred-an-hour level."

Marni nodded, then leaned her head on his shoulder.

Her touch disturbed Paul, but he didn't falter. "I'm less of an expert when it comes to your personal life. I can't tell you what to do about Ian, except don't rush things. And I can give you even less help in your problem with David."

: 140

"I know what I really need," she murmured, and looked up at him, her eyes luminous.

Instinct told him what was coming, and he braced himself.

"There isn't much glamour when you reach the top in modeling. There's just viciousness, hard work and a lot of money you're too tired to enjoy. Katya kicks the tensions by sleeping around town, but I can't do that. I'm not promiscuous. What I need is one man who'll guide me and console me and help me."

"Honey," he said, hearing a tremor in his own voice, "I've worked with more beautiful girls than I'll ever be able to count, and you're the loveliest of them. You're giving me an excruciating choice."

"Barbara."

"I wasn't thinking of her just now, only of you. We couldn't have a one-night stand, like Katya's affairs. Neither of us is built that way. I can't let myself get together with you under these circumstances." The intense hurt in her eyes jarred him, and he had to get a stronger grip on himself. "You're badly upset and whirled around by many things these days. So you're groping. You're also vulnerable, and much as I want to live with you, I've got to live with my own conscience first."

"A very neat put-down, Mr. Howell," Marni said limply. "It serves me right."

"I've never had to make a tougher choice," Paul said angrily, then forced himself to speak more calmly. "Recover your balance, honey, and gain some perspectives. My own system is to get into some hard work, but that might not be the way for you."

"What else is left?"

"When you're on your feet again, let's see if you feel the way you do right now. I'm inclined to doubt you will, but if you do, we'll cross that bridge when we come to it. Meanwhile this talk will remain strictly between us."

Marni nodded, then quickly turned away and opened the door.

"I'll send the agency a letter outlining the terms of our work agreement with you," he said formally, "and I'll expect to see you every month at the Clothco employees' school."

Again Marni nodded without looking at him and hurried off down the corridor.

Paul left the door open and returned to his desk, but before he could call his secretary and tell her to send in his next visitor, Carlo Bennett stepped inside.

"Having fun with the old man's dream girl?"

"Miss Kendall," Paul said coldly, "was here on business."

"Sure, no offense meant," Bennett replied. "But you don't have to climb onto the ramparts to do battle for Mack the Knife. He looks out for himself, that one, and when you feel the blade sinking eight inches between your ribs, don't say that you weren't given a tip-off." He vanished as suddenly as he had appeared.

Paul closed the door, returned to his desk and, buzzing his secretary, told her to put off all his appointments until the next morning. Walking to the windows, he stared out at the silhouettes of the city's skyscrapers at dusk, at the lights glowing in high buildings and the shadows in the canyons of steel and concrete and glass that no light reached.

His session with Marni had shaken him, and he thought it unlikely he would ever stop regretting the impulse that had led him to reject her, no matter how honorably he had behaved.

Bennett's brief interruption had disturbed him too, and he realized he was growing tired of the man's unpleasant innuendos and dark hints. Paul was relishing his experience at Clothco, and he hated the faint but unquenchable feeling that his luck was too good to last. Bennett, catching him off guard so soon after his meeting with Marni, had momentarily upset his own balance, and he told himself he would be wise to ignore the uneasiness that stirred deep within him.

"I'm almost twice your age," Ian MacDonald said, facing Marni Kendall across his spacious living room. "And for years I've had a sort of private joke that I've told the few people I've liked well enough. I always say I have to order specially made mirrors for my bathrooms so the glass doesn't crack when I look into them."

"I don't think that's even a little bit funny." Marni wished she could change the subject, but the knowledge of what he intended to say seemed to paralyze her.

"I'm not fooling you or anyone else, least of all myself. I come close to being a freak."

"That's not true," she protested feebly, and although she was trying to appear composed, one hand kept smoothing the pleats in her short skirt of violet silk.

"So I know I have my nerve approaching the greatest beauty of the day—"

"I'm no such thing!"

"Who is the number one model in town, at the highest prices? And don't tell me it's Katya."

"I may not last."

"Suppose you don't. That doesn't mean a thing." He paused for a moment, then resumed his carefully prepared speech. "Nerve is one thing I've never lacked. Or the courage to take chances, when the stakes are high enough. Or an instinct for making money. So, in spite of all my handicaps, I'm not coming to you empty-handed."

Marni wished she could clamp her hands over her ears.

"I'm not exactly a poor man, and I'm not lacking in influence. I could give you everything you've ever wanted if you could persuade yourself to become my wife." Aware of the heavy beads of perspiration on his forehead, he wiped them away with a neatly folded handkerchief.

"I wish I knew how to answer you, Ian. I—well, I haven't been thinking of marriage to anyone. Now that I've climbed to the top of the modeling mountain, I want to see if I have what it takes to stay there for a while."

"If you wanted to continue working," he said, thinking fleetingly of Barbara Howell, "I wouldn't mind. You'd be free to do whatever you pleased."

"For one thing, I'd never know whether I was being hired for myself or because I was Mrs. Ian MacDonald. Besides, it wouldn't be fair to you. Your position deserves to be treated with dignity, and you wouldn't have it if your wife were a model."

"I don't see why not. Anyway, if it didn't bother me, why let it get you?"

"I'd better stop making excuses," Marni said. "My real reason is that I don't love you."

"I'm not asking for your love," MacDonald said. "I'll be satisfied with a great deal less."

"I won't, because I can't. I'm afraid I've grown up in the romantic American tradition of movies and TV plays and ladies' fiction. Love has to conquer all and that kind of jazz. I won't marry anyone unless I love him."

MacDonald opened his mouth to counter her argument, then closed it again and shrugged, spreading his hands in a helpless gesture.

"It isn't just you, Ian. I'm not in love with anyone."

"Well," he said, with forced heartiness, "that's something of a relief."

"Let me be as honest with you as you've been with me," Marni said earnestly. "I'm not even sure I'm capable of loving anyone except myself. I suffer from the model's syndrome, you know. The one person in the world who fascinates me is Marni Kendall. I can sit in front of a mirror for hours, fiddling with my makeup and hair. I can spend just as long admiring myself in new clothes and jewelry—"

"I could buy you enough to keep you happy in front of that mirror for years." MacDonald leavened the remark with a broad smile.

His grin made him look particularly ugly, and Marni couldn't stop looking at him. "You'd grow tired of that kind of a wife. I know nothing about business, or finance, and I couldn't talk to you about them—"

"There are nine members of my board, an office full of business-men and financiers, and executives in thirty-two cities I can see when I want to talk business."

Marni tried another tack. "The difference in our ages would up-set my parents, but it doesn't bother me. Of course, I've always assumed that when I marry I'll have children, and I don't know whether that fits into your concept of marriage."

"I've always wanted a son who could carry on with what I've built. If he doesn't resemble me too much. And I'd love to have a daughter—if she looked like you."

"I find it very difficult to debate with you, Ian. You're too clever for me."

"I'm not trying to be clever, and I don't want to talk you into anything, Marni." Unable to sit still any longer, he began to move around the room, picking up cigarette boxes and ashtrays, then putting them down again. "Above all, I want to see you happy. You have my oath that whatever may come, I'll never hurt you. Or let anyone else hurt you."

She knew he would keep his word. "In some ways," she said slowly, "I think more of you than of any other man I know."

He misinterpreted her declaration. "I wouldn't force myself on you," he said painfully. "I wouldn't be greedy and make too many intimate demands."

"I wasn't even thinking about that," she said in embarrassment.

MacDonald saw she was being truthful, and his heart leaped. This loveliest of creatures wasn't repelled by his ugliness, and the realization gave him grounds for hope that, with her, he could overcome his impotence. "I've never had much love," he said, "so it wouldn't take much to make me happy."

Marni understood precisely what he meant, and the rapport with him that she felt aroused her somewhat from her lethargy. "In many ways we're more alike than you know. That's why I don't want to reject you, Ian, any more than I can accept."

He stared at her. "You're telling me I have a chance."

"Be patient with me," she replied, nodding. "You see, I don't want to hurt you, either."

"You couldn't."

"Don't be too sure. Narcissists can be cruel. Sometimes we don't even know it."

"I'll take my risks." His spirits rose. "All this time I've been sure your life was filled with other men."

It hurt her to think of Paul, then of David. "Right this minute," she said, "there's no one."

"Ah!"

"But I can't promise you there won't be."

"I've never been afraid of competition." He thought it diplomatic to refrain from adding that when he had a head start in a race, no one could catch him.

"You'll give me time to see how far I can go in my work—and straighten out my thinking?"

"All the time you'll need and want." Although he knew almost nothing about women other than prostitutes, his instinct told him to hold Marni on a loose rein. "I won't even mention the subject of marriage again. I'll wait for you to bring it up."

His consideration touched her deeply, and she could only say, "Thank you."

MacDonald, pausing directly in front of her, saw the expression in her eyes and hesitantly drew her to her feet.

She recognized curiosity and compassion among the motives that impelled her to move closer to him, her face lifted, and she closed her eyes when he kissed her. His touch was unexpectedly gentle, and she was astonished to discover that his ugliness did not repel her. If anything, it gave their light and brief embrace an additional, exciting dimension.

Paul held a three-hour meeting with the designers and architects supervising the rebuilding and redecorating plans for the stores in the Clothco chain, and by the time they left his office a mountain of other work had piled up. The mail was unusually heavy, his secretary handed him a mound of telephone messages, and he had not yet read the regular weekly reports from the personnel managers of each of the stores. He had hoped to clear time to wrestle with a complicated set of budget figures he was expected to present the following afternoon at a vice-presidents' meeting, but resigned himself to the probability that he would have to work on them that evening at home, or, if necessary, lock his door in order to do the job in the morning.

He quickly leafed through the telephone messages, and one in particular caught his eye: "*Mrs. Howell wants you to call her as soon as possible. She has phoned twice.*"

He picked up his telephone and dialed his home number on his private line. This was no day to listen to Barbara's complaints about some picayune grievance, and if she became long-winded he would cut her off.

"Hello." She sounded breathless.

"You wanted something, Barb?" Paul was unintentionally brusque.

"You certainly took your time getting back to me. I was afraid I'd have to leave before you called."

"I've been jammed. I'm having one of those frantic days." He tried to curb his impatience.

"Well, I won't keep you long. I'm dropping the kids off at my

147 :

mother's. She's going to feed them dinner, and then she'll bring them home and put them to bed. Maybe you'd like to go there for dinner, too, or grab a bite somewhere else, if you'd rather. I expect to be back around ten or ten thirty."

"You know I hate to impose on your mother, so I can eat anywhere. What's up?" She rarely made plans of her own for an evening, but he was only mildly curious and continued to glance through his other telephone messages.

"I'm doing a fashion show at the Rotterdam House." Barbara tried to speak calmly, but could not conceal a feeling of triumph.

Paul was so stunned he could think of no reply.

She waited for a few moments on the silent line. "Have you fainted, or something?"

"What kind of a fashion show?"

"A big one. For the American Couturiers Association. They'll have an audience of about four thousand in the ballroom."

Paul's mind began to function again. "Models are always booked well in advance for the ACA shows, so the clothes can be fitted on them."

There was a trace of nervousness in Barbara's giggle. "I know. I've had three fitting sessions in the past ten days." She seemed to gather courage. "This show isn't the only thing I'm doing. I've been booked for a kitchenware ad layout at an advertising agency tomorrow, I'm being tested for a TV commercial and I'm doing a two-hour show tomorrow afternoon for a Seventh Avenue evening-gown house."

"In other words, you've gone back to modeling."

"It would seem that way, wouldn't it?" She sounded almost ingenuous. "Everything has been happening so fast that I hardly know where I—"

"Knock it off, Barb!" Paul said savagely. "Nobody who is starting from scratch can get this many bookings overnight."

"Well, nearly." Thrown onto the defensive, she became plaintive.

: 148

"And you just finished saying you started fittings for the ACA ten days ago."

"What of it?" Barbara was cornered and felt compelled to fight. "Do I have to tell you every single thing I do all day?"

"Hardly. But a return to your career is a major step, and you damn well know it. What's more, we've been discussing the subject for months."

"And getting nowhere," she retorted. "I got sick of nothing but talk while you kept dreaming up new ways to deprive me of what I've wanted."

Paul's temper flared, but suddenly he felt very tired, drained of all emotion. "I've never denied you anything you've really wanted, Barb." That, he thought, was the heart of the problem. He had been so indulgent that she believed it was her right to act like a spoiled and irresponsible child.

"If you really mean it, then you won't try to stop me, Paul."

"I'd have hell's own time trying, wouldn't I? You made up your mind, and you went ahead on your own."

"The reason I didn't tell you I'd actually gone back," Barbara said lamely, "is that I was afraid of what you'd do."

"It's too bad you didn't show a little more confidence in me."

She shifted ground. "As long as you approve now, everything is all right."

He knew she was using subtlety and was in no way as naive as she appeared. "I haven't indicated whether I approve or disapprove. I don't know what I think. However, it's done. So my opinions are irrelevant."

"They're not. I want you to be proud of me."

Long and painful experience had taught him that any failure to bolster her fading beauty's ego could result in a prolonged drinking bout. "If it's what you really want, I certainly won't try to stand in your way. I just don't want to see you fall on your face, which could hurt."

"That won't happen." Again she sounded breathless. "I'm starting off like an atomic explosion."

149 :

"So it would seem." He made an effort to reconcile himself to the inevitable. "Who is handling your bookings?"

"I am."

"You set up these jobs yourself?" The possibility seemed remote, but in all fairness he had to admit that she might have accomplished the feat.

"Yes, I did," she replied promptly, having been prepared for the question and knowing that it would cause too many complications to tell him that Ian MacDonald had done more than help, that he had been responsible for all of her bookings to date.

"A fluke like that can't last," Paul said. "You need representation."

"I'd be happy to sign up with the Howell Agency," Barbara said gaily. "I hear they're pretty good."

"You can't go anywhere else. It would make me look foolish. But I'm not in a position to speak for the agency anymore, remember."

"If they don't want me, there are plenty of others."

"I didn't say they won't want you. You seem to forget that Harriet is in charge there now, and she's perfectly capable of making up her own mind."

"I can't see her turning down a request from you. After all, you're still the principal owner, and nobody there is going to antagonize you if it can be helped."

Paul knew a great deal more than he was admitting to her. Even without his active intervention, Harriet and the other members of the agency staff would accept Barbara as a client, regardless of whether they thought she would be a money-maker. But he had no intention of creating additional difficulties by revealing too much to a wife whose stability was in a perpetual state of delicate balance. "Does your mother know?"

"I told her when I called her a little while ago and asked her to take the children off my hands. But you know how she is. Old stone face didn't react. All she said was had I told you about it and what did you think? No matter what I do, it's never right according to her."

He had no time now to explain again, as he had done so often in the past, that she completely misinterpreted her mother's quiet responses. "We'll talk about all that when you get home tonight." Reluctantly, knowing the offer would please her, he asked, "Do you want me to pick you up?"

"I'm not sure exactly what time we'll beak," Barbara said, "so I wouldn't want you hanging around. Thanks anyway. I can get a taxi."

After Paul rang off he had to force himself to concentrate on his work for the rest of the day. He did not pause to analyze his reactions to Barbara's startling and unsettling news, in part because he was afraid he might judge her too harshly, partly because he knew his own selfish interests made it impossible for him to view the matter dispassionately. Her secrecy infuriated him, but of far greater significance was his conviction that, at her age, she could not make a success of her return to modeling. If he was right, the blow to her vanity would be devastating, and the consequences well might destroy a marital relationship that was already badly eroded.

He worked at a furious pace for the rest of the day, and breaking a lunch date in order to spend more time at his desk, sent out for a sandwich, but was so busy he ate only part of it. Although he put Barbara into the back of his mind, he continued to feel nettled, and by late afternoon his dissatisfaction made him restless. He was determined to clean off his desk, however, and, in no hurry to leave the office, asked his secretary to stay late.

By six o'clock they had made appreciable inroads in the mounds of reports and other documents but were interrupted by the arrival of someone in the reception room and looked at each other in surprise.

"I'll see who it is," the secretary said, and hurried out.

Paul immersed himself in another personnel report.

151 :

The secretary returned, closing the door behind her. "A model named Cleo is here to see you. She says she had a late appointment about part-time faculty work at the charm school."

Paul glanced at his calendar pad and groaned. "It's a good thing we stayed. This was the only time Cleo could come in, and I agreed to a late appointment, but I forgot all about it. Why don't you clear out of here, Edie, and save your husband the price of a divorce? I'll lock up when I go."

She departed, first ushering in Cleo, who looked chic in a beige-dyed calfskin minicoat with high matching boots and shoulder bag. Greeting Paul effusively, the model made a thorough inspection of his office, and, admiring everything she saw, was particularly impressed by his private bathroom.

"How often do you take a shower here?" she asked.

Paul laughed. "I haven't used it yet, but it gives me a good feeling to know it's here if I'm ever stuck overnight."

"Man," Cleo said, looking out at the lights of the city, "if I had this view—and the private john—I'd get me a hot plate for breakfast coffee and I'd never go home. Think of the rent you could save." She unfastened her belt.

Paul took her coat from her then stopped short. Cleo was wearing a short dress of transparent beige silk, and beneath it, a coffee colored body stocking that matched her skin tone. The effect was spectacular.

Aware of his attention, she modeled for him, walking and twirling with practiced ease.

"What are you trying to do in that outfit—start riots in the streets?" he demanded.

"It gets 'em where they live, baby," she said contentedly and posed for him.

He waved her to a chair and returned to his seat behind the desk. "That combination will get you any booking in the business."

"That's why I wore it today." She made herself comfortable opposite him, showing no self-consciousness in the presence of this man who had been responsible for her success. "The agency sent me on a tryout for a speaking part in a TV show this afternoon. I'm no actress, and the way I read lines is a fright; so I had to compensate by showing off my other assets."

He was amused, and for the first time since Barbara had telephoned him he stopped glowering. "Did you get the job?"

"You can bet your sweet bippy I got it! Along with a proposition from the assistant producer and a dinner invitation from the director. All I accepted was the job."

"This is your day for bookings, Cleo." Paul carefully explained how he intended to utilize the services of several models in monthly visits to Clothco stores around the country.

"Sounds pretty good," Cleo said.

"The change of pace might make it fun for you, and you'll have a chance to travel all over the United States."

"Do you have many stores in the South?"

"A few, but they'll cause no problems, Cleo. If you'd rather skip the South—"

"I wouldn't want to miss one of those stores, not me."

"Then that's settled. You'll get five hundred a day plus expenses."

"Five hundred? I'm still in the sixty-an-hour league, and we get three hundred and fifty, in case you've forgotten."

"My memory is holding up, Cleo. You'll soon move up to the hundred-an-hour class, and in any event, I wouldn't want you making less than Marni and Katya when you'll be doing the same work."

"You're a good man, Paul. Any time I can do you a favor—"

"Maybe you can." He remembered what Marni had told him about Cleo and David Bernstein and thought this an opportune time to bring up the subject, but didn't want to discuss it in the office. He glanced at his watch, then realized there was no reason for him to hurry home. "If you have time for a drink, I can tell you about it."

"Sure, baby, if you'll buy me a champagne cocktail to celebrate my first speaking part on TV."

153 :

"You can have a bucket of it if you like." He helped her don her coat, then took his own from the closet.

The outer office was deserted, and Paul made certain that the door to his suite was locked. They were the only passengers in the self-service elevator, and as they walked through the empty lobby of the building, he asked, "Any place special you'd like to go?"

Cleo took his arm. "It's your party, baby."

The Merry-Go-Round was convenient, he decided, and they walked the two blocks to the place, which featured a merry-go round bar surmounted by billowing, tentlike roofing in striped pink-and-green satin.

Cleo let her coat fall open and automatically struck a pose on the landing as she surveyed the room. "This is cool," she said. "I haven't been here before, but I'll like it—if we don't have to sit at the bar. I'd rather get dizzy from champagne."

At a word from Paul the headwaiter escorted them to a table against the pink-and-green banquette.

The girl was silent as Paul, true to his word, ordered a bottle of champagne and seemed to have withdrawn when he held his lighter to her cigarette. She inhaled deeply, then exhaled in a thin stream. "If this is the most civilized, best integrated city in the country," she said in a low tone, seething, "may the Lord preserve us from American tolerance."

"What's eating you?"

"Didn't you see the looks we got when we came across the room? Just open your eyes, baby—they're still at it. Sophisticated, smug—and white."

Paul waited until they were served their champagne before he replied. "You ought to be used to it by now. The day people stop staring at a model, she knows she's had it."

"Those are the million-dollar stares, and I'll take all I can get." Cleo was still indignant. "These are the nasty kind. All of them—and the women are worse than the men—are thinking that the only reason you're out with me is because you're going to take me to bed. The hypocritical white punks, looking at us through that microscope of racial superiority."

"Here's to you, Cleo, and to television stardom, if you'd like that." He drank, then tried to calm her. "I can hardly blame anyone black for being hypersensitive, but in all fairness I don't think color has anything to do with the look you describe. I've had lunch or drinks or whatever with one hell of a lot of models through the years, and people always have that expression stamped on their faces when they see a man with an exceptionally attractive girl."

"It's possible," she admitted grudgingly as she sipped her champagne.

"Then there's something else. That outfit you're wearing gives people ideas."

"You mean I look like a whore in it?"

"Certainly not. I'm no expert on that subject, but I think most whores dress fairly inconspicuously."

"Then I don't qualify. If any clothes have ever had pzazz, this little outfit is number one." She pushed her empty glass toward him.

He refilled both glasses, but decided to wait until he was certain her mood had improved before mentioning Marni and David, and instead exchanged casual gossip about models and modeling.

"Did you mean it about that bucket?" Cleo interrupted. "This bottle is empty."

Ordinarily Paul enjoyed a considerable capacity for both hard liquor and wine, and it did not occur to him that, because of the very light lunch he had eaten, he was already feeling his drinks. Instead of replying, he signaled to the waiter.

"You're lovely to do this for me," Cleo said.

"Why shouldn't I? You're one of my discoveries, honey, and I make the flat prediction you'll make it to the top of the heap."

She squeezed his hand in appreciation, then glared at a nearby couple who had seen the gesture. "Rubbernecking bastards," she muttered.

The fresh champagne arrived, her mood improved and Paul decided to lead into the subject that had brought him here. "Your future depends on a lot of different things, of course," he said, "and one of them is the stability of your private life."

Cleo laughed, her false eyelashes fluttering. "What private life, baby?"

Paul had often thought it remarkable that so many models, the most desirable and glamorous of young women, often spent most of their evenings sitting at home alone. But beauty, as he well knew, could frighten away all but the most intrepid and self-confident of men. "You don't see Julius anymore?"

"Oh, that ended a long time ago."

"That gorilla was bad for you, Cleo."

"You're telling me. Anyway, there's been somebody else since Julius. Another football player, but this one has brains."

She was making it easy for him. "Sounds interesting."

"It was."

"Past tense?"

"Oh, we had a ball for a month or two, but both of us knew from the beginning that it wouldn't last, so there were no hard feelings when we called it off. Recently. He's reached the stage where he's ripe for marriage. You know what I mean?"

"No."

Cleo's smile was superior. "A woman would. I'll try to explain it like it is. A man tomcats around, but then he gets tired of the bachelor life and he wants to settle down with one girl. Dig?"

"So far I'm with you," Paul said.

"Usually the new feeling hits him before he has the girl. First he wants marriage, then he hunts around for the wife to go with this wanting. But he doesn't know that's how he feels. He's ripe, you see, and a girl who realizes it can get him, if she doesn't lose her cool."

"Now I see. But you didn't want this fellow?"

"I'll get my kicks with Whitey when I feel like it, but I won't dance up that aisle with him. When I stop taking the pill, my husband will have a permanent suntan. Kids have a rough enough life without making mongrels of the little bastards."

Paul knew too little about mixed marriages to express himself, particularly in a discussion with a young woman who had given the subject her deepest consideration. But for Marni's sake he was relieved to learn that Cleo had terminated her relationship with David Bernstein. If Marni wanted to explore the possibilities of the future with him, there were no obstacles to halt her.

"Now that I've delivered my lecture for the day, would you like to kiss me?" Cleo's shoulder touched Paul's, and her face was close to his.

He was startled, and glanced at the rapidly disappearing wine. "Are you sober?"

"Sober enough. Our friends are still watching us like they're expecting to see a dirty exhibition, so I figure we ought to give them a thrill or two for their money."

Her childish motive was typical of the adolescent attitude he had known in so many models, and although he couldn't blame her for feeling as she did, the Merry-Go-Round, one of the city's more cosmopolitan bars, was no place to stage a scene.

But Cleo gave him no opportunity to plead for reason. Long, pearl-enameled fingers slid up around his neck, and as she tipped his head toward her, their lips met.

Paul reacted physically and emotionally before he had a chance to think. Cleo's lips were soft, her touch was expert and sudden desire flared within him. Instinctively he took command and became the aggressor.

She was aware of the change in him, and her lips parted to admit his probing, darting tongue.

His kiss became more passionate, and he had no idea he was grasping, then caressing her smooth thigh.

At last they parted and looked at each other wide-eyed, their faces still only inches apart. At the moment neither realized that most of the Merry-Go-Round's patrons were ogling them, but, even if they had known, they would not have cared.

157 :

"Zap, powie, wham!" Cleo murmured. "Baby needs a drink, but fast."

"Another bottle will put us under the table." Paul tried in vain to pull together his disordered mind.

"That might be fun, too," she said with a giggle. "All right, we'll be sensible. Let's make it a couple of double champagne cocktails instead of a bottle."

He gave the order, then turned to find her liquid, mascara-fringed eyes still studying him.

"You switched me on, baby," she said.

Ever since Paul had first opened his agency he had made it an inviolable rule to keep his distance from all models. Business and sex didn't mix, he had claimed, especially when the commodity he had been selling was beauty. Now he was breaking his own cardinal rule, and it did no good to argue that he was no longer a models' mentor. If the Howell Agency made money, a substantial share of the profit would be his. Equally important, Cleo would become his employee when she joined the Clothco charm school faculty.

"What do you think you did to *me?*" he demanded.

"Once in a million years it happens like that. You get together with somebody. Unexpected. And there's an explosion."

Paul tried to get a grip on himself. "Chromosomes can be tricky little things, I guess. But I suspect that if you get any reasonably attractive man and woman together under the right circumstances, it will happen."

"You and I know we're both more than reasonably attractive," Cleo said firmly. "And we also are big boys and girls, so we damn well know it happens once in that blue moon you hear about in the soupy old songs."

Their drinks arrived, and Paul took refuge behind the rim of his glass as he sipped his champagne cocktail.

"I never would have suspected it," she murmured, her hand groping for his.

He realized the gesture might commit him to innumerable complications but felt powerless to resist and took her hand.

: 158

"You felt it too." She paused, then challenged him. "Well, baby?"

"I don't trust my judgment after I've had this much champagne," Paul said.

Cleo squeezed his hand, her many rings biting into his flesh. "Are you chicken?"

His inner war intensified. "Maybe."

She disengaged herself and wiped her hand on his, as though drying it. "The color," she said, her voice taking on the quality of that used on stage by an amateur actress playing a Shakespearian role, "doesn't come off."

Her misinterpretation of his reluctance astonished him, and he wanted to protest that their racial difference had no bearing on their relationship. But honesty forced him to reconsider: to what extent did it influence him?

The fact that Cleo's skin was black made her no less appealing. In fact, as he had known only white women, her color gave an erotic fillip to the potential they faced.

What really bothered him was a more subtle question: would he be equally wary, equally hesitant if Cleo were white? Certainly the pigmentation of her skin and his had no connection with an unsatisfactory marriage that had just taken a sharp turn for the worse. And the increasing tensions he felt each day at Clothco were irrelevant to Cleo's blackness and his whiteness.

"Maybe you don't know it," he said, facing the girl, "but my lack of color won't wash you out."

Cleo started to reply, but Paul gave her no chance. Roughly pulling her to him he gathered her in an enveloping embrace, and his savage, demanding kiss made conversation impossible. The abrasiveness they had created, combined with the champagne they had consumed, made their mutual desire all the greater, and the intimacy of their sudden lovemaking caused the other, embarrassed patrons of the Merry-Go-Round to turn away and ignore them.

Holding the girl close, Paul could feel her warmth through the thin fabric of her dress and body stocking. His masculinity was irresistible, and Cleo responded to it with a yearning just as ravenous. They drew still closer, their bodies straining, and began to caress each other.

The maître d'hôtel knew that Mr. Howell was a steady and important patron but debated whether to intervene.

Cleo had to free herself in order to breathe more freely. Sucking in air, she panted, "Double powie. Double wham-bam."

"There's enough electricity in the air," Paul said, "to frizzle an ox." He drained his drink, called for his check and paid it.

The girl took her time repairing her makeup, and looked collected, but Paul noted that her hand trembled as she applied her lipstick. When she was done she put away the small standing mirror she carried in her oversized shoulder bag, cleaned off the tiny brushes that she then placed in a slender, waterproof container and ran a comb through her short hair, quickly rearranging it.

Paul had seen thousands of women primp, but watched in fascination.

Cleo closed her shoulder bag and twisted on the banquette to face him. Her features were composed, but her eyes were shining, full of promise, and she unconsciously moistened her lips with the tip of her tongue. "Well," she said.

"Finish your drink," he told her gruffly.

"I can take a hint, baby." Cleo emptied her glass.

"Ready?"

"Mmm. Am I, ever!"

Her candor was provocative, and the tension in his responding laugh indicated his appreciation. He stood and moved the table aside so she would be able to emerge.

At the same instant they became aware of the renewed interest being shown by their fellow patrons. Paul could feel his face burning and held himself stiffly erect as he walked toward the exit.

But Cleo, who was preceding him, seemed to accept the challenge. Moving with short, mincing steps that caused her hips to sway, she appeared to be wriggling rather than walking to the door.

"That was bitchy," Paul told her as they waited at the check-room for their coats.

"You noticed, baby?" Cleo was delighted.

"Even people with peripheral eyesight were knocked out of their seats. There ought to be a city ordinance, or—even better—a state law to outlaw that kind of walk."

"It got to you, huh?" Cleo clung to his arm, snuggling close, as they emerged onto the street.

"It was a ridiculous caricature of a sexy walk, and, yes—it got to me. Now it's my turn for a question. Do you want some dinner?"

"Later. What I need right now isn't food."

Paul made no reply as, the Merry-Go-Round doorman having disappeared, they started toward the corner to find a taxi. He realized he was deliberately becoming enmeshed in an affair and knew he had no excuse other than his overwhelming desire for the girl. Cleo's insistence that together they created something explosively unique was accurate, and the knowledge further whetted his appetite.

Was this erotic hunger sufficient justification for a relationship that would defy every principle he had long observed? He neither knew nor cared but told himself he wouldn't be able to blame the champagne for his indifference. Although he had consumed far more than he could handle on an empty stomach, he was still sober enough to be aware of what he was doing and to weigh the consequences.

The truth, as he saw it, was that Barbara had gone too far in the way she had chosen to flaunt her independence. He had remained sexually faithful and emotionally loyal to her over a long and difficult period, and the least she had owed him in return was the maritally honorable gesture of sharing her plans and accomplishments with him. That lack of trust, as he saw it now, freed him to seek whatever he might want. Two wrongs didn't make a right, to be sure, but he was finding the first measure of relief from the pressures that had been piling on him since he had joined Clothco, and he relished his new-found exuberance.

A taxi slowed as it approached the corner, but the driver picked up speed again when he saw that the pair waiting on the curb were a mixed couple.

"Racist," Cleo said.

Paul flagged another taxi, close behind the first, and it pulled to a stop.

As Cleo climbed in she gave the driver the address of an apartment building in the east Seventies. "I'm what makes the place integrated," she told Paul. "I just moved in, and I'm not sure I can afford the rent, but the neighborhood is so jazzy that it sends a kid from Harlem."

"Is that what you really want?" He put an arm around her shoulders and drew her close.

"What I want right now—"

"I know. That isn't what I meant."

"I can't answer you, baby. I don't know what I want. You tell me I'm close to joining the hundred-an-hour club—"

"I can guarantee it, honey, and not because of me. Strictly on your own merit."

"That much I know, and it's been my ambition for a long time. But after I've passed just about every good-looking white girl in the horse race and I have millions of Whiteys wanting me and their wives envying me, then what? Is there any place to go from the top—except down?"

"Sure. Either you fight to stay at the top, or you find your ambition changes and broadens."

"How?" she demanded fiercely. "Into what?"

"I've had too much champagne to give you a sensible answer, and you've had too much to make it hang together if I did."

"Check," she said, and curled her arms around his neck.

Somehow her minicoat had opened, and as Paul kissed her his hand cupped over a firm breast. Never had he known a woman to react as quickly; almost immediately, under his touch, he felt the nipple harden and grow.

: 162

Cleo reluctantly ended the kiss. "What are we—a couple of teenagers who can't wait?"

"It seems that way," Paul said, and removed his hand.

"Too bad. That was groovy." Cleo fell silent for a few moments. "Sometimes I wonder if the man who invented the shape of these taxis was a leg man."

Paul didn't know what she meant, but joined her in creating a diversion. "I know he assumed that people are double-jointed acrobats. You can't get in or out without jackknifing."

"At heart, though, he's a leg man who spends all his spare time riding around in taxis and staring at the legs of the helpless females he takes with him. It doesn't matter how a girl sits in one of these contraptions. There can be no such thing as modesty, and you let everything show."

"If every girl had legs like yours, there would be no complaints."

"You're not just saying it, baby? You honestly think mine are all right?" Her model's narcissism demanded a fresh compliment.

"If I start telling you—and showing you—what they do to me, we'll be at it again in no time."

She laughed breathlessly and peered out of the dirty window. "I guess we'll have to wait. We're almost there."

Neither spoke on the rest of the ride, and after Paul had paid the driver they remained silent as they crossed the small, modern lobby of the building. A new tension gripped them in the elevator, and they refrained from looking at each other or touching. Cleo unlocked her door, opened it and snapped on some lights, and Paul, close behind her, was surprised by what he saw.

The living room was large and the massive, ornate furniture was in the style that had come to be known as Mediterranean. The color scheme was a harmonious blend, and the chairs and tables, sofas and lamps, rugs and wall decorations were in perfect balance. The overall effect was one of beauty and style, and Paul was impressed.

"This is great," he said.

"Thank you." There was a new dignity in Cleo's tone. "I've

163 :

been working on my decor in the last three places I've lived, and I'm finally getting what I want." Her manner was somewhat formal as she took his coat and put it on a hanger in the vestibule closet.

Paul wandered around the room, examining everything he saw. "You did the whole job yourself?"

"Natch. That's been the fun of it."

"You have a real talent for decorating, Cleo. You were wondering what you'll do when you grow tired of modeling. Maybe you should go into interior decorating."

"That was my first ambition, but I've never thought I was good enough."

"You are. You ought to take classes evenings, in your spare time." He still did not look directly at her.

She avoided his gaze too. "Wouldn't that be something? Here, let me show you through the rest of the place, such as it is."

The kitchen and dinette corner were done with humor and taste, and every inch of the cramped room was used. Cleo had transformed a tiny chamber into an unusually attractive dressing room to hold her extensive model's wardrobe, and the bathroom, crowded with a profusion of plants, resembled a Mediterranean garden. The bedroom, however, was surprisingly simple, almost severe, and here the rococo atmosphere was replaced by a purity reminiscent of a Castilian convent or seminary in the Middle Ages.

"No professional decorator could have done better," Paul said when they came to a halt in the bedroom. "You have a real flair for this sort of thing, honey, including imagination and the courage to carry it out."

"All that's missing is the education and experience," Cleo replied with a harsh laugh.

"Take some classes, as I told you. Decorating is a little out of my line, except that I'm involved in it these days, in a supervisory capacity. I can get you together with some of the best experts in the business if you'd like. People who are doing over all the Clothco stores."

Cleo faced him at last, angrily, her feet planted apart. "Is that your idea of repayment—for this?" She gestured toward the bed.

Her sudden, inexplicable hostility baffled Paul, and he stared at her. "Hey, what did I do wrong?"

"Nothing, yet. But I'm not giving you the chance. It's customary, I believe, for a white gentleman to pay off a nigger girl who gives him some tail."

She was even more vulnerable than he had thought and had become defensive in advance, before he could hurt her. "Any help I give you is given freely, for two reasons," he said, his voice calm. "First, you have talent. You're more than a beautiful girl, and talent deserves to be recognized and nurtured and developed for its own sake. Second, I like you. I mean as a person, and this has nothing to do with any man-and-woman relationship. Believe me or not, as you please, but I'll prove my sincerity very easily. I'll talk to the Clothco decorators in the morning, and I'll set up an appointment for you through the agency strictly at your convenience, in your spare time. Now, so my motives aren't misunderstood, if you'll give me my topcoat I'll be on my way."

"Baby, you have what it takes." Cleo's belligerence had disappeared, and she stared down at the sand-colored Castilian rug. "I'm sorry, but sometimes I get sort of kooky ideas. It comes from too many Charleys wanting to lay me and promising me presents if I'll spend the night with them or go off for a weekend. All of a sudden I got scared."

"I can't make promises," Paul said gently, "but I'll try very hard not to hurt you."

Cleo returned his steady gaze. "That's good enough for me. Wait!" she commanded when he started toward her.

Paul halted directly in front of her.

"No ties, no strings, no commitments from me either. Okay, baby?"

He nodded. "And not too many regrets either, I hope."

"We'll have to take our chances. It's worth them." She laughed ruefully. "I swore off, but this thing we have going mustn't be wasted. If you'll forgive the language, it's that old black magic working overtime."

Paul grinned and reached for her.

But Cleo eluded his grasp, and, retreating several paces, undressed, every move calculated for his benefit. In a sinuously graceful gesture she removed her dress, pulling it over her head, and then bent to take off her stockings. Finally, her sense of the dramatic strong, she peeled off her body stocking, performing the deed with such consciousness of her sexuality that, although she was almost boyishly slender, she gave the impression of being voluptuous.

With artful simplicity Cleo stood before him, posing in the nude, her half-smile and stance, her eyes and the way she held herself indicating a sense of erotic abandonment.

Paul had removed his own clothing, and with one accord they moved to the bed, virtually leaping at each other as they kissed and embraced. Their mutual desire was so great that neither felt any inhibitions, in spite of the fact that this was the first time they had become intimate. Paul's hands roamed incessantly, caressing and exploring, and Cleo was not slow to follow his example. He reveled in the firm perfection of her body, and she, even as she became increasingly aroused, managed to minister to his needs.

At last their desire overwhelmed them, and they became one. Cleo uttered a soft but piercing scream and dug her long fingernails deep into Paul's back, drawing blood, but this moment of erotic climax was all-encompassing, and he felt no pain.

When their passion was spent they fell back, exhausted, and lay side by side in a loose embrace, quiet hands stroking gently as their excitement subsided.

"That was fabulous," Cleo murmured.

"I've never known anything like it," Paul agreed.

"And I came to the agency three years ago. Think of all the time we've wasted."

"No, we haven't," he said. "People react to each other in different ways at different times, depending on all kinds of factors in their lives. A year ago you and I might have been a dull flop to-gether."

"I can hardly believe it, but I guess you're right, baby."

"Or a year *from* now."

Cleo raised herself on one elbow. "I catch on. Do you always say it the way it is?"

Paul opened his eyes to see her face looming above his, her expression mocking. "I try."

"Fair enough, because that's how I am too. And I warn you— I'm going to need plenty more with you before I get tired of it."

"I can't even think that far ahead," he said with a laugh.

"Good. Because the way we do it is the way the book says it ought to be."

"But we have one fault in common. We talk too much." Pulling her to him, he began his love-making again. To their surprise they became aroused even more quickly, and he took her savagely.

Again they rested, and when they overcame their lethargy Paul began to dress.

"If it's different but just as good every time," Cleo said, hauling herself from the bed, "we'll be at it day and night. We'll never do anything else."

"We're going to do something else right now." He glanced at his watch, and saw that it was almost ten o'clock. Barbara would be coming home soon, but he had no desire to hear a detailed account of her return to modeling. "Are you hungry?"

"I'm ravenous. But," Cleo added delicately, "you have other things you have to do."

"I intend to eat before I do anything else."

"I could fix us something here—"

"You're in no mood for a kitchen."

"How did you know?" She sat at her dressing table and with nimble, experienced hands began to repair her makeup. "There's a jazzy little place around the corner. Their food isn't bad, and the service is fast. I know you're in a hurry, so I won't be long."

He was amused to see that, although she raced, she would tolerate no makeup flaw. And, rather than wear the same clothes, she donned a body shirt and wide-legged pants. Only a model, going out for a bite to eat would insist on appropriate attire and perfection in her appearance at a moment like this.

Cleo was concentrating on what she was doing, and, seemingly absorbed, did not speak again until she was almost ready to leave. "We'll get together again, won't we?" she asked suddenly.

He recognized a generic trait, the basic insecurity of a model. "You can count on it."

"I just wanted to hear you say it." She used a comb to give her black hair a tousled look.

"In case you don't realize it," Paul said, "I get as big a charge out of all this as you do."

"I'm glad." Cleo turned to face him. "You have no regrets, baby?"

Paul knew he was still in a state of euphoria, that a reaction hadn't yet set in, to be followed by the torture of guilt. "Not yet," he said.

"Rosalie isn't home," Marni said, and tried to close the apartment door.

David was too quick for her and, seemingly without effort, held it open. "I'm not a carrier of communicable diseases, and I ask only two minutes of your time."

Rather than create a scene she opened the door, but remained unwilling to admit to herself that she was pleased to see him. "If you must. I'm going out soon."

She looked delectable in a short cocktail dress of green silk, and David's admiration was frank. "You look wonderful."

"Two minutes," Marni said, ignoring the compliment and ostentatiously studying her wristwatch.

"You and I," he said, "got our signals all loused up. You blew your cool over something that wasn't my fault or anybody else's. And then I got sore when you went to such extremes to ignore me. So my conduct was just as infantile as yours. How much more time have I got?"

"One minute." Her expression and voice were wooden.

"All I need is thirty seconds. I haven't been able to get you out of my mind all this time, and I hope you've had the same experience. It's enlightening. So I suggest we stop acting like children, and see each other occasionally. How about it?"

"Why should I?" Marni's facade crumbled, and she faced him angrily.

"Why shouldn't you?" David countered. "I lack the clairvoyance to know what you'd gain, but I can't see what you lose."

"You've been going with somebody else." Fortified by a telephone call the previous day from Paul, Marni was on sure ground, and spoke emphatically. "You've just broken up with her, so you're at loose ends right now, and you're shopping around for another girl to take out."

She knew more about him than he had imagined, but he recovered swiftly from his surprise. "First, I am not shopping around. Second, any dates I may have had with one or more other people are irrelevant to our situation."

"You didn't just date Cleo," she cried. "You had an affair with her."

"I refuse to dignify the accusation with either an affirmation or denial." David was secretly elated by her agitation, which indicated that she wasn't as indifferent to him as she had seemed. "And I can't deal with the issue in terms of other personalities. The principle of privacy is at stake, as much for other parties concerned as for myself. Let me illustrate. You're going out for the evening shortly. I'm not asking you to identify your escort—"

"That's good, because I wouldn't."

"Nor do I intend to inquire, either directly or otherwise, whether you're sleeping with him."

"You wouldn't dare!" Marni whipped herself into a fury. "Of course I'm not, but it isn't any of your business."

"Precisely my point. It's none of my business. When two people see each other socially, on a voluntary basis and without the free assumption of moral and ethical responsibilities inherent in a more permanent union, the scope of their relationship is limited to their own exclusive sphere." He grinned at her. "I didn't do badly, did I? Sounded like a sociologist lecturing a class of sophomores."

It occurred to Marni that she was behaving foolishly, and she had to admit that David's engaging smile and sense of humor attracted her. "No girl," she said, "likes to think she's lost a man to someone else."

"And no man," David replied, "willingly admits the existence of a rival. This raises a matter of some urgency. Your date will be here at any time, and if I see him I'll be strongly tempted to punch him in the teeth. The modern male—at least, this modern male—finds he hasn't been able to rid himself of vestigial traits of the jealousy that handicapped his uncivilized ancestors. I might add that I've exceeded my time limit, and I appreciate the tact you've shown by not reminding me of the error."

To her astonishment he walked quickly to the door.

"Goodnight, Marni," he said, smiling broadly, and was gone.

She stood for some moments, staring at the closed door. David hadn't spent much more time with her than the two minutes he had requested, and his abrupt departure had startled her. She was grateful for the tact he had shown in leaving before Ian appeared, but she knew enough about men to realize that a more fundamental motive had been responsible.

He hadn't indicated that he would telephone her or call again, but that had been a wise tactical maneuver, as he hadn't wanted to run the risk of a refusal. She felt certain he would call, and, for the first time, she opened her mind to the possibility that she would forgive him. A very few dates well might determine whether a further development of their relationship would be worth the time and effort or whether she should devote herself exclusively to Ian.

: 170

Paul couldn't rid himself of a feeling that he was harassed, and it was small comfort to realize that his own actions were at least partly to blame. He continued to enjoy his work at Clothco and took pleasure in the knowledge that he was solving the problems that the corporation had made his responsibility. But some of the fine edge of his enthusiasm for his job had been honed away, and it was a constant annoyance that he couldn't analyze the reason. His sense of foreboding about his future at the company persisted, even though he had established solid relationships with his colleagues and knew that Ian MacDonald and the directors approved of his accomplishments.

He often thought that Barbara's complete indifference to his vocational existence was one basic root of the trouble. She neither knew nor cared what happened at his office and was so wrapped up in her own return to modeling that nothing else, including her home and children, held any interest for her. To be sure, a man worked in order to achieve results and satisfy his own pride, and the applause of his wife wasn't essential; but Barbara's lack of concern was an unending source of irritation.

Paul had to admit that she was obtaining far more bookings than he had believed possible, and a telephone call to his former subordinates at the Howell Agency confirmed her contention that there was a steady, if not heavy demand for her services. "I don't understand it, either," Harriet had told him, "but the calls for her keep dribbling in—a fashion show here, a photography call there. She's no threat to Katya or Marni, but she's averaging three or four hours of bookings a day, and that's pretty darn respectable for a gal in her midthirties."

Barbara hadn't looked as attractive in years, but Paul knew of no other benefit resulting from her return to work. Her preoccupation with herself and the consequent neglect of her family had created many inconveniences, among them Paul's loss of his study, which was being used as a bedroom by the full-time maid it had been necessary to hire. He could not determine whether Barbara's drinking had diminished, although she certainly had not become abstinent. In years past she had spent hours each evening sitting in front of her mirror after over indulging, and there were no visible changes in her habits, even though Paul had no idea how much liquor she had consumed.

His continuing affair with Cleo made his burden no easier to bear, in spite of the fact that he rationalized his infidelity. Perhaps Barbara was an even less satisfactory wife now than she had been, but no matter how inexcusable her conduct, his breaking of his marriage vows was unjustifiable. He and Cleo had formed an attachment because they gave each other great erotic pleasure, yet he could tell himself she really meant nothing to him.

Nevertheless the conscience of a man who had always believed in monogamy—and practiced it—gave him no peace. He was making no attempt to terminate the affair and felt contempt for what he considered a weakness, his feeling in no way alleviated by the realization that his sensual pleasures remained undiminished.

He became increasingly irritable and moody, which did not improve his already shaky relationship with Barbara, and one spring evening, as they walked across the East Side, he felt particularly out of sorts.

"You can never get a taxi in this town when you need one. And why are we going out in the first place? Just because Audrey and Lou Burns snap their fingers and demand to see us is no reason we've got to jump. We haven't seen them for months, and I don't understand why it's so important to go running over there the minute they call."

"Aunt Audrey was very apologetic on the phone, and she kept

saying she knew she was imposing on us, but it was important."
Barbara's mind was elsewhere, and she seemed tranquil.

"All the same, they must have known before dinner that they
wanted to have us over. Unless there's been a sudden crisis, like the
Third being suspended from college."

"You've never liked my cousin." Her voice became ugly.

Paul knew she was spoiling for a fight. "I've never had anything
against little Louis, although he's a worthless kid. It gripes me because he shows no interest in Schwartzman-Burns."

"Maybe that's why I've always been so fond of him," Barbara
said. "The Third and I are the only members of the family who
don't think the universe revolves around that store."

"He'll inherit enough to do whatever he pleases with his life,"
Paul said. "But I wish I'd had his opportunities. Handed to me on
a sterling silver platter."

Barbara was bored by the subject. "Should I have worn my pants
outfit from Pakistan instead of this suit?"

Paul glanced at her gold-buttoned suede jacket and miniskirt.
"What's wrong with what you're wearing?"

"Well, it really isn't new."

"You mean you've gone out in it three times."

The irony escaped her. "At least four."

"What difference does it make? This is just a family visit."

"It's important to me," she replied stiffly.

"So I've discovered."

"There's no need to get nasty."

"What you wear isn't a matter of life and death!"

Barbara became testy too. "Who said it was? All I'm saying is
that my clothes mean something to me. And I'm buying all of my
own these days, remember. I've earned every penny's worth."

Paul felt his temper slipping. "That's your own choice, and you
goddam well know it. You could save your earnings or blow them
on something else. I kept you in a fancy wardrobe for years, and
I'm in a better position now than I ever was, so you don't have to
spend your own money on clothes."

"If my wardrobe was rather special," she said sweetly, "it's because I got the family discount at the store."

Paul knew they would bicker all evening unless he gave her the last word, so he fell silent, and they did not speak again on the rest of the walk.

The lobby of the Burns's apartment building reeked of ostentation. The ceiling, walls and floor of the lobby were done in a ceramic tile and featured scenes of vaguely Oriental men and women playing what appeared to be a Far Eastern version of croquet. But the effect was spoiled by indirect lighting that was inadequate, panels of incongruously modern mirrors and an ornate Persian rug that obliterated the most amusing portrayals of the croquet players.

Barbara automatically paused to study her reflection in a mirror, then immediately went to work with eyeliner brush, lipstick and a tube of a transparent, shiny substance she used to highlight her cheekbones.

Paul had been forced to wait while she had primped interminably just before leaving home, but a critical word might spark a quarrel that Barbara would make no attempt to conceal from her relatives, so he merely tapped a foot until his wife deigned to stroll to the elevator.

She bestowed a bland artificial smile on the elderly, uniformed operator who had been watching her with open interest, and Paul's irritation increased. This, he told himself, was a night he should have stayed at home, no matter how flimsy his excuse.

Audrey Burns, elegant in hostess pajamas of ivory lace, greeted her guests with the practiced finesse of a lifelong hostess, offering a cheek to Barbara while simultaneously grasping Paul's hand in both of hers and somehow drawing them into the extensive foyer, then into her husband's book-lined study in what appeared to be a single, uninterrupted movement.

"I'm so glad you could dash over on such short notice," she said, "and you'll never know how much we appreciate it. But I've always believed that blood is thicker than water."

Paul, who saw her no more than once or twice a year, couldn't remember whether her conversation was always cliché-studded.

"You're looking well, Paul, and as handsome as ever," Audrey said. "Your new job must agree with you."

"I like it very much," he replied politely, and felt like a small boy being complimented by an elder.

"Someday soon you must tell me just what it is that you do. All sorts of exciting things, I've heard, but I've never had much of a memory for business."

Barbara resented her absence from the spotlight. "How do you like my outfit, Aunt Audrey?"

The older woman gave her a cursory glance. "You always look enchanting, dear."

Barbara seethed. "In my opinion a suede suit is smart, and if it's worn with an air it can be dashing. But, enchanting? Never!"

Audrey was bored. "Paul, what will you drink?"

"A light bourbon and water, please."

"Barbara?"

"I feel like gin, I think."

Paul wanted to announce that she always wanted gin, but refrained.

Audrey went to a small bar in a corner. "Lou will join us as soon as he finishes a long-distance call." She busied herself with bottles, ice and glasses. "Poor Lou. Do you want your gin straight, Barbara?"

"A dash of tonic or Tom Collins mix would be nice."

"I asked, dear, because I didn't know."

If the women continued to throw knives at each other, Paul told himself, he would find a reason to walk out. "What's wrong with Lou?"

"We'd rather he tell you about it himself." Audrey looked serene as she handed them their drinks.

"I haven't seen him for a long time," Paul said.

An expression he couldn't define crept into Audrey's eyes. "I know."

She had no intention of explaining; and there was a moment of

175 :

awkward silence, which was broken when a small door at the rear opened and Louis Burns came into the room, his shoulders sagging and his walk weary.

Paul was stunned by his appearance. His hair had become white, his face was heavily lined and there were deep hollows beneath his eyes. He had been transformed into an old man, and an overly hearty, "Lou, how are you?" sounded an obviously false note.

Burns aimed a kiss at Barbara's forehead and limply shook Paul's hand.

"Give the bartender your order," Audrey said.

He waved her away from the bar. "I'll just pour myself a glass of celery tonic. Maybe it'll help settle my stomach. Funny, I've been drinking it ever since I was a boy. The Schwartzmans always gave it to me when I went to their house. Sometimes I think I'm half-Jewish."

Paul realized that something serious was happening, and his own restless dissatisfaction faded, but he could not make small talk.

Burns made a ritual of opening a bottle of celery tonic, pouring a glass and tasting it. "Everybody watches me. When I belch, the performance will be over. Pay your quarters to the doorman as you file out."

The crisis, Paul thought, was major.

Burns consumed about half of his drink, then hooked his thumbs in his vest pockets. "You two," he said, looking first at Barbara, then at Paul, "are the last couple in New York I wanted to see."

"I knew you were mad at us." Barbara sounded like a little girl. "What did we do wrong, Uncle Lou?"

He ignored the question. "But I have no choice, and at my age, when my back is to the wall, I have to forget my pride."

Paul had the sense to say nothing.

Suddenly Burns pointed a forefinger at him. "You like it in that house of crooks, huh? Working with MacDonald and the rest of them who should be behind bars!"

Paul kept his head. "To the best of my knowledge," he said, "there's nothing crooked about the Clothco operation."

"That's your excuse, too, is it?" Burns's voice shook. "I might have known. Oh, sure—it's legal, all right. Anybody with enough money can find smart lawyers who'll keep him out of jail. But are your friends honorable? And ethical? I defy you to give me your honest opinion!"

"Sit down, dear. Now." Audrey took her husband's arm and guided him to an overstuffed leather chair.

"Lou," Paul said, "I have no idea what you're talking about."

"Neither do I." Barbara was close to tears.

Burns glanced at his wife and shrugged.

"Ann has been telling us for weeks that they have no idea," Audrey said.

Burns grimaced. "You couldn't believe her, either."

"My mother knows something that I don't?" Barbara sounded indignant, but no one paid any attention to her.

"An explanation," Paul said, "might help. I haven't been able to figure out why you've been treating me like someone in an advanced stage of leprosy."

Burns gripped the arms of his chair. "Clothco," he said, "meaning your boss, MacDonald, is making an all-out effort to buy up Schwartzman-Burns stock and force me out."

Paul caught his breath.

Barbara's totally unexpected giggle broke the silence, and everyone looked at her, but she offered no explanation. Now she knew why Ian had been so helpful, calling scores of friends and acquaintances to obtain modeling bookings for her. He was clever, she thought without rancor, but she was getting the better end of the bargain, so perhaps he had outsmarted himself.

Paul slowly pulled himself to his feet. "I don't mean to insult your intelligence, Lou, but you're sure of this, obviously. How long ago did MacDonald start?"

"A year, as close as I can figure it." Burns watched him closely.

"Before he hired me?"

"Long before."

Paul's eyes hardened, and his voice became metallic. "I'll see him first thing in the morning. A great many little bits are falling into place right now, and I suspect that a number of people have gone out of their way to keep this information from me."

Burns took a deep breath. "If I've misjudged you—"

"That's unimportant. Are they swamping you, or are you holding them off?"

"By the time I discovered what was happening," Burns said, drinking the rest of his tonic, "MacDonald had a real toehold. In the past few months I've been devoting all my time to rounding up support, and right now we're at a stand-off."

"But you didn't come to Barbara." Paul glanced at his wife, who seemingly had lost interest in the conversation and appeared to be daydreaming as she took quick, nervous sips of her Tom Collins.

"At the beginning of this crisis," Burns replied wearily, "I naturally assumed that any member of the family would back me all the way, and I thought I could count on the stock of my niece as much as on that of my own children."

Barbara's empty glass thudded on the table beside her.

Audrey took the hint and went to refill it. "Another for you, Paul?"

"No, thanks. Go on, Lou."

"Then you went with Clothco. A big job, a fancy salary, all the trimmings." Burns paused and became defensive. "If our positions had been reversed, Paul, you'd have reacted as I did. It seemed very plain to me that MacDonald was sewing up Barbara's vote. What else could I think?"

"I knew nothing of the situation, and neither did Barb," Paul said, and everyone turned to her.

Accepting her fresh drink from her aunt, she shook her head. "How would I have found out?" she asked plaintively. "Nobody ever tells me anything."

The embarrassment of the others created a painful silence. Paul was so irritated he thought it best not to address her. "Lou," he said, "my head is in a real spin. All I knew was that the company has been making strenuous efforts to find a New York outlet, and the directors are willing to pay a fortune for it. The buying policy has been hampered by a lack of a leader store here, and it hasn't been possible to create a solid national image for the corporation itself without—"

"Sure, I know MacDonald's problems. Two years ago, when Silverman and Sons went out of business, he stood on his head trying to buy the name and the property. But the real estate had already been snapped up by a combine, and the Silverman boys finally decided to expand their suburban chain, so MacDonald was frozen out. That time he was too eager with his left hand and too slow with his right. But I'm not worrying about his headaches when he's giving me enough of my own." Burns took a cigar from the humidor beside him and began to unwrap it.

"You shouldn't, Lou," Audrey said.

He looked at her blankly.

"The doctor told you to cut down."

"Nobody is going to deny me the last of my pleasures, and it'll be good riddance if something happens to me." Burns stared gloomily into space, then clipped off the end of the cigar and reached for a table lighter.

Audrey subsided with a sigh.

"What's the picture right now, Lou?" Paul asked.

"I'm coming to that. It's the reason I wanted to see you two tonight. I had to take the chance that Ann was right about your innocence."

"I feel," Paul said, "like a woman who has been tricked into becoming a streetwalker without even knowing she's prostituting herself. If anyone had told me I'd land in this spot, I'd have said I couldn't be this naive."

"Don't blame yourself," Burns counseled. "If MacDonald didn't take you into confidence and I was afraid to trust you, the only way you could have learned anything was to pick up a rumor on the street."

"It doesn't really matter whether I've been slapped in the ego and whether the bruises show," Paul said. "Is Clothco in a position to force you out?"

"No, but I can't get MacDonald off my back without more help, either," Burns said. "We're running a dead heat, and Barbara's vote is going to be the deciding factor."

Barbara immediately became the center of attention. Burns peered at her anxiously, Audrey's face was veiled and Paul, as usual, was looking at her with what she called his "superior expression." Enjoying the suspense she was creating, she languidly took a cigarette from a case in her handbag and lighted it. "If you please, Aunt Audrey, I'll take just one more drink, a tiny one, and then I've got to get home. I'm making some photograph tests early tomorrow morning for a face powder campaign, and I'll need plenty of rest."

Paul couldn't help grimacing.

"It's terribly important," Barbara flared. "You may not care if I get the booking, but I do."

Her seeming stupidity galled him; he knew she was intelligent enough to realize that she was in a position to determine the fate of Schwartzman-Burns.

Her uncle waited until she had tasted her refill and had found it strong enough. "Well, Barbara?" He tried to sound jovial, but his voice was too hoarse. "Are we going to keep your father's and grandfather's store in the family?"

Barbara relished both the spotlight and the tension. Sipping her drink, she stared up at the ceiling, then smiled blandly at each of the others in turn, her eyes noncommittal. "I have no head at all for business, which isn't news, and I'm always frightened half to death by complicated things like stocks and voting. But as anybody who knows me ought to realize, I intend to do what I believe is right."

"I have a mean schedule this morning," MacDonald said on the intercom, "but if it's important, I'll cancel my lunch date and we can get together then."

"It's so urgent that I must ask you to mess up your schedule," Paul replied, his mouth close to the microphone-speaker.

MacDonald's faintly exasperated sigh floated through the intercom. "Come ahead, then, and we can talk while I'm looking at my mail."

Hurrying down the corridor to the president's office, Paul told himself that precious little mail would be read in the next half hour.

The secretary in the outer office of the presidential suite gaped as Paul strode past her. Everyone at Clothco knew that no one entered the inner sanctum without being announced, and the new vice-president had been around long enough to have learned the house rules. But he opened and closed the door before she could halt him.

MacDonald was surprised, too, but his expression indicated nothing but mildly preoccupied geniality as he glanced up from a letter. "Good morning," he said. "I didn't know anyone could develop serious problems this early in the day."

Paul dispensed with both amenities and preambles. "The company," he said harshly, "is trying to buy Schwartzman-Burns."

MacDonald felt as though an electric current had shot through him, but continued to smile calmly. "So we are. It's been one of my major projects for the past six months. Sit down, Paul." He waved toward a chair.

"I just learned about it last night." Paul continued to stand.

"Sit down." MacDonald's voice became a trace firmer, and he

waited until the order had been obeyed. "May I ask who told you?"

"Lou Burns."

"Ah, yes. I've sometimes wondered why he hadn't said anything to you."

"Because," Paul said, successfully making the attempt to remain civil, "he didn't trust me. He was positive I'd sold out to you."

MacDonald managed to look both startled and amused. "If I had stopped to think about it, I might have guessed that would be Louis Burns's reaction. I've never agreed with some of the crowd around town who claim he's strongly paranoid, but he does display a tendency to see conspiracies in strange places."

"On the basis of what little I know at this point," Paul said, "I'm in no position to point a finger at anyone and shout, 'Conspiracy.' But I do think I look like a horse's ass."

"You've had one of those nights where everything gets out of focus when you can't sleep," MacDonald said, becoming sympathetic. "It happens to me, too, and by the time I drag myself out of bed in the morning my vision is psychedelic. You need some coffee."

Paul felt himself losing the initiative, and tried to protest.

But MacDonald would not listen. "It's my usual time for it," he said, speaking briefly to his secretary on the intercom while continuing to return his visitor's steady gaze. "Forgive me for a minute while I get off a teletype to the store managers."

Paul had no choice, and watched the other man, who was taking his time, scribble a message on a memo pad. Perhaps MacDonald was stalling, preparing a defense after being caught unexpectedly, but there was no way to call his bluff. The man's request was reasonable, and he was on his home ground, where he was privileged to make the rules and set the pace. It might have been wiser to accept his original suggestion and meet him for lunch at a neutral spot where the odds might not have been tipped in his favor.

The secretary came in with a tray, which she placed on the coffee table in front of the sofa, and Paul, in spite of his agitation, was aware of the splendor. The handsome sterling silver service and bone china had appeared so quickly that it was apparent they were used regularly, rather than for the purpose of impressing a presidential guest.

MacDonald handed the girl the message he wanted dispatched on the teletype network that provided instant communication with the stores of the company's chain and then went to the sofa. "Cream and sugar?"

Paul realized it was useless to insist that he wanted no coffee. "Just black, thanks."

MacDonald made a little ritual of pouring the steaming brew, adding both cream and sugar to his own cup and stirring gently. His movements were deliberate, but he finally looked up and smiled.

It would have been impossible to converse with him while remaining near the desk, so Paul had to move to a chair placed at right angles to the sofa.

"I have my own blend ground for me at an old shop near the Battery. I hear I've been criticized for what some people call an affectation, but after you've tasted the coffee I think you'll agree it's worth the trouble."

Paul realized it was useless to press ahead at his own tempo, and decided to play a variation of the other's game. He picked up his cup, sniffed and took a tentative sip. "A gourmet would have me drawn and quartered," he said, "but I need a cigarette to bring out the flavor of coffee." He took his time drawing one from the pack in his pocket, tapping it on the table and lighting it.

MacDonald's quick grin indicated his appreciation of the younger man's gesture.

Again Paul sipped, and sat back in his chair. "You're right," he said. "I can't remember when I've had better."

"I'll have a bag sent to your office this afternoon, along with a breakdown of the blend."

"Wonderful," Paul said with simulated heartiness and made no further attempt to converse. Eventually the topic of coffee would be exhausted, and MacDonald would return to the subject at hand.

MacDonald knew it would be ludicrous to drag out the small talk and, realizing he had been checked, took the plunge. "Ever since we've grown into a major operation," he said, "we've had a need for a New York store. In the past few years that need has become desperate."

"One of my first recommendations after I joined you," Paul said, "was the acquisition of a Manhattan store, preferably one on Fifth Avenue."

"I haven't forgotten the recommendation."

"Your answer was a red herring. You told me about negotiations for a couple of outlets—"

"Legitimate negotiations, as the files will prove."

"—but you made no mention of Schwartzman-Burns. I assume that by then you were piling up shares of stock."

"We had cornered about forty percent by then, estimating roughly. Maybe a bit more." MacDonald spoke cheerfully, with seeming candor and was completely at ease as he drank his coffee.

"Presumably a number of company officers knew what was happening."

"A very few. Only those who had to be told. The same is true of the board. Most of the directors know nothing—to this day—about our efforts to gain control of the store."

Paul had the feeling that his case was being weakened, but he hadn't yet brought up the heart of his argument. "I'll grant you that a new man, no matter what his responsibilities, deserved no priority over those who outranked him."

"I'm relieved that you can see the corporate point of view," Mac-Donald murmured.

"On the other hand, my situation was rather special, since I had an intimate personal connection with Schwartzman-Burns. You know that my wife is closely related to Louis Burns, and you must have known—since you were tracing shareholders and buying them out—that she owns a substantial chunk of stock in the store."

"How could I have failed to know all that?" MacDonald

: 184

countered. "The facts of life, as we might call them, were in my mind from the day I offered you a place here."

Paul's mouth tightened. "I see."

"Do you? I wonder." MacDonald decided to draw some heat from the confrontation. "More coffee?"

"Fine," Paul said, wanting to avoid another diversion.

Again the older man went through the ritual. "I must confess this is one of my extravagances," he said as he drank.

Paul remained silent, using the same technique he had previously found effective.

MacDonald resumed where he had stopped. "Your family connection with Louis Burns was a factor long before I spoke to you. It played a part in our thinking from the time we began to consider you for a vice-presidency."

Rigid self-control helped Paul maintain a facade of calm, but he reached for another cigarette.

"The others—two or three of them—believed your relationship with Burns was a black mark against you. I disagreed with that opinion and still do."

The confrontation was veering off into an unexpected channel, but Paul forced himself to remain silent and put the full onus for an explanation on MacDonald.

"They took my word, of course. I gave them no choice." The ugly face twisted in a leering smile. "You may have heard it whispered around here that I'm inclined to be bullheaded on occasion."

Paul nodded and allowed himself a faint smile to indicate his appreciation of the other's ponderous humor.

"My faith in you has been justified, although that's neither here nor there."

"Quite so," Paul said crisply, letting him know that compliments were wasted.

"As a safety measure, and for no other reason, my advisors asked that you be told nothing about our efforts to gain control of a working majority of Schwartzman-Burns stock. I didn't think the precaution was necessary, but I went along with it. It will interest

185 :

you that one of the men involved has come to me recently and indicated he sees no need for continuing secrecy. He trusts you too."

Paul knew that some gesture of response was required, so he inclined his head slightly.

"There's only one thing it would be impolitic to tell you at present," MacDonald said. "As a member of the top echelon you're working with others on the team, and there have been none of the personality clashes that can ruin any corporation. You might resent the advice I was given—by men who didn't know you at that time, remember. Even under those circumstances it would be only human if you developed grudges against them."

"I don't care who advised you or what they thought of me," Paul said, cutting off another diversionary advance.

"Well, then. You have the whole story, and I hope you're satisfied. I apologize for any slight you may have felt, but I hope you can see and understand the spot I was in."

The time had come for Paul to strike. He stubbed out his cigarette and leaned forward in his chair, but did not raise his voice. "I understand everything you've said, Ian, but you've only scratched the surface, and I'm no more satisfied than I was when I came storming in here."

"What more can I say?" MacDonald spread his hands in the helpless gesture he had so often found effective.

"It seems to me," Paul said, "that I was hired because of my wife's Schwartzman-Burns stock. I was given a high salary and many other benefits in what appears to me to be a blatant attempt to buy my influence."

"My God." MacDonald stared at him, open-mouthed.

"There you have it. If I could persuade Barbara to vote with Clothco against her uncle, I'll have been worth many times what you've been paying me."

MacDonald stood and paced the length of the large office, occasionally clasping and unclasping his hands behind his back. He had grown pale, and the expression in the small, sharp eyes behind his glasses indicated that he was in a turmoil of some sort. "I can't blame you for feeling that way," he said at last, speaking in a choked voice. "I'm trying not to be hurt by your lack of faith in me, but I realize you've had no real reason to trust me. And I can see how this warped idea took hold in your mind."

His sincerity was open to question, but in any event the histrionics left Paul unmoved.

MacDonald came to a halt beside him and dropped a hand onto his shoulder. "You've had a nightmare. Forget it."

"I find this distasteful, too," Paul said. "Can we confine ourselves to facts, Ian?"

MacDonald immediately resumed his seat. "Of course," he said quietly.

"You deny that I was hired because of Barbara's stock."

"Categorically. And your record since you've come to us proves your worth to Clothco. There are damn few executives of your caliber anywhere, and I can assure you the directors of this company will fight to keep you here."

Paul remained unconvinced. "I find it impossible to believe that my presence here has no connection with my wife's stock."

"We'd want you if she sold her stock tomorrow. Or gave it away."

"I think it unlikely that she'll do either," Paul said wryly.

"I sincerely hope not," MacDonald replied in the same tone. "It's too valuable. But," he added with emphasis, "that has nothing to do with your place in the corporation. We'd want you here even if your wife had never owned a single share of Schwartzman-Burns stock."

"It's senseless to argue a theoretical question," Paul declared. "The facts of the situation are undeniable. I'm an officer of a company that's trying to buy out a department store. That store can be a major factor in carrying the corporation into a new, higher category. My wife owns a significant interest in the store. At present her stock is vital. If she votes with her husband's company, it gets the store. If she swings the other way, it stays in her family, where it has been for several generations. I've been put in an untenable position."

"Only if you insist on maneuvering yourself into it, Paul. I have no desire to debate theoretical questions either. What I'm willing and eager to do is demonstrate my complete faith in you, regardless of the question of Barbara's stock. Clothco will tear up your present contract and give you a new one for ten years instead of five. Will that convince you that I'm not trying to trick or con you?"

"It's a powerful argument." Paul was shaken and made no attempt to conceal his feelings.

"You'll have the new contract as soon as the lawyers can draw it up. Today, if possible, and it shouldn't be too difficult, as they can use the same language practically word for word and just change five years to ten." He extended his hand.

Paul drew in his breath, then shook MacDonald's hand.

"You've had rough sailing, boy!" MacDonald clapped him on the back.

"I'm still feeling the ship's motion." Paul told himself he had solid cause to feel relieved. He had been treated honorably and generously and could assure himself that his integrity was not being threatened. But the hard lump that had formed in the pit of his stomach had not dissipated, nor had his uneasiness.

"Why don't you play hooky for the rest of the day? The morning is pretty well shot anyway."

Paul was tempted to call Cleo to learn if she was free. An afternoon of uninhibited sex might rid him of what MacDonald had just proved to be an unwarranted fear, and a prolonged romp with a mistress whose vigor and appetite matched his might dispel his lingering depression. But he could not allow himself the luxury of such undisciplined behavior. "I have too much to do," he said, shaking his head. "My desk is piled so high that if I goof off today, I'll pay for it tomorrow."

"Now," MacDonald said, "you know why we want you here. How I wish we had a few more with that attitude."

Paul started toward the door, then paused. "It isn't the extension of my contract that convinced me Clothco wants me for myself. You must be pretty anxious yourself, but you haven't once asked me which way Barbara is going to vote her stock."

"It didn't cross my mind."

"I don't believe in playing cute games, either, so I'd tell you, Ian, if I knew. But whatever she's decided—if she's decided—she's keeping to herself."

When the door closed MacDonald returned to his desk and slumped in his chair, exhausted. Then, rousing himself, he polished his glasses, and after satisfying himself that they were clean, he flipped an intercom switch. "Come in here!" he ordered, his voice grating.

Almost immediately Carlo Bennett appeared, and knew from his superior's manner that this was not a moment for informality. "Yes, sir?"

"Barbara Howell is somewhere around town, making the rounds of the modeling circuit. I want you to find her. Discreetly."

"You bet."

"Hear me out, and don't interrupt. You'll have to be more careful than you've ever been, Carlo. While you're looking, don't identify yourself or me. I want no one—and I mean that literally—to connect this company with our interest in her. Got it straight?"

"I think so."

"You Neapolitan blockhead!" MacDonald shouted. "Think! If you've got to phone, let her agency or whoever believe that you're a client. A photographer, maybe, or an advertising agency talent supervisor."

"Now I see what you mean." Bennett's saturnine face cleared.

"I'm not done. When you find Mrs. Howell, speak to her alone. If she's with other people, get her aside. But make sure the others don't know you. I can't afford to take even a very small risk. No one must know that I'm looking for her."

"I've never failed you yet, Ian." Bennett had jumped to his own conclusions regarding his mission, and his grin was suggestive.

"When you're able to speak privately to Mrs. Howell, ask her to call me. She knows my private number. Tell her it's important—"

"Oh, I will!"

"—but make it plain that all I want is a few words with her. I have no intention of seeing her."

Bennett became confused. "We aren't going to have one of our special parties?"

MacDonald half-rose from his chair. "No!"

His assistant shrugged.

"Just follow my orders to the letter. They're simple enough, but a mistake could cost us millions. This is the most important assignment you've ever had."

The fitters balked, refusing to make the final adjustments on the clothes until the designer returned from lunch. Maurice, they insisted, was so temperamental that the risk of being subjected to one of his rages wasn't worth the length of a hemline or the fit of a dress across the bosom. Maurice's assistants privately agreed, as they, too, had no desire to face the master's wrath, so all activity in the large hotel suite came to an end.

So the models, lounging in various stages of undress in the hotel bedroom set aside for them, were required to wait too. They had ordered cottage cheese or sandwiches made with diet bread from room service, and after eating they smoked, rested on the beds and sipped low-calorie soft drinks.

Barbara, in a bra and half-slip, was conscious not only of being much older than the others, but of being in a unique position. Although she liked to think of herself as just another model, the others did not regard her as a full-fledged member of the sorority. To them she was Mrs. Paul Howell, and they could not let her forget it, either.

Karen and Freddie, a young blond and even younger brunette, were awed by her and kept their distance, remaining at the far end of the room and talking to each other in whispers. Occasionally they glanced in Barbara's direction, making her believe they were discussing her, and she couldn't decide whether to feel annoyed or flattered.

Katya, stretched out on a bed in a half-bra and bikini panties, was friendly enough, but took care to watch her language when addressing a direct comment to Barbara. Marni Kendall, in a model's smock, was the most relaxed with the older woman, but even she adopted a respectful attitude. Cleo, who was also wearing a smock, was strangely aloof, and although she replied civilly when Barbara spoke to her, took no conversational initiatives of her own. Yet Barbara repeatedly found Cleo staring at her, inspecting her critically with hooded eyes, and found the experience disconcerting.

At times such as this, when other models were involved, it wasn't easy to return to one's past, Barbara decided. Certainly she didn't enjoy these assignments as much as she did the jobs she worked alone.

"The slob," Katya said to no one in particular, reaching the climax of a long story she had been telling, "offered me a blue fox cape. Street length! Not even a long one! And in return for three whole days!"

Several of the girls smiled, and Cleo, who was wandering restlessly around the room, asked, "What did you tell him?"

"That I hated Miami Beach. What else could I say? The cheap bastard!"

Although Barbara had never condemned the morals of others, she was startled by Katya's casually mercenary attitude toward sex. Apparently, she didn't realize she was a high-priced prostitute, a woman who put a price on her body. When Barbara had first gone into modeling she had known a number of girls whose approach had been similar, but she hadn't been bothered and actually had accepted their philosophy as long as it hadn't applied to her. Perhaps the passage of more than fifteen years combined with what felt like a lifetime of marriage made the difference.

To be sure, her relationship with Paul left a great deal to be desired, and she certainly wouldn't characterize her marriage as a happy one. The hard-driving qualities that others admired in him made him less than an ideal husband. Demanding perfection from himself, he was so critical of her that she wanted to scream, most days, and often was in despair because he was never satisfied with anything she did or said. And when he wasn't blasting at her, he was looking down, sneering, from the heights of his intellectual, masculine superiority.

Nevertheless, although there were times when she not only hated him and wondered how she could have been in love with him so long ago, she found marriage a safe and comfortable institution. Admitting she was smug, she found it somewhat more difficult to see that she was growing increasingly conservative as the years passed. All the same, she found Katya's attitude disgusting. The girl might be a hundred-an-hour star, the reigning queen of the profession, but her type gave all models a bad name.

"I can't wait much longer for Maurice," Marni said. "I have another booking."

"The high price of fame," Cleo said. "Only you superpopular people get jobs late on Friday afternoons. Everybody else may as well go home and start the weekend."

"When I accepted Maurice's fashion show," Marni said, "I made it plain that I couldn't stay later than two thirty today for fittings."

Katya opened her eyes for a moment. "Maurice doesn't care about other bookings, darling. He thinks you've gone to heaven when you wear his clothes, and if you leave one minute early, he'll throw a tantrum."

"Let him," Marni said, looking at her watch.

Katya's smile was catlike. "First he'll skin you, and then he'll try to blacklist you in the industry. You just don't know how vindictive that little monster can be."

Barbara realized that some aspects of modeling were unchanged. Katya, like other reigning queens before her, resented the rise of another girl to stardom and was losing no opportunity to denigrate a rival.

But Marni proved she could look after herself. "You're one of Maurice's old-timers, Katya, so he'll listen to you. Would you be an angel and explain to him that I'm on a spot?"

"I've done his shows for five years, that's all." Katya was sputtering. "Is that what you call an old-timer?" She controlled herself, then seemed to relent. "I'll do what I can for you, darling. But he hates an unprofessional attitude."

Marni appeared unaware of the jibe. "Thank you," she said sweetly, and, although continuing to address Katya, appeared to address the others as well. "You're lucky you have no conflicts this afternoon."

The redhead jerked to an upright position. "I told the agency this would be my last today! I've had so many bookings this week I need a little time to myself."

The queen, Barbara knew, was in great danger of losing her throne.

Before Katya could goad her rival into an open squabble, the others simultaneously began to chat, motivated less by a desire to protect Marni than to prevent a scene in which they might become involved. Everyone had seen Katya at her worst, and although she herself could still find work, someone whose name became linked with hers by the industry gossips might find herself shunned as a trouble-maker.

The bathroom door opened, and Fran Black emerged, wearing only pantyhose and shoes, but unconcerned about her near-nudity. She had done a thorough but unnecessary job of repairing her makeup, and the mascara on her lashes was too heavy, her eyeline too broad, her lipstick too thick. "Guess what, kids!" she called. "I just got weighed on the scale in the john, and I'm down eight pounds since I started freelancing."

No one paid any attention to the interruption, and Barbara felt sorry for the girl. Models were hypersensitive to class distinctions, and Fran was out of her league. No one objected to her past as an employee of a lingerie manufacturer; many models had made the transition to freelance work and had been successful in the more difficult and exacting realm. But the self-employed who made good acquired a patina that set them apart from their lesser sisters: they were better groomed, more expensively dressed, more subtly made up. They were the elite of the profession and acted accordingly, but Fran seemed incapable of making the grade.

Barbara, who felt that she herself was something of an outsider, sympathized with someone excluded from the circle. "Congratulations," she said. "How did you do it?"

Fran responded like a hungry puppy being offered a biscuit and came to her. "I starved myself, for all the good it did me, and then I went on the wagon. Now I eat anything I please, but I don't touch booze."

"That's the rough way," Barbara said, and wondered if she had the strength to stop drinking.

"Booze isn't one of my hangups," Fran said, perching on the arm of her chair. "Ask me to give up nooky, and I'd rather get fat." She laughed heartily at her own joke.

Barbara was disconcerted by the proximity of the girl's bare breasts to her face, and it occurred to her that Fran might be a Lesbian. It seemed more likely, however, that she was one of the new breed who didn't know the meaning of modesty.

"Anything else, I'm willing to quit," Fran continued. "You're Mrs. Howell, aren't you?"

"Yes. Barbara."

"Well, your husband did it to me, Barbara."

"I beg your pardon?"

"I only met him a couple of times before he left the agency, but he was the one who told me I had to lose fifteen pounds to be in freelance. And that's worth almost any kind of sacrifice."

"I know what you mean," Barbara said with sincerity, and felt a bond with her.

: 194

The violet eyes studied Barbara curiously. "Doesn't it make you up-tight? Like, being married to him?"

"I don't—dig you." The current vernacular didn't come easily.

"Not his being famous and important and all. That isn't what I mean. Like, he's such a gorgeous piece of man."

Barbara couldn't express herself too freely to someone she didn't really know. "Oh, I guess I just got used to his good looks, and take them for granted. The way he does mine." She noticed that Cleo had stopped conversing with several of the others and was staring at her again, but she told herself that if the black model had nothing better to do than eavesdrop, she supposed she didn't mind.

"Like, if he was mine," Fran said, "I'd put a chain on him. And a chastity belt."

Barbara was tempted to reply that, to her relief, Paul was so absorbed in his work he had lost interest in sex. "I suppose I'm one of the few women in this world who doesn't have to worry about her husband."

Marni was listening, too.

Aware of her audience, Barbara raised her voice. "Beautiful models have always been Paul's business, not his pleasure. He was surrounded by them for so long that they're a commodity to him, and when he looks at an attractive girl he sees only dollar signs."

Cleo quickly turned away, and Barbara, catching a glimpse of her expression, wondered briefly what she had said that had caused the black model to smirk.

"Everybody except you," Fran said with a laugh. "Like, you're still stacked, and you have the face to go with the body. So he knows you're around, I bet."

The talk was becoming too intimate, and the embarrassed Barbara groped for a suitable reply.

Marni came to her rescue. "I'm sure Barbara won't mind my saying this, but I've seen the Howells together, a number of times, and Paul appreciates his wife. Every woman," she added, not realizing she sounded wistful, "wishes a man would look at her that way."

"You couldn't be hurting," Fran said, delighted at the development of a general conversation in which she could participate. "That was some man who dropped you off here today. I was coming into the hotel at the same time, and I saw you with him. When they're that husky they don't send me, but for anybody who wants them big, that one was a mountain."

Cleo exchanged a glance with Marni that was knowing, sympathetic and slightly amused.

Fran realized there had been a communication of some sort and hastened to include Cleo. "You, too," she said.

"I've been sitting on the bench ever since I sent Julius back to his coach," Cleo said. "I almost forget what it's like to have me a man."

"What do you call the fellow you were having dinner with on Tuesday night?" Fran's crude teasing sounded more like an interrogation.

Cleo stiffened. "Tuesday?" she asked vaguely.

"At the Merry-Go-Round Club. I saw you while you were having dinner, but you and your fellow were too busy making out to see me."

Cleo became rigid and tried in vain to hide her distress.

"I couldn't get a good look at him. There was a post in the way, a column, like," Fran said. "The next time I looked over, you were gone. You left early."

"I remember now," Cleo said, taking care to avoid Barbara's eye. "That was just an ordinary date. I thought you meant somebody special."

Fran's whooping laugh was raucous. "If that was ordinary, I'd hate to see you with somebody special. Man, were you two making out!"

Recovering from her fright, Cleo smiled, her expression indicating that the other girl's exaggerated observation should be discounted. Barbara, she saw, had lost interest in the interchange, and she was indifferent to the reaction of anyone else.

The door opened, and Maurice's principal assistant stood in the frame. A tall, raw-boned woman in her midfifties who always dressed inconspicuously, she adjusted her steel-rimmed spectacles on the bridge of her nose and raised a hand for silence.

The models, who despised her dictatorial manners, continued to chat.

"Ladies!" she called imperiously, and at last the talk died away. "I have just received a telephone call from Monsieur Maurice. He has been delayed by a matter that could not be postponed and will not arrive for another hour."

"That's too long for me," Marni said, going to a rack for her clothes. "The agency said you'd promised I'd be free by two thirty."

Katya catapulted herself from the bed. "Maurice is a half hour late now, and another hour is too much. I won't wait that long for any man."

There was a swelling chorus of high-pitched, angry agreement.

The assistant had to call, "Ladies!" repeatedly before she could make herself heard. "Monsieur Maurice expresses his regrets, and assures you that you will be paid your full fees, not half-fees, for the time you have spent here today. He also requests that you arrange time on Monday for the fittings. We will settle the details with your agency."

Marni was dressing rapidly. "I'm sorry," she said, "but I have no time open on Monday."

Katya zipped herself into an abstract print dress that bore the signature of a famous designer. "Neither do I. If you and Maurice can't work the fittings into our schedules, you'll just have to hire other girls with our measurements."

Maurice's assistant stalked out of the room, damning the independent insolence of high-priced models.

Marni and Katya, drawn together by their status and mutual indignation, left together.

Cleo departed a few moments later, followed by the younger girls, and Fran, after donning a low-necked, snug-fitting dress, went to the mirror and began to take cosmetics from her handbag.

Barbara was in no hurry and dressed slowly. She had no other assignments for the day, no calls on potential clients to make, and, less than eager to return home, was killing time. "Fran," she said, "may I make a suggestion?"

"Why not?"

"Use less makeup, not more. Here, let me show you." She thinned the girl's eyeline with a tissue, then studied the result. "That's better. I can't do much about the lashes, though. Clean them when you take them off tonight, and try them with about half as much mascara. Now scrub off your lipstick."

Fran reluctantly obeyed.

"We'll try mine."

"But you're a blond and I'm dark."

"That doesn't matter. This silver-transparent goes with anyone. That deep red you've been using makes you look old."

"They keep telling me these things at the agency, but I've been making up one way, and it's hard to change."

"Stop talking." Barbara busied herself with the lipstick. "There," she said at last.

Fran examined her reflection. "I always feel funny this way. Like I'm naked."

Barbara looked at her in the dress that left little to the imagination and restrained a laugh. "Believe me, it's an improvement."

"If you say so."

Barbara knew that whether she liked it or not she had made a friend.

They left the suite together, and Fran talked animatedly all the way down the corridor and in the elevator, keeping up the pace after they reached the lobby.

Barbara listened patiently and waited for a chance to break away. Ordinarily she would have suggested going somewhere for a drink, which would have used up another hour, but she couldn't face the prospect of drinking with Fran. The girl's loud voice attracted attention, and her skimpy attire combined with the way she carried herself seemed to draw to her every man in search of a pickup.

Within a few minutes three of them came up to her, but she waved them away without pausing in her monologue.

Wanting to get out of the uncomfortable spotlight, Barbara began to drift slowly toward the hotel entrance, and was dismayed when Fran continued to walk with her. When they turned a corner she saw the door that led to the drugstore located in the hotel, and that gave her an idea.

"I'll say goodbye to you here," she said. "I've got to make a phone call."

Fran delayed her still longer with an elaborate farewell.

At last Barbara was free, and as she started toward the drugstore, a man came through the door and approached her.

Carlo Bennett had obeyed his instructions meticulously, and had waited until Barbara was alone before speaking to her. "Mrs. Howell," he said, "I'd like a quick word with you."

Fran Black turned to wave and call a last goodbye. Her eyes met Bennett's, and at the same instant they recognized each other.

The walls of Andrew Reilly's office were lined with framed covers of every issue that *Chic* had published since its inception a half-century earlier. Every available inch of space was being utilized, and the covers of recent years had overflowed into his secretary's office, the executive reception room and the corridor connecting the suite with the magazine's main offices. It was a standing joke among the company's employees that *Chic* would be forced to move to new quarters when Reilly no longer had the space to continue the custom started by his father.

Visitors from the outside, who expected to find the publisher ensconced in modern splendor resembling the Furnishings section of *Chic*, were surprised to find his office curiously old-fashioned. He used a large and cumbersome rolltop desk that had belonged to his grandfather, the founder of the family fortune, and the chairs, tables and small sofa, although comfortable, were old and plain. The oriental rug that covered the better part of the inexpensive wall-to-wall carpeting was, in the opinion of older employees, a key to Andrew Reilly's character. They swore it had seen service in his mother's dining room for many years, which may have been an exaggeration, but it was undeniably worn, slightly frayed and rapidly growing shabbier.

Reilly, they said, was a penny-pincher, his own custom-tailored personal appearance to the contrary notwithstanding. He kept a sharp watch over the magazine's income and expenditures, frequently questioned expense accounts and granted salary increases only when cornered. It was said, without proof, that he sometimes roamed through the offices at night, checking outgoing mail to make certain that employees did not use the company's postage meter machines for their private mail.

When Didi Martin was summoned to the front office she assumed she would be forced to justify her photographic safari to San Andros, which had been more expensive than she had anticipated, so she armed herself with proofs of the sixteen-page spread that she intended to run in a forthcoming issue. The photographs were among Gary Carey's best, the series covered a wide variety of beach attire, and the two models Didi had used came across subtly to the reader without projecting their own personalities too strongly, so she was satisfied that no fashion editor could have done better. The spread, Didi was convinced, spoke for itself and was worth at least double the sum she had spent.

But Reilly surprised her by making no objections to the expense of the trip. He had already seen the proofs, and complimented her on the series, saying that the advertising department was particularly pleased because she had used products made by seventeen different manufacturers of beachwear, shoes and accessories. He seemed to be in no hurry to discuss the business that had caused him to send for her, and instead he chatted amiably about a recent Broadway opening, a new restaurant and a charity costume ball both had attended.

The more relaxed the publisher appeared, the more Didi's suspicions were aroused. The last time she had been subjected to the "chums" treatment, as his excursions into informality were known, Reilly had postponed consideration of her long overdue pay raise. So she braced herself for another rejection.

"I see you've brought your San Andros proofs with you," he said at last. "May I see them again?"

Didi handed them to him, and he spread them on a cork board he kept for the purpose, expertly pinning them into place. "They're striking shots, Didi. What makes them is the way your white model and your black are juxtaposed. And your costuming is marvelous. You did it yourself?"

"Of course, darling." Didi's wariness mounted.

"You've always been a first-rate editor, and you've been improving every year. I can't risk losing you, Didi, so I've sent through a memo that'll bring a twice-monthly recognition of *Chic's* appreciation."

"Aren't you sweet." She couldn't remember anyone on the staff getting a raise without hounding him for it.

"I wish," Reilly said, a shade of appropriate regret in his voice, "that I could have made it for the three thousand a year you and I were discussing a couple of months ago."

Here, Didi thought, was the catch.

"I went to bat for you, but they wouldn't buy that big an increase. They insist our profit margin just won't stand that much of a strain on the budget right now."

The mythical "they" were never identified, as Didi well knew. Her employer liked to maintain the fiction that he was not the final authority in such matters, but had to refer requests to a nameless, faceless group to whom he was allegedly responsible.

"The most they'd grant us at the present is fifteen hundred, but if circulation and advertising keep growing, they've promised that you'll be the first to get another raise, so the additional fifteen hundred shouldn't be too far behind."

"I hope not. And thanks, darling." Didi hadn't done too badly.

An increase of fifteen hundred was all she had expected, really, and at least she would be in a position to remind him of his vague promise to double the sum.

Reilly continued to study the proofs. "Your black model has just the right balance of pizazz and elegance. Will her agency give you a twelve-month fashion exclusive?"

"I suppose they would if I asked." Didi wished Reilly wouldn't interfere in her realm. She had more or less made up her mind not to use Cleo again, blaming the girl for influencing Marni against her on the San Andros jaunt. She knew Cleo frequently had referred to her disparagingly and could think of no other reason for Marni's painfully obvious efforts to avoid her.

"Ask," Reilly said.

"There are a half-dozen other black models who are very effective, Andrew."

"This one," Reilly said, "has the *Chic* look."

"Very well," Didi replied sulkily, wondering if he was developing a personal interest in Cleo. It was just her luck to be stuck for a whole year with a model who claimed she wouldn't take another woman as a lover, and the pleasure Didi had felt when she learned of her salary raise began to evaporate.

"This Kendall girl is superb, isn't she?"

"She's gorgeous, Andrew, and she's going to be number one." Didi's spirits lifted a bit.

"You've already tied her up under a fashion exclusive, I presume."

"Naturally. With the usual guarantee."

"Good."

"If I do say so, I can take some of the credit for Marni, you know. The bikini shot in the current issue that's causing so much comment was strictly my doing."

"So I've gathered," Reilly said. "I can't blame her or the Howell Agency for being unhappy, even though our circulation department is ecstatic. That photograph has an explosive erotic quality,

Didi. There would have been far fewer repercussions if she had posed in the nude."

"I honestly do pat myself on the back, Andrew. Marni has always done the young-lady things, but I was the first to discover she has sex; so now she can run the whole gamut."

Reilly knew what lay behind Didi's sex "discoveries" and glanced at her, but her expression remained smugly bland. "She isn't going to be running any gamuts. From now on she'll go back to the lady-like photos."

Didi was startled and annoyed. Her publisher had no right to interfere, and she would have to put him in his place.

"I'm afraid," Reilly continued, "that our exclusive will have to be subassigned. Now, wait. Before you go flying through the roof, let me explain."

"Never, in all the years I've been in publishing," Didi said, "have I heard of a model's exclusive being subassigned. Marni Kendall is a *Chic* protégé, Andrew. Her image is our image, and she belongs to us."

He raised a hand to stem the torrent. "She won't be seen in any other magazine. That's part of the deal."

"How dare anyone make a deal behind my back?"

"The deal was made by me. Because I had no choice. If you'll just simmer down—"

"Andrew, how could you?" she wailed. "Marni is the new Katya, and you know how *she* helped our image until she began to look too hard and sleazy."

"I've had a personal request from Ian MacDonald," Reilly said flatly. "He intends to use the Kendall girl in Clothco advertising. Ads that will appear only in *Chic*."

"He can't have her!"

"Like hell he can't. Every one of his thirty-two stores runs its own advertising campaign. Clothco is going to start a new institutional series, too. And to top it off, they expect to add another store to the chain that'll be advertising more heavily than any of the others. Start counting up the advertising dollars, Didi, and be thankful MacDonald is coming in all the way with us instead of giving the lion's share to our competition."

"This is outrageous. Clothco has no right—"

"MacDonald is taking the right. He was very blunt with me, as he can be when he wants something. He realizes we have an interest in Kendall, and he's protecting us by using her in *Chic*, but nowhere else. He's also made it very clear that we aren't going to lose anything. He'll increase his advertising appropriation for *Chic* very handsomely."

"There's always been a clear-cut line of demarcation that separates editorial from advertising, Andrew. We've never been the handmaidens of the advertising boys, and I don't propose to start giving up my editorial freedom now. There's a principle at stake, Andrew. Freedom of the press."

"You're getting hysterical, Didi," Reilly said coldly. "There's nothing involved here but your own pride. You lose nothing, really. At the worst, one might say you lose the editorial services of a model, and what's one model, for God's sake?"

"This one happens to have unique qualities—"

"Are you sleeping with her?" he interrupted.

"What a nasty question!"

"That means you aren't, but you want to. Sorry, Didi, but you'll have to make your pitch without the benefit of photographic sugar plums to hand out to Kendall."

"How can you be so insulting?"

"How can you be so stupid? No magazine could afford to turn down an offer like this!" Reilly began to lose his poise.

"If you're willing to give up the basic right of a free press—"

"Bullshit," he said, and shocked her into silence. "No one is dictating or even suggesting changes in my editorial policies. Clothco is increasing its advertising, that's all, and will observe our usual rules of taste and style. All they want from us—and we're happy to oblige them—is to grant them the exclusive fashion-magazine photographic rights to a model. The issue, if it is one, simply isn't worth the stink you're making."

"You make it sound simple, which it isn't," Didi said, and sniffled.

"If it weren't for this deal, I couldn't give you a nickel's worth of salary raise, and it isn't just you. When I give you more, I've got to give it to eight or ten others at the same time."

Didi was near tears. "What you're trying to tell me," she said, "is that I must accept a bribe in return for giving up Marni Kendall. I could do it without a murmur if I didn't have an active conscience—"

"If it'll make you happy to twist a minor transaction into a major crisis, be a masochist, for all I care!" The publisher stared at her in exasperation. "I still congratulate you, you idiot. You made this whole deal possible by getting exclusive fashion-photography rights to Kendall from her agency."

"The bikini shot of Marni was my big mistake. It was so erotic that it gave Ian MacDonald ideas." A malicious gleam lighted Didi's eyes. "But he's wrong—as he'll find out! And what will happen, I'd like to know, when he learns she isn't the type she seems to be in that photo? He'll throw her back to us, and he'll cancel his fat advertising contracts."

Reilly's anger gave way to helpless laughter.

"MacDonald is a dirty old man, and you're acting as his procurer."

"You have a genius for turning facts upside-down, Didi. Ian raised hell over the bikini photo. He said it hurt her professional stature, and he told me confidentially that his advertising department was a bit reluctant to accept her."

"That was just front and pretense."

"You wouldn't have thought so if you'd heard him. He sounded like the girl's maiden aunt trying to shield her."

"All men are alike," Didi insisted. "When you see a ravishing young woman looking ravishable, you want to ravish her."

"That's very clever, but you're not writing glib fashion copy for *Chic* right now. MacDonald didn't build his corporation by using it to further his personal affairs. He's a shrewd cookie who sees the high-class qualities the Kendall girl projects and wants to use them to improve the image of the Clothco stores."

"That may be a by-product, but it isn't his real motive, and *Chic* is going to regret this bargain. I accept your decision because I have no choice, but I certainly don't thank you for it, Andrew, and neither will Marni. I just wish I could make all this up to her."

"You will, Didi," he said. "You'll find a way."

Barbara hesitated in the doorway, but MacDonald guided her into the foyer and almost forcibly helped her out of her jacket. "I have a martini waiting for you," he said.

"Then you really must have raced over here after I phoned you."

"Not at all. I could understand your reluctance to discuss important and confidential matters on the telephone, so I simply dropped everything at the office and came home. Let me give you your drink and show you the view."

Barbara walked reluctantly down the steps into the sunken living room. "I'll skip the drink if you don't mind, but I do thank you for it. The view is lovely; but I've seen New York before, so I'll skip the tour, too."

MacDonald watched her as she wandered around the living room, occasionally reaching out with a tentative hand to touch the back of a chair or a piece of bric-a-brac. "You seem upset."

"A little out of sorts would be more like it."

"I hope I haven't had a hand in it."

"Oh, it isn't your fault, Ian. I happen to be one of those women who can't talk about anything meaningful on the phone. So, when I suggested it might be easier if we got together, I—well, I assumed we'd meet at a hotel bar or someplace like that."

"It bothers you to meet me here."

"I know it's ridiculous of me to be so old-fashioned," Barbara said with an embarrassed laugh. "Nothing could be more innocent than this. I mean, you're my friend, and you're Paul's boss, and all. But I haven't been in the habit of meeting any man at his apartment, so I feel guilty, as though I were doing something wrong. Forgive me for being so ridiculous." She sank into an easy chair, but immediately sat upright and began to tug in vain at her short skirt.

He took care to keep his distance from her when he selected a chair for himself. "It was for your sake," he said, "that I asked you to meet me here. So much is happening that your motives might be misinterpreted if you were seen with me in public."

"Oh, dear." She became even more disturbed.

"I don't mean what you think. I'm sure you're above personal suspicion—"

"As if any woman could be."

"But there are other things, equally damning, that could be said about you." MacDonald saw that she looked blank. "You just learned last night, I believe, that my company is making a bid for Schwartzman-Burns."

"So I did, but I forgot all about it today. Maurice was supposed to have a fitting for his semiannual fashion show, but he didn't show up after keeping us waiting for hours, and I've been so furious that everything else was driven right out of my mind."

Either she was more naive than he had imagined, MacDonald thought, or she had found a clever protective device. "An experience like that must be frustrating," he said, sparring until he could learn more about her attitude. "Now you know why we don't stock Maurice's styles. If he isn't in the mood, he doesn't deliver, and our stores need merchandise to exist."

"If I were a businessman, I'm sure I'd agree with you, but Maurice's creations really are divine."

"A great many women who can afford his prices feel that way, which is why Louis Burns always keeps a line of Maurice clothes. We'll have to do the same, if we take control of the store."

"I can't imagine Schwartzman-Burns without Maurice originals," Barbara said. "It wouldn't be the same store."

"Clothco," he said, groping cautiously, "intends to make no changes of any kind there. When a store is that profitable and has that much prestige, you keep everything exactly the way it was."

She nodded, but he couldn't tell whether she was impressed, comforted or indifferent.

"In fact," he said, his sudden enthusiasm indicating that an idea had just occurred to him, "it would be great if we could persuade Lou Burns to stay on. We'd even give him a free hand to run the place, just as he does now."

"Uncle Lou wouldn't work for anyone but himself," Barbara said. "He's been the whole works ever since Grandpa's last illness, when I was a little girl. Even my father had absolutely nothing to say about policy, you know. He told me one time, shortly before he died, that he wasn't much more than an office boy."

MacDonald wondered if she might resent her uncle on her father's behalf, but he didn't dare run the risk of making even a mildly derogatory remark in order to find out.

"If Uncle Lou loses the store," Barbara continued, "I'll make you a bet of almost anything that he won't even stay in the city. They'll close up their apartment, and Aunt Audrey will drag him down to their Florida place."

"His son might not like that," MacDonald said casually.

"Oh, the Third will shoot off fireworks all over the Princeton campus. If he had voting rights in the stock his father has set aside in his name, he'd jump right onto your bandwagon, Ian."

"I naturally assumed that anyone named Louis Burns III would—"

"You'd be wrong. The Third wants out."

MacDonald found the attitude incomprehensible, but was anxious to pick up any information that might prove useful. "Some other line of business interests him, no doubt."

Barbara shook her head. "He wants to teach anthropology."

Any young man who would willingly permit a gold mine like

Schwartzman-Burns to slip out of his grasp didn't deserve to keep the place, MacDonald told himself.

"You know, maybe I'll have that martini after all, Ian. But just one. I don't want to be late getting home this afternoon."

"I give you an ironclad guarantee not to let you drink more than one." He went to the bar, where a pitcher was chilling in ice, and poured her a generous double martini in an old-fashioned glass. "The modeling is coming along these days, is it?"

"I'm building, thanks to you." She raised the glass in a toast as he handed it to her.

MacDonald's bow was courtly. "You certainly look like a professional, with that big tote bag and the portfolio of photographs. Yes, and your makeup, the way you dress—everything."

"You don't miss much, Ian."

His modest shrug was self-deprecating.

"And you've been so good to me that I've wondered why," she said, her tone and expression blandly innocent.

MacDonald's covert glance told him nothing. "I explained my reasons when I offered to help you," he said.

Barbara smiled. "But there was another reason, that you didn't mention."

When forced onto the defensive, he instinctively counterattacked. "You believe I've wanted to put you in my debt."

"Of course."

"In my book, friends do favors for each other when the occasion arises. And when the spirit moves them." He spoke lightly, his manner impersonal.

"That's what friendship ought to be," she agreed, but a hint of hard metal crept into her voice and gave her away.

MacDonald heard the warning and immediately altered his tactics accordingly. "You know the gravity of the situation," he said solemnly. "Clothco wants and needs that store. I won't bore you with the details, but Paul can explain them to you. Louis Burns wants—just as hard—to keep the place. After more than a year of maneuvering, we've reached a showdown."

"It's very dramatic," Barbara said, lighting a cigarette and sipping her drink.

"And all of a sudden, out of nowhere, you find yourself in the middle."

She laughed as though she had no cares. "I know, and it's so silly. I'm just not the type."

"That's true," he conceded.

"All I want is to prove that someone of my age can still make the grade as a model."

"Which you're doing, thanks to your looks and your figure and your sense of style."

"All of those things—and the tremendous help I've been getting from you, Ian. If it weren't for you, I'd be making a little dent in the ice, and that's about all."

"No matter how you decide to handle this situation," MacDonald said, "I hope you know I'll continue to help you rebuild your career."

She realized that, no matter what his intentions, he was compelled to make her the promise. If he antagonized her now, she would be certain to vote against the Clothco merger. But she remained wide-eyed as she said, "I just knew you'd feel that way!"

"Then we really are friends." He studied her surreptitiously.

"Naturally. You've proved that." As soon as she spoke the words, Barbara knew she had erred. The light that appeared for an instant in MacDonald's eyes told her she had given him the opening he had been seeking.

He had no intention, however, of trying a direct approach. "I believe I can give you even more concrete proof," he said. "Your investment in Schwartzman-Burns will be trebled, perhaps quadrupled, after a transfer to Clothco stock. Assuming, of course, that we take over the store."

She was on safe ground now and said truthfully, "I don't know anything about finances. I've never thought about those things."

MacDonald felt a surge of hatred for this woman who possessed, in such abundance, all that he had ever craved and had fought so hard to acquire. Money, the root of power, meant nothing to her; wealthy at birth, she had taken position as well as the luxuries of life for granted. Funds were available for the indulgence of her whims, and she neither understood nor sympathized with the desire of the ambitious to accumulate—and use—a fortune.

What infuriated him above all else, however, was the sense of lofty superiority that her beauty gave her. Pretty from birth, she had become increasingly attractive as she had grown to womanhood, and the accident of her bone structure enabled her to remain handsome in maturity. The anguish of the homely was beyond her understanding, and although she might feel an occasional stab of pity for those whom nature had treated less generously, she considered herself above them, believing that the beauty of her face and form made her a higher order of being.

MacDonald knew his unreasoning resentment was senseless, that his desire to hurt Barbara grew out of frustrations and yearnings unrelated to her. She was no more responsible for her own beauty than he was for his ugliness, and he could not blame her, logically, for her marriage to a handsome male who made him feel inadequate.

Why, he wondered, did he feel such intense dislike for the Howells but have such a totally different reaction to Marni? It was because Barbara and Paul unconsciously patronized him, he told himself, while Marni, seeking an understanding of the man behind the mask and sympathizing with him, no longer appeared to notice his ill-proportioned features.

Conscious of his silence, Barbara became uncomfortable. She was feeling her drink and warned herself not to accept another. She was aware of MacDonald's driving dynamism, sensed his ruthlessness, and instinctively felt another quality in him, something she couldn't define but that, nevertheless, made her slightly queasy. Long accustomed to the use of her beauty as a weapon to soften men, make them malleable and bend them to her will, some mechanism within her warned that it would be dangerous to flirt with MacDonald. Every girl learned there were males to whom one did not make unspoken promises without delivery, and every woman realized there were males it was wise to hold at arm's length.

"I wouldn't presume to advise you," MacDonald said at last. "It would be presumptuous of me to assume your husband's prerogative, and in this situation I couldn't act impartially, since I have such a high stake of my own. I just hope you're giving the matter very serious thought."

"Is that why you wanted to see me, Ian? The way you tracked me down, I thought it was something earth-shattering."

"To be frank, I've hoped that, if you've already made up your mind, you'll tell me your decision."

"Until last night," she said, "I didn't even know there was a problem at the store."

He waited for her to continue, but she evidently thought she had given him a full explanation. "I can see," he said, "that you're pulled in opposing directions."

"No, I'm not," she replied with a laugh, "because what happens to Schwartzman-Burns doesn't mean as much to me as it does to Uncle Lou. Or to you."

MacDonald found her frivolity maddening, but managed to smile. "It wouldn't, of course."

"So I'm just not thinking about it. There's no rush, is there?"

"I suppose not, from where you sit." His facade cracked open for a moment, but he quickly closed it, making his face impassive again.

"For once in his life, Paul was right. He told me last night not to make up my mind too fast, because I don't want to make a mistake I'd regret. So I'll take my time, which won't be hard, you know. I have plenty of other things to think about. And eventually something will happen that will make up my mind for me."

"I'm sure it will," MacDonald said.

Cleo, in minirobe and clogs, stood at the counter measuring coffee into a percolator, and Paul, in his shirtsleeves, sat at the kitchen table, watching her and absently turning his highball glass. "For a smart girl," he said, "you sure showed rotten judgment when you picked a lover."

Preoccupied with her counting, she laughed.

"I mean it."

"Stop feeling so sorry for yourself, baby. You're no freakout." As she turned to face him her robe started to fall open, revealing expanses of coffee-colored skin, and she casually belted it again.

"You don't have to be nice to me," he said bitterly.

She came to him and put a hand on his shoulder. "It isn't the end of the world, baby, and you're not the first it ever happened to. You're tired, and you've got a lot on your mind."

"My mind is about the only place I've got it right now." Paul stared past her at the far wall.

"So you couldn't make the grade."

"You make it sound like nothing."

"Didn't it ever happen to you before?"

He shook his head.

"They haven't been chopped off. You'll recover."

"I suppose. What gets me is that it wouldn't work, even when we tried all the fun and games."

"When you aren't with it," Cleo said matter-of-factly, "you can't take a trip with kinky sex any more than you can with straight."

"You've summed it all up. I'm a mess."

She sat down opposite him and, putting her elbows on the table, rested her chin in the palm of a hand. "You're in a mess or two, maybe, but you aren't one. What's bugging you?"

"I've already indicated to you that there's a business situation I really can't discuss—"

"I'm not trying to find out more than you want me to know, baby. But it isn't *all* business, right?"

"Everything is connected."

She debated whether to replenish his drink and decided against it. "With Barbara?"

He focused on her, glaring.

"Tell me I'm a meddling black bitch, if that'll make you feel better. And then answer my question. I haven't made any demands on you, but I have the right to know that much."

"Sure it's Barbara," he said sullenly. "What else?"

"Now I'll really give you the excuse to kick my ass." Cleo crumpled an empty cigarette pack, then rose and wandered around the kitchen.

"Here." He offered her one from a package he carried in the breast pocket of his shirt.

Cleo accepted it, found a match and then paused before lighting the cigarette. "How long since you've done it with her?" She became very busy with the match and cigarette.

"I've never been very good at arithmetic," Paul said.

"That long, baby?"

"Goddammit, what are you driving at?"

"Barbara," she said, "isn't exactly a beat-up old wreck. Walk her through a room full of men, and nobody will fall asleep. We're doing Maurice's semiannual show together, and I took some good looks at her the other day when we were waiting for fittings. She's pretty—she has the kind of face that never changes. And she has class. The same kind Marni has."

It hadn't occurred to him that Barbara and Marni might be similar, but he didn't want to think about either of them. His life would be infinitely less complicated if there were no women in it.

"She has the bod, too," Cleo continued, "and I don't just mean she has a shape that's good for somebody who is getting older. Line for line, lean for lean and bulge for bulge, she can compete with me any day."

"Once, maybe, but not anymore." Paul had no desire to pursue the subject.

"Let's cut the crap, baby," Cleo declared. "A million men would hop into the hay with that bod, if they had the chance."

"By any chance," he demanded sarcastically, "are you trying to send me back to my wife?"

"I'm trying to dig why you ever left her, that's all."

"No one has left anybody. We sleep in twin beds four feet apart, but it might as well be four miles. Heard enough?"

"No," Cleo said, and for some moments there was no sound in the room but that of the coffee bubbling in the percolator.

"When a woman loses interest," he said bitterly, "a man learns to take the hint."

She went to the stove, turned it off and poured two steaming cups of coffee. Adding sugar to one, she placed it in front of Paul.

"None for me," he said.

"Drink it."

"You think I need sobering up?"

"It can't do you any harm, baby."

He sipped the scalding coffee. "Maybe," he said, "I couldn't satisfy Barbara anymore, just as I can't satisfy you."

"I read in a psychiatry book one time that it's a woman's fault when a man can't come across for her, but the book was written by a man. Me, I think that sometimes he fails because he doesn't want her anymore."

"Meaning I lost interest in Barbara?"

Cleo placed her cup on the table opposite him, then shrugged. "Or me. Or both of us, maybe."

"I'm not sure what you mean," he said angrily, clenching his fists, "but I don't like it!"

"I've been hating every minute we've spent together this past week," Cleo said.

"That's good to hear."

"Baby," she said earnestly, "you and I got together because we had something going. The animal attraction of a beautiful black for a beautiful white, and vice versa."

"Now, wait."

"That's what it was, baby, no matter how hard you deny it. And for a while it was fun. The best I ever had, and the same goes for you."

His affirmation was a grunt.

"But you don't give a damn for me. As me, I mean. You've used me as an outlet for your tensions, and I'm not complaining. I got my kicks out of it. But now your problems are getting bigger, so big that I can't offer you the relief from them you need. Lately we've been bickering. Over nothing. And you know what that means."

"Suppose you tell me," he demanded.

"I'm not doing you any good, and you're not exactly manna from heaven for me, either." Cleo jumped to her feet so abruptly that some of her coffee spilled into the saucer. "When things get this way between a man and woman, it's better to blow the whistle on the ball game. In sudden-death overtime you can get badly hurt."

Paul watched her in silence as she mopped up the coffee with a sheet of paper toweling.

Cleo looked straight at him. "I hope you understand," she said, "why I'm copping out."

He hauled himself to his feet and went into the bedroom, where he hastily donned his necktie and jacket.

Cleo awaited him in the living room, where she held his topcoat. "Tell me straight, do you dig me?"

"Sure, you're breaking off because I've fizzled."

"God preserve me from a dim-witted man! If you hadn't dried up, I'd have copped out days ago, but I didn't want to hurt your feelings."

Paul snatched his coat, then slammed the door as he left the apartment. The shelter he had built as a refuge from his worries had collapsed, leaving him unprotected and vulnerable to the storm.

PART
THREE

Andrew Reilly's interoffice memo to the *Chic* staff, which gained its author unintended publicity when it was excerpted without authorization by a nationally syndicated gossip columnist, was succinct in both purpose and tone: "*It would be impertinent of me to suggest there is no connection between nudity and morality. The pages of this magazine will at no time reflect any such connection, however, and for our editorial and advertising purposes, it will at no time be intimated that there might be a conflict between the two in today's world. Nudity is natural, normal and healthy, a desideratum of every chic woman. I can best illustrate our situation by reviewing, in a word, the recent history of the monokini, or lower portion of a bikini bathing suit. A single editorial paragraph in our pages launched the monokini as the most desirable of beach styles, and a new fashion was born. We will claim, therefore, that we originated the monokini, along with all similar styles."*

It would have been gratuitous for Reilly to add that eight bathing suit manufacturers, each acting independently of the others, already had reserved space for full-page monokini advertisements in *Chic*, and a dozen others were expected to follow their example. Meanwhile Didi Martin, with the enthusiastic approval of the publisher and advertising director, began to prepare a twelve-page section in full color on the subject.

As yet America and the world knew nothing of the new style. The exhibitionists were somnolent, contenting themselves with transparent blouses, skirts and pants. The consciences of those who followed the new fashions remained untroubled. The nation's police continued to concern themselves with other matters, as did the clergy and judiciary. The managers of beach clubs, along with the proprietors of hotels and motels with beach rights or swimming pools, still led blissful, uncomplicated lives. The editors of *Life*, *Look* and the news magazines, aware of what was ahead, confidently anticipated sharp circulation increases.

The full fury of the storm had already struck the modeling industry. Marni Kendall, afraid she might be asked to pose in a monokini, had already informed Ian MacDonald, Paul Howell and the Howell Agency that under no circumstances would she be available for the purpose. Most of her colleagues told each other they would decline monokini modeling offers, but those who received bids happily and hastily accepted them.

Barbara Howell was pleasantly surprised when a bathing suit manufacturer asked her to appear in his monokini ad, and indicated that she would accept, but at the last minute she lost her nerve, and with it the goodwill of the manufacturer. It was rumored that Katya had agreed to do a monokini ad, but she herself would neither confirm nor deny the story.

The year's prize assignment, that of being featured in the *Chic* spread, was won by Cleo. By the time the job ended, after a week of hard work, she and Didi were no longer on speaking terms, but the photographs were spectacular, successful beyond the fondest hopes of everyone connected with the project. As a result, and in anticipation of the new renown—or notoriety—she would achieve, Cleo's fee was raised to one hundred dollars per hour. She was the first black model to reach the pinnacle.

Thereafter every advertiser, every fashion editor and every designer showing new fashions clamored for Cleo. Her popularity was so great, in fact, that Marni wondered if she had been wrong to reject monokini work before she had even been approached to do it, thereby slamming a door in her own face. Both in private and professionally she tried to justify her position on the twin grounds of morality and good taste, which was not difficult, but she secretly condemned herself for being an inhibited coward whose position as the industry's top model was being threatened.

Paul was only vaguely aware of the furor, and was indifferent to it. His own problems preoccupied him to the exclusion of everything else, and his dilemma was compounded one morning by Ian MacDonald, who stopped in at his office for a brief, ostensibly casual chat.

"You need to get your worry about your wife's stock off your mind so you can concentrate on your own work," MacDonald said. "You know my stake in all this, so I certainly can't pretend I'm disinterested, but even if I were an outsider, I know the advice I'd give you. Lou Burns isn't your relative, he's your wife's. You're obliged to protect her financially, and you know she'll do better if she goes with us than if she rides with Lou. And don't forget that a man has to look out for himself. The better Clothco does, the higher you'll climb, and it won't do you any harm to be vice-president of a chain that has Schwartzman-Burns in its fold. After all, you owe Lou nothing. If he had been loyal to you or thinking of your future, he could have offered you a spot, long ago, on his management team."

Paul realized it was too late for him to balk. Had he intended to fight MacDonald, he should have done it at the time of their first confrontation, and he knew that by remaining at Clothco and taking no firm stand with regard to Barbara's shares in Schwartzman-Burns he had tacitly compromised himself.

His conscience would not allow him to dismiss Louis Burns from his mind, however, and after tormenting himself for days, a new thought occurred to him. It was so obvious he wanted to kick himself, and delaying no longer, he called Audrey Burns and told her he wanted a private talk with her. Sounding surprised, she agreed to see him that same afternoon.

Paul reached the Burns apartment promptly at four o'clock, and Audrey, wearing an off-white hostess gown she had obviously donned for the occasion, received him in the drawing room, a formal chamber whose authentic Louis XV decor, combined with a number of incongruous but exorbitantly expensive original paintings by leading French Impressionists, had always overwhelmed him.

"I always have tea at this time of day, but if you prefer a drink, I'll have one with you, in honor of this very special occasion."

"Tea will be fine, thanks," Paul said stiffly.

As she rang for her maid, Audrey glanced at him in amusement. "Are you afraid of me?"

"No, I just find it a little strange that after all these years of being related by marriage, you and I don't really know each other."

"And that's a pity. When a man has your looks and build, I can't help wishing I were twenty-five years younger." She ignored the maid, who entered with a tea tray and placed it on a low table. "I don't suppose you'd believe I was once considered beautiful."

Paul waited until the maid left the room and closed the door behind her. "You *are* beautiful," he said.

Audrey's laugh was dry, very brittle. "Some women fade gracefully, but I've turned into an old scarecrow. I wear outrageously expensive clothes, which confuses people a bit, and I draw attention away from myself by living in two of the most overdecorated houses in America. But nothing really helps, you know. When a woman has lived on her beauty for years, she feels lost after it goes.

I don't know why I'm telling you all this, except that you're allegedly an expert on the subject of women."

"Not really." He felt increasingly uncomfortable.

"No, that isn't my reason. I've chosen a rather clumsy way of saying I feel sorry for Barbara. She may be an idiot who drinks too much, but I can understand her despair when she looks in a mirror. Burns women, whether by marriage or birth, have never been distinguished for their inner resources. Lemon or cream?"

"Neither, thanks. Just a spoonful of sugar."

She dropped in the sugar and handed him his cup. "What brings you to see me, Paul?" she demanded abruptly. "I've been dying of curiosity all day."

"Barbara's stock. I've been trying not to influence her, but Mac-Donald has been putting some fairly subtle pressure on me—"

"Why tell me about it?"

"It occurred to me I could get the straight pitch from you about Lou. I know what he wants, but what's best for him in this situation? What do *you* think about it and want?"

Audrey astonished him by laughing aloud. "You're priceless, and I'll remember you in my will. All through this whole, insane crisis, no one has bothered to ask my opinion."

He was too embarrassed to comment and bent his head over his cup.

"In all the years Lou and I have been married, I've decided nothing more important than the guest lists and menus for our dinner parties. I've been a semiprofessional hostess because I've had no other way to fill my time. I've also served on just about every good works committee in town, and you have no idea how many of them there are. Shall I tell you something, my dear? Ever since my children started school, I've been bored to extinction. Every moment of my life."

Paul still didn't know what to say.

"Would you like to know what I've really been doing for this past year? Praying. Praying that Lou would be forced to give up control of the store to that dreadful MacDonald. I'm sick of being married to a Fifth Avenue retail institution, and, if it's not too late, I want a husband instead."

"Doesn't Lou know how you feel?"

"I've bitched for so long that I doubt if he's heard a word in years."

"Maybe if he understood—"

"He refuses. The very thought that someone might not be in love with Schwartzman-Burns is beyond him. But the insane part of it is that he has a marvelous time whenever I can drag him down to Florida. Thank God I put down my size eight—in better shoes, third floor, the sizes are flattering—he'd have opened a branch in Palm Beach if it had been up to him. That was when I threatened to leave him."

Paul began to regret the impulse that had led him to get in touch with her.

"He swims in our pool, and he loves it. He not only plays a respectable game of golf, but he beats me, and I'm good. He adores fishing, which I've learned to tolerate, just so we can do it together. And he enjoys our dinner parties instead of going through the automatic motions of being a host."

"I can see why it would be better for you if Lou retired to Florida," Paul said carefully.

"It would also be better for him," she retorted. "Infinitely. He barely exists here too, and you needn't look so skeptical. The store doesn't offer him challenges anymore. He lives in a comfortable rut, and it's easier to follow routines than stir himself up. Lou is a perfectionist and a collector, you see. He had to own the best department store in town. He had to have the most exquisitely furnished living room. And he had to own the most beautiful wife. But when something becomes his, he takes it for granted. He has no real appreciation of beauty. His only thrill is the knowledge that something or someone is his property."

Her bitterness ran deep, but Paul suspected there might be a strong element of truth in what she was saying.

"If he caught the biggest fish ever landed off the coast of Florida, it would give him as much pleasure as he gets out of the store."

Perhaps she exaggerated, Paul thought, but, on the other hand, he had to concede that she knew her husband.

"Then there are the children. Lou had it all planned, naturally. The girls would marry Schwartzman-Burns vice-presidents, and the Third would inherit the throne. It was a lovely dream—for Lou—but the children had their own. Both the girls married doctors, and I've always suspected they chose husbands who couldn't, much less wouldn't, go into retail merchandising. The Third is something else." Audrey peered at her guest. "You don't know the Third very well."

"Barbara is very fond of him," he said diplomatically.

"As well she should be. But you think he's a snot. Don't shake your head! Of course you do. That's his defense. Ever since he's been a small boy he's wanted to be an anthropologist. He dreams of going off to some ghastly little chain of islands south of Australia and studying the natives there. I can think of nothing worse, but it's his life, and he has the money to do what he pleases. So why shouldn't he? I can't for the life of me see why he must—absolutely must—be forced into the traditional Burns mold."

In spite of her emotional approach, her arguments were valid, Paul told himself.

"There you have it all, my dear. If Barbara could be persuaded to vote for the Clothco merger, there isn't anything I wouldn't do for her. Very privately, of course. Because if you dare to quote me to anyone, I'll swear you're a liar."

The Front Parlor occupied the ground floor of a rickety old building off St. Marks Place in the East Village and although dingy and difficult to locate, with little to commend it other than its ornately old-fashioned Tiffany shades that diffused the light and made it possible for the proprietors to serve carefully diluted drinks, every straight-backed kitchen chair at each of its imitation marble tables was occupied every night. The Front Parlor had been "discovered" by a celebrated homosexual pair, a playwright and his lover, who was a dress designer. Word had spread by means of the instant invisible communications network employed by New Yorkers in the know, and for a brief moment the bar had become one of the most prominent of the city's "in" night spots.

"I think it's noisy and crowded and stupid here," Marni told David Bernstein, "but it really does help me to be seen in places like this. I've already counted three people who can hire me for important assignments. And they will, because they've seen me."

David grinned at her as he poured more soda into their glasses of light vermouth. "You're the most ambivalent girl I've ever seen. You want to be number one in your profession, but at the same time you hate everything you're doing."

"That's not true," she replied indignantly.

"Sure it is. Look at the way you're dressed. You're with it, but your heart isn't in it."

Marni glanced down at her close-fitting, transparent body shirt, slit to the waist, which was daring enough to be appropriately fashionable, but knew what he meant. Beneath the shirt was a flesh-colored bra that belied the exposure of the shirt, and although her skirt was very short, her opaque pantyhose, in an abstract print, afforded her complete protection.

"You'd be annoyed if you couldn't get a table at a hole-in-the-wall like this dump, and you enjoy being recognized and shown to a table—"

"Sure, I get a blast out of it. But what's wrong with that?"

"Let me finish. Once you're actually here, sitting at the table, you think the place is stupid, crowded and noisy. That was your description, not mine."

Marni turned her glass slowly, watching the ice cubes bob up and down. It bothered her that this independent, ruggedly masculine male should sometimes be able to read her better than she knew herself. Marriage to him would be an uncomfortable challenge. "I don't mean to hit below the belt or bring up the past," she said, "but I don't see why I have to live up to my public image, the way Cleo does. Ever since she did that monokini spread for *Chic*, she wears clothes that show her breasts. I'm not condemning her for it, but I'm not going to do it, even if a model is supposed to be sexy and glamorous."

"In the first place," David said, "you're raising the legitimate question of whether the exposure of a woman's body *is* glamorous. You think it isn't, and you're entitled to your opinion. Parenthetically, I happen to agree with you. In the second place—and this is seemingly irrelevant, but isn't—you've developed a strong dislike for Cleo."

"But I haven't! I'm very fond of her."

"You were, maybe. Perhaps you don't realize it, but you've mentioned her several times tonight, always disparagingly."

"No, I didn't realize it, and I really don't see why I should feel—"

"It screams, Marni, and it's part of your ambivalence. You liked Cleo as long as you could look down a step at her. But she's come up into your class now. She's your competitition for number one."

"If you want to be technical about it, I'm sure Katya still rates as number one."

"From what you've told me, Katya has had it. So it's either you or Cleo. You spend your evening here, and she's showing herself off at another dump like it. You're running hard on the fastest treadmill in the rat race, and sometimes you get a little out of breath."

"Most of the time," she admitted, and wished she knew what she really wanted.

David started to speak, but was interrupted by someone looming above him.

"Good evening, Marni."

"Ian! Hello."

"I saw you, and couldn't resist coming over." MacDonald's eyes were wary, but his smile was genial.

"Mr. Bernstein, Mr. MacDonald."

"How do you do." MacDonald made a close inspection of the younger man.

David stood but ignored the other's outstretched hand. "I saw you earlier tonight. You were sitting in a taxi across the street from Marni's apartment. When we were leaving."

"Won't you join us, Ian?" Marni asked hurriedly, hoping David would lower his voice if they were seated.

MacDonald quickly took an empty chair from an adjoining table, mumbling an apology to the couple sitting there.

David sank back into his chair, which squeaked beneath his bulk. "You followed us." He made a flat statement rather than an accusation, certain in his own mind that he couldn't be mistaken about the ugly little monster. "Friend of yours, Marni?"

"Yes, we're good friends." Her fear of a scene mounted.

But MacDonald proved equal to the situation. "The whole story is so complicated it isn't worth the telling," he said, dismissing the awkward subject. "Marni, you look lovely, as always. Mr. Bernstein, I hope you don't mind my barging in on you like this."

"Suppose I do?" Although David remained belligerent, he lowered his voice.

"Then I hope you'll let me make amends. I'd like to buy you a drink, although I must say the liquor here is awful. I'm sure they water it. Perhaps I could persuade you to drop up to my place, where I can guarantee both the quantity and quality of what I give you. I'm not suggesting you stay for the evening. Just have one drink with me, and then you two can be on your way."

David opened his mouth to reject the offer.

But Marni cut in before he could speak. "We'd love it, Ian."

MacDonald's expression, admitted no recognition of his victory. "I'll go ahead and get a taxi," he said. "They aren't easy to find in this part of town." His steady smile as diplomatic as his gesture, he threaded his way toward the door.

David looked hard at Marni. "What is this?"

"I saw him earlier, too. He didn't mean any harm by it."

"To hell with him. We'll stay right here, and if he annoys you again, I'll—"

"No, David." She put a restraining hand on his arm. "Ian is my most important client. His company has signed me for exclusive fashion photography in *Chic*."

He glanced at his clenched fists. "There's nothing like slapping a pair of handcuffs on a fellow."

"It won't be too awful, I promise you. Ian is charming, a brilliant man, really. And his apartment is worth seeing."

David started to speak, but checked himself. He was willing to accept MacDonald's importance to Marni in business, but that did not explain her familiarity with the man's apartment. Making no further comment, David paid his bill and followed the girl out of the room, but could take no pleasure in the stares of admiration she attracted.

MacDonald was waiting for them in a taxi and kept up a smooth flow of talk on the ride uptown, lightly criticizing establishments like The Front Parlor, yet keeping his remarks impersonal. He observed the amenities gracefully, and if he was exerting more than ordinary effort, nothing in his demeanor revealed it.

Marni did not lose sight of the fact that he had created the situation, but she couldn't help admiring his poise and self-command. As an admirer of willpower, she was impressed by his control of himself as well as his ability to handle others.

David, on the other hand, had withdrawn. He feigned polite interest in what was being said but made no attempt to join in the conversation, and only his alertness to unspoken nuances prevented his attitude from resembling that of a sulky little boy.

Marni realized she was being unfair to him, yet his failure to cope with the unexpected annoyed her. It occurred to her that she

229 :

wanted him to gain the advantage, to put Ian in his place. Her own inability to free herself from an ever-increasing emotional entanglement with a man older than her father had been disturbing her, and she knew she had accepted this confrontation in the hope that David would restore her perspective. Perhaps she was foolish to have established rules she was keeping hidden from the contestants, but she nevertheless felt a growing sense of disappointment in David.

When they reached the apartment, Marni went off to the guest room to repair her makeup, and David duly noted that she had no need to ask directions. MacDonald disappeared in the opposite direction, and David wandered aimlessly around the living room until Marni returned.

"The view from those windows is just gorgeous," she said.

David shrugged. "The combined efforts of the world's most talented and imaginative architects can't miss. That view has earned a profit for many people."

She made another effort. "I think this painting is just darling. Come over and look at it."

He glanced at the far wall. "I'm not qualified to comment on a modern representation of the seventeenth-century neoclassical."

"Is that what it is?" she murmured. "I wondered."

His laugh was harsh. "It would appear, however, that I'm better qualified than our good host."

Marni thought his comment was lacking in sportsmanship and frowned.

MacDonald chose that moment to return.

David realized he had been eavesdropping, but could find no immediate way to turn that knowledge to his own advantage.

"What will it be?" Ian asked. "I can give you bourbon, Scotch, Canadian, rye, gin, vodka, rum—"

"You wouldn't have a simple, old-fashioned brew called beer around the place, would you?" David heard the stridency in his own voice but could not curb it.

MacDonald's smile was gentle. "Domestic or imported, in bot·

tles, cans or on tap? The Dutch and German are the best, I always think, and the Czechs still make a first-rate Pilsener. I'm rather partial to a West Indian beer, although it has a trace of a bite in the aftertaste. Or you might like to try a wicked Malaysian beer, but I warn you it may stay with you until tomorrow."

David felt himself shrink, and knew the man was making him look like a fool. "Any kind," he muttered.

MacDonald gave no indication he had won a round, but returned to his attack as soon as he had made all of their drinks. "May I ask what you do, Mr. Bernstein?"

"I teach." David knew he was behaving like a boor.

"He's too modest," Marni said. "He's a history professor, and until a short time ago he was a famous defensive halfback with the Giants."

"Linebacker," David said.

"I must confess I know nothing about sports," MacDonald said. "It's obvious I couldn't have been an athlete, even in my younger days, and I've always been too busy earning a living."

David dug himself in deeper. "I played for money, not fun. Now I'm doing what I've always wanted to do."

"I suppose I was lucky," MacDonald declared. "Necessity forced me into my vocation as a stockboy, and it never crossed my mind to search for another line of business. You might say I made up my mind not to stray, not to waste time, and I forced myself to find out all there was to know in my own field. I do envy professional athletes their freedom—"

"Self-discipline is the key, Mr. MacDonald," David said sharply.

"—and I have a great respect for anyone who teaches."

David thought he saw an opening. "Do you have a degree?"

MacDonald's broad grin was disarming and made him look like a caricature. "It's rather funny, now that I can look back at all those years of anxiety and sweat, but I was determined to get a degree, and I finally eked one out through a combination of correspondence courses and night school. The work helped me gain some of that discipline you just mentioned, but it did me no other good."

David saw that Marni, to his distress, was impressed by Mac-Donald, so he struck again. "An education shouldn't be measured in dollars, in terms of jobs and advancement."

"My point precisely," MacDonald replied. "The goal of all learning must be education for its own sake, and that's why my efforts were wasted. I was concentrating so hard on earning a living that the courses I took meant nothing to me. It wasn't until many years later, when I could afford the leisure time, that I began to pick up the rudiments of an education."

Marni was listening avidly, David saw, and knew he had lost another round.

MacDonald seemed to remember her presence for the first time in some minutes. "We've been neglecting you," he said. "I happen to have the first proofs of our new *Chic* campaign here. I brought them home from the office this evening. Would you like to glance at them?"

Marni eagerly studied the photographs, asking David to sit beside her on the couch and inviting his comments.

He admired her in a variety of costumes, but didn't know what else to say.

MacDonald, however, discussed the flaws in a number of photographs, which he said would be done again, and he launched into technical explanations of the advertising layouts and copy.

David lost interest in the subject, and eventually he inadvertently yawned.

"I'm sorry," MacDonald said. "I'm boring you. And I've horned in enough on your evening. You two run along."

David immediately rose to his feet, realizing belatedly that he had been outmaneuvered and should have matched the other's gracious warmth.

"Please come again," MacDonald told him as he accompanied his guests to the elevator.

David's recognition of his own failure infuriated him, and he was so angry he compounded his errors. "I'll have to do that very thing," he replied.

Not until he caught a glimpse of Marni studying him as they descended in the elevator did he become aware of the extent of the damage he had perpetrated. He deserved her contempt, but the indifference he read in her eyes was as shocking as it was unexpected. He tried to tell himself he had no one else to blame, but he had the uneasy suspicion, which he could not prove, that MacDonald had tricked him in unseen ways. As he should have remembered from his football days, one of the best ways to win a game was to force one's opponent to lose it.

Paul waited for the right time to hold a serious discussion with Barbara, but she was preoccupied with modeling all evening, and no propitious moment presented itself. Unwilling to tolerate another delay, he drifted into their bedroom as she sat before her mirror, patting a thick cream into her face and taking an occasional sip of a Tom Collins.

"I've been thinking quite a bit about your Schwartzman-Burns stock lately," he said, dropping into the room's only easy chair.

"That's more than I've been doing. Paul, I forgot to tell you a priceless story about Cleo."

"You've got to consider what's best for everyone concerned, and that concerns your uncle, your aunt—and your favorite cousin."

"Let me tell you. She's never been reluctant to do bra advertising, you know, but I heard she turned down a bra booking today. She said it would spoil her new image. Because of the whole monokini uproar," she added, when he failed to respond.

He laughed lamely, but was still sensitive to any mention of Cleo, and in any event, he was trying to direct the conversation into a more important channel. "About your stock," he said. "If you voted with Clothco, Lou and Audrey could live it up in Florida, and Little Louis—"

"Oh, the Third could do what he's always wanted. I already know all that." She dismissed the matter with a wave of a cream-covered hand. "Some of the girls say it was sheer luck that shot Cleo up to the top bracket."

He knew he had to dispose of the topic before she would listen. "Don't you believe it. She's worked damned hard."

"Of course, but so have a lot of others, and they say her figure is no better for photography. You don't suppose she's made it because being black is so fashionable these days, do you?"

He didn't want to be drawn into a long diversion, but was annoyed. "Any girl who hits the hundred-an-hour class gets there on merit," he said flatly.

"What I mean is, she's nothing super if you start adding up. She has a long waist, but who hasn't? Her breasts—"

"Put her curves together and she has a sensational figure, Barb."

"For my taste she's too angular."

"The clients like her, and that's what matters," Paul said with finality. "Now, about that stock—"

"Must we? I know you want me to vote for the merger with Clothco."

Her sensitivity surprised him. "It's in our own best interests, you know. Joint and separate."

Barbara seldom had been given the opportunity to keep others dangling, and she enjoyed the sense of power that her present position gave her. So she wanted to prolong the suspense. "When I make up my mind, which I'll do in my own way and in my own good time, I'll let everybody know. Maybe I'll even take an ad in the *Times*. But right now I'm going to get some sleep. I'm up for three possible jobs tomorrow, and one of them is a national ad."

Paul watched her in frustration as she wiped her hands on a tissue, went to her bed and turned off her night light. Any attempt to reason with her, much less force her to make a decision now, he knew, would succeed only in setting off another of the bitter arguments that had already destroyed the intimate fabric of their marriage.

: 234

Although it would be humiliating, he had no choice, and in the morning he would tell Ian MacDonald he was incapable of influencing his wife's decision.

Maxine Holland's Restaurant had catered to the upper middle-class suburban housewife for twenty-five years, and the backbone of the establishment's clientele was made up of regular customers who ate generous portions of well-cooked foods. The menu featured a variety of low-calorie dishes, too, which insured the restaurant's continuing popularity.

A scattering of men could be seen in the place at noon, the majority of them tourists accompanying their wives, and usually they looked as out of place as they felt. Few New York businessmen ever went there, but the ladies, many of them en route to matinees, paid no attention to the two quietly dressed middle-aged men at the corner table. Perhaps they didn't belong at Maxine Holland's, but they were minding their own business, disturbing no one's routines; so the ladies returned the compliment by ignoring them too.

"For years my wife has been raving about the soup here," Louis Burns said. "Try the soup."

"I think I'll have the shrimp cocktail," Ian MacDonald said.

"So will I." Louis was silent for a moment, glancing at the menu but too tense to read it. "And an omelette."

"Sounds fine."

"I should have asked you if you wanted a drink, Ian."

"Not for me, but you go ahead."

"I'll skip it today."

They looked at each other for an instant, then gazed elsewhere, and the tension increased.

"I suggested meeting here," Louis said, "because somebody

would be sure to recognize us anyplace else, and then the gossip would start. My God, would there be talk!"

"As I told you on the phone when you called me, it was an inspired idea. I've passed this place a thousand times without ever coming inside. Now I know what it's like."

A uniformed waitress took their order, and again there was silence. "Would you like to talk now, or after we eat?" Louis asked.

"Suit yourself." MacDonald managed to sound at ease.

"Okay, now. Ian, we're both on hot seats, waiting for my niece to tell us what she's going to do. Being an imbecile, she probably doesn't know. So last night I said to myself, why stew forever, waiting? Maybe Ian and I can get together and settle this whole thing."

"Anything is possible," MacDonald said, and smiled.

"I said to myself," Louis continued, speaking too rapidly, "that two reasonable men can always work out compromises. A deal, after all, is a compromise that makes everybody happy."

"Provided both sides want the same thing."

Louis was puzzled, but concealed his nagging concern. "In this business of yours and mine, we both want the same thing. I believe. What is it, *exactly*, that you want, Ian?"

"It's more than wanting, Lou. Clothco has a definite need. The expansion of our chain makes it necessary for us to have a prestige store that's a proven and continuing success as our house leader. Our buyers are screaming for it, our branch managers are demanding it, our comptroller is threatening to resign if we don't get it."

It was difficult for Louis Burns to smile. "So Schwartzman-Burns fills the bill perfectly. There isn't a store in town with more prestige than mine. The Gimbels know Saks Fifth Avenue doesn't rate higher, even if they wouldn't say it out loud, and Andrew Goodman might admit—privately, maybe—that our prestige is equal to Bergdorf-Goodman's. As for our success, the books tell their own story. Last year's profits—"

"You don't have to sell me on Schwartzman-Burns, Lou," MacDonald interrupted dryly. "I'm very much aware of your prestige, and I've seen all your figures for the past twenty-five years."

"Someday you'll have to tell me how you got them." Louis paused, but MacDonald merely smiled. "I would have bet ten thousand dollars that our treasurer's office was leak-proof. Come to think of it, I did bet—and I lost."

MacDonald's laugh was restrained. Any advantage he held at the moment was psychological rather than financial, but he was bearing down, utilizing his hastily conceived tactics for all they were worth. Burns's nervousness indicated that the tactics were effective, so MacDonald had no intention of revealing his own eagerness. The initiative that had brought about this unexpected confrontation had come from Burns, so it was fair to guess that he intended to make a proposal of some sort that would end the impasse.

Above all, MacDonald was sure of only one thing: although he had not yet won the fight, he hadn't lost it, either, so he had no intention of yielding anything. Burns wouldn't have suggested the meeting if he hadn't been frightened, and a show of firm strength might force him to capitulate. There was nothing to be lost by trying.

It was possible, of course, that Burns knew something about Barbara Howell's decision, but MacDonald was inclined to doubt it. After Paul had revealed to him that she was procrastinating, refusing to take a stand because she enjoyed the attention both camps were giving her, MacDonald had felt certain she would make no move whatever until forced to act.

Their first course was served, and Louis, who was not an accomplished actor, ate one shrimp, then pushed his plate away.

MacDonald, however, made a show of eating, even though the food made him slightly queasy. "You haven't spelled out what it is that you want, Lou," he said.

"In the best of all possible worlds, I want everything to stay the way it was. I own the most beautiful store in the world, and I want to keep it."

The thought occurred to MacDonald that, in his own way, Burns was a worshiper of beauty; but the notion had no immediate bearing on the issue, so he tucked it away in a corner of his mind. "It appears," he said, "that we do want the same thing."

"The way I see it, we can both get what we want."

That would be the neatest magic trick of the decade, MacDonald thought.

The waitress arrived, and after removing the remains of the first course, served their omelettes. "Didn't you like the shrimp?" she asked.

"They were delicious," Louis assured her.

Her shrug was eloquent, indicating that she preferred her regular customers to men who allowed business discussions to ruin their appetites.

Louis waited until she was out of earshot. "First, I want to take care of my son."

"Naturally." MacDonald felt an unreasonable surge of hatred for the boy whose future was assured for him by a doting father, but he quickly conquered his emotions.

"The money isn't important. He inherited plenty from his grandfather, and he'll get more from me, so he'll never starve. But we've always taken it for granted in the family that someday the store would be his. Now I've had to think in other terms, maybe."

MacDonald felt a surge of hope.

"Suppose we could work out a deal that satisfied both of us in other ways. Could you find a good spot in your organization for my boy?"

Contempt for Burns mingled with MacDonald's growing sense of elation. The man, for all his professed paternal concern, was willing to sacrifice his son's business future in return for the protection of his own. MacDonald deliberately dangled tempting bait. "Under the right circumstances we can always find a place for a good man, and I believe I could persuade our board of directors to offer your son a Clothco vice-presidency."

"Wonderful!" Louis beamed.

"That point is settled. We can either make it a tacit understanding between gentlemen, or we could include it in a written agreement."

"As far as I'm concerned, Ian, your word is good. But my wife doesn't understand business, so for her peace of mind I'd like it in black and white."

"Of course." Burns didn't trust him, which he knew, and MacDonald couldn't blame him. But the request for the inclusion of this minor matter in the formal agreement could have been made with a little more finesse.

"You have no idea how this relieves my mind," Louis said.

"I can imagine." MacDonald's smile was bloodless.

"Now, for the main problem. Suppose I sell you all the Schwartzman-Burns stock I control."

"You mean your own stock?"

"Mine, the Schwartzman family's, the odd shares that our retired executives own. Everything."

"So far it sounds good."

"Schwartzman-Burns then belongs to Clothco."

"Obviously."

"But I stay on as president and active operating head of the store."

MacDonald sat for a time, pondering. "Suppose you and Clothco disagree on a question of policy. How is it decided?"

"I've run the store all my life. I'll continue to run it. After I'm dead, the Clothco management can try to do better. Which all your merchandising experts put together couldn't do, Ian."

"It might be an awkward arrangement."

"I think it would be perfect. For my lifetime we'd be partners. After I'm gone, your bright boys and your wise guys can take over, and we'll see whether they run the place into the ground. Which wouldn't surprise me."

"I see a natural conflict, Lou. You're accustomed to the planning and operating of a single store. We're in the business of planning for a chain of more than thirty stores."

"All of them are different. In San Francisco and St. Louis you're at opposite ends of the merchandising game—"

"True. There are differences. But we're coordinating our operations, and we intend to pull the reins much tighter. The more we streamline, the more efficient we become and the greater the annual profits we show." MacDonald saw nothing to be gained by feigning interest in his food and pushed his plate away. "Tell me truthfully, would you be able to subordinate the interests of Schwartzman-Burns for the larger interests of the whole Clothco chain?"

"You and I have known each other for a long time, Ian. We're friends."

"Friendships have been known to break up when business interferes."

"What could cause such a great hassle between us?"

"Let's try an example. We're planning to use the Schwartzman-Burns sportswear department as the leader for the sportswear in all the other towns. Could you change your buying patterns to fit the needs of the chain? Not a major change, you understand, but consonant with the needs that the main office would relay to you?"

Louis blinked indignantly. "My sportswear departments are known throughout the whole country. What's right for them should be right for every store."

As MacDonald had known, it would be impossible to work together, but some facets of the offer were still intriguing. Giving no hint of his reaction, he asked, "How would you square this setup with the Schwartzman family and your retired executives?"

Louis shrugged. "I don't see why I'd have to account to anybody for what I'd be doing. Their stock will still pay good dividends. I mean, Clothco is in business to make money, the same as I am. I assume you'd give them the right to trade in their Schwartzman-Burns shares for Clothco stock."

"Yes, we have something like that in mind."

"Well, then." Louis spread his hands.

"Naturally, we'll buy the stock of anyone who doesn't want to be a Clothco investor." MacDonald was amused: Burns's willingness to sacrifice the Schwartzman heirs and his former employees for the sake of his own interests was in no way surprising and confirmed MacDonald's cynical view that any individual, when backed into a corner, would look out for himself at the expense of others, even those who had placed their trust in him.

"Then they've got no kick coming," Louis said flatly.

"I'm glad you feel that way." MacDonald dropped his bomb very gently. "The offer includes you, Lou. If you don't want Clothco stock, we'll take your Schwartzman-Burns shares off your hands for cash."

"Why would I want cash when we're going to be in business together? The way I see it, I'm taking in a new partner, Clothco. Partners have got to have faith in each other."

"I'm afraid that wouldn't fit our system. Our directors insist we observe certain policies, you see." MacDonald preferred to detonate the bomb obliquely. "In fact, the directorate makes certain that no outsiders ever control large blocks of our stock. Whenever someone begins to get too many shares for our comfort, we buy him out."

Louis looked as stricken as he felt.

"We don't want the rug pulled out from under us. I'm sure you can appreciate our attitude more than most."

Louis's mind was whirling, and he was incapable of grasping subtleties. "What in hell are you talking about, Ian?"

"I can't blame you for wanting to keep operational control of the store, Lou. But we don't work that way. We'll put in our own general manager, who will take his orders from the headquarters office in all things. We'll set his budgets, we'll tell him what merchandise we want him to buy, we'll supervise his advertising. We'll also do the hiring and firing of his key executives."

"That's being a puppet."

"I suppose you're entitled to look at it that way. We call it maintaining central control of our retail outlets."

"My God, Ian, I can't work that way. After all these years, I

241 :

know what's best for my store. Why should I take orders from some young punks who don't know anything about my business?"

"What I'm trying to tell you," MacDonald said patiently, "is that it won't be your business, Lou. When Clothco moves in, we take over. Completely. Schwartzman-Burns will become the most important store in our chain, but it will still be part of an integrated operation. We don't believe in separate kingdoms."

Naked hatred blazed in Louis's eyes. "You son of a bitch."

"Everybody hates to lose." MacDonald spoke quietly rather than retaliating in kind. Not only was it less of a strain, but it was his theory that one never knew when it might be necessary or desirable to do business again with an enemy of the moment. So, when it could be avoided, he never slammed doors.

But Louis was too incensed to be tactful. "If you don't want a peace treaty, we'll have a war."

"Why should we fight, Lou? Just because I can't accept your terms doesn't mean we've got to break off negotiations."

"I made you a fair offer, the only offer that would be fair to both of us. I know your kind of terms. I'd be giving you my store. To hell with that. You forget something, MacDonald, when you get so damn high and mighty."

MacDonald raised an eyebrow.

"My supporters—and they're loyal to me, so don't think you can wangle voting proxies from them—will see me through. You talk as though you've already stolen my store from me. But you haven't, and you won't!"

MacDonald felt no reply was necessary and remained silent.

"I've seen a dozen of them like you," Louis said, indifferent to the stares his loud voice was attracting. "You're all alike, you hotshots. For a little while you're lucky. A few years here, a few there, and you're the geniuses of the business. Then you come up against the people who really know merchandising, and you fall on your damn faces. Now it's your turn. I'll still be running Schwartzman-Burns long after those tricky deals you make have sent you into bankruptcy."

MacDonald felt goaded almost beyond endurance but limited his reply to, "We'll see."

It was almost unbearably hot under the dazzling lights in Gary Carey's studio, and Marni, muffled in a long mink cape with a matching hood and thigh-high leather boots, felt she was suffocating. Even when the photographer's assistant came to the prop sleigh on which she was perched and patted her face, removing streaks of perspiration, there was no respite. It was agony to hold a pose that a contortionist would have found difficult to assume, and she had been smiling steadily for so long that her face ached, too.

"It won't be much longer, sweetie," Gary called.

"Why the inquisition?" Marni demanded. "Why couldn't you use your strobe flash instead of all the lights the power company has been collecting?"

"I needed precise lighting to pick up the glisten of the artificial snow and the gleam of all that phony ice behind you. We spent six hours setting the lights, so don't begrudge us a couple of measly hours, angel. That's it. Steady. Smile."

Marni managed another brilliant smile.

"Hold it. Good. Hold it. All done. Now, that wasn't a bad half-afternoon's work, was it?"

Marni shed the cape, handing it to the assistant as she moved out of the circle of light and gratefully accepted a frosty soft drink. "I'm soaked."

"Don't stand around in this air-conditioning or you'll catch pneumonia," a young feminine voice said.

Still blinded by the bright lights, Marni blinked repeatedly and finally recognized Cleo, wearing a white ermine cape and hood, awaiting her turn under the lights. "Hi, darling. How are you?" It was impossible to speak warmly to a rival, and although Marni heard the stiffness in her own voice, she felt powerless to pretend.

Cleo was feeling the strain too and found it difficult to observe the amenities. "You looked lovely in that outfit."

Marni removed her mink hood. "Thanks. I don't envy you your turn."

"We're being punished for our sins."

Gary, who was adjusting lights on the set, half-turned and calling in a jeering tone, "My poor heart bleeds for you two! It wasn't so long ago you'd have posed for me for nothing, just so you'd have some pictures to include in your composite. Now, between you, you're costing me four hundred dollars for the afternoon!"

Ordinarily one or the other of the girls would have replied in kind, but the reminder that they were in the same, top bracket increased their mutual self-consciousness; and although both tried to smile, their efforts lacked conviction.

"You look gorgeous in the ermine," Marni said.

"The white brings out the best in me."

"Maybe they'll sell it to you for half-price. That's how Katya got her sable."

"But she didn't pay for it herself, you can be sure," Cleo said, "and earning money her way is too much for *me*."

Marni wondered if she were being overly sensitive and reading an unintended slur into the remark. "I never get that sort of offer," she said, determined to meet subtlety with subtlety.

"It shouldn't be very difficult, if that's what you want, dear." Cleo's dark face looked feline encased in the white ermine hood.

"Oh, I manage quite well the way I'm doing."

"So I noticed the other evening when I saw you with Ian Mac-Donald."

"Oh, I enjoy his company." Rather than defend herself, Marni switched to a counterattack. "Who was that fellow you were dating? He didn't look like anyone in the business I know."

"He isn't. He plays professional basketball."

"You really go for the athletes, don't you, darling?"

: 244

Cleo studied her rival, slowly looking her up and down.

Marni was conscious of every flaw in her appearance, from her damp, bedraggled hair and streaked makeup to the wrinkled dress of white wool she had worn beneath the mink cape.

"What type turns you on, baby? Don't tell me it's that animated cartoon, MacDonald."

"I like to think I've always had taste," Marni replied loftily. "In some girls it's a natural instinct, others acquire it—and some never pick up the knack."

"The trouble with professional virgins is that they don't know the difference between a living room and a bedroom. They don't know that the men who can talk pretty usually don't know how to perform."

"The trouble with amateur playgirls," Marni retorted, "is that they don't know where to draw the line between fun and work, and pretty soon they aren't amateurs at anything."

They glared at each other, neither speaking, both of them consumed by a jealousy neither had known before joining the ranks of the highest paid models.

Gary, who had been listening to the exchanges as he had worked with the lights, came between them. "Mirror, mirror on the wall," he said mockingly, and sighed in exaggerated exasperation. "Women," he said, "make me want to puke. You're both beautiful! Isn't that enough to satisfy you? You're living in the real world, kids, where there's no immutable law that says there can be absolutely no more than one Miss America at a time."

Cleo's eyes glittered, increasing her resemblance to a cat, and she stalked onto the lighted set, where she angrily brushed aside the assistant who tried to help her climb onto the prop carriage.

Marni's principal concern was her own behavior and how it influenced the regard in which others held her. "Don't blame me," she said, "or Cleo, either. You're more at fault than we are, Gary. You and everyone else in the glamour business. From the time a girl is a little child she has one question drummed at her: who is the fairest flower of all? In my saner moments I know that no one is, and that it doesn't matter, because no two judges have the same standards of beauty. But the hell of being told you're beautiful—and, in my work, of being paid for it—is that pretty soon you believe the propaganda and you start competing. When that happens, you're hooked, and you don't even know any other approach to life."

Fran Black let her miniskirt ride very high, and twisted slightly in her seat on the couch so that one unencumbered breast almost escaped from her low-cut blouse. "We never see each other anymore," she complained. "Have I got something that even my best friends won't tell me?"

Ian MacDonald went through the motions of appreciating her appearance. "You look great," he said. "I wouldn't have thought you had to lose any weight, but you really are improved, no question about it."

"It's a relief you think so. I was beginning to wonder if I'd ever hear from you again. Anyway, this place hasn't changed much, except you have a new easy chair and table over in the corner." She refrained from mentioning the framed photograph of Marni Kendall on the table.

Her powers of observation were more acute than Ian recalled. "It is a rather unusual chair-and-table unit. If you'd like, I'll have our custom furniture department send a unit over to your apartment."

"That would be nifty!" Trying to appear enthusiastically grateful, Fran thought that, so far, he was following their usual routine. When he had telephoned, asking her to come to his apartment, she had been somewhat surprised, as he had never before made a morning appointment with him. Since he reputedly never missed a day at his desk, she had assumed that something out of the ordinary was taking place, but perhaps she had jumped to conclusions.

"How is the freelance world treating you?" He took a seat opposite her.

"Not bad. Pretty good, really. I'm making more than I did, but I have to hump my rear end more to make it."

"You have the essential equipment." He made a show of peering at her bottom.

She laughed heartily, wondering why even the cleverest of men considered themselves wits when making the crudest of obvious remarks.

"You like your agency?"

"Yeah, they're with it, and they've hustled a lot of jobs for me. Of course," she added quickly, "I'm not exactly rolling in money yet, and I'm always seeing something new in the stores that I want to buy."

He handed her a card and a pen. "Write your size on this, and give me all the particulars—height, weight, measurements of bust, waist, hips. All the details."

She complied, asking no questions in spite of her curiosity.

"I'll have a summer wardrobe sent to you," he said. "If there's anything in particular you want, like sports clothes—"

"There's only one sport I like," Fran told him. "I'm strictly a city kid. Since you're giving me a choice, I need town stuff, mostly, with a lot of pizazz."

"I know what you like, and I'll see to it that you get samples of the more extreme things our buyers are picking up."

"You've just switched me on, Ian." Never had he treated her this generously, which made her wary, and she wondered what sort of freak-out he expected in return. It disturbed her that he hadn't offered her a drink, which was contrary to his custom, and she knew she'd have to ask for liquor before playing one of his nutty games. At best it was difficult to stage a show on request, and she definitely needed a few stiff belts when Ian became an audience of one and watched the performance.

"Well," he said, "I do hope I can ask a little favor of you in return."

"Sure, honey." Scarcely aware of what she was doing, she glanced around, half-looking for Carlo Bennett, who should have been making his supposedly unexpected appearance right about this time.

Ian smiled. "I'm not expecting anyone else."

Fran tried to cover for herself, but failed.

"I'd like a different kind of favor today." He paused, then said casually, "I've heard that you've become rather chummy with Barbara Howell."

She immediately thought he wanted her to recruit Barbara for one of his crazy sessions, and although she didn't shock easily, an expression of horror appeared on her face.

"Don't jump to conclusions," he warned.

"Oh, I'm not." She knew she was an inefficient liar.

"According to my book, friends never measure what they do for each other."

Feeling queasy, Fran could only nod.

"As it happens, I have a very minor request to make of you."

"Anything at all," she said faintly.

"You still haven't told me whether it's true that you and Barbara have become pals."

"Not really. I mean, we get along fine when we run into each other on jobs, and all, and sometimes like, we have a cup of coffee together. But I don't rate in her crowd socially. You know that, Ian. Her husband is one of your important guys at your office, and he also owns the agency I'm with."

"Those things aren't important. What does matter is that you know Barbara well enough to drop in at the Howell apartment—"

"I've never been there!"

"—telephoning her first, to say you want to talk to her about something."

Fran waited tensely.

"You've got to be convincing when you see her. That's all. She's got to believe you've come to her because of your friendship for her. It isn't farfetched, you know," Ian continued persuasively. "You'd go to her on your own initiative if you thought you could be of real help to her."

"I guess." Fran was so worried she forgot about keeping a breast half-exposed.

"All I want you to do is to tell her something as though it came direct from you, not from somebody else." Ian paused, then said slowly, "I want you to tell her that her husband has been having an affair."

"Jeez, that's a filthy trick!"

"It happens to be the truth."

Curiosity and distaste for the assignment warred within her. "I never thought he was that kind."

"Then you were wrong."

She pondered for a few moments. "This could be serious. Suppose it breaks up their marriage?"

"That isn't your responsibility."

Fran swallowed hard. "She'll want to know more."

"I hadn't finished. I want you to identify the woman. Tell her it's Cleo."

The girl was stunned. "You're kidding."

Ian shook his head. "It often surprises me that people can get away with anything in this town. Of course, Paul Howell can be seen in public with a beauty, and no one thinks twice about it. It's even easier for him to cheat than it is for the ordinary married man."

Fran hadn't yet recovered. "If this isn't the end. He was in my book as an iceberg Joe. And Cleo, that smug bitch. If she weren't black, she'd never in a million years be earning the top fee. She isn't worth it!"

Ian had no intention of discussing the personalities involved. "Barbara may need convincing."

"Then what do I do?"

"Convince her. Tell her you've seen them together, but not too recently. They haven't been visiting any of their usual haunts, so it may be they've stopped seeing each other."

Again Fran became thoughtful. "If Barbara won't believe what I say to her—"

"You can't very well offer her proof. It'll be enough if you sound positive and insist that a great many people know about the affair. She may say she doesn't believe you, but she'll certainly take the news to heart."

She peered hard at him. "You've got to level with me, Ian. Are you planning to get her up here for one of your little parties with Carlo?"

His face hardened. "No," he said sharply.

"Because, if you are, I can't go through with this for you. I'd love a summer wardrobe, and that chair and table are cute, but I can't cooperate in any stunt that would—"

"I've already answered your question, Fran." Ian's anger was unfeigned. "I can't blame you for having a rotten opinion of me, but I'm not that low." There was no need, as yet, for him to bludgeon Barbara in that way.

"I said what I thought, that's all." When she remembered the power he exerted, the harm he could do a model who antagonized him, she became nervous. "And I don't have a rotten opinion of you, honest. I just came out with the first thing that entered my head."

"We've now settled all that to your satisfaction," Ian said.

Fran was still troubled. "But if that isn't your reason, why would you go to all this bother?"

He glared at her in silence.

She retreated hastily. "Okay. There are things in this world that are none of my business, right?"

"Right," he said.

"So I guess it's a deal." Fran wished she hadn't answered his summons.

: 250

Ian's chilly smile indicated that a bargain had been struck.

"I'm sure to run into Barbara someday this week, either on a job call or up at the agency."

"Do it right now." He was unyielding. "Call her from here, and then go straight up to see her."

"You don't waste time! Maybe she isn't home—"

"She is." He had no intention of explaining that, thanks to his foresight, Barbara's morning was free, and she had no appointments scheduled until afternoon. "I'm assuming she's at home," he said, amending a declaration that had been too emphatic. "It won't take much effort to find out."

His stare made her so uncomfortable that she stood, absently tucking her blouse into a broad belt made of several connecting links of imitation coins.

"You'll find a telephone book and the phone in the guest room down the corridor," Ian said, giving her no respite. "Shall I show you?"

"I've been there," Fran told him, with a slight return of her spirit and gave him the benefit of a hip-swaying walk as she left the room.

MacDonald paced up and down, going over their conversation again in his mind. He had covered every angle and had told the girl all that it was safe for her to know. He hated to resort to desperate measures, but time was running out, and he was afraid that if he delayed, a rebuffed Louis Burns would bring extreme family pressure to bear on his niece.

The knowledge that Paul had been unfaithful to her, and with a younger, more attractive woman, might be enough to jar Barbara's composure. With luck, the loss of at least a measure of her self-confidence might cause her to stop dangling her stockholder's vote as a prize she would award to the side that paid her the most attention.

If she seriously contemplated a marital separation after learning of her husband's infidelity, she might become more concerned about her own future. Under those circumstances, with her bank account at stake, she would be inclined to accept the higher offer for her stock, and Ian was prepared to outbid Burns, no matter how high the ante became.

It was impossible to guess how Barbara might react, and Ian did not intend to speculate on details. Whether she and Paul remained together was irrelevant for his purposes. It would be enough that she was shaken out of her childish attitude and would become more amenable to dealing seriously with a problem that was of vital importance to Clothco. Certainly, with so much at stake, he felt that his interference in the private lives of the Howells was warranted, and his conscience was untroubled. When a man had an empire almost within his grasp, he could not pause too long to examine scruples under a microscope.

Fran returned to the living room, her manner tense. "I'm ready to go," she said, and went up the stairs to the front hall closet for her lightweight jacket.

Ian tried to show unconcern as he followed her, but the effort was too great. "Well?" he snapped. "Did you reach Barbara?"

"Yes."

"Must I drag the details out of you?"

"There's nothing to tell. Like, she was kind of surprised to hear from me. But she said, sure, come on up. So that's what I'm going to do. Okay?"

Ian nodded, and put a hand on her shoulder. "Don't mess up this assignment," he said.

Fran imagined that a creature out of a nightmare was digging long talons into her flesh, and she squirmed in an effort to free herself. "I'm wearing some strapless bras at a show this afternoon, so go easy, will you? I can't afford black-and-blue marks up there."

He tightened his hold. "I'll be right here, waiting," he said. "As soon as you leave Barbara, go straight to a pay booth and call me. Remember everything—what she says, how she looks, what she does."

"Jeez, all right! I'm not stupid!" She wrenched away from him and rubbed her shoulder. "You play rough."

Her response was precisely what he had wanted. "I get much rougher when people I trust fail me."

Fran became frightened by the bright intensity of the eyes that peered at her from his grotesque face. "I'll do what you want."

"See that you do. And keep a tight hold on your girlish feelings. I wouldn't like it in the least if you felt so sorry for Barbara that you told her about this little meeting."

"I wouldn't have the guts to cross you," she confessed.

Having applied the stick, it was time to offer her the carrot. "That wardrobe," he said, "will be the best in our stock. I know the next half-hour or so won't be very pleasant for you, but you'll be the best-dressed model in town."

Fran brightened. "I do love nice clothes," she said. "Digging them is my weakness."

Ian released her with what he hoped was a paternal, benign smile.

She remained in good spirits until she left the apartment building, hailed a taxi and started the ride uptown. Had she known she was going anywhere but Ian MacDonald's place she would have worn more suitable attire, and certainly she wouldn't have dreamed of paying a visit to Barbara in what she privately called one of her "tramp outfits." But she had no time to dash home and change, so she could only hope that the news she was bringing would distract Barbara and cause her to forget what someone else was wearing. Unfortunately, all models had uncanny memories for such things, and she wanted Barbara to like her. On the other hand, she couldn't afford to make Ian her enemy; she felt sorry for anyone who let him down.

Barbara was waiting at the door after Fran had announced herself from the lobby, and several factors combined to dispel, in part, the visitor's uneasiness. The apartment, contrary to her expectations, did not overwhelm her. It was furnished in good taste, but

253 :

less expensively than she had imagined, and aside from a few objects of bric-a-brac and a brocaded divan, it contained no items that she herself might not have owned. She was relieved, too, that Barbara was wearing a low-plunging body shirt not unlike her own and with it wide-legged denim pants and sandals with medium heels. And the finishing touch, which reduced Barbara to human dimensions, was her chipped toenail polish.

They weren't sufficiently close to touch cheeks in the ritual kiss of greeting, but knew each other too well to shake hands, so they exchanged warm smiles as Barbara ushered her guest into the living room. "Would you like some coffee?" she asked. "I always keep a pot on the stove."

"I don't think so, thanks. I've already had plenty today."

"I know what you mean. It's too late in the morning for coffee and too early for serious drinking. Why don't we have a couple of Bloody Marys?"

Vodka was a lifesaver for the model who didn't want liquor on her breath. "Just one," Fran said. "I'm working this afternoon."

"So am I." Barbara went to the small bar in the corner of the room and expertly made their drinks.

Fran's tension began to mount again, and although she knew she should keep up a conversation, she could think of no small talk. Her mind had gone blank.

Barbara sensed her uneasiness, and enjoying a rare feeling of superiority, tried to make the guest feel at home. "Try the divan," she said. "It's the most relaxing piece in the room, especially if you stretch out."

Fran kicked off her shoes and sat on the divan, tucking her feet beneath her. "This is great," she said.

"I had it redone in an expensive material to discourage the children. They sprawled all over it every time they came into the room, but the brocade discourages them."

"Are the kids around?"

"Oh, no. They're at school."

"It's funny, but I don't think of you as being a mother."

"Neither do I, when I can help it." Barbara brought their drinks to the divan, and removing her own shoes, curled up at the other end.

"I mean, like, you don't look like somebody who has had kids. Do you have to work at keeping your figure, or—"

"I work at it, every day of my life, from thirty minutes of exercises to watching every bite I eat."

"That takes willpower. I know how tough it's been for me to get rid of those extra pounds."

"The effort was worth it, Fran. You look marvelous." Barbara took a large, free-form ceramic ashtray from a table behind her and placed it between them on the divan. "I've never really noticed your legs until just now. They're good."

"Yeah, they slimmed down too."

"I hope you won't be offended if I ask you something? Why do you wear that pearl anklet?"

Fran laughed. "I guess I'm proud of my legs and want to call attention to them."

Barbara was reluctant to tell her in so many words that the ankle bracelet of imitation pearls was tawdry. Realizing that the girl knew no better, she used a more subtle approach. "You might try a plain gold anklet. It will pick up light and will be more effective without being obvious."

"Thanks for the tip." Fran studied her legs, her mission momentarily forgotten as she studied herself. "I've been wondering whether I should make a pitch at leg modeling. I hate being typecast as a breast model, and I'm sick of all those bras and the necklines down to my navel."

"I don't blame you. I've never done legs myself, I've heard from some of the girls that it's the hardest kind of modeling. They have to stand for hours, holding crazy positions, and it hurts. Their ankles swell, and when their veins bulge, they have to hold their legs in the air for a while until they can get on with the job."

"That wouldn't bother me. Anything for a change of pace, and all the specialty work is in demand. There's as much call for legs as there is for bosoms."

"I believe so. I've never done anything but general modeling, so I'm no authority."

"You could do legs! They're out of this world."

They stared at Barbara's legs, neither of them realizing that such concentration by two grown women was faintly ludicrous.

"I thought about it one time," Barbara said, "but a photographer told me my ankle bones aren't rounded enough. Yours look just right to me, but you might want to check with a photographer to be sure before you go out on a limb."

Fran nodded gravely. "That's what I'll do."

Barbara realized her joke had been wasted, which was fair enough. Any model's sense of humor was limited when she was discussing the physical attributes that enabled her to earn a living.

Appropriate compliments having been exchanged, the time had come for Fran to reveal the reason for her visit. Again she became tongue-tied, and fumbled in her shoulder bag for a package of cigarettes. Then she was unable to find matches.

Barbara came to her rescue, handing her a table lighter.

Fran took her time lighting the cigarette, but realized she could not procrastinate indefinitely. "You've been decent to me," she said at last. "Some of those snots won't even talk to me, just because I came into freelancing from lingerie."

It would have been possible for her to overcome that handicap, as many others had done, but Barbara knew that some models automatically excluded the girl from their circle because of her flashily cheap appearance. She hadn't yet learned how to show herself off without being crassly obvious. "I haven't done much of anything, Fran, except pass along a few hints, for whatever they're worth. You'll do the same, someday, for somebody else who is just breaking into freelancing work."

"Sure I will, anytime. But that isn't what I mean. You've been my friend."

"I'm glad," Barbara said, and meant it. The admiration of another, younger model was flattering.

"I'm here," Fran said painfully, "because I want to do something for you. Only I'm scared it won't seem like much of a favor, maybe."

Barbara tried to encourage her with a smile.

"It's—about Paul." Fran sucked on her cigarette and stared at an oil portrait of her hostess that occupied the place of honor over the mantel.

Barbara relaxed as she sipped her drink. All through the years other models had fallen in love with Paul, and so many had come to her with confessions that such scenes bored her. Ordinarily she would have become curt in order to hold the discussion to a minimum, but her sympathy for someone she was beginning to regard as a protégée impelled her to deal gently with Fran. "He's a very attractive man," she said.

"That's putting it mildly. All he has to do is walk into a room, and every girl in the place turns on. If a man can be beautiful and still be a man, that's what he is."

"I know." This was going to be easier than Barbara had expected. "One of Paul's problems is that he's always had this magnetism of his. He was born with it. Way down inside him, he's always aware of it, I suppose, but not on the surface. He thinks about his work and his family—all the usual things a man thinks about. Any ordinary man, that is. Most of the time he actually doesn't realize he's a devastating female slayer."

Fran giggled nervously. "You sound so calm about it. Like you weren't talking about your husband."

"In marriage, one becomes accustomed to many things," Barbara said serenely.

"When all these gals make such a big thing about him, doesn't it give him a big head?"

"No bigger than it already is. He expects their tribute."

Fran was becoming desperate in her efforts to find an opening wedge that would enable her to reveal the news. "Most guys would go leaping from one bed to the next."

"Not Paul. His vanity is satisfied when whole platoons swoon over him. He already has such a high opinion of himself that he doesn't need sex with them to prove to himself that he's a man."

Fran took a deep breath. "Maybe he's that way most of the time. But not always."

"Some women," Barbara said gently, "like to imagine their relationship with him is something very special. He grew so accustomed to dealing with models, you see—their appearance, their personal problems, everything in their lives—that he gives every woman the impression he's interested only in her. Actually, it's the other way around."

Her refusal to understand was making Fran's task virtually impossible. She thought of giving up, but could not face the prospect of returning empty-handed to MacDonald. Maybe, she thought, she would break through the protective shell if she tried an entirely different approach. "Any man can be had," she said, "and that isn't news to you. Catch him at the right time, and he'll do a flipper. When he's worried about his job or has had a big fight with his wife or is bored with what she feeds him in bed. Whatever. It doesn't matter. He gets like a little boy again, and he'll make an ass out of himself over any girl who smooths his rooster's feathers."

Barbara froze, her glass halfway to her mouth, and looked hard at the younger woman. She would have sworn that Fran was too blatant in her appeal to attract Paul, but it was true that a man's standards frequently became lower as he grew older and felt his magnetism weakening.

Fran knew she had finally scored. "I think," she said weakly, extending her glass, "I could stand a refill."

Barbara drained her own drink, rose and went quickly to the bar, where she mixed two more Bloody Marys, stronger than the first. Her visitor was silent now, obviously in extreme discomfort as she pretended to concentrate her full attention on the oil portrait.

Studying her with care, Barbara was sickened by Paul's lack of taste.

It was possible that he had strayed on occasion throughout the years, and she had forced herself, long ago, to accept as almost inevitable the hard fact that a man surrounded by beautiful girls might give in to temptation. But there was a difference, at least in her own thinking, between a brief, virtually meaningless liaison and a genuine affair that lasted for any length of time. He was an honest man, basically, which was one of his greatest charms, and she believed he was incapable of dissembling. Even though their marriage had been in increasingly great distress during recent years, she was convinced he had been as faithful to her as she had been to him. The vanity of a woman intent on proving she had lost none of her beauty would permit her to reach no other conclusion.

Returning to the divan, Barbara thrust the fresh drink at her guest.

"Thanks," Fran said miserably.

"If you had a quickie with him," Barbara said curtly, "I don't want to know about it."

"Oh, no—"

"And I refuse to believe you've really meant anything to him. I do know Paul too well for that."

"It isn't me!" Fran cried.

Barbara gaped at her.

"Jeez, now I see why the temperature dropped in here." Fran laughed shakily. "Paul hardly even knows me. And listen to me calling him Paul. When I've seen him, which is only a few times, I call him Mr. Howell."

Barbara laughed, too.

"Anyway, you're my friend. I don't steal the man of a friend, not even part-time."

"I'm sorry," Barbara said, and patted the girl's leg before taking a long swallow of her drink. "Apparently I jumped to a wrong conclusion."

"For all I know, you slipped a Mickey into my drink. Or rat poison." Fran demonstrated her trust by gulping her Bloody Mary, but spoiled the dramatic effect by choking on the pepper-laden concoction.

An unspoken question remained in Barbara's eyes.

"He did it," Fran said, "and it was no one-shot. The way I heard it, and I'm not the only one, they were in and out of their playpen like a baby learning to climb."

"Do I know the woman?"

Fran nodded.

Barbara's composure deserted her. "Who is it?"

"Look, doll, I don't want to hurt you, and the only reason I've come to you—"

"Who?"

"Cleo," Fran said, unable to catch her breath.

Barbara neither spoke nor moved. Her face became ashen, and her eyes were as blank as her mind.

Fran wanted to hold and comfort her, but stayed at the far end of the divan. "I couldn't believe it at first, either, but the word is out all over town. It has to be true."

Eventually Barbara stirred. "How long has it been going on?" she asked listlessly.

"I never know anybody's anniversary."

"You're sure it's a real affair, Fran?"

"I don't have affidavits or pictures or witnesses, but they've been seen different places together for some time. I can't say exactly how long. I'm not reliable when it comes to counting weeks and months. Look, doll, maybe the whole thing is just a lot of gas. I thought you ought to know the story that's making the rounds. It's your right. But a story isn't the same as evidence in court."

"There's always been talk about Paul," Barbara said. "Cleo has just moved up to the top level, and that sort of thing takes all kinds of planning. Perhaps Paul has been helping her, and people who've seen them together have misunderstood."

"Could be," Fran replied, aware that MacDonald wouldn't be

satisfied unless Barbara became convinced that a real affair was in progress. "Only, Paul isn't running the agency anymore."

Barbara took a long swallow of her drink. "I have no color prejudice, although I wouldn't go to bed with a black man, no matter what. So why did he pick Cleo? It would have been humiliation enough if he'd taken up with Marni Kendall or Katya."

She was taking a wrong approach, Fran realized. "He wasn't thinking about *you*, doll."

That possibility was as insulting as the revelation of the affair itself, and Barbara could not accept it. "I've read that when a husband is unfaithful, he's thumbing his nose at his wife."

"I don't know anything about headshrinkers, but I do know men," Fran said. "And all you have to do is take one look at Cleo. When a man starts to wrestle with her, he'll forget more than his wife. By the time she lets him up for air, he's lucky if he can remember his own name."

Her crudity made Barbara wince, but she couldn't accept the notion, even by indirection, that her beauty was inferior to that of Cleo. "She's attractive enough, I suppose, but take her apart, and what has she got?"

"Everything, doll. The same perfect features that Marni has, plus all the sex that Marni doesn't have. Breasts as good as mine, although I hate to admit it. The smallest waist I ever saw, and a rear as high and tight as Katya's used to be. Plus a pair of absolutely gorgeous legs."

"But her personality—"

"A man goes to bed with a beautiful body that he thinks is sexy, not a girl's personality," Fran said with authority.

"I don't know why a man acts as he does." Barbara tried to shake off a sense of helplessness. "But I intend to find out."

Paul was tired after a long day at his desk, and it was a relief to snap off the lights in his office. He had made no major decisions, done nothing inspiring or accomplished anything visibly constructive, yet the day had been important. Outsiders failed to understand that one of an executive's principal functions was that of supervising the necessary routines of a business operation, making certain that his subordinates performed their appointed tasks efficiently, with a minimum of friction.

Since early morning he had held many staff conferences, had spoken to key officials in most of Clothco's branch stores and had signed scores of letters. He had dictated many others, made a final, intensive check on the curriculum of his employees' school and had managed to break away from his own department for two high level meetings with colleagues. If challenged, he would be unable to tell anyone how he had spent his day, although he knew that, in the long run, his area of responsibility would benefit from his efforts.

He was still tense on the taxi ride home, but looked forward to a stiff drink and a filet with a baked potato. Last night he had accused Barbara of neglecting to serve anything but short-order meals since she had returned to work, and after the usual exchange of bitter words, she had sworn that tonight she would give him a dinner he'd remember. She knew his favorite was filet mignon, a baked potato stuffed with bacon crumbs and a huge salad, and he'd found himself thinking about the meal at odd moments throughout the day.

His cigarette had a stale, almost rancid taste, so he threw it away after paying the taxi driver and walked slowly into the apartment building. His legs were heavy, and he looked forward to an evening of reading in his easy chair. In fact, he would turn in early, knowing he was so exhausted he would enjoy an uninterrupted night's rest.

The dining room table was not set, and Barbara was nowhere in sight, but he found her with the children, watching a television program. He made no comment in front of the children, however, but waited until she accompanied him to the living room, where he mixed himself a drink.

She gave him no chance to strike first. "You're late."

"I called you from the office to say I'd be tied up. I had stacks of mail to sign and a couple of reports to read, but I couldn't do any of it until the phone stopped ringing and the hired help went home for the day."

"I waited as long as I could for dinner," she said, "but I was so starved I felt ill, so I ate with the kids."

"Fair enough, but I hope you saved me something."

"What would you like?" Barbara asked mechanically.

Paul put the steak, baked potato and salad out of his mind. "Anything at all, it doesn't matter."

"We have several kinds of cold cuts, or I could make you scrambled eggs and bacon."

"Don't bother. A sandwich and a hunk of raw tomato will be fine."

A shout from the television room interrupted them. "Hey, Mom! You're missing the best part."

Barbara looked only faintly apologetic. "It's a program I've wanted to see, and I told the children I'd watch it with them."

"Go ahead. I'll manage." He watched her leave the room, and only his weariness prevented him from reminding her of the promise that, obviously, had gone out of her mind. An accusation would start a fresh fight, however, so he refrained.

Determined to follow his usual routines, he sat in his easy chair while drinking his bourbon and water, but he seethed over Barbara's casual indifference and could not relax. He discovered he was smoking too much, so, after pouring himself a stiffer-than-usual second drink, he went out to the kitchen and searched through the refrigerator.

Nothing was in its right place, which had become the norm since Barbara's return to modeling, but he found some sliced ham and eventually located a loaf of white bread, although he wanted rye. There were tomatoes in the vegetable bin, but they were soft, overly ripe, so he opened a jar of stuffed olives instead and ate a few with his sandwich, which he consumed at the kitchen table. The television program, he gathered, was a long one, as no other member of the family appeared.

Paul ate quickly, then returned to the living room. There was no need for him to be alone, and he knew he could join his wife and children; but he was in no mood to watch a television program, and he had no desire to read, either. For want of anything better to do he poured himself yet another bourbon, which he drank too quickly, and it occurred to him that the liquor, combined with his weariness, had made him sleepy. He closed his eyes, and a few moments later he drifted off.

Someone was speaking to him, and Paul struggled in vain to wake up.

"That's no place to sleep," Barbara said.

Something alien in her voice aroused him, and when he opened his eyes he saw she had changed for the night. What surprised him was her unusually elaborate attire: she was dressed in the peignoir he had given her for her birthday, and he could see that beneath it she was wearing a transparent black nightgown. His nose told him she had used liberal quantities of her favorite perfume, too, and when he focused more clearly he saw that she had not removed her makeup.

"You've been dead to the world for two and a half hours," Barbara said.

Paul hauled himself into a more comfortable position. "I always take a nap after I eat too much at a banquet," he replied.

She ignored the remark. "I'd have let you sleep still longer, but I've got to talk to you before it gets too late."

His head ached dully, and he hoped she didn't intend to quarrel with him.

"Is it true," she asked calmly, "that you're having an affair with Cleo?"

The last vestiges of his sleepiness vanished. He wanted to lie, but knew there was nothing to be gained by postponing a revelation of the truth, so he steeled himself. "Put it in the past tense," he said. "I did have an affair with her, but we cut it off weeks ago."

Barbara continued to stand. "Thanks for the honesty. Now, do you mind telling me why?"

Her self-control astonished him, but after a moment he considered the question. "I wish I knew," he said. "It wasn't planned, and I didn't do it to spite you."

"Really?"

"Really. It was a crazy chemistry of the moment, and nothing else."

"I find that hard to believe."

"Sit down, Barb. It isn't easy to talk with you looming over me."

She continued to stand.

Paul hauled himself to his feet, vaguely brushing his rumpled suit, and went to the bar with his empty glass. He seldom felt an actual need for liquor, but right now he craved a shot of straight bourbon. He took care, however, not to offer Barbara a drink. She seemed completely sober, which might account for her calm, but she would be sure to create a wild scene if she started drinking.

She was watching him, her expression unfathomable.

He deliberately returned to his chair.

"I think it had everything to do with me," Barbara said.

"Not directly. Oh hell, Barb, you and I had been moving apart for a long time. I was under all kinds of strains in a new and demanding job. I'm not making any excuses, mind you. I'll take the full blame. I'm just trying to explain the way it all happened, as nearly as I can fit it together."

She nodded, her lips compressed.

"I guess I needed a sympathetic female to listen to my troubles. It's that simple. You were just going back to your modeling, so you had your own problems to think about. And I'm not throwing that in your teeth, either. I claim no extenuating circumstances. We got together at a time when both of us were vulnerable."

"But why was it Cleo? I can't see her being sympathetic and feminine."

"She was. That's all I can say."

"Then she stopped being the eternal woman, is that it?" Barbara's tone was mildly mocking.

Paul shrugged. "The chemistry wore off." Suddenly he straightened. "Look here. Even though you and I haven't been making out very well together, the last thing in the world I wanted to do was to hurt you. I don't expect an apology to compensate for whatever you've been suffering, but for whatever it may be worth to you, I'm sorry."

She inclined her head a fraction of an inch, then raised it again, her chin jutting forward.

He spread his hands. "What do you intend to do about it?" he asked slowly. "It's your ball game now."

She took a seat opposite him. "All sorts of thoughts went through my mind at first," she said, carefully arranging the peignoir's puffy sleeves. "But I tried to be honest with myself, and I've got to share the blame with you. Until I went back to modeling, I was letting myself go. I looked dowdy and plain. Frumpy."

He wanted to protest that the opposite was true, that she had never failed to give most of her attention to her appearance.

"So I can't blame you too much. Even though you went into an affair after I started back to work, you were still thinking of me as a plain housewife."

It was impossible for Paul to destroy her illusion without inflicting even more damage on her.

"I think we've got to be fair to each other," she continued. "For the kids, of course, but even more for ourselves."

He had to admit she made sense. "Spell that out."

"If we can get along together, it would be better than breaking up."

"Of course," Paul said, surprised by the lack of jealousy she had shown. He had assumed she would be angry if and when she learned of his affair, and her maturity, if not a pretense, meant he had underrated her. In fact, her behavior was far more adult than his had been. "A lot of things made us go sour, and both of us know what they were, so there's no need to add up the score."

"Good. I'm tired of fights. Either we try to get along together or we call it quits."

He took a deep breath. "It takes only one of us to walk out, but we'll have to work together if we want to continue."

"Which do you really want, Paul?"

"If you can live with me in spite of my mistake and provided we can stop squabbling over everything and nothing, I'd like to hang on. I don't like being a loser at anything, and I hate seeing all these years go down the drain."

She nodded, but remained silent.

"What about you, Barb? I've given you cause for divorce, if you want it—"

"If I had, I'd be gone by now. I just can't face finding a new place to live for the children and me—"

"Keep this apartment, if that's what you want."

She shook her head. "It's everything. My career is picking up momentum, and it would be the end for me if I had to start making a different kind of life for myself."

He didn't know whether modeling or her need to lean on someone was responsible for her reluctance to leave him. Perhaps both factors influenced her.

"So I vote for trying to stay together," she continued. "What do we lose?"

Paul regarded the question as rhetorical and did not reply.

"I think," Barbara said, "I'll have a drink now."

He watched her as she went to the bar and had to force himself not to comment when she poured a large quantity of vodka into a highball glass, then added a splash of coffee liqueur. Her version of a Black Russian was as strong as three or four ordinary drinks.

"Here's to us," she said, raising her glass.

He lifted his own in response.

"Beginning tonight."

Her words, combined with her seeming calm, and, above all, her provocative night attire suggested what Paul should have known from the moment she had awakened him, and he blamed his grogginess for his failure to understand earlier. After living apart for months under the same roof, she was inviting him to share intimate relations with her.

She couldn't have chosen a less propitious time. He was tired, so that his desire was dulled, and the shock of discovering that she knew of his affair numbed him. Her stiff drink was another inhibiting factor; he realized, as she obviously did not, that liquor was an anesthetizing agent and that she derived no pleasure from sex when she had been drinking.

Paul found it impossible to speak his mind candidly, however. If he suggested a postponement because of his emotional and physical state, she would be certain he was rebuffing her, and if he urged her to drink moderately, she would become furious, since she liked to believe she could handle liquor in any quantity without harmful effect.

Realizing he was trapped, he returned her smile.

"Let's finish these in the bedroom," she said.

He followed her down the corridor, and knew it was his place to take the initiative. Barbara had done her part by indicating her willingness to remain married to him, and her unspoken invitation was a concrete gesture of forgiveness. He could not ask her to do more, and it was up to him to create an appropriate romantic atmosphere.

He removed his rumpled jacket, and throwing it onto a chair, went to her, intending to embrace her.

But Barbara, unaware of what she was doing, sidestepped him as she bent to pick up his jacket, which she carried to a small table. "Your suit will have to go to the cleaner's tomorrow," she said.

Paul tried to ignore the interruption. "Barb," he said, "I want to tell you something."

"Just a minute. Do you want it cleaned or just pressed?"

"Cleaned. I hope you realize I've never stopped loving you. It might not be easy for you to believe—"

"Don't talk about all that, please."

He was forced to comply, but nevertheless went to her and kissed her.

Barbara suffered his embrace, but held one arm rigidly extended. "You almost spilled my drink," she said when he released her.

"Sorry," he muttered.

"That new powder I got does wonders for spots on rugs, but I'm glad I didn't have to use it."

He couldn't help wondering whether she was deliberately avoiding him or, at the least, trying to spoil the mood for love play with chat about domestic trivia. "To hell with the rug."

She looked at him over the rim of her glass. "That isn't what you said when I bought it. What a fuss you made, telling me no rug was worth that much—"

"I remember." He cut her short, hoping she would drop the subject. Her ability to dredge up old, presumably buried conflicts and air them anew was one of her more annoying traits, but he could not allow himself to dwell on the failure.

Switching off the stronger lights, he undressed rapidly, wishing his legs would stop aching. He happened to glance at Barbara just as she absently flicked cigarette ashes onto her precious rug, a sure sign she was feeling her liquor. Everything was going wrong, he thought, but doggedly refused to hint that another occasion might be more appropriate.

Barbara was waiting for him in front of the full-length mirror set into the back of the bathroom door, always an important prop in their love-making. For years, at her instigation, Paul had undressed her before the mirror while she watched, and on the infrequent occasions when she came to life, she invariably showed signs of response at the mirror.

He slowly removed her peignoir, interrupting himself to stroke her repeatedly, and when it fell to the floor he allowed her to stand for some moments while she studied her reflection. Then, his caresses becoming firmer and more insistent, he took off her flimsy nightgown and dropped it, too, onto the floor. Again he permitted her a glimpse of herself in the mirror before kissing her, lifting her into his arms and carrying her to the bed.

Barbara was weaving slightly in the moment before he picked her up.

Paul's performance was not flawless, either. His wife was a dead weight in his arms, and he stumbled slightly as he carried her to the bed.

As they kissed and embraced, their bodies pressing against each other, he tried to put these minor absurdities out of his mind. More important, he made an attempt not to recognize the possible significance of her complete failure to respond in any way while standing before the mirror.

All at once Barbara freed herself. "Do you want me as much as you wanted Cleo?"

"More, much more," he replied honestly, realizing she had not dismissed his affair from her thoughts.

"Am I as attractive as she is?"

"Of course," he lied.

"But her figure is better," Barbara persisted.

"Not to me." It dawned on him that she did not regard intimacy as a sign of forgiveness, but had suggested it as a basis of comparison, as a way of reassuring herself that she was still beautiful.

"But her waist is much smaller."

He could not imagine a less appropriate time for an analysis of relative merits and flaws in the figures of his wife and his former mistress. "I like what you've got just fine," he said gruffly.

"Even though I measure at least two or three more inches around the waist?"

"I don't take a tape measure to bed with me." Unless she desisted, he was afraid that what little sense of desire he felt would disappear.

"I'm not the exotic type, though, and she is," Barbara said.

"I've always preferred your type, and still do," Paul replied, his voice rising. "Now shut up, will you?"

For a few moments she endured his caresses in silence, her body limp, but her curiosity was too overpowering, her need for reassurance too great. "Is there something that's—well, different—about a black woman? I mean, do they do things that we don't even know about?"

He held his exasperation in check. "Well," he said, "they do know when to stop talking."

Barbara accepted the rebuff, but her mind still lingered on a comparison, and she showed no interest in Paul's renewed lovemaking.

He became increasingly disturbed by his inability to become aroused and became more persistent.

"I think," Barbara said at last as she wriggled away from him, stood and moved across the room, "that both of us need another drink."

"No," Paul said. "Come back."

She paid no attention, and, stark naked, went off to the living room, returning with refilled glasses.

He saw she had again poured herself a too generous quantity of vodka. But he knew that, beyond all doubt, she would make a scene if he asked her not to drink too much.

271 :

A cigarette in one hand and her drink in the other, Barbara perched on the foot of the bed. "From what I can tell in the mo-nokini pictures," she said, "Cleo's breasts are just gorgeous. Are they?"

"She's a 34B, just like any other first-rate model." Paul took ref-uge in an impersonal, professional attitude.

"She looks much bigger."

"That must be because of the way she holds herself in front of the camera."

"Doesn't she seem bigger when you're with her?"

"I never thought of it, one way or the other."

Barbara consumed a considerable quantity of her drink in a sin-gle swallow. "I always thought my breasts were pretty good."

"They are."

"But I'll bet the monokini wouldn't have caught on if I had done that layout."

It was impossible to reply intelligently to such an inane specula-tion, but Paul knew he had to keep up his end of the conversation. "I'm sure you'd have created just as big a sensation."

"Well, it's true I haven't sagged or anything." She was silent for a moment, still dissatisfied. "My body doesn't give off that exotic air in a photograph the way's Cleo's does."

"That's a matter of opinion. I happen to think you're even more exotic, but in your own way, naturally." He did not know how much longer he could juggle words.

"In person I don't."

"Wrong again. You do."

"Well, I don't think so," she said with finality. "Her tummy is so flat. A woman can't look exotic when she has a rounded stom-ach."

Paul felt so frustrated he wanted to shout at the top of his voice. "Go to the Metropolitan or any other art museum, and look at the paintings of nudes. You'll see that every woman has a rounded stomach."

"Styles of beauty change," Barbara said stubbornly.

"True enough, but—"

"And today a flat tummy is in."

"The only women past the age of eighteen who have them are the models in their early twenties. A woman can stay slender, which you've done, and she can be remarkably attractive, which you are, even though nature takes its own hand in shaping her figure as she matures."

"I still wish I could get rid of that last little bulge." Barbara sighed and took another swallow of her drink.

Paul's bourbon and water remained untouched on the night stand, and he no more wanted it than he felt any desire for intercourse. But he realized that only love-making might silence her, and he reached for her.

She eluded his grasp. "I'm thinking of changing my hair style. Should I?"

A reply was obligatory. "To what?"

"I'm not sure. More like Cleo's, maybe."

"The basic style you've used this past year has been very effective, Barb."

"I'm sick of it. I'm restless, and I want a change, but I can't make up my mind between a dozen styles."

"Go to a wig place, then, and rent all twelve. Have yourself photographed in each of them, and it'll be much easier to spot what's best for you."

She remembered that in recent years he had urged many of his agency's models to utilize that system of selecting a hair style. "Is that what you did with Cleo when she signed with you?"

"I can't possibly remember. But if you really want to know, I suppose Harriet must have a notation in her files. You might ask her the next time you drop up to the office."

"It isn't worth the bother. I'm worried about my own hair, not somebody else's." She yawned, then shivered.

"Get under the covers," he told her.

"I didn't realize I was getting cold." She drained her drink and climbed into bed.

The last remnants of Paul's desire had vanished, but he joined her and resumed his love-making. The first contact told him that Barbara had far exceeded her capacity for liquor: she remained immobile, unresponsive to his touch. A burst of frenzied energy enabled him to overcome his weariness, and, simulating passion, he kissed her lips, throat and breasts until the muscles around his mouth ached.

Barbara's eyes were closed, her breathing was deep and even, and she lay motionless on the pillow.

Paul extricated himself, left her bed and went to his own. His guilt made it impossible for him to blame Barbara for this latest in a long series of failures. He wished she had chosen another time to express her curiosity about Cleo's attributes, yet he realized that a woman crippled by an ever-present sense of inadequacy was incapable of demonstrating such judgment.

He stretched full-length in his bed, then tried several changes of position, but the aching sensation in his legs did not dissipate, and the dull throbbing of his temples told him his headache was returning. Although he rarely indulged in self-pity, he drew the inescapable conclusion that the future was as bleak as the present, and he told himself he was growing old.

Barbara moaned in her sleep, turned over and began to snore gently.

Even her snores were genteel, Paul thought, and winced. It occurred to him that her problem was insoluble. Even now, after spending years demanding recognition of her beauty, she did not understand that self-recognition was an ingredient of beauty and that the salute of others depended upon the confidence the beautiful individual manifested. Barbara was too inhibited, too much of a lady to expose her soul as well as her face and body for the admiration of others.

In spite of Paul's exhaustion, his mind continued to churn, and not until an hour or two before he had to haul himself out of bed for another day of work did he drop into a light, troubled sleep.

: 274

Marni felt as giddy as she looked in her multicolored tunic and matching pants, done in a wild, abstract print on raw silk. Her hair flying freely, her shoulder bag swinging, she laughed aloud for no apparent reason. "If I start to skip," she asked, "will you turn and walk the other way, or will you just pretend you don't know me?"

"Neither," Ian MacDonald said, his grin and the squint caused by strong sunlight making his face resemble the stiff, lined features on a shrunken head. "Just so I don't have to skip with you."

She promptly skipped several yards down the gravel path, causing a young couple giving their baby an airing in Central Park to stare at her with astonishment, while two old men playing chess on a board spread out between them could not believe the evidence of their own eyes. Halting, the girl waited for her companion to catch up. "I'm disgracing you," she said.

"Not at all. You're having fun." Ian's associates at Clothco would have been astonished by his benign tone.

"An afternoon in late spring or early summer in the city always does things to me," Marni said. "Much more than in the country. I suppose it's because I'm always surprised by really beautiful weather in town. Except when it's raining or snowing, I never think of weather in New York." She saw a vacant bench ahead and walked more rapidly. "I've been dragging you through the park for more than an hour and a half. Don't you want to sit for a few minutes?"

"If you like." He carefully spread a handkerchief on the dusty bench for her, and her quick smile of appreciation was his reward. "Here," he said, taking a bag of peanuts from a jacket pocket. "For the squirrels."

"Where on earth did you get them?"

"From a vendor, while you were busy watching the seals at the zoo."

"Ian, you really are something else."

"Again, please, in English. I'd rather not interpret the day's slang myself."

"Sorry, I keep thinking you belong to my generation."

The inadvertent compliment delighted him.

"What I was trying to say is that you're so sweet and considerate." Marni flicked a long strand of blond hair out of her face. "Rosalie is always telling me she hears dreadful stories about you, and other people say the same sort of thing. But you aren't that way at all."

"You don't know that side of me, the only side most of the world sees." He hunched forward on the bench, staring at his fingers as he laced and unlaced them. "I've heard some of the stories myself, and most of them are true. When I want something, I can be ruthless and hard and conniving. A bastard who doesn't give a damn, but who gets what he's after." The act of making a confession to her gave him a feeling of relief.

"I guess I caught a small glimpse of that Ian MacDonald," Marni said. "That night with David."

"Your gladiator-professor." His tone was casual. "How is he?"

"I have no idea."

Ian tried in vain to look regretful.

She laughed and shook a finger at him. "Anyone who says you're inscrutable is silly. I can see through you, so don't pretend you're sorry when you deliberately showed me how small he is."

"You knew that's what I was doing, then," he said, and chuckled.

"Not at first, but it didn't take a computer to figure it out. Here, help me feed that pair of squirrels."

They sat in easy silence, opening shells and throwing peanuts to the scampering animals.

"I believe there's a law against feeding them," Ian said.

"Oh-oh."

"But it's what you want, so don't give it another thought. I've broken worse."

"I'm not sure I want to know anymore," Marni said.

"One of these days I intend to tell you the worst."

"I wish you wouldn't."

"But it's necessary. I can't come to you under false pretenses. You and I face enough handicaps."

Marni wasn't prepared for a serious discussion of a possible joint future and abruptly veered away from the subject. "I'm sorry my quick job this noon and the quicker one coming up this afternoon spoiled a day in the country for you."

"It wouldn't bother me if I never got out of the city," he said. "I'm not inspired by trees or grass, and I've never considered flowers beautiful. I've spent so many years breathing contaminated city air, what's more, that my lungs would be shocked by any other kind."

"Just when I think I'm beginning to understand you, I don't dig you at all. I didn't know until you suggested a drive that you own a car, much less a house in the country."

"When a man is alone, he talks himself into all sorts of idiotic things. I became convinced, don't ask me why or how, that a man in my supposed position needed the usual status symbols. So I have a car that gathers dust in the garage of my building, and a house out on Long Island I almost never see. A caretaker looks after it for me."

"That's wasteful, Ian."

"I dare say, but automobiles give me no thrill, which probably makes me un-American, and aimless driving gives me no pleasure. I bought the car to take me out to my house and back, but I find eleven empty rooms too depressing."

"This is none of my business, but why don't you sell the place?"

"I intended to put it on the market before you came into my

life." Ian brushed peanut crumbs from his hands and turned to face her. "When I suggested we drop out there today, I had a reason."

"I'm beginning to think you have a reason for everything you do," Marni said faintly.

"So I do. I know you'd find my waterfall and woods pretty—"

"Ian! You have your own woods and waterfall?"

"Well, it's a fairly extensive property. And I decided that if you found the whole place attractive, I'd keep it."

"That's a responsibility I can't accept."

"I'm not asking you to assume any burdens, Marni. I want to relieve you of them."

"I'm a coward when I avoid talking about us. You could be going with famous, brilliant women, Ian, the most talented women in a city filled with bright, creative people. Why should you be interested in a girl who is a nobody?"

"Is that how you think of yourself?"

"Of course. I've fought my way to the top of a little mountain that's called glamorous, but the harder I struggle to stay at the peak, the more I wonder if the reputation is deserved. One of these days my looks will start to fade, and it won't take as long as you might think, because the altitude takes it out of you. Look at Katya, and the girls who went before her. Then what'll I be? A woman of no particular distinction, with no talent, an ordinary mind and a figure like anybody else's. I'll have gained a taste for expensive clothes and high living, and that's about all, which isn't an asset. So I can't see why one of the country's most important men in retail merchandising should look twice at me."

"It seems to me," he said, the sunlight reflected in his glasses hiding the expression in his eyes, "that you haven't really cared whether you became the number one model in the industry."

"No fair! You're digressing, Ian."

"We'll come back to me. What's your real goal, Marni?"

She rested the weight of her outstretched legs on the backs of her heels and, twisting a long strand of hair around a finger, looked like a little girl. "I've asked myself that question many times, and all I know is that I had to reach the top in modeling because I wasn't qualified to do anything more lasting or meaningful. Maybe that's why being on top doesn't satisfy me."

"If you played the piano, you'd seek recognition as a leading pianist. Or if you painted, you'd want to become a great artist. Is that it?"

"Sort of," Marni replied, shaking her head, "but not exactly. I don't know all that much about music or art, but I don't imagine a pianist or a painter swings much weight—"

"Stop right there," Ian said sharply.

It was the first time she had heard him use a tone of command, and she glanced at him in surprise.

"I'm not being an amateur psychiatrist," he said. "But it seems to me you're saying you want influence over other people."

"You could be right, but I don't know. Do I have any influence as a model?"

Ian laughed. "Millions of women copy your makeup and hair styles. They imitate the way you dress, everything in your appearance. And I couldn't begin to estimate the number of men who pin your photographs on their walls, not to mention those—like me— who trot around after you like obedient puppies."

"I hope I'm not as awful as you make me sound."

"Your ambition is legitimate, and you're fulfilling it legitimately. There's no reason you should feel in the least ashamed."

"Well," Marni said, "that's good to hear."

"The reason modeling gives you no contentment is because you've achieved a temporary goal. You'd be much happier if you could stay young and beautiful forever, and keep your place on the top of the mountain."

"It's hard to imagine something like that, but the way you put it is logical."

"What you're really saying is that you want power. You've called it influence, but I'm being more accurate."

"I—I'll have to think about all this, Ian. I don't know if you're right or not."

"I'm being so positive," he said, "because I know and recognize all the symptoms. What would you do if someone got in your way?"

Marni laughed dryly. "Well, lately I've been tempted to slit Cleo's throat."

"It wouldn't take much to make you ruthless, too. Good!"

She laughed again, this time with real amusement.

"I know what I'm saying, Marni. You see, power is my hangup, too. There, you've got me talking your language."

Marni became confused. "But you already *have* power, Ian."

"Not enough. It's never enough. I'm on the verge of pulling off a deal that—if it materializes—will do tremendous things for Clothco and for me, personally. I'll need a year for consolidation, and then I'll start hunting for still bigger game. I know me, and that's the way I operate."

Marni found his ambition fascinating and wondered if he might be right about her own desire for power.

"Now let me show you where you come in. I'm never satisfied with less than perfection. In my business, my house, my car, whatever. Or you, the only woman who has ever come up to my standards."

She forced herself to return his gaze, realizing the time had come to clarify their relationship, no matter how great her reluctance to face the issue. "Why me? If you're looking for beauty, there are a dozen models who—"

"Just you," Ian said. "You're not only beautiful, but I don't scare you away. I'm sure that every one of the others you could name would either laugh at me or run screaming because I look like an ogre."

She hadn't expected him to speak so frankly of his ugliness, and was too embarrassed to reply.

"Don't be upset, Marni," he said quietly. "I've known, all my life, that I'll never win any beauty prizes."

"I don't think of you as homely, Ian, not anymore. I see *you.*

"Oh, I'm saying it all wrong—"

"Never mind. I understand what you're trying to tell me. Your actions prove it, and there you have some of the reasons I want you. Now that I know what I suspected, that you're hungry for power, too, I'm convinced that, together, we'd make an unbeatable team."

Marni was silent for a few moments and then jumped to her feet. "Let's walk again."

He rose too and folded the handkerchief on which she had been sitting.

"If we go over to Fifth Avenue, you could put me in a cab, and I can meet you back at my apartment in time to go out for dinner."

"Would it bother you if I came along for your photography job? I've never watched you work."

It had not occurred to her that he might enjoy seeing her perform in front of a camera, and she felt flattered. "If it wouldn't bore you. It's a simple little assignment and won't take more than an hour."

"I can think of few ways I'd rather spend an hour on a Saturday afternoon," he said, matching his pace to hers. He glanced at her, then spoke again, sharply. "Don't let me scare you off, Marni."

"I—I won't," she replied, startled by the abrupt change in his manner.

"I promised you I wouldn't push too hard, and I'm trying to keep my word."

"I know, and I'm grateful to you, Ian. I feel like a bitch, keeping you dangling."

"I want you to be sure of what you want. That's the only way you and I could work out together."

"Thank you."

"I try to explain things about both of us so you'll find your right road more easily."

Marni nodded, realizing he was hoping to influence her decision and that she would have to sift anything he said to her.

"I could walk into a studio anytime you're doing a Clothco assignment, and no one—the advertising agency, the photographer or even you—could stop me. But that would be inviting you to a contest, and one power-hungry person doesn't challenge another unless he's prepared to make war, which I'm not."

"Thank you, but I wouldn't mind, Ian. Truly." Marni smiled at him. "Since we're both letting our hair down, I'll confess to you that I like having an audience. Applause and admiration are food and drink to my narcissistic soul, and I can't get enough of either. You'll never know how much I demand."

"But I do know," Ian said, "because I've had the same hunger. Insane, isn't it, that the ugliest man in New York has a craving for the unattainable?"

"You're not the ugliest—"

"As soon as I was old enough to go out on the streets alone, I had fights with other kids about it. I had hell knocked out of me until I learned how to slug, and then I became the neighborhood terror. I looked for insults, and it got so bad I'd start a scrap if I didn't like the expression on some other boy's face. And all the while what I really wanted was to hear some girl tell me I was handsome. What a crazy dream. I was so afraid of girls I wouldn't even talk to one."

Impulse led Marni to take his arm and squeeze it.

"I'm not telling you all this to win your sympathy," he said harshly.

She realized he was being scrupulously fair and was impressed.

"When you go in front of that camera," he continued, "I'll be realizing part of my dream, if that makes sense to you. It would be like—well, watching a beautiful woman and a handsome man making love, let's say. I mean that because you and I have a tie and are growing closer, I'll get a great kick out of watching you pose."

Marni was unable to follow his complicated line of thought, but was unconcerned. It was enough that the head of a large corporation had such a high regard for her that he could actually derive

: 282

pleasure from the sight of her at work, and for the moment it did not matter that she found modeling stultifying.

Barbara was in a quandary and sat for a long time at her dressing table. Pulled simultaneously in several directions, she made an uninterrupted effort to clarify her thinking by examining each facet of her overall problem as a separate entity.

Her marriage didn't rate first in importance, but she decided to get her analysis of it out of the way so it wouldn't clutter everything else. It wasn't easy to pinpoint her feelings, she knew, because she resented Paul as much as he bored her. It was his fault that she had consumed a little too much liquor the night of their lovemaking, and she certainly couldn't be blamed for falling asleep. He had accused her of passing out, but that was just another of his exaggerations and could be ignored. What had happened was plain, although he refused to admit it: he had been impotent, and in order to cover for himself, had fed her too much to drink.

In any event, they hadn't made another attempt to go to bed together, which was just as well. She had to admit to herself that she had no more interest in sex with her husband than with anyone else, and she couldn't remember when someone had last attracted her. It was even possible that she recoiled more from Paul because of his affair.

In one sense she didn't resent his intimacy with another woman. If an occasional, casual fling kept him away from her, she was almost grateful. What she could not forgive was his choice of a partner. It was bad enough that Cleo was black. It was worse that she was a model and therefore was Barbara's direct competitor. What made the whole thing so infuriating was the girl's current status as one of the undisputed queens of the profession, and nothing would convince Barbara that Paul had slept with Cleo for any reason other than to thumb his nose at the wife who was making such a great effort to reestablish herself in modeling.

She was willing to concede that he might have tried to rationalize and find other reasons for the affair, but she was convinced that the coincidence was too great. It could not have been accidental that the most glamorous of current models had been his partner and that he should have engaged in his only protracted affair at the precise time that his wife was trying to regain a foothold in the vocation she had abandoned for his sake.

In spite of her anger, however, Barbara had no intention of terminating her marriage. She had not yet achieved a resounding success in her comeback, and she realized it would be wise to keep her life as a housewife in reserve. It wouldn't be easy for a woman in her midthirties, with two growing children, to find another husband, even though she had retained far more of her beauty than most of her contemporaries.

She was willing to grant that the present arrangement was unsatisfactory, but considered it fortunate that Paul was making no complaint. So they could drift this way indefinitely, until their marriage either improved or she found something better to take its place. She wouldn't mind drifting—once she repaid Paul for the insult his affair had inflicted on her.

Of far greater importance to her was her career itself, and she studied her reflection in detail, critically examining each feature, every portion of her body. She was far more severe in her self-condemnation than anyone else would have been, because she alone knew all of her flaws and tended to magnify them. Nevertheless she reached the inescapable conclusion that she still had it. Oh, she couldn't compete with the very top girls who were in their early twenties, but she could outshine the majority of young models, and as a more mature beauty she was in a class by herself.

So it was inevitable, she thought, that eventually she would be in steady, heavy demand again. Photographers, advertising agency men and television producers, as well as dress designers, manufacturers and the key fashion-magazine people were unaccustomed to dealing with models of her age, so she had to educate them. Little by little, as she found more and more work, they would recognize her worth. Surely it couldn't be accidental that some of the people who were hiring her these days were calling her back for additional jobs.

One basic fact was difficult to face, even when alone: Ian Mac-Donald was primarily responsible for the comeback she had made so far. In fact, without his help she would be an abject failure.

She could not feel grateful to Ian, however, knowing that neither friendship for her nor a desire to give a hand to the wife of one of his key executives was responsible. Ian was a clever devil, and from the outset she had recognized his motive. He would do anything for her in order to swing her Schwartzman-Burns stock into his camp.

It amused her that everyone else thought her decision in the matter was as difficult as it seemed momentous—to them. She secretly relished the knowledge that it had been absurdly easy to make up her mind. She owed Uncle Lou nothing and saw no reason to show more loyalty to him than he had demonstrated toward her. Lately, after making it clear he wanted her support, he could have shown a little savvy by saying a word or two to his buyers. That's all it would have taken, and with virtually no effort on his part she would be modeling in every fashion show that Schwartzman-Burns staged. She knew that two departments there had held them in recent weeks, because she'd seen the call on the bulletin board at the agency. But Uncle Lou hadn't lifted a finger on her behalf.

On the other hand, what Ian MacDonald had done for her career spoke for itself. His past favors were not the determining factor, to be sure. What concerned her was what he could and would do for her in the future, and his hold over her was a subtle one. Until she reestablished herself on a truly solid basis as a model, she needed Ian's continuing assistance.

Therefore she would vote in favor of the Clothco merger.

The game of hard-to-get she had been playing had lost much of its savor, so she saw no reason for protracting her delay. There was something else she had to remember, too: if she read Ian's character correctly, he could be a vindictive bastard, and she would need his continuing goodwill after he pocketed her vote. So it would be wise not to try his patience too long.

Ian's telephone call of this morning had been the danger signal, and she hadn't realized, in fact, that he was desperate in his desire for her support. Just exactly how far he was prepared to go was a tantalizing, intriguing question.

Certainly his motives had been obvious enough to her when he had said, "This is an odd call, and I have a rather strange request to make of you. I'm embarrassed, so I hope you'll hear me out. Someone who has been associated with me for many years is your ardent admirer. Now, please don't get me wrong. I'm not suggesting that you be disloyal to Paul, any more than I'd double-cross him. But Carlo—Carlo Bennett, you've met him, I believe—sees Paul daily at the office, too, which makes things a bit awkward. So I wonder if you might be willing to drop up to my apartment this noon. You and Carlo and I could have lunch together there. It's all innocent and rather adolescent, and I know Carlo would be overwhelmed by the chance to chat with you for an hour."

Barbara's vanity had prompted her to accept, but she realized instantly that the invitation might not be as blandly harmless as Ian had indicated. It was possible that he might try to compromise her in order to obtain her support, and she thought him capable of staging just such a maneuver. But she believed she could take care of herself, so she wasn't concerned.

Just to be on the safe side, she had signed the stock proxy ballots that Ian had mailed to all Schwartzman-Burns shareholders and had already tucked them away in her shoulder bag. At the end of lunch, after she discovered what, if anything, they intended to do in order to obtain her votes, she would present Ian with the proxies.

No matter how she looked at the date, it promised to be fun.

Bennett wasn't her idea of a Greek god, although she had to admit he was rather exceptionally good-looking. Girls who were drawn to Latin types probably fell all over him. On the basis of her slight acquaintance with him, Barbara considered him rather crude, but perhaps she was mistaken. However, he was a member of her own generation, perhaps a few years older, and it certainly was possible that his admiration was genuine. So she was going to enjoy eating a meal with someone who paid more attention to her than to his food.

The unexpected invitation delighted her, too, because of the opportunity it gave her to repay Paul, at least in part, for his infidelity. She had no intention of developing a relationship with Carlo Bennett—or anyone else—that might lead to an affair, but the knowledge that another man found her desirable would be balm enough. A flirtation that went a trace beyond the bounds of discretion would be the most effective of medicines in the healing of her wounded ego. And if Ian gave her a moment or two alone with Bennett after lunch, she would be tempted to permit her admirer a farewell kiss.

Barbara really knew she was being unrealistic, that she was guilty of romantic daydreaming a modern teenager would shun. Ian had millions of dollars at stake and was playing no girl-and-boy games; furthermore, both he and Bennett were men of experience. A woman who wanted respect had to earn it, and no one would erect a pedestal for a matron who agreed to a private lunch party with an alleged admirer.

In brief, Barbara was taking chances, and knew it. That realization, however, gave the date its ultimate appeal. She couldn't be certain why she felt as she did, but the longer she contemplated what might be ahead, the greater her excitement became. Perhaps her long abstinence had whetted her appetite, and she remembered, from the bygone days before her marriage, that she and her friends had sometimes referred to someone as "ripe for it." At the time she had agreed with her mother that the phrase was crude, but a restless sensation, a yearning she could not define, kept growing within her, and caused her to suspect that she might indeed be ripe.

Related to this feeling was another, which also contributed to her anticipatory pleasure, although it defied reason. With her eyes open she was walking into a situation beyond her control. She could only guess Ian's intentions, and Bennett's, but didn't really know them, yet it was they, not she, who were making plans and would decide what happened at the lunch.

Her reaction to this situation surprised her. As far back as she could remember, she had demanded control of her own destiny, and she knew that her return to modeling had been sparked in part by her insistent desire to regain the feeling of independence she had always cherished. Nevertheless she was willingly—eagerly, she had to admit—allowing herself to be handcuffed today, and the prospect of being at the mercy of others added to the zest of the occasion.

A glance at the clock beside her bed told her it was time to get ready, and she made her preparations with unusual care. She poured a strongly scented oil into the tub and soaked for a long time in the bath. The makeup she applied was as heavy as she would have worn for participation in a major fashion show, and although she had no need for false eyelashes, it amused her to wear them. Everything that added glamour to her appearance would make the day more memorable.

The problem of what to wear vexed her, and, as usual, she made several false starts. Bennett was an unknown quantity; but she knew herself, and certainly Ian was a solidly respectable businessman, so it was unlikely that anything really untoward would happen. "All the same," she said aloud, "I want to *feel* wicked."

The day was hot, with a muggy lifelessness in the air that could make city dwelling a torment, and the weather gave Barbara the excuse to be more daring than she otherwise would have been. Perhaps it was an unwritten law that ladies—and models, regardless of whether they were ladies—always wore stockings, but the heat gave her a perfect out, and she didn't even open her pantyhose drawer.

This was one day she would wear neither stockings nor panties.

Working her way slowly down the line of hangers in her closet, she came upon a dress that seemed precisely right. The top was a transparent linen with a plunging neckline and large, double-material pockets intended to conceal the wearer's breasts; the knife-pleated skirt, although short, was very full and created a demure illusion. It too was made of two layers of linen, and the color, a creamy white, was young and fresh.

Barbara put on a short, lace-edged half-slip and went through an inner struggle trying to summon the courage to wear the dress without a bra. Although she recognized the folly of drinking too much today, she couldn't resist taking a nip of vodka from a bottle she kept hidden at the bottom of a lingerie drawer in her dresser. Then, trying to postpone a decision, she doused herself in perfume and added a few touches to her makeup.

The ringing of the doorbell forced her hand. Quickly tying a chiffon scarf over her face and head to protect her makeup, she pulled on the dress, adjusting it and removing the scarf as she answered the summons.

"I hope you don't mind my blowing in like this," Fran Black said. "I just dropped off a set of my composite pictures at a photographer's studio a couple of blocks from here, and I thought I'd take the chance and see if you were home."

"Come in." Time was growing short, but Barbara was pleased to see her. "In the bedroom, if you don't mind. I'm getting ready to go out."

"I hope I'm not interrupting."

"Not at all. I'm going to fiddle with my hair, and then I'll be done."

Fran inspected her with interest. "Jazzy," she said.

A wave of uncertainty rolled over Barbara. "I wonder if it's too much. Or too little, I should say."

"Not on you. If I wore something like that into the agency, Harriet would scream and send me home to put on some underwear. But you're the dignified type, like, that can get away with it."

Barbara's laugh was shaky as she brushed her hair and sprayed it.

"Big job today?" Fran's curiosity was friendly.

"Mmm."

The lingerie model sniffed appreciatively. "That perfume is too expensive for me, but I love it. You must have used a gallon of it."

"Help yourself." Barbara handed her the bottle.

Fran applied a small amount. "This stuff is so sexy it's a waste to use it for a modeling job. It ought to be saved for dates."

Barbara could feel color rising to her face and was horrified.

The girl was aware of her flush and immediately desisted. Fran would have sworn that Barbara wasn't the kind who played around, but you never knew about another woman, particularly when her marriage was on the rocks.

Barbara felt the need to fill the conversational gap. Opening a huge wicker case of costume jewelry and peering into it to avoid looking at her guest, she said, "I should have called you after your visit, but it wasn't easy."

"You didn't owe me anything."

Barbara donned an upper-arm bracelet of white enamel. "Whether I'm indebted to you or not, and I believe I am, I want you to know that Paul and I are staying together. At least for now."

"I'm glad. Provided that's what you want. You deserve the best. Of everything." Suddenly Fran's tone changed. "Hey, not too many of those junk rings."

Barbara, again in the grip of her reckless mood, demurred. "They're fun."

"Sure, but not with that dress." It was obvious to Fran that her friend was unaccustomed to such daring attire. "Your wedding and engagement rings are enough on your left hand."

Barbara had forgotten she was wearing them and studied her hand for a moment. "They aren't right, either," she said, and removed them.

Fran watched her fling them into the wicker basket with a careless, almost abandoned gesture and drew her own conclusions. What Barbara did was her own business, but it was plain that any woman who handled her wedding and engagement rings with such contempt had not reached a real understanding with her husband.

"There, I'm just wearing the snake rings and the three white ones that match my bracelet. Okay?"

"Better," Fran conceded.

Barbara glanced at her reflection in the mirror, giving her hair a final pat, and was startled. The blouse pockets partly concealed her breasts, but anyone who looked at her would know she was not wearing a bra; and perhaps it was her imagination, but she, at least, could tell from the hang of her skirt that she was wearing a minimum of undergarments beneath it.

But she refused to give in to cowardice and back down. Slinging her bag over her shoulder, she grasped the strap and struck a model's pose. "How do I look?"

"If I were a man—yum!" Fran said emphatically.

Barbara hurriedly changed the subject. "I'm sorry there isn't time to offer you a drink or coffee. I'm taking a taxi down to midtown. Can I give you a lift?"

"Sure, I'm headed that way too."

On the ride they chatted about clothes, gossiped about other models and jointly damned a photographer who had rejected both of them for an assignment. Barbara felt such intense excitement it was difficult for her to concentrate on the conversation, but she made the effort to create the impression that this was just another, ordinary day. At one point she was afraid she had left her Schwartzman-Burns proxy ballots at home and felt a surge of panic, but grew calmer when a quick glance at the contents of her bag reassured her that she was carrying them.

Fran was mildly aware of her tension but thought nothing of it and was so immersed in the girl-talk that she paid scant attention to their surroundings as the taxi headed down Park Avenue.

"Driver," Barbara called. "Let us off at the corner, please. That's fine." She paid the man before they emerged.

Fran had been telling a story, and they stood for a few moments on the sidewalk as she finished it.

"It's been good to see you," Barbara said in a rush, "and we'll have to get together soon. For a nonmodeling day. I'll call you." She smiled, nodded and hurried away.

Fran turned, but something odd struck her, and she halted, looking back over her shoulder. Barbara was heading in the direction from which they had come, and when she entered an apartment building it occurred to Fran that they had passed the place in the taxi, but she had not asked the driver to stop there.

Then it dawned on Fran that she knew the building, and everything else left her mind. Ian MacDonald lived there.

Perhaps it was just a coincidence, but Fran suspected that the provocatively attired Barbara was paying him a visit, and the girl was stunned. Unless she was crazy, totally incapable of judging people, she was positive that Barbara Howell wouldn't be party to one of Ian's nutty merry-go-rounds. In fact, Fran doubted that Barbara had ever heard of such warped activities. And Ian, whose only weapon was his wealth, could have no hold over a woman whose husband earned a large income and who was financially comfortable in her own right. This just didn't make sense.

Fran's instinct told her to forget the matter and go about her own business, but she hesitated. Barbara was her friend and might be getting into water that was deeper than she realized. A woman who had just learned that her husband had been unfaithful to her wasn't necessarily the most stable of people.

"Jeez!" Fran murmured aloud, when she remembered the most important part of the puzzle. It was Ian who had sent her to Barbara with the news of Paul Howell's infidelity, Ian who had paid her absurdly well in return for acting as a messenger in accordance with his exact instructions.

Fran felt certain she had pieced together the whole picture. Ian had wanted Barbara for one of his I-spy sessions, so he had made certain she had learned of her husband's affair. In some way—it didn't really matter how—the clever bastard had even persuaded her to show up for the party skimpily dressed, which was one of his requisites.

Maybe Barbara knew what she was doing, but just in case she didn't, Fran was reluctant to desert the woman who had befriended her. She didn't quite know how Ian would react if she followed Barbara to the apartment, but she didn't want to find out; and although the sun overhead was softening the pavement, she shivered.

Only one course of action remained open, and Fran took it. A small tavern was located around the corner on the crosstown street, and she knew from experience that the entrance to Ian's building was visible from the small table nearest the window. Maybe she couldn't do Barbara much good, but at least she'd be nearby.

Her decision made, she went into the bar, sat at the window table, and, ordering a glass of beer and a package of cigarettes, settled down for her vigil.

Meanwhile Barbara, announcing her identity to the attendant on duty in the apartment house lobby, felt more secure and slightly let down. She wasn't sneaking into the place after all but was coming here openly as an honorable, married woman. She had been silly to let her imagination run so wild.

The attendant checked on the telephone, then turned back to Barbara with a smile and a bow. "Go right on up, ma'am," he said, holding the door of the self-service elevator for her. "Apartment 14-A."

The elevator ride seemed very long, and Barbara found herself wishing she had dressed more conventionally. It was easy to argue that nudity was fashionable, and had no connection with morality, but she had maintained that there was a vast difference between modeling outrageous attire and wearing it nonprofessionally. It had been her contention that a woman who was too scantily clad was asking for whatever she got, but this was not the time to remember her homilies.

Ian was waiting for her in the open door of his apartment, and his welcoming smile grew broader as she walked toward him.

Barbara thought she saw a quick flicker in his eyes as he took in her appearance, but she couldn't be certain.

"This is sweet of you," he said in a conspiratorial tone. "You're a good Samaritan as well as a very lovely one."

Her laugh was unconvincing.

Carlo Bennett stood near the living room windows, where he seemed to be looking at the view, but he turned as Barbara came into the room. Going to her, he bowed from the waist and raised her hand to his lips in Continental fashion. "Mrs. Howell," he said, "I'm obliged to you."

Barbara wanted to giggle, but managed to keep a straight face. "Barbara, please. Let's not be formal."

"Thank you," he said. "Paul is my friend as well as my colleague, and I have great respect for him. But for a little while it will be pleasant not to be reminded of him."

Barbara wondered whether he was an accomplished actor, but came to the conclusion that he was being sincere.

"You probably think I'm some kind of a kook, and maybe I am," Carlo continued. "I've only seen you a few times, and I doubt if we've said a hundred words to each other, but I believe you're unique, Barbara."

She turned in embarrassment to Ian, who followed her into the room. "Listen to him," she said. "He doesn't waste time, does he?"

"Carlo has been practicing his little speech for the past half hour," Ian told her, chuckling. "Let him finish it, and then we can all relax."

"I know you have been married for many years," Carlo said earnestly, "and have two children who will soon be in their teens. But you don't look old enough to vote."

"Except for your store stock," Ian said quietly from the far side of the room.

His assistant ignored the interruption. "I've been in awe of you, Barbara. But I hope I'm neither a moron nor a sentimentalist. I've gathered from Ian that he didn't tell you my real purpose in wanting to meet with you."

Barbara glanced at the host, whose shrug seemed to confirm that there was more to the story than he had indicated.

"I don't cast myself at the feet of happily married women," Carlo said, and grinned.

Feeling more at ease, she smiled at him in return.

"I earn my living working for a large chain of department stores. Our cosmetics department is one of our largest and most profitable. Maybe you know from Paul—there I go, mentioning him again—that the cosmetics manufacturers in the United States earn more than two billion dollars a year—that's gross income, of course —and the figure soon will go up to three billion."

Barbara's half-formed dream of a romantic interlude began to fade, and she felt vaguely disappointed.

"Anyway, women spend enormous sums of money every year trying to do what you've actually done. You've discovered the fountain of youth, Barbara, and if we can reduce your system to a formula, we'll be rich beyond anything we've ever imagined. Host," he called, "what do you think you're doing?"

"Mixing drinks," Ian replied.

"Something very mild for me, please," Barbara said.

He nodded but did not pause.

"What I'd like to do today," Carlo told her, "is pump you. Anything and everything you can tell me may be of help."

"I'm sorry to disappoint you," Barbara said, flattered by his interest in her beauty, even though his motives were financial. "But I'm sure I do the same things a lot of other women do. I'm sure I use the same night creams, all that sort of thing."

"There must be differences," Carlo insisted. "The results are so dramatically different."

"I've tried to convince him," Ian said, coming to them with a tray of drinks, "that maybe nature has been kinder to you than to most, but he won't hear of it. Incidentally, there's a good reason we didn't ask Paul to sit in with us. We didn't want you to be self-conscious in front of your husband while Carlo plays district attorney. Naturally, we'll fill Paul in this afternoon."

Barbara accepted the martini he handed her, forgetting she had asked for a mild drink.

Carlo took a folded sheaf of neatly typed papers from his pocket. "As a preliminary," he said, "we could run through these questions I've worked up. Most of them are rather obvious, but don't let that throw you. I'm hoping you might come up with an unexpected answer or two that could open some doors for us."

"Easy, there," Ian told him. "Don't be in such a rush. Give the poor girl a chance to catch her breath." He raised his own glass in a toast.

Barbara was grateful for the drink as well as his solicitude. Her tension was dissipating, but she was annoyed with herself for having taken Ian literally when he had told her that Carlos was her admirer. The skimpiness of her attire continued to make her self-conscious, and she hoped that Carlo, who was a stranger, wouldn't think her cheap or bold. She had no idea what might be going through Ian's mind either and could not let herself forget that he was both her benefactor and Paul's employer. A swallow of the martini gave her a momentary feeling of relief, however, and she managed to look at ease as the attentive Carlo lighted the cigarette she took from a box on the table beside her.

"I see you have my brand, Ian," she said. "You really are marvelous about remembering little things."

"Oh, I'm taking no chances these days," he replied genially. "I'm wooing you madly."

"But as soon as I vote my stock, I suppose you'll forget I exist."

"You're wrong. I'll continue to think of you with great affection. Whether it will be in happiness or sorrow is something only you can decide."

"I've decided," Barbara said quietly.

He stiffened and waited for her to continue.

Carlo, who had less at stake, had no difficulty in dissembling and appeared slightly amused.

Barbara wanted to prolong the drama until the end. "I'll tell you after lunch, just before I leave. How's that?"

"I'm delighted." Ian sounded pleased, but his eyes narrowed and his smile became fixed.

She realized he had jumped to the wrong conclusion, that he believed she was delaying because she intended to vote against the merger and therefore was afraid the atmosphere would become strained if she revealed her position now. Perhaps she was being unfair, she thought, knowing that a word now would not only clear up his misunderstanding but cause him to rejoice. On the other hand, she could not resist the temptation to wait. Never had she exercised this much power over any man, and he would regard her no less highly once he learned that she had made her decision in his favor.

"If no one minds too much," Carlo said, "I'd like to get started on this list." He rattled the sheaf of papers.

Ian recovered his aplomb. "We've taken it for granted that Barbara doesn't mind, but for all we know she resents being used as a guinea pig."

She saw both men looking at her, awaiting her reply. "I've never been bashful about my appearance, but I honestly don't believe I'm all that beautiful."

"If you won't take my word for it, spend a little time in front of a mirror," Carlo told her.

"Better than that," Ian said, "I'll let you in on a little business secret. We've allocated a quarter of a million dollars for the experimental development of a new line of cosmetics, diet aids and whatever, if something comes out of this interview. And if our research looks promising, we'll sink a great deal more into it. So your beauty isn't a matter of personal opinion or taste. You're the all-important essential in an enterprise that might earn very large sums of money."

"You do make me seem important," she said with a laugh, and drained her drink.

Carlo immediately refilled her glass from a pitcher on the tray. "Tell her the rest, Ian. It's only right."

"I guess it is. I was going to surprise you with this, Barbara, but you should know. If we're able to develop a product—or several, or whatever—that we can either manufacture ourselves or license to one of the big cosmetics companies, we'll make you a shareholder in the new corporation we'll form for the purpose."

"That's very thoughtful. Thank you," she said politely, unable to muster the interest in money that most other people displayed.

Her reaction did not surprise Ian. "We're also thinking of putting your name on a line of cosmetics."

"That would be wonderful!"

"I knew you'd like the idea. It would be premature to go into details now, but keep it in mind."

"Oh, I will."

Carlo unfolded the papers and glanced at one. "Let's start with diet. Are there any special foods you eat to help you stay slender?"

"Not really," Barbara said. "I've been careful for so long that I automatically skip starches, and if I'm still hungry at the end of a meal, I'll eat more meat or fish. Almost any kind of fish is particularly good for holding down weight."

He made a scribbled notation in the margin. "What about drink?"

She raised her glass and giggled. "I'm lucky, I guess, but I seem to burn it off. I know liquor is supposed to give you a tummy, but I metabolize it." She absently patted her stomach.

"Could I impose on you to stand for a second or two?" Carlo looked embarrassed. "I'd like to see how flat you really are, and please don't haul in your breath or anything like that."

Again Barbara felt a wave of self-consciousness and tried to tell herself this was like a modeling assignment. Taking a quick gulp of her drink, she rose to her feet.

"Fantastic," Carlo said, his pencil busy again. "You weren't exaggerating."

"I do spend a half hour exercising every morning," Barbara said, resuming her seat.

"Ah!"

"But I can't possibly stretch out on the floor and illustrate. Do you want me to describe the exercises?"

"By all means."

She launched into a detailed explanation, and Carlo wrote rapidly as she talked.

Meanwhile Ian picked up the pitcher of martinis and topped her drink.

Barbara was aware of what he was doing and, not wanting to interrupt her complicated recital, made a vague gesture indicating she wanted no more. Two drinks were her limit at noon, and she was afraid she might get stoned if she didn't know how much she was consuming.

Ian smiled reassuringly and refilled her glass to the brim.

"Your exercises make you firm but don't give you muscles?" Carlo asked.

"No, I'm careful not to do too much," Barbara said.

Smiling apologetically, he reached out and felt the muscle of her upper arm, slid his hand to her lower arm and then moved upward again. "You're absolutely right," he said. "I wouldn't have believed it." His hand lingered for a moment or two before he resumed his writing.

His touch had felt like a caress, but Barbara told herself not to let her imagination get out of hand. Just because she'd had a couple of drinks was no reason to start convincing herself that he had made a subtle pass at her.

"I hadn't prepared any questions on this," Carlo said, "but what kind of care do you give your skin? It occurred to me just now."

It was obvious why the subject of her skin had crossed his mind, and although she was enjoying the close examination of her beauty, she felt another twinge of discomfort. "I use face creams and body creams every night, and I stay out of the sun."

"That doesn't account for your youthful skin. You don't have a wrinkle anywhere."

"You need glasses," Barbara told him.

"I wear glasses," Ian said, "and he's right."

"We'll probably find the clue somewhere else in our study," Carlo said. "Let's drop it for the moment and come back to it later. Now, I hope you don't mind very personal questions, but there's no other way, I'm afraid."

"Fire away," Barbara said, and fortified herself with another swallow from the glass that, miraculously, seemed to stay filled.

"What figure aids do you use?" Carlo asked. "I'm thinking of special girdles, the type of brassiere you use and so on."

"I've never in my life worn a girdle," Barbara said proudly. "Some designers and photographers say it makes a smoother line to wear one, and when they've made an issue of it I've simply let them think I've worn one for them. They've never known the difference."

"Amazing."

"And sometimes," she continued, growing more reckless, "I don't wear a bra, either."

Carlo appeared incredulous.

Had Barbara been sober she would have realized that a single glance would have verified her assertion. "Why are you so surprised?" she demanded.

"I thought that just about every woman over thirty develops bulges and starts to sag."

"Here's one who doesn't bulge or sag!" Barbara jumped to her feet, staggered slightly before regaining her balance and then paraded up and down the room, giving her audience of two the benefit of her smoothest and most accomplished model's walk.

"I told you she had a perfect figure!" Carlo exclaimed.

"Well, I don't pretend to be an expert in these matters," Ian said, sounding amused, a trifle bored and somewhat self-deprecatory.

"My boss is too old and crotchety to appreciate you, Barbara," Carlo told her, rising as she returned to the divan. "There's a gold mine in your figure if we can duplicate it, and that much he can appreciate. Turn around for a second, will you?" He caught hold of her arm and faced her in the opposite direction.

The experience, she thought, was identical to that of modeling.

"Her posture is part of the secret," Carlo said. "See the way she holds her shoulders back? But that's only part of the story. She really doesn't need a girdle."

She felt him passing his hand down her buttocks, then across them, but his tone was so impersonal that she didn't want to make an issue of the matter.

Again he turned her toward Ian and, standing directly behind her, slipped his hands beneath her arms. "If we can duplicate this effect, without a brassiere, every woman in the United States, Canada and most of Europe will scream for our product."

Barbara felt his hands half-cupping her breasts as he illustrated his words. She wanted to break away, but Ian was regarding her impersonally too, and it would have been embarrassing to make a scene.

"All the research analyses prove that the primary body concern of most women as they mature is their breasts," Carlo continued. "Now, this is the basic effect that most brassiere manufacturers try to achieve. Our job is to do the same thing, without tricks. No building in of brassieres in dresses. Exercise and diet are the answers, I suspect. Right?"

She felt his hand closing over her breasts, holding them firmly but gently, yet his manner was so lacking in intimacy that she felt confused. And she realized, too, that the sensation was pleasurable. "I know there are special breast exercises," she replied, trying to match his tone. "Luckily, I've never had to do any of them. But it could be that some of the other exercises I use have an effect."

"They must." Carlo continued to hold her.

She was uncertain whether she had shifted her position slightly or whether his hands were moving almost imperceptibly, but she couldn't help shivering when the touch of his fingertips through the thin fabric of her dress caused her nipples to swell.

301 :

"I assume," Carlo said, "that your bustline is as perfect in profile as it is in a front view." Giving her no chance to reply, he swiftly pulled her dress down, the shoulder straps pinning her arms to her sides.

Mortified because her nipples were enlarged, she stood rigidly, frozen and unable to move.

"We'll want a dummy made to her precise measurements," Carlo said. "This is the line we'll want to copy, and it can't differ from the original by as much as a millimeter."

She was aware of his fingers again, tracing the outline of her breasts and, without pausing, delicately manipulating the nipples.

Ian glanced at his watch. "You two will have to work out these details without me for a few minutes while I make a long-distance call." He rose and quickly left the room.

Carlo took a step backward. "I hope I haven't embarrassed you," he said.

Barbara didn't want him to know he had aroused her and tried to speak casually too. "That's all right." The shoulder straps still held her arms against her sides, and she decided this was not the moment to struggle too obviously into the upper part of her dress. Perhaps his touch had been accidental, and her instinct, although dulled by the gin she had consumed, told her that her only protection was the shield of pretense. So she continued to stand for a moment or two, unmoving, before she reached for the shoulder straps.

Carlo gave her no chance to pull them up, however, and grasping her arms above the elbows, immobilizing them, he suddenly bent down and kissed her breasts.

Barbara was caught completely off guard, and felt powerless to resist him. His flicking tongue expertly caressed her breasts, and the desire that welled within her made it almost impossible for her to think coherently. She realized she had been tricked, that Carlo had planned his moves from the outset with great cunning, and that Ian, who had vanished so abruptly at the critical moment, had been a party to the scheme.

Carlo's ministrations became more demanding.

For a brief moment Barbara went limp. Then, in spite of herself, she managed to raise her hands and press his head closer.

Her original hunch had been right, and she had been invited to play the principal role in a seduction. Ian, the bastard, was responsible, and she realized he was even more desperate than she had thought possible, that he would do literally anything to obtain her proxy vote. But she was enjoying the last laugh, and it would be comical to see his reaction when he discovered that she had already voted her stock in his favor.

As for Paul, who was an even bigger bastard, she was winning the ultimate victory, repaying him in kind for his infidelity. What really pleased her was the knowledge that she was retaliating so swiftly, and she intended to let him know, in some subtle way, that she had not only evened the score but would do it again if he repeated his error.

Neither Paul nor Ian was her principal concern, however. This experience, for its own sake, meant far more to her, and she relished the intimate attentions of this attractive stranger, whose ministrations were a tribute to her beauty. His ardor fed her ravenous vanity, and the feeling that she was trapped, unable to resist, inflamed her own desire. Her lethargic indifference to the demands of her own body had vanished, and she found herself yearning to be ravished by this man whose love-making was so much more polished than Paul's.

Carlo, sensitive to every nuance, instantly recognized the change that took place within her. He knew at once that this woman had become his eager victim, and it was no longer necessary for him to overwhelm her. Deliberately adopting a more leisurely pace, he raised his head, and, his mouth seeking hers, he fondled her breasts, his touch light but confident.

Barbara realized dimly that she was doing what she had always condemned in the models who, according to her standards, were wantons. But she no longer cared, and it did not even occur to her that she was casting aside the values that, in her own opinion, set

303 :

her apart from the girls with pretty faces and supple bodies whose lack of integrity made it impossible for them to become truly beautiful. It was enough that Carlo wanted her, that his passion awakened her own.

The vague thought crossed her mind that he might believe her abandoned when he discovered how little she was wearing beneath her dress, but she happily dismissed the notion. A man who toyed with her as he was doing, bending every effort to awaken her erotic yearnings, would be pleased if she were a wanton, and Barbara threw herself into the role, neither knowing nor caring whether she was in earnest or merely playing the part in which she had been cast.

She pressed against Carlo, her body undulating, and neither then nor later did she know whether he carried her to the divan or pushed her onto it. It was enough that he was stretching her out on it, and she shuddered when she felt his hand start to travel, very slowly, up the inner side of her thigh.

"Carlo, the proxies," MacDonald muttered impatiently.

The sound of his voice jarred Barbara. She opened her eyes and tried to sit up, but Carlo pinned her to the divan, and she redoubled her effort.

He made a game of it, holding her on her back with one hand while the other continued to inch up her thigh.

Over his shoulder she caught a glimpse of Ian MacDonald, his eyes glistening behind his thick glasses, a drink in his hand as he sat only a few feet from them, taking in every detail of the spectacle.

The shock sickened Barbara, and her euphoria, created by sex play and liquor, instantly evaporated. Until this moment she had loved the feeling that she was behaving wickedly, but the realization that she and Carlo were performing for an audience of one made a travesty of the erotic adventure. She struggled still harder, but the flailing of her arms and thrashing of her legs accomplished nothing.

"You heard what the man said, sweetheart," Carlo murmured.

"First you sign some little pieces of paper, and then I'm going to ball you. Everybody's going to have a good time."

Barbara's one desire now was escape, and nothing was farther from her mind than her shares of Schwartzman-Burns stock. "No!" she cried.

Carlo misunderstood. "You heard what I said, sweetheart, and don't play innocent. You knew what to expect when you came here today."

What had been a sexual daydream was transformed into a nightmare, and there was no way she could free herself from his groping hand. Making a supreme effort to gather her disorganized thoughts, she remembered she had already signed the documents that Clothco had sent her. "The papers—are in—my bag!" It was difficult for her to catch her breath, even more difficult to speak.

Ian leaped to his feet, tore open her shoulder bag and, his facade cracking, said exuberantly, "She signed them, and even dated them!"

"Congratulations, sweetheart. Welcome to the team." Carlo laughed, then lowered his face to her breast.

"Let me go!" Barbara gasped.

Her partner's love-making immediately became more persuasive.

"Please!" She saw Ian, clutching her signed proxies, return to his chair.

Carlo was active in earnest now, and was trying to remove her dress and half-slip.

"You have what you want. Now let me go!" Barbara heard her voice becoming hysterical.

Ian, his triumph complete, leaned forward in his chair, drinking in every detail.

Carlo's touch became still firmer as he ignored his partner's protests.

Barbara was trapped in a conflicting agony of mounting desire and increasing revulsion. The balance maintained itself for what felt like an eternity, and she writhed in the helplessness she had wished on herself.

Ian's low laugh of satisfaction filled the room.

The sound of his voice broke the spell, and Barbara's sense of degradation snuffed out the erotic flame that had been burning brighter. The difference between consent in sex relations and outright rape became clear to her, and her terror became as great as her shame.

She fought harder, and when she could not escape, a shrill scream echoed through the apartment.

"Shut her up!" Ian said urgently.

Carlo was aware of the change that had taken place in her, and if left to his own devices would have released the woman, knowing neither could derive pleasure from the experience. But he, too, was trapped in a situation not of his own making, and, incapable of questioning the order, he hastened to obey it. It was not easy to subdue a woman whose frenzy had endowed her with greater strength, but he managed, nevertheless, to clamp a hand over her mouth.

Instinct alone guided Barbara, and she sank her teeth into the offending hand, biting so hard she tasted blood.

Carlo howled in pain, and with great effort finally succeeded in extricating his injured hand. In his rage the last of his caution deserted him, and he reached out with his free hand, slapping her across the face so hard that she tumbled from the divan onto the floor.

Barbara's panic gave her a resilience she had never before possessed, and she rolled out of Carlo's reach, hauled herself to her feet and made a wild dash for the front door, tugging up her dress as she ran in an attempt to regain a respectable appearance.

Ian shouted in alarm.

Carlo needed no warning, and, jumping to his own feet, ran after the woman.

But her desperation enabled her to accomplish what would have been impossible under ordinary circumstances. She opened the door and fled down the outer corridor to the elevator, and there, after frantically pressing the button to summon the cage, she managed to pull on her dress.

Carlo followed her into the corridor, intending to haul her back into the apartment, but Ian called something to him, and he desisted. His eyes black with hatred, he stood, nursing his injured hand and glaring at her.

Not until the elevator door closed behind her was Barbara able to take stock of her situation. Her half-slip was torn, but, as nearly as she could see, only an inch or two showed at one side beneath the hem of her skirt. The detail was trivial, however, and she was grateful that the dress itself seemed intact, so she could appear before others in it. She was still wearing her shoes and, as nearly as she could remember, had not removed them while in the apartment.

Unfortunately she had left her shoulder bag behind, but nothing would induce her to return for it, even though she wasn't carrying a penny. She had money at home, and the taxi driver who took her there would simply have to wait while she went upstairs for it. The side of her face burned, too, but she was scarcely aware of the discomfort and shrugged it off.

All that mattered to her at this moment was that she was safe, with her battered honor relatively intact. Her shame still enveloped her, but not until later would it overcome her; and it had not yet occurred to her to regret, with all her heart, that she had signed the proxies Ian MacDonald had wanted so badly. Not until she relived the scene would she realize that she could have achieved the final victory had she denied him his great prize by supporting Louis Burns.

The elevator came to a halt, the door opened and as Barbara emerged into the lobby of the apartment building, the real world took possession of her. She became conscious of her bedraggled appearance, and knew too that her walk was unsteady. But fear still gripped her, and she made her way to the street as quickly as she could.

The doorman frowned but having seen her come out of the building could not ask her to move off, and when she told him to summon her a taxi, he was compelled to obey.

Barbara stood at the curb waiting and tried in vain to shut out the stares of passing pedestrians. Everyone was gaping at her, she believed, but she could not hide and was as helpless now as she had been in Ian's apartment. For a few moments she closed her eyes, not realizing she was swaying perilously, and prayed that a taxi would stop for her.

She had no way of knowing, of course, that far fewer people even glanced in her direction than she imagined. Nor did she realize that one spectator, however, took in every detail of her appearance and situation.

Fran Black's vigil was rewarded, but she was stunned when she saw Barbara, whose smudged mascara, tousled hair and raw lips told their own story. It was obvious to Fran that her friend had consumed too much liquor. One of her shoulder straps was broken too, and a ragged length of her slip showed below her short skirt. One side of her face was suspiciously red; in short, she looked like a whore who had been on a binge.

Suddenly it occurred to Fran that Barbara was not carrying her white shoulder bag and probably needed money. The girl hastily left the tavern, but before she could reach the corner she saw a taxi pull up to the door of the apartment building, and Barbara drove away. Watching the taxi until it was swallowed by the Park Avenue traffic, Fran realized she knew too much.

She felt sure she could guess what had happened upstairs. Ian and Carlo had staged their usual act, and had used force when Barbara hadn't wanted to play. But there seemed to be nothing Fran could do to help her friend, and she decided that for the present she would keep her information to herself.

"The sons of bitches," she said aloud, surprising several pedestrians who thought she was addressing them.

PART
FOUR

Clothco sent out more than two thousand invitations, but no one was surprised when four thousand guests appeared, filling the first three floors of Schwartzman-Burns. They ate and drank vast quantities of canapes and liquor, and they kept scores of special police busy when, instead of using the many ashtrays provided for the occasion, they threw burning cigarette butts onto the rugs. Society leaders and politicians, dress designers and manufacturers, the staffs of fashion publications and business journals, celebrities from every walk of life and virtually everyone of importance in retail merchandising mingled with the many hundreds of flashily dressed nobodies who had a genius for showing up at such functions.

311 :

Everyone came to see and be seen, and at one time or another even the most insignificant of the guests were mistaken for fashion leaders, rock singers or collectors of ultramodern art. All of the in groups publicized by newspaper columnists were represented in strength, as were those who assiduously avoided the light of print. The expensively attired stood shoulder to shoulder with those who merely looked as though they had spent a fortune on their clothes, which was a far more difficult feat to achieve, and everyone tried to guess the price of what everyone else was wearing. So, in all, the cocktail party celebrating Clothco's acquisition of a major New York outlet was a resounding success.

Ian MacDonald and the corporation's directors held court near the jewelry department on the main floor, while the company's vice-presidents and other executives wandered where they pleased, looking after the guests whose welfare was important to their departmental activities. Paul Howell found himself burdened with few responsibilities, and after making certain that the architects and decorators with whom he was working had been given food and drink, he was on his own.

He deliberately shunned the larger presses of guests, and, staying in some of the outer aisles, was able to avoid the crowds. Occasionally he spoke briefly with one or another of the extravagantly dressed models whom he knew, but he, of all those present, did not feel in a celebratory mood.

He still associated Louis Burns with the store and couldn't help thinking of the man to whom the sale was a major tragedy. He hadn't seen Lou since the transfer but understood from his mother-in-law that the former owner was suffering his loss in stony silence and had become so lethargic that he had agreed without protest to move permanently to Florida.

But it was a personal problem of his own that occupied Paul and was in large part responsible for the sense of depression he could not shake off. Barbara, who was responsible for the store's sale, was conspicuous by her absence from the party, and those who missed her simply assumed that, as a member of the Burns family, she had diplomatically elected to remain at home rather than risk spoiling the party for those of Lou's friends who might be sensitive to such nuances. Paul allowed anyone who made the assumption to remain in ignorance.

The truth, which he revealed to no one, was that Barbara was too drunk to leave their apartment. The whole summer had been a nightmare, and he hadn't even allowed himself the hope that she might pull herself together for the occasion.

What he hated to admit to himself was that he couldn't tolerate much more of Barbara's outrageous conduct. He had no idea why she had suddenly slipped, given up her modeling and spent her days alone, drinking herself into a stupor. In fact, he couldn't be certain that any one incident or experience had sparked her fall from relative grace. It was Ann Burns's theory that her attempted comeback as a model had been a heavier strain on her emotions than anyone had realized and that she had cracked under it.

So far the two physicians treating her had been unable to bring about any improvement in her condition, and Paul was growing desperate. He had sent the children off to camp for the summer, which had provided a temporary solution for a delicate domestic problem, but they were returning home in a few days; unless Barbara made a miraculous recovery, which he considered highly improbable, he would be forced to send them to his mother-in-law's house to live for the present.

"Hi, Mr. Howell."

Paul came back to the present and smiled at the girl in the low-cut peasant blouse, who looked vaguely familiar. Her makeup and bearing identified her as a model, and all girls represented by the Howell Agency automatically assumed that he remembered them, even though he took no active part whatever in the business.

"I guess you don't remember me. I'm Fran Black—I came into freelancing from lingerie."

"Oh, sure. You've changed your makeup."

"Well, I'm wearing less of it. And I've had my hair cut—more like Barbara's."

313 :

He recalled, dimly, that before dropping her career Barbara had mentioned having become friendly with the girl.

"I've been looking for her today, but I haven't seen her around."

"She stayed at home," Paul said politely.

Fran cast a nervous glance over her shoulder. "Is she still—sick, Mr. Howell?"

"I'm afraid she isn't feeling any too well." The girl's expression told Paul she knew Barbara had been drinking.

"I've called her any number of times, but she just hasn't been well enough to get together for lunch or anything."

"We're hoping she'll be improved soon." Wanting to escape, or at least change the subject, Paul thought it odd that the girl should keep looking back toward the crowd in the center of the store.

"Mr. Howell, can I get together with you one of these days for a talk. I've had a rotten summer, and—"

"I'm afraid I have no hand in booking models these days."

"Oh, work is great, and since I've gotten thinner I'm doing lots of photographic modeling too. It isn't that. I—I just thought maybe you could drop up to my apartment for a few minutes after you finish at your office some evening."

Rarely had any model made such a direct pitch, and he wondered how to slam the door without hurting her feelings.

"It isn't what you think," Fran said. "I'll call you."

Before he could reply she was gone, and he noted with amused wonder that she chose a circuitous route to return to the group bunched in the jewelry aisle. In all probability she'd had a drink too many, he thought, but dismissed her from his mind when he caught a glimpse of one person he was pleased to see, emerging from the throng, and he hurried to her. "Marni!" he called.

Looking around in every direction but the right one, Marni didn't see him until he approached her, and she greeted him with equal warmth. "A real human being in all this mob!"

"You're looking lovely," he said, and meant it.

"I've always thought black was too severe for me, but Rosalie said chiffon has a softening effect, even in black, and she was right."

"You'd look terrific in anything." He noticed she was holding an empty highball glass. "May I get you another drink?"

"No, thanks. It's just ginger ale, anyway. I can't stand liquor at brawls like this."

Paul couldn't help wishing that Barbara felt as she did. "Aren't you enjoying yourself?"

"Don't tell anybody, but I'm having a horrible time. Maybe I'm just up-tight these days, but this is one of those times when everything bugs me. First I was standing with Ian, and it made me sick to hear the insincere slop all those people were handing him. Really, it's disgusting the way they fall all over him."

"That sort of thing has to be expected, Marni. Ian has become a very powerful man in the industry."

"Well, I couldn't listen to it, so I made the mistake of joining that other mob over there. And do you know what's going on in that ring of the circus?"

She was no less beautiful when she became indignant, Paul thought, but the essence of her charm was altered, and she looked like a little girl. "I can't imagine," he said, enjoying his first genuine chuckle in many days.

"Cleo is holding court. And it isn't that I'm jealous or anything, but she's become too much. It's a warm night, but the way she's dressed is outrageous. She's wearing a turban with a huge jewel set in the middle of it, and some furrier loaned her a fantastic floor-length leopard cape. Honestly, she looks like an African princess who has stepped right out of the jungle."

"Well," Paul said, "don't forget that being noticed is part of her job."

"But nobody wears a tight-fitting turban and a long leopard cape in the summer. She makes all models look ridiculous."

"Did you say you weren't jealous, Marni?" he asked quietly.

She stared at him for a moment, then reddened. "For one counterfeit subway token, I'd have myself some real hysterics, right here."

"Because Cleo has taken the spotlight away from you tonight?"

"Not really. It's—well, everything."

"I know what you mean."

Impulsively, she laid a hand on his arm. "I know, and I'm sorry, Paul."

He stiffened.

"Ian told me about Barbara. In confidence. I suppose he shouldn't have, but he knows I'm really fond of her."

"Don't worry about it. A secret like that is impossible to keep."

They looked at each other in silence, two troubled people drawing the balm of sympathy from each other.

"Paul." Marni became breathless. "Would you do something for me?"

"Anything I can."

"Take me out of here."

"Of course." He'd thought of asking her to have dinner with him, but had assumed she had come with Ian. Come to think of it, no harm would be done by clearing the air first. "You didn't come with anybody?"

"Not exactly, and I'm free to leave whenever I please."

"All right. We'll have dinner somewhere—"

"That's part of what I had in mind. I mean, it's an off-beat idea."

He guessed she intended to suggest one of the new restaurants that specialized in a weird setting.

"I thought we could stop at a supermarket that's open late, and get all kinds of things we like. Then we can take them back to my place, and I'll cook dinner for us."

"I don't want you going to all that trouble, Marni."

"But it wouldn't be trouble, and I'd really like to do it. Honestly, Paul. I'm fed right up to here with all the chi-chi people and empty talk and insincere kissing everybody else hello. And I just couldn't eat if I saw this same crowd in a restaurant, which is what would happen. Everybody looks alike these days."

"By all means, then, we'll go up to your apartment."

"This is just what I need." Marni linked her arm through his, and they started toward the men's wear section, where a cloakroom had been set up. "You can't imagine how much I've been longing for home cooking—even my own—in a kitchen that needs to be painted."

They retrieved her lightweight wool shrug from the cloakroom and made their way through the crowds toward the store's main exit on Fifth Avenue.

They were not able to leave without attracting attention, however. Ian MacDonald had been keeping Marni in sight, and when he realized she was departing he murmured an apology and excused himself from a group that included a member of congress, the board chairman of a rival department-store chain and a middle-aged motion-picture actress whose appearance in a hit Broadway musical had revived her career.

Carlo Bennett, always on duty as a major functionary, immediately detached himself from a small group nearby and joined his superior.

"Marni is going." In spite of his extreme agitation, Ian remembered to keep his voice lowered.

Carlo glanced toward the cloakroom, then averted his face to conceal his secret smile of pleasure. "So she is," he replied calmly.

"With Paul Howell."

"Yes, I see them, Ian."

"Do something about it!"

Carlo did not move. "What would you suggest?"

"There must be some way." Ian was growing frantic.

"Sure, I can think of plenty. I can slug Howell, which would create a distraction. Or I could try dragging her back here by the hair, in which case he'd slug me." Carlo was enjoying a rare opportunity to strike back at his employer and was making the most of it.

"I won't tolerate this!" Ian, always in command of himself, was in danger of losing his temper.

"What's happening, boss? Is your bird standing you up?"

"Marni is not my bird. And we had no formal engagement for this evening, but I was taking it for granted that she'd have dinner with me after the party."

"It looks," Carlo replied, no hint of his gloating attitude in his voice, "like she wasn't taking it for granted and had a few ideas of her own."

"But with Howell!" Ian hated all handsome men.

Carlo could not resist his chance to unleash a knockout punch. "Well, maybe he's got something you haven't."

Ian became waxen. "What's that supposed to mean?" he demanded, clenching his fists.

Carlo shrugged.

"Answer me, you goddam—"

"Calm down, Ian. People are looking at you."

"I won't take that kind of insult from anyone."

"You don't have to—from anybody but me. You and I are the only ones who know certain—ah—facts of life, so don't get into an uproar. That couldn't be why the Kendall broad is leaving. She doesn't know that side of you. Yet."

"She never will."

Again Carlo shrugged, and then spoke softly. "Has it struck you, the way it just did me, that maybe Howell has picked up some of his lush wife's story?"

"Of course not. That's why she's drinking." Ian could not think of Barbara without feeling upset.

"Don't be so damn sure. Howell is as smart as they come, and maybe he's found a way to hit back that'll really give it to you."

Ian made no reply, but looked as though he had been kicked in the groin.

Carlo had observed him in many situations through the years, and had come to believe him impervious to the emotional weaknesses that plagued other, lesser people. It was obvious that Marni Kendall had penetrated the armor of his self-reliance and had exposed him as vulnerable to the pain that ordinary mortals felt.

Two large candles furnished the only illumination, and Paul used the closer on his side of the kitchen table to light their cigarettes. "That's the first time in weeks I've had any appetite."

"Me too," Marni said. "My weight will be up tomorrow, and I'll hate myself."

"It wouldn't do you any harm to put on as much as two to three pounds."

"I like to hold myself a little under my ceiling so I can splurge every once in a while on a meal like this. I hadn't touched potatoes in a year."

"And what potatoes. I've always loved them with bacon, but you really shoot the works. Onions, cream—"

"Stop, Paul. I was just beginning to feel comfortable again."

"Okay, you've got to save room for some of that cognac we brought back."

"Cognac on top of the Bordeaux is too much."

"A little won't hurt you, and neither will I. You don't have to be on your guard with me, Marni."

She met his steady gaze. "I know," she said. "Thank you."

"Your danger from me is far more subtle, but it isn't a safe subject. Where did you learn to become such an expert cook?"

"My mother brought me up to be a solid, middle-class Ohio housewife, not a symbol of glamour to empty-headed females who don't know any better. Now, what's my danger from you?"

Paul twirled his empty wineglass. "You must realize that Barbara and I have about had it. Maybe the fault is mine, and sometimes I kick myself for not giving her encouragement and help when she tried to go back to modeling—even though she claimed she wanted no help from me. But even if I'm to blame—"

"I don't see how you could be."

"—I can't go on this way without losing my own sanity. And that leaves me wide open, Marni." Paul fished another cigarette from his pack and lighted it. "I don't wear tin wings, and I don't own a halo. As you may have heard, I did some playing around not long ago."

Her silence indicated that she knew of his affair with Cleo.

"I don't regret what I've done, and I offer no excuses. The only reason I'm even mentioning it is because I'd be tempted to have an affair with you too, but I wouldn't."

She tried, feebly, to make a joke of the assertion. "Should I be insulted?"

"You aren't mistress material," he said, refusing to be distracted. "You're the marrying kind."

She became tense too. "So I've been learning."

"But regardless of whether you'd want me," Paul continued doggedly, "I don't know whether I'll ever be in a position to offer marriage to anyone. I have no idea what will become of Barbara, and I'd be the worst kind of heel if I divorced her when she's sick. Not to mention the fact that I'm one hell of a lot older than you and have two growing children."

"That's the nicest nonproposal I've ever had." Marni sounded wistful.

"You and I have had a potential for something, and I've recognized it for a very long time."

"So have I."

"I've seen that too," he said.

"At first I thought it was just the mutual attraction of two narcissistic, beautiful people who could feed each other's need for admiration. But it's much more than that. We have an instinctive two-way sympathy that almost makes it possible to read each other's minds."

She was exaggerating, Paul knew, but he recognized the enthusiastic prerogative of youth and did not correct her.

"I know where I stand with you," Marni said, "which is more than I know about anything else in my life. Which is why I'd probably agree if you tried to make out with me."

"Don't say things like that." He started to reach across the table for her hand, but drew back. "Make another leading remark like that, and I won't be responsible for the consequences."

Her weary smile suddenly made her look much older than her years. "Oh, I'm just playing at being daring. Rosalie is due home at any time, so I know I'm safe."

He had completely forgotten her roommate and was simultaneously relieved and disappointed.

"To me," Marni said, "the danger I'm in is that it would be easy to convince myself I'm in love with you."

"Now it's my turn to be insulted."

She smiled fleetingly, but immediately sobered again. "You're the only man I've ever known who understands and accepts me the way I am. All the others fall into categories. There's my father's type. They think beauty is a lot of bilge water, and they not only can't appreciate my need for admiration, but they insist I conform to the old virtues. Which I can't, much as I respect them. Then there's David's type. They intellectualize everything and try to destroy the beauty myth by rationalizing it to death. Except when it comes to the admiration they need. Hurt their egos and they wither away."

She was proving herself a better judge of character than Paul had realized.

"And the most complicated is Ian's type. They build up the glamour cult and make more of it. I shouldn't talk about Ian, but I know I can trust you. And he's even more complex than the others who are like him, sort of. In some crazy way I don't dig, he associates himself with the admiration I get for being pretty."

"That makes sense," Paul said. "The best way for him to avoid the curse of his ugliness is to be seen with someone who looks like you."

"Oh, there's more to him than that."

"I'm aware of a great deal more," Paul replied dryly.

"May I tell you something? I will, anyway. Ian wants me to marry him, and sometimes I think I'm weakening."

Paul was startled. "But he's years older than I am."

"This sounds nutty, I know, but I don't think of him as being so much older, any more than I see his ugliness."

"There's more than his physical appearance. I've seen him at close quarters for some time, and I don't mind telling you he's an operator, who can be mean and tricky when he's crossed."

"Not to me. I've never seen him that way."

Paul stiffened. "I'm wasting my breath if you're in love."

Marni laughed. "But I'm not! How could I be?"

He watched the second hand on the electric clock over the stove make a complete cycle. "Let's have that cognac, shall we?"

She took two miniature snifters from a cupboard and wiped them, while he uncorked the bottle.

They resumed their seats, and after pouring brandy into their glasses, Paul offered a toast. "Here's to you and me, two people who'd have been far happier in life if we hadn't been cursed from birth with good looks."

They took small, ritualistic sips, and then Marni placed her glass on the table. "I'd like to explain something. The way I see it, I could live a well-balanced life as Ian's wife. I could work or not, as I see fit—"

"If you're tired of modeling, quit. You needn't escape into marriage to a wealthy man."

"That isn't it, Paul. I don't know what I want to do about my career. I love all the glamour, phony though it is, but I hate the scratching and gouging. If it isn't Cleo I'm battling, it will be someone else."

"How would you stop all that?"

"Ian could keep me at the top through his own advertising and through his friends."

"For a time."

"Long enough to satisfy me. And after I retire I'd have all the admiration I want and need from him. Meanwhile I'd be giving him what he seems to want so badly, a tie with beauty."

"Ownership, I'd call it." Paul was concentrating, and couldn't appreciate the aromatic cognac. "I dislike clichés, but I don't know any other way to say this. You pay for whatever you get in this world, and beauty isn't an expendable commodity."

"But it is, if you can buy security with it, and alternatives that give you freedom of action, and all the adulation you crave."

"That's a big 'if,' " he said.

"I haven't mentioned happiness," Marni protested. "For a little while, anyway, I'd be much happier with you."

"Sure, we'd be ecstatic—until we began to compete for the spotlight."

"Is that what happened to you and Barbara? Forgive me for being tactless—"

"We're both being honest, so it's a fair question. No, you and I wouldn't turn sour in the same way. Our problem is that our strength would be our weakness. We're far too much alike. Even our ambitions are similar—we want recognition more than achievement. After a couple of years we'd hate each other."

Marni's deep sigh indicated her reluctant agreement.

"I'm not going to predict what would happen to you if you married Ian MacDonald. But I do warn you to think carefully before you make the wrong move."

"Oh, I will. And maybe you and I might find a way together, in spite of all the obstacles."

"I know why you said that. You know I can't start to make love to you right now, no matter what, because you just heard your roommate coming in the front door. But one of these days both of us may weaken at the same time—and then—look out!"

Louis Burns stretched out on the chaise beside the swimming pool, the New York newspapers on the grass beside him, his face raised to the sun. His sports shirt, shorts and knee socks were new, but he spoiled their effect with a shabby pair of bedroom slippers, and clouds of smoke that were emitted from the cigar held in his clenched teeth occasionally obscured his face from the bright Florida sun.

"Here you are," Audrey said, standing over him. She, too, was wearing a shirt and shorts, and she thumped a bag of golf clubs on the ground for emphasis.

"Where else would I be?" Her husband did not open his eyes.

"You ought to put something on your nose, or it will peel again."

"Let it peel. That way we have something to talk about." He blew another cloud of smoke.

She studied him in silence for a moment. "I'm glad you're wearing your new outfit."

"It was the best way to make you stop hounding at me." He took a pair of dark sunglasses from his breast pocket and put them on before opening his eyes, even though he knew they annoyed her. Allegedly they hid his expression, but, as he had told her, there was nothing for her to see. "We carried shirts like this for eight to ten dollars less, and the shorts I wouldn't have had in the store. Some of the merchants down here are digging their own graves, getting pirates' prices for shoddy products."

"I know you stocked that brand of shorts," Audrey said sharply, "so don't make another issue out of absolutely nothing, Lou."

"Anything else?"

"Yes, I hope you aren't going to play golf in those disreputable slippers."

"Who says I'm going to play golf? I think I'll stay right here all morning. When a man is retired he can do whatever he wants. I read that someplace."

"Lou, you promised!" She looked at him in concern. "You won't get any pleasure out of anything unless you stir yourself. The cook told me you didn't eat your bacon and eggs—"

"In climate like this, I don't have an appetite. Up home, it'll be getting cool soon. There a man could eat!"

"Do you want to go back? We still have the apartment." Audrey's voice was unexpectedly gentle.

"No," he said sharply. "We kept the apartment for the children, so let them use it. We're here now, and here we'll stay."

She sat on the foot of the chaise and put her hand over his. "I was watching you from the bedroom."

"Don't tell me you're that desperate. You must have something better to do."

"Lou, you were reading the accounts of MacDonald's party at the store again. I'm going to burn those newspapers."

"All my friends showed up," he said angrily. "Not one of them had the decency to stay away."

"Barbara didn't go. Ann said so in her letter."

"Barbara. Maybe she was choking on her guilts." His cigar had gone out, and he took his gold lighter from his pocket. "What kills me is thinking of what that mob did to my carpets and drapes. The liquor stains, the ashes, the cigarette butts—"

"They're MacDonald's carpets now. Let him worry about them."

"Do you realize," he demanded, "that in the second-floor Designer Salon I paid $18.95 a square yard for the carpets, and that was the wholesale price?"

"Lou!"

He pocketed the lighter unopened and dropped the cigar into a large ashtray on the ground. "Say it. I'm getting senile. But old habits die hard."

Audrey stared at a rustling palm frond. "I'm going to order us a fishing boat for tomorrow morning. What time would you like to go out?"

"I'll make the arrangements."

She was pleased by his sudden spark of interest.

"But not for tomorrow. Next week, maybe. Besides, what good are more fish? The freezers are filled, and there's no more room on the walls for more mounted specimens."

Audrey's expression became bleak.

"I'm a trial, I know." He stroked her hand. "Stop fussing over me, and you'll be happier. Why don't you give a little dinner party some night next week?"

"You hate them."

"At least we'll be seeing people, and for one night we won't be snapping at each other."

"Is there anyone you'd particularly like me to invite?"

"Out of season we've got to take what we can get. But we're lucky. That fellow Johnson from the bank in New York is down for a visit—"

"We don't know either of the Johnsons very well."

"Ask them," he said, an unexpected note of authority in his voice.

She found his vehemence surprising, but made no comment.

"We owe a couple of the Miami department-store owners, too," he said.

"But you've been avoiding them. You said you didn't want to be reminded—"

"I can't avoid them forever, and I have a right to change my mind."

Audrey looked at him.

Louis immediately averted his gaze.

"Lou!"

Slowly, with great reluctance, he turned back to her.

"What are you up to?"

"Nothing. Yet." For the first time he became animated, and a smile spread across his face. "All that money I got from MacDonald when he bought me out is just sitting, not doing anybody any good. So I've been thinking."

She watched him apprehensively.

"I've got a couple of ideas. But right off, let me tell you I know you won't approve. MacDonald tried to get a promise out of me—in the agreement of sale—that I wouldn't go into business in any other New York store. But I told him to stuff it, and he was so anxious to buy me out that he went ahead anyway."

"No, Lou. You can't—"

"I happen to know that Johnson is close to the owners of a couple of major retail stores. And I can't see *any* store turning down a combination of my know-how and an investment of several million. I'd give MacDonald a run for his money! In two years—three, call it, to be on the safe side—he'd be losing so much he'd have to sell Schwartzman-Burns or close down."

"If you start all over again, you'll kill yourself in a year. You wouldn't live to beat him."

Louis was so engrossed in his own thoughts that he did not hear his wife's protest. "There's only one trouble with the idea. I'd need complete control, one hundred percent, to handle operations in my own way. But you know how orthodox that New York crowd is, and nobody would want to start a feud with Clothco. So I might not get the kind of deal I'd want."

Audrey grew a trifle calmer. "It certainly doesn't sound that way."

"All the same, it can't do any harm to look into the situation, so I thought I'd have a little talk with Johnson and ask him to do some snooping for me."

Audrey realized what she should have seen instantly, that he was indulging in a daydream to cushion the blow of his involuntary retirement. "By all means," she said, "talk to Mr. Johnson and explore the idea with him. I'll definitely put the Johnsons on the list for next week's dinner."

"Well. You've come around to my way faster than I thought you would. Doing nothing for the rest of our lives doesn't appeal to you so much either. Huh?"

"I hadn't thought about it in those terms," she said, "but you may be right."

Louis sat upright, lowering his feet to the ground. "Listen to my other idea. I can't use the Schwartzman-Burns name in New York. But what's to stop me from running a store down here and calling it Schwartzman-Burns? Nothing!" He was enjoying his small triumph.

"The Schwartzman family—"

"I'll give a few shares to some of them," he said carelessly. "For a couple of bucks they'll jump through hoops for me."

Audrey now knew, beyond all doubt, that he was weaving a fantasy out of whole cloth. The Schwartzman heirs despised his arrogance, and for a decade their relations with him had been strained. They had supported him in his unsuccessful effort to retain control of the store only because they had been convinced that their best interests had been identical to his own. But those ties no longer existed, and Audrey felt positive they would refuse to become associated with him in any new venture.

Her husband was both lively and genial, however, and she had no intention of spoiling his mood with a dose of reality. "You've always known how to handle them," she murmured.

"You bet I have! Now, here's the best part. I'm not stupid, so I know that at my age it would be too much of a struggle to open a brand-new store down here. There's too much competition. So I'll do something much better. I'll make a deal for a first-class store that's already in business and making money. I'll let the present owners keep a minority interest to shut them up. Then Clothco had better watch out!"

He was becoming so expansive that Audrey confined herself to an encouraging smile and nod, but said nothing.

"A Schwartzman-Burns in Florida can become the showplace retail store in America," Louis declared. "I'll use so many merchandising innovations that the industry will be dizzy. And what will MacDonald be doing? Sweating plenty. Everything I do will be different from the way his chain does it. Thousands of the New York store's customers come down to Florida every year, and they'll go back home expecting the same service and prices I'll give them here. I'll turn MacDonald's whole operation inside out, and he'll have to change every last one of his policies. I'll guarantee it!"

She watched him as he exuberantly unwrapped a fresh cigar and lighted it. "You built your reputation on solid merchandising ideas," she murmured, parroting a phrase she had heard him use many times.

"Exactly!" He beamed at her. "This is the best tasting cigar I've had in weeks."

"I'll certainly ask the Miami store people to dinner too. If you like, we can have a series of small dinners, inviting just one store couple at a time. Then you can concentrate better."

"That's my girl," he said fondly.

Audrey returned his broad smile. "Of course," she said carefully, "I'm sure you know you won't get results overnight."

"When I'm onto something good, I don't waste time."

If his bubble broke too soon, he would become even more unbearable than he had been, and her one desire was to nourish the dream. "What I mean," she said, "is that a Miami store owner won't want to sell out to you. At least, not at first."

"Look, I know from my own experience how they'll feel. I'll have to use plenty of persuasion, but I'm good at it."

She agreed and was relieved when he failed to detect her lack of sincerity.

"When I make up my mind that I'm going to get something, I don't let anything stand in my way. So it's as good as done." Louis stood and stretched. "Who did you get to play with us this morning? And we'd better hurry over if we're going to get to the first tee on schedule. You know how fussy the club gets when members are late."

Few members of Clothco's office staff had ever seen Ian Mac-Donald remove his glasses for more than the few moments it took him to clean them. But a handful of employees who had joined the corporation at its inception claimed that in the early days, when the company's future had been questionable, the president frequently had dropped his glasses into a pocket at times of great crisis.

Everyone joked about the topic, and Paul remembered the feeble humor when Ian came into his office quite early one morning, made a few comments about inconsequential matters and then, sitting abruptly, put away his glasses. "Paul," he said, "I've been going through hell trying to decide whether to have a very private chat with you. But I've finally come to the conclusion that I must, even though I know you'll resent me for it."

Instantly on his guard, Paul nevertheless observed the amenities. "Why don't you try me and see?"

"I will. My interests give me no choice. I thought of sitting down with you elsewhere than in the office, since this has nothing to do with Clothco, but I didn't want to magnify something that can be handled very simply."

"We're all inclined to complicate our problems," Paul said, making conversation.

"At our cocktail party the other evening, I saw you leaving rather early. With Marni Kendall."

So that was it. "Yes, we felt we'd outlived our usefulness there."

"I know you're a happily married man, so I don't want to appear critical," Ian said. "But I couldn't help wondering whether Marni's reputation was damaged."

"What we did was her business and mine," Paul declared, his calm unruffled.

"In a sense, it's also my business. You see, I've become very much interested in Marni."

"So I understand," Paul said, but did not elaborate. It was obvious that MacDonald wanted to ask what Marni had said about him, but knew he would be rebuffed if he went that far.

"Then you see my position."

"No, all I see is that her reputation wasn't what worried you. I'd say you're afraid I've interfered with whatever claim you believe you may have."

"That's putting it rather crudely, perhaps—"

"How would you put it, Ian?" In spite of his determination to control his temper, Paul felt annoyed. His dislike for MacDonald was so intense he wished they could confine their relationship to matters that directly concerned Clothco.

"Marni's welfare has become vital to me. I'll grant you that she's given me no right to act as her protector—"

"But you'd like to assume that right."

"Well, yes. In a manner of speaking."

"In that case," Paul said, "I have seniority. Let me remind you that Marni is represented by the Howell Agency—"

"In which you're no longer active."

"You're right, I'm not. But I broke Marni in as a model, and I advised her on every step that led her to the top."

Ian sat back, relief in his myopic eyes. "Then your relationship is financial."

"I'm taking only a token percentage of the agency's profits these days. What I get from Marni's income wouldn't buy her one good dinner."

Hatred appeared in Ian's eyes for an instant, but he quickly masked his feelings. "You confuse me."

"You confuse yourself by snooping. If Marni were my mistress, which she isn't, that would be her business and mine, and your interference would be unwarranted."

"I'd do anything I thought necessary to break up an affair."

Paul realized he wasn't threatening, but was stating a fact. Marni's life would be unenviable if she married a man with his violently jealous disposition, and for her sake it might be wise to put the record straight. "Long before she met you, Marni was my good friend as well as my client. And whenever she marries, no matter whether it's you or someone else, I hope we'll still be friends."

"I've always questioned the friendship of a man and woman, especially when they're both handsome."

He had a valid argument, but Paul wasn't willing to concede it. "Everybody is entitled to his own standards."

"We're getting nowhere." Ian reached into his pocket for his glasses, and his manner became more authoritative when he donned them. "I was hoping you'd agree to stop seeing her—socially, that is—when you knew my intentions toward her and became aware of your own somewhat compromising position."

"I don't give up important friendships for the convenience of third parties."

Ian's face darkened. "You make this difficult for all of us."

"If it means so much to you, why don't you speak to Marni?" Paul knew he was being cruel, that MacDonald wouldn't have the courage to suggest openly that Marni should stop seeing a friend.

"I came to you as one gentleman to another," Ian said, rising, "and I hoped we could reach an understanding in a spirit of accommodation for Marni's best interests."

"We may not agree on what's best for her, and since she's an adult, I prefer to let her make her own decisions."

"I keep my private life and Clothco's affairs separated," Ian said loftily, "but I won't forget this."

The door closed and Paul laughed; but his irritation was unalleviated, and he found it difficult to keep his mind on his paper work. MacDonald's gall was boundless, and it wasn't easy to understand what any woman could see in him. Other than his money. Certainly Marni was too good for him, and Paul promised himself that, if another opportunity arose, he would use whatever influence he exerted to persuade her not to marry the man.

His secretary buzzed him. "That model, Fran Black, is calling you again, Mr. Howell."

"Get rid of her," Paul said.

"I've used every excuse I know, but this is at least her sixth call in the past couple of days, and—"

"All right, I'll do it myself." He flipped a switch. "Yes?"

"Mr. Howell, I'm not chasing you," Fran said, hoping to make her point quickly. "This is about Barbara. I went up to see her day before yesterday, and—well, I hadn't known how bad off she is. I've got to see you. About her."

Paul sighed, glanced at his watch and knew the morning was shot. "Where are you now?"

"At home. I—"

"What's the address?" He scribbled her reply on a scratch pad. "I'll be there in ten minutes." Hanging up, he told himself he was wasting time. But on the other hand he wasn't accomplishing anything constructive at the moment, and he could always tell himself, later, that he had done everything within his power for Barbara.

Crosstown traffic proved to be light, and he reached the brownstone building a block from the East River without delay. There were five apartments, one on each floor of the old, narrow structure, but Paul was not fooled by appearances. In any other city the building would be classified as near-slum housing, but here, because of its location, it was in great demand. Fran Black undoubtedly paid a large rent, so perhaps she had been telling him the truth about her improved modeling situation.

The girl greeted him in a sweater and pants cuffed with frivolous bells that were in striking contrast with her grave demeanor. "You'll have to excuse the way the place looks," she said, "but I just moved in recently, and I don't have everything straightened out yet."

The decor of the apartment meant nothing to him, and he said so.

"Could I get you a drink or some coffee, maybe?"

He started to refuse, but she was so nervous he took pity on her. "Coffee would be fine," he said.

"It's ready." It pleased Fran that he had accepted her hospitality, and she managed a smile as she hurried off to her small kitchen, returning in a few moments with two steaming mugs. "Sit there," she said. "It's the most comfortable chair in the house."

Paul thanked her and tried to curb his impatience.

"Day before yesterday I finally got tired of the runaround Barbara was giving me, so I went up to see her. She was bombed out of her mind."

He hoped she hadn't brought him here to tell him the obvious. "She's that way every day."

"I know why," Fran said, and waited until he stared at her. "Before I start, I need your promise that you'll never tell anybody I talked to you. Anybody at all."

Apparently she was one of those girls who needed to inject drama into her life, and he was willing to oblige. "Fair enough," he said.

"Before I started to make out in freelancing, I had to scrounge around for a buck sometimes. Like, when I was in lingerie."

"I understand."

She sucked in her breath, making it evident she was wearing no bra beneath her sweater. "How well do you know Ian MacDonald, Mr. Howell? Or his pal, Carlo Bennett?"

The unexpected questions startled him.

"That chair you're sitting in was a present from Ian. So are most of the other good pieces I have. I call them presents, I mean, but that's a gasser. I earned them. On my back."

Her confession made him uncomfortable.

"No matter what you're thinking, that isn't how it was." Fran launched into a detailed account of what had been required of her on her visits to the MacDonald apartment.

Paul's growing disgust made him restless.

: 334

Aware of his reaction, the girl cut short her recital. "Now we come to Barbara," she said.

His expression mirrored his feeling of disbelief.

"I've got to tell it to you like it was. From where I saw it. Until the day before yesterday, I thought they were after the usual. Only, when I saw Barbara and told her I had an idea of what happened, she said something about stock. She was so stoned she made no sense to me, but maybe you know."

"Schwartzman-Burn stock?" Paul's mind was racing.

Fran shrugged.

"Tell me in your own way."

"You see all the furniture on that side of the room?" she asked, her manner apprehensive. "I got that as a bonus, and a whole new summer wardrobe, too, for doing a different sort of job for Ian." She could not meet his gaze, and, her voice dropping, she told him how she had been required to carry the news of his affair with Cleo to Barbara. His silence was even more unsettling than the wild anger she had anticipated, and when she finished her story she stole a glance at him.

Paul sat motionless, his face drained of all expression.

"I didn't want to do it. But Ian is an arm-twister, and I was afraid to turn him down. Even so, if I'd known what—"

"Tell me everything," Paul said, biting off each word.

She resumed with an account of what had taken place on the day she had dropped in on Barbara, omitting no detail.

Paul continued to sit very quietly after Fran described her friend's appearance upon emerging from MacDonald's apartment house.

"That's it, Mr. Howell. The very next day I called her to see if she wanted to make the rounds of the photographers with me. She said she wasn't feeling so good, but I didn't know until later that it was then she started the boozing."

He nodded and stood.

Something in his manner that Fran could not identify caused her to shiver. "I'm sorrier than you'll ever guess, Mr. Howell."

"If it hadn't been you, they'd have found somebody else." He was unaware of the hoarse, metallic quality of his own voice. "You were stuck, and I'm not blaming you."

"Jeez, I thought I'd have to get another agency—"

He interrupted her with a reassuring pat on the shoulder. "That won't be necessary. There isn't much loyalty in the world, and I'll see to it that you won't suffer. But stay away from MacDonald and his boy from now on."

"You don't have to tell me that!" She didn't know whether to laugh or cry.

He walked to the door and opened it. "You and I haven't seen each other," he said, and was gone.

Fran leaned against the wall, rubbing her arms and feeling unaccountably cold, even though her sweater was made of thick wool.

Paul couldn't remember walking several blocks until he found a taxi, and he had no memory of his ride home. When he opened the door of his apartment, however, everything came into sharp focus, although he had formed no plan of speech or action.

He found Barbara in their bedroom, still in her nightgown and negligee. She was sitting at her dressing table, making up, and the streaked base and smudged eyeliner told him she had already started her day's drinking.

She achieved a wan smile. "You're home early. Aren't you feeling well?"

"I know, Barb," he said.

She continued to look at his reflection in the mirror for a moment or two, and then, her gaze faltering, she covered her face with her hands.

Paul went to her and gripped her shoulder. "People who live in glass houses are in no position to take baths in the window. You'll hear no sermons from me. We'll manage."

Barbara trembled and was unable to lift her head.

"You don't have to talk about it."

"There's just one thing," she said, speaking with difficulty, "I'd like you to know. I didn't quite—go all the way. No credit to me. Because I might as well have."

Paul swallowed hard. "Was it your Schwartzman-Burns stock they wanted?"

"Partly, but I'd already signed the proxies and gave them to Ian. He didn't even have to ask me for them."

He still didn't understand MacDonald's motives but was afraid to ask any more questions when Barbara was in such an emotional state.

"I guess," she continued, her voice so muffled that he could scarcely make out what she was saying, "they wanted more than the proxies. Me."

The pity she aroused in him was deeper than anything he had felt in a long time. "You'll have to stop living with this thing," he said. "We could take a trip—"

"There's no place I want to go."

He stared at the back of her head, and, knowing she had only one real interest, tried again. "If you'll let me help you, we can plan a campaign for you—"

"No!" Barbara raised her head, and still unable to face him, looked with bleary, unseeing eyes at the far wall, where a number of her framed magazines covers from earlier years were on display. "Ian got me every last job I had. That's the worst of it. I wouldn't have been hired by anyone if it hadn't been for him. I've had it! So why substitute your influence for his? Nobody wants a model who has grown old and plain."

She wouldn't believe him, Paul knew, if he tried to convince her she was still beautiful.

"Anyway, why should you help me? Oh, I know you were no saint, but you didn't run off to orgies. When I let you down, I made a total mess of everything."

"Both of us need new perspectives—"

"I can't listen now." She clamped her hands over her ears.

He realized she was inundated by new waves of guilt in the wake of his discovery, and needed time to regain some measure of balance before she would be able to take part in a sensible and realistic discussion of the future.

Barbara started to speak again but bit her lip instead. Then, pushing back her chair, she sought the refuge of her unmade bed, where she buried her face in her pillow.

For a long time Paul looked at her, his own thoughts confused. Perhaps it was just as well that he would never know what had happened at MacDonald's apartment. In spite of his own shame and anger, he had no desire to hurt her. He had no reason to be surprised by her inability to protect herself from emotional injury or to handle the disposition of her store stock in an adult manner. She had been an adolescent when he had married her, and through the years she had shown few signs of maturation. She needed someone to take care of her, but she alone could decide whether she wanted him to bear that responsibility.

Her deep, even breathing indicated that she had fallen asleep, so it was possible that she had consumed more liquor than her condition had indicated.

"I'll be back shortly," Paul said as he started toward the door.

Barbara neither replied nor stirred.

On the taxi ride back to the Clothco offices in midtown, Paul's mood changed, and he discovered that his spirits were rising. The doubts of months were clearing away, and he knew not only what had to be done, but what he wanted to do. The fog had lifted, and his relief was so great that a hint of a smile appeared at the corners of his mouth.

First he went to his own office, and after sending his secretary to fetch several cardboard cartons, he methodically packed his personal belongings. Then he removed his jacket, placing it on a hanger in his closet and went down the executive corridor in his shirtsleeves. Ian MacDonald's office was his goal, but he saw Carlo Bennett at work and revised his schedule, not caring which of them he confronted initially.

Carlo saw him, grinned and waved.

Paul stepped inside the office, closing the door behind him. "Stand up!" he commanded.

Carlo blinked in astonishment, but made no move.

Paul rounded the desk, hauled him to his feet with his left hand and struck simultaneously with his right. The blow traveled only a short distance, but there was so much force behind it that, catching Carlo on the cheekbone, it sent him crashing against the wall.

He stood there, stunned.

"A woman who opens herself to seduction, no matter who she is," Paul said conversationally, "gets what's coming to her. But I don't like it when my wife is made to play dirty games against her will." Not waiting for a reply, he lashed out again at short range, his left driving into the pit of the other man's stomach, his right again finding its target on his cheekbone.

Carlo clamped a hand to his bruised face. "You've got it all wrong. It isn't my fault that—"

A sharp left jab to the mouth split his lip and silenced him. Paul followed with a flurry of blows, but felt no satisfaction in administering the beating. Although he hadn't used his fists in years, he instinctively recalled his college training as a boxer, and discovered he was as interested in his own technique as he was in the punishment he was inflicting. Bennett was a puppet who didn't deserve even contempt wasted on him.

Even puppets reacted to pain, however, and Bennett at last retaliated with a succession of right hooks.

But Paul fended off the blows without difficulty and was privately elated that he was fighting a man who telegraphed his punches. They circled the office, knocking over chairs and a standing ashtray, both men weaving and ducking, although only Paul landed substantial blows.

Blood streamed from Carlo's swollen upper lip and a cut on his cheekbone, and one eye was half-closed. But he continued to absorb punishment, returning again and again for another exchange.

Paul had formed no precise plan in advance, and even now he had no idea when he might call a halt. In one sense he had already won the unequal fight, but he had no desire to stop and dimly realized he would not feel any real gratification until he knocked the man unconscious.

A clicking sound, soft but distinct, cut through the heavy breathing of the two men, and something gleamed in Carlo's right hand.

Almost too late Paul realized his foe had produced a switchblade, and when Bennett slashed at him in a vicious, sweeping arc, he barely managed to catch the wrist and lower portion of the hand that held the knife.

Cursing and sobbing, Carlo tried to break free and strike again.

But Paul knew that the fist fight had degenerated into a far more serious contest, that his life might depend upon his ability to gain control of the blade. Although Carlo was pummeling him with his free hand, he paid no attention to the blows and concentrated on the knife.

They fell to the floor together, rolling over and over, and Paul finally managed to pull the blade from his opponent's grasp. It fell to the floor, and Bennett made a frantic effort to retrieve it. But Paul reached it first and threw it across the room. It clattered against the wall, then bounced under the desk, coming to rest out of the antagonists' sight.

The nature of the fight was changed again, and Paul held a natural advantage, but Carlo's desperation gave him added strength, and he punched, clawed and kicked violently, even trying to bite Paul's ear as they grappled at close quarters.

Until now Paul had been able to maintain a rigid self-control, his only feeling the mild satisfaction of a man who was seeking and obtaining some measure of justice. But his temper snapped under Bennett's vicious, unorthodox assault, and a cold fury possessed him. No longer thinking coherently, he was filled with an overpowering desire to crush his opponent, and he became indifferent to questions of right and wrong, good and evil.

He could satiate his blood lust only by destroying his foe, and he lost consciousness of his reasoning skill as a boxer. All of his strength went into every blow as he drove his fists into Bennett's face and body, and when he broke free, he quickly rose to his feet.

Carlo remained on the floor, a low moan indicating his willingness to concede the victory.

But Paul still yearned for the ultimate gratification. Hauling Bennett to his feet, he propped the man against the wall, then sent him crashing to the floor with a hard right that deepened the cut on his cheekbone.

Carlo sprawled on the carpet, his blood staining the fabric. He lay very still, and Paul, thinking he had killed the man, quickly regained his senses, a feeling of relief flooding him when he realized that Bennett was breathing.

There was a faint, almost imperceptible sound on the far side of the office.

Turning quickly, Paul saw Ian MacDonald leaning against the closed door. Apparently he had witnessed at least part of the fight, neither of the antagonists having been aware of his arrival. Even more startling than his presence was his appearance. He was gaping at the fallen body of his assistant, completely absorbed by the spectacle, his eyes glassy and his rapid breathing shallow. It was obvious to someone who had learned of his character peculiarity that he was in the grip of his voyeuristic trait, and his expression was that of a gladiator who had himself just won a smashing victory.

All at once he became conscious of Paul's stare. He raised his head, grew pale and although his fear immobilized him for a moment, he recovered before the younger man could move toward him. Evidently afraid that he too would be subjected to a beating, he reached for the doorknob, ready to shout for help if he should be attacked.

Paul continued to stare at him.

"You had no right to do that," Ian said, barely able to speak.

"You had a good time, did you?" Paul asked, his voice brutally contemptuous.

Ian was unable to reply.

"Which of us were you, Bennett or me?"

Again there was no answer.

Never had Paul felt such disgust for another human being. Mac-Donald's ugliness, which had always been a symbol to him of evil strength, was reduced to a petty shabbiness. Momentarily stripped of his power, he was revealed as a pathetic little man who was the victim of his own impotence.

Recognizing the other man's loathing and scorn, Ian seemed to shrink still more.

Paul glanced down at his hands, realized his knuckles were skinned, and was so surprised to discover he felt no physical discomfort that he laughed aloud.

Ian took a firmer grip on the doorknob, ready to hurry out into the corridor should it become necessary. "I can testify for him," he said hoarsely. "I saw what you did."

Paul walked around the desk, picked up the switchblade and drove the knife deep into the wood of the desk. "For a great many reasons," he said, "Bennett isn't going into court, and neither are you, MacDonald."

Ian began to recover his courage. "If you think you can walk in here and attack—"

"There are all kinds of attacks," Paul cut in.

Ian caught his breath.

Paul nudged Bennett's body with his toe. "At least he's man enough to lay a woman when he's given the chance, and he fights his own battles. Maybe he's a dirty fighter because he doesn't know any other way."

Certain now that he would be assaulted, Ian opened the door.

Paul reached past him and closed it again. "When I'm speaking to you, don't walk out on me. It isn't polite."

Ian shrank against the door.

Paul rubbed his chafed hands, almost as though he were washing them.

The gesture appeared to fascinate the older man, who stared at the other's hands.

Paul was able to read his mind. "I wouldn't soil my fists on you, MacDonald," he said. "For all your front, and your money, and your power, you're a sad punk, a nothing." Opening the door wide, Paul stalked off down the corridor, and although he did not deign to look back, he knew that MacDonald had suffered a devastating blow.

Most of the secretaries and other employees in the executive wing had gone to lunch, but the few who remained stared wide-eyed at Paul. Apparently they had heard the sounds of the fight but had not dared to intervene, and even now they asked no questions as they watched him.

He went to his own office, where his secretary was nowhere in sight, so he scribbled a note to her: "Send the belongings in the cartons on my desk to me at home."

Retiring into his own office, he quickly donned his jacket, and when he washed his scraped hands he looked at his reflection in the mirror. The only signs of battle were a scratch on one side of his neck, where Bennett had clawed him, and a red spot on his cheek. Even his hair had not been mussed, and there was no need to comb it.

Clothco, he thought, could mail him his terminal salary check; for that matter, he didn't care if he never received it.

The lunch-hour traffic was heavy, and Paul's taxi crawled through midtown, but there were fewer cars in the Sixties, so he reached his own apartment building without further delay. Using his key to let himself in, he thought Barbara might have remained in bed, so he did not call out to her as he walked to their bedroom. The door was still closed, so he opened it softly and stepped inside, then stopped short.

Barbara was sprawled on the floor directly in front of him, an overturned vodka bottle and a pool of dripping liquor on her dressing table. She had passed out again, and he started toward her, intending to carry her to her bed; but for a second time he halted, his flesh crawling.

In her right hand Barbara was clutching a pair of thick kitchen scissors, and only a miracle had prevented her from suffering severe injury when she had fallen unconscious. But the deliberate damage she had inflicted on herself was bad enough. She had cut off most of her hair, and there were blond tufts everywhere, on the table, the floor and even on her bed. Only ragged clumps remained on her head, most of them only a fraction of an inch long; elsewhere her scalp was bare. The mutilation had destroyed the last illusion of her beauty, and she looked like a broken, discarded doll.

"For the past ten days I couldn't decide whether to stop seeing you altogether, so I made excuses whenever you telephoned." Marni could not sit still and wandered around the living room of her apartment, straightening the pictures on the walls and aimlessly moving ashtrays.

Ian MacDonald sat very still, making no comment, watching every move she made.

"I finally decided I wasn't being fair to you or to myself and that I owed you the courtesy of hearing anything you might want to say."

This was Ian's opportunity to take the offensive, but he did not respond to the challenge.

"There are so few of us in freelance modeling—no more than about four hundred who actually earn a living at it—that gossip makes the rounds fast. Everybody heard that Barbara Howell had a mind-blower breakdown and was taken off to a sanitarium somewhere in Connecticut. I don't know if it's true that she was carted away in a straitjacket, but details like that really don't matter. All I do know is that she's in a bad way."

Ian resembled an unblinking, stone gargoyle.

"And everybody knew that Paul had left Clothco and had taken charge at the Howell Agency again. It wasn't just a rumor, you understand, it was definite information, and I had it straight at least twenty-four hours before Paul called to tell me."

He managed to find his voice. "The grapevine is the same in any business," he muttered vaguely.

"I was on a job when Paul tried to reach me, and by the time I got back to him, he'd spoken to a number of others. I knew right off that he was upset, but he wouldn't admit it until we had dinner together that evening."

Ian couldn't help growing rigid when she confirmed what he had assumed, that she and Paul had been seeing each other.

"Anyway, he told me a long, complicated story. I listened, naturally, for his sake and Barbara's, as well as my own. I found some of it hard to believe, but if I believe anything in this world, I'm sure Paul wouldn't lie to me." Marni forced herself to sit facing Ian, and, flicking back a long strand of hair, looked straight at him.

He made a visible effort to compose himself. "I was distressed when I learned that Barbara had been placed in a sanitarium, but that's irrelevant. Far more to the point is that I can't—I refuse to accept responsibility for her breakdown. Ever since I first met her she was unstable, and she had been drinking heavily for a long time. In fact, I've been assured by two physicians who specialize in treating alcoholics that any serious emotional crisis could have upset her very precarious balance."

Marni listened intently, her lovely face masked.

"*Any* crisis," he repeated. "Any upset that threatened her security."

"Then you deny—"

"So far I've denied nothing." Ian showed a little more spirit. "I spent months trying to win Barbara's goodwill and place her in my debt. It was absolutely necessary that she vote her Schwartzman-Burns stock my way if I was to gain control of the store. The entire future of a major American corporation depended entirely on the whims of a neurotic woman. Clothco wasn't in an enviable position."

"Neither was Barbara," Marni said. "She must have felt frightful pressures."

"Her collapse proves she did." Ian tried to smile, but his voice was ragged. "Did Paul Howell tell you how she made a game of her vote, tantalizing Clothco—and Louis Burns, too, I dare say?"

"Paul didn't put it that way, but he did mention that she couldn't or wouldn't make up her mind for a long time."

"She delayed beyond the point of endurance. A company worth four hundred million dollars was being endangered by an alcoholic who wouldn't give anyone a direct answer."

"I hadn't looked at it that way," Marni said.

"The method I chose to force her hand was rough, and I admit it. Without making excuses, we had tried literally everything else, including her husband's persuasion. I hope he told you about that."

She nodded.

"What we did was unethical, raw—call it what you will." Ian's manner hardened. "I don't know how to be more honest than this. I'd do the same thing again to get those proxies."

"I'm not blaming you, exactly, for that part. Since I'm inclined to be soft myself, I admire a ruthless quality in someone else. As you know."

He was pleased, but remained wooden-faced.

"There's something else I don't consider your fault. Paul didn't know any details, except for a couple that seem significant, like Barbara purposely underdressing the day she went up to your apartment."

He felt he could make a point by seemingly giving it away. "Seminudity no longer means what it did. I'm astonished by the merchandise our stores all over the country are selling."

"A girl like Cleo doesn't mind appearing in public half-naked," Marni said, a sudden bitterness in her voice. "It's her stock in trade these days. But Barbara didn't go in for that sort of thing, not in all the times I saw her. I wouldn't know whether she had a reason for wanting to look provocative. Maybe she was just looking for a charge. But I can say to you what I couldn't mention to Paul. A woman who is asking for trouble, even if she's neurotic, doesn't deserve all that much sympathy when the trouble comes."

: 346

Ian saw himself gradually assuming control of the situation. "Not many woman would be fair enough to see that side of the coin."

"On the other hand," Marni said, "it doesn't justify what happened to her. Especially when the same trick has been played on others."

His hopes suddenly collapsed.

"That's the part I don't dig. Paul wouldn't tell me any other names, but he insisted he could prove Barbara wasn't the only one who went up to your place, and—"

"There's no need for him to prove it. There were others," he muttered.

"Is that—what you had in store—for me?" Color stained her cheeks beneath her makeup base.

His head jerked upright as though pulled by a rope. "Never!" he said fiercely.

"I—I didn't think so. Not after all this time. I mean, you had plenty of chances."

"Not you, Marni!" He peered hard at her, the fear that she might not believe him plain in his eyes.

She accepted his declaration with a slight bob of her head, and her belief in his sincerity became stronger when she saw his relief. One question remained unanswered, however, and she knew it had to be faced. "But why did you and Carlo do it that way with the others?"

Unable to tolerate her steady gaze, Ian rose and walked to the nearest window, where he stood for a long time, looking out at the wall of another building. "I had to have some way," he said at last.

All at once Marni understood the hints and innuendos she had shrugged aside for months. His ugliness, which had sparked and fueled his long drive for power and wealth, had left him crippled in his private life. But, if she interpreted him correctly, she provided the ingredient that restored him, that made him whole again.

Ian realized she was displaying no overt hostility toward him and reacted instantly. "Save me," he begged. "Only you can do it."

Marni told herself she was insane to listen to him, much less consider his request. But she knew people with worse hangups, and it was flattering to think she enjoyed that much power over another person, particularly someone as important as Ian.

He sensed her hesitation, and knew this was not the moment for subtlety. "You won't regret it," he said.

She was torn and tried to weigh the offer.

"I'm not rushing you," Ian said. "Take all the time you want, and if you'd rather not see me while you think it through, I won't pester you. I'm not trying to defend myself, and I think, by now, that you know me."

"I thought so too, but these past few days I haven't been so sure."

"Nobody is selfless," he said. "I want your happiness because I can find my own through you. In return, I'll give you whatever in this world you want, and I can't imagine anything that would be beyond my reach."

"I guess I do need a chance to sort things out in my own mind, Ian."

He followed his gambler's instinct and, picking up his hat, walked to the door. "I won't try to get in touch with you again. Whenever you're ready, I hope you'll let me know. In an imperfect world, you and I, together, could be invulnerable. But if you're willing to settle for less with someone else—or with no one—I'll wish you well." Making no attempt to touch her, he bowed and quickly departed.

Marni couldn't decide whether she felt sorrier for Barbara or for Ian, but she suspected she was devoting so much emotional energy to herself that there was very little left for anyone else.

Andrew Reilly rarely entertained at home, so most of his guests were seeing the Victorian town house for the first time. Built by his grandparents before the turn of the century, when only the daring had moved as far uptown as Murray Hill, in the east Thirties, the carved woodwork, marble sinks and elaborate chandeliers once again were fashionable. The home-decorations editor of *Chic* had assured her employer that his house was smashing, and Reilly privately considered the pendulum swing fortuitous. A man who hated to spend money had cause to rejoice when the three hundred guests who filled all three parlors, the dining room and library all chanted the same admiring refrain.

Even Reilly's competitors had to admit he was lucky. There were rumors to the effect that he had owned a share of Schwartzman-Burns stock, which he had voted in favor of the Clothco acquisition, and had been rewarded with a larger number of shares in the chain-store corporation. But the publisher, having quietly sold his stock for a handsome profit, was in a position to tell anyone who broached the subject that he considered it inappropriate for the owner of any fashion magazine to hold a financial interest in a corporation that could benefit from such an association.

"Freedom of the press," he said, "is far more important than money."

The many skeptics in both publishing and retail merchandising noted, however, that Clothco consistently placed more advertising in *Chic* than in any other fashion magazine.

None of the cocktail party guests mentioned the subject, but a number of significant glances were exchanged when the host and Ian MacDonald greeted each other with the warmth that good friends habitually reserve for one another. There were other fascinating phenomena to observe too. Paul Howell, making one of his first social appearances since his return to the active management of his agency, escorted one of the most glamorous of his models, Marni Kendall. And as all readers of the gossip columns knew, not only had Paul left Clothco abruptly, but Marni, who appeared in the company's major advertising, was no longer seen in public with MacDonald.

Virtually all of the guests except the cynics were disappointed when the seemingly explosive situation produced no fireworks. Those who witnessed the confrontation of the trio reported that mutual constraint was evident in the greeting of Howell and MacDonald. But they were on speaking terms, and both were civil. As the cynics pointed out, they needed each other: Clothco was a major employer of models, and so both men were forced to observe the amenities.

What surprised everyone was the warmth that Marni and MacDonald displayed toward each other. Their parting, obviously, had been friendly, and they spent several minutes chatting amicably. The only crumbs of comfort the gossip-mongers could pick up resulted from their interpretation of Howell's reaction, and they were agreed that he appeared somewhat disgruntled while Marni and MacDonald conversed.

The arrival of the other star in the Howell Agency stable diverted the attention of the entire assemblage. Cleo arrived in a white velvet cocktail suit with a neckline slit to the waist, and immediately took the spotlight away from Marni, whose Russian Cossack outfit, although original, was less spectacular. The girls, it was noted, were barely on speaking terms, although Paul made a valiant effort to bring them together. Those within earshot said that Cleo was haughty and somewhat condescending to her rival, while Marni's attitude appeared to be one of bored indifference.

Didi Martin's observation quickly made the rounds. "Cleo is the most beautiful woman here, and who can blame her for knowing it? Marni lacks the ultimate chic that makes a great model, and it's strictly her own fault. Natural beauties are so common that no one gives them a second glance, and if Marni is too lazy to develop more than a pretty face, she deserves oblivion."

Those who were aware of Didi's personal tastes raised their eyebrows and interpreted her remark in their own way. She had been rejected by Marni, but was either getting what she wanted from Cleo, or at the least hadn't lost hope.

Within an hour of the time the party started the crush became so great that it was impossible for anyone to see beyond his immediate neighbors, whose drinks and lighted cigarettes constituted a peril. In spite of the autumn chill, windows were opened, but the odors of perfume, tobacco and liquor remained strong. It became increasingly difficult to obtain a drink from the waiters who tried to make their way through the throng, and trays of canapes vanished as soon as they appeared from the kitchen. But no one left, and the party was a great success.

Paul was too busy to drink, and had no interest in food. At least a score of major clients, both active and potential, were on hand, and he made it his business to have a talk with each of them. Eleven of his major models were in attendance, along with several whose careers were expanding, and he had reason to feel satisfied with his representation. The thought occurred to him when he saw Ian MacDonald that it was good to be his own master again, but he was too preoccupied to dwell on personal matters. The Howell Agency, now that he was in command again, was enjoying its greatest boom, and he hoped to increase his gross income by at least thirty percent within the next six months. The goal was ambitious, but he needed the challenge to compensate for his lack of a private life.

He wasn't complaining but at odd moments had to admit that his present existence was lonely. Since he was swamped with work he had little time to spend with his children, and they were continuing to live with their grandmother. They came home for a visit one night every weekend, when he took them to dinner, and occasionally he felt he was failing as a father. But he took solace in another, brighter thought: in spite of his heavy expenses he was putting aside more money than he had ever before saved, and someday the children would thank him for it.

A casual exchange with the creative director of a large advertising agency promised to develop into far more, and Paul arranged for a meeting the following day at the agency. At that time, he was convinced, he would sell a team of models for a major campaign, and he quietly patted himself on the back.

Someone tugged at his arm as he tried to make his way through the crowd in one parlor to that in the next. "Paul, may I have a word with you?"

He frowned at Marni, who should have been making time on her own.

"Are you going to stay on here much longer?" she asked.

"I hadn't even thought of leaving." Her increasingly defeatist attitude annoyed him, and he told himself he had been mistaken when he had imagined they might share a future. Marni lacked the persistence necessary for real success, and he couldn't help wondering if she might be far more dependent a woman than he had believed.

"Have you made any plans for later?"

"Not yet. Has something come up for you?"

She nodded.

"Then go ahead, by all means." He hoped he wouldn't have to spell out the obvious, that there was nothing personal in his gesture of acting as her escort. She was free to leave whenever she pleased.

"Thank you." Marni hesitated for a moment. "I don't want you to get the wrong idea."

"Why would I?"

"Well, I'm going to dinner with Ian."

Paul was too startled to reply. He had assumed that she had seen the last of MacDonald, and he couldn't imagine why, knowing what she did about him, she would consent to go anywhere with the man.

Marni answered his unspoken question. "Clothco is still my biggest account."

He smiled cynically. "You're protected by contract, and you've been producing for them. There's no law that says you've got to date the president."

"I don't want to be cruel to Ian."

Paul saw the handwriting scrawled in large graffiti on the wall. "You know the score, honey. Do whatever you think best."

"Oh, I have no intention of getting involved," Marni said. "It's just that I feel sorry for him."

Paul patted her on the shoulder and released her. Watching her as she pressed through the crowd to join MacDonald, who was waiting for her in the foyer outside the parlor, he took another drink from a tray carried by a passing waiter.

"Beauty and the beast." Fran Black came up beside Paul and stood with him as Marni and MacDonald disappeared in the direction of the front door.

Paul grinned at the girl, then looked her up and down in swift approval. Her improvement had been steady, and, thanks to a less blatant approach, she was earning a steady seven hundred and fifty dollars a week.

Fran was unaware of his scrutiny. "Some chicks don't know when they're well off."

"I think she does know what she wants, although she doesn't realize it yet."

"That slob? With all she has to offer?"

"He has a few assets himself," Paul conceded, sipping his drink.

"Sure, tons of bread, and enough influence to keep a model busy for as many hours a week as she wants to work." Fran was contemptuous.

"I've been given to understand he also exercises quantities of personal charm."

"When a man has what you've got, which is everything, you couldn't be jealous of that psycho."

"I'm not," Paul assured her, speaking too quickly.

"Take it from a gal who knows, he's nothing but a dirty old man. I wouldn't go out with him no matter what he offered me."

"Some people can't afford your kind of independence."

"It's way out, isn't it? Money stops being important to some of us when we begin to make it, but others can't ever get enough. I'll bet when our friend looks at him, she doesn't see how ugly he is. All she sees are those beautiful millions."

"You've changed."

"Like you just said, I can afford it."

"In many ways."

Fran ran a hand down her figure-hugging, silk knit dress. "If I get any skinnier there won't be anything left."

"There's enough," Paul said.

She studied him, trying in vain to determine whether his comment was professional or personal.

"You've been one of the more pleasant surprises of this past year. Stop in the next time you come to the office, and we'll see what we can do to put you into the four-figure-a-week bracket."

Fran's laugh belied her suave appearance. "Isn't this great? When I sleep with somebody these days, it's because I want to. And you know who did it?"

"You."

"I didn't know enough to do it by myself. Two people helped me. You. And Barbara. How is she?"

Of all the many friends and acquaintances at the party who knew Barbara, Fran was the first to mention her name to Paul, and he felt certain that only a few were being circumspect. The others had forgotten his wife's existence. All the same, he could report so little that he found Fran's interest embarrassing. "I go up to the sanitarium twice a month, but most of the time she refuses to see me."

"Jeez, then she's as bad off as ever?"

"No, the doctors tell me her hostility is a healthy sign, proof that she's improving."

"I don't get it."

"Neither do I," Paul said bleakly.

The girl hesitated. "Will she ever be okay again?"

"So they say, provided she learns to accept a life without liquor and can find something as a substitute emotional prop. But the director of the sanitarium can't give me as much as a target release date, so I'm afraid Barb will be there for a long time."

"That's tough."

He shrugged.

"All around, I mean."

"She's getting good care, the kids are fine and I'm surviving." He wished she would change the subject.

"That's what I mean. Surviving isn't living, and I'm not being fresh or nosy." Fran moved closer, which wasn't difficult in the crowd, and lowered her voice. "Like, you have to want it, the same as everybody else. But a chick expects romance, and that's dead the minute she hears you've got a wife locked away."

Her bluntness was unsettling, but Paul had to admit there was an element of truth in what she said.

"Maybe I could help, and being Barbara's friend and all, we wouldn't have to pretend to anything that wasn't."

Paul was simultaneously amused, flattered and alarmed. "Thanks all the same."

Fran did not recognize the rebuff. "Oh, we wouldn't be doing each other any favors. When a man oozes your kind of masculinity, I wouldn't be making any sacrifices."

He realized the offer was sincere, made within the limitations of her emotional and intellectual sphere. "It wouldn't work," he told her gently.

"Because of Barbara?"

"Exactly." This was the easiest way out; she would be hurt if he indicated that mere beauty, as such, no longer attracted him. "But you're a good kid."

Fran accepted the rejection cheerfully, and after exchanging a few desultory remarks with him, allowed her attention to be claimed by a photographer who, six months earlier, would have snubbed her.

Paul watched as she and the photographer tried to work toward the bar that had been set up in the dining room. In girls like Fran, he thought, beauty was an acquired characteristic, and her sincerity made up for her lack of finesse, even though she would never reach the heights of the model who achieved the ultimate glamour, the sheen that the uninitiated mistakenly identified as charisma.

There were remarkably few in the business itself, he reflected, transferring his gaze to the ravishing Cleo, who was holding court on the far side of the parlor, capable of recognizing the artificiality of beauty. Regularity of feature and form had become routine in an age when all but the most impoverished were denied medical and dental care, balanced diets and the knowledge that enabled them to stay healthy, vigorous and slender.

Yet it was strange that beauty, although a man-made product, was essential to the well-being of the individual who had acquired a taste for it. Paul continued to ruminate, still staring at Cleo, until she became aware of his gaze and raised her head. For a long moment their eyes met and held, and then he pushed through the crowd surrounding her.

"Gentlemen," he said, "you're denying my top model the oxygen she needs for her lung and skin care." Casually tucking her arm through his, he led her away.

The dark eyes set in a deep fringe of false eyelashes regarded him solemnly, but with a hint of humor. "When you want to, you sure can pour it on."

"Watching you perform just now gave me some ideas. I think we can put you out of reach of any other girl on any agency's list— for the next five to ten years."

"I'm listening, baby."

"The crowd here is starting to thin out. Do you have a date?"

"Nothing I can't break."

Paul indicated with a gesture that he would meet her in the

entrance hall, and after they thanked Andrew Reilly for his hospitality, they found themselves on the sidewalk.

"If you can take another drink," Paul said, "I know a nice little bar a couple of blocks from here, on Madison. The only trouble is that you'll freeze without a wrap. There isn't a taxi in sight."

Two young men in a passing automobile slowed down and whistled at Cleo.

"That," she said, "is what keeps me warm."

They walked rapidly, arm in arm, saving their breath but enjoying the wide-eyed stares of virtually everyone they passed. They created a minor sensation at the crowded bar, where they found the last unoccupied stools and grinned at each other.

"This is like old times," Cleo said, expressing the thought in both their minds.

Half-forgotten habits returned automatically, and Paul ordered without asking what she wanted to drink. "You really brought that party to life," he said. "It was a great exhibition."

"I didn't do too badly," Cleo replied complacently. "It was a matter of timing, you know, and I got there just as everybody was starting on the second drink."

"I noticed." He enjoyed her complete, dedicated professionalism. "It's that outfit, too. Every time I think you've run the whole gamut, you come up with another. Where did you get this one?"

"Didn't Little Miss Muffet tell you?"

"Who?"

"The one who wasn't frightened away by the spider, but went off with him instead."

"What does Marni know—"

"Her roommate Rosalie made this for me. She does most of my things. She's good for me because she has imagination, she can achieve the high-couture look—and she's cheap. And I give her creations plenty of free advertising, so everybody is happy and satisfied. Except Little Miss Muffet, who is so freaked out that she's thinking of taking an apartment alone. Rosalie wants to get rid of her and would like me to move in, but I'm not sure. I'm thinking about it. One of the reasons it appeals to me is that it would be a kick in that bitch's pretty teeth."

"It's beyond me why you two should dislike each other so much," Paul said. "There's plenty of room for both of you at the top."

"Where I'm headed, which is nearly in outer space, there's only room for one," Cleo said calmly.

"Then there should be even less friction. Marni isn't giving you more than token competition these days, and you ought to know it. Katya told me in so many words that she was getting married and retiring because you had taken three of her best accounts. Marni didn't land one of them."

"I can recite all the logical arguments too, but that doesn't stop me from hating her."

The longer Paul dealt with beautiful women, the less he understood them.

"It's her holy-holy attitude that revolts me. She acts like a professional virgin, but anybody who runs around with that Mac-Donald isn't. I don't know or care if some of the rumors I've heard about him are true. But it wouldn't surprise me if he and Marni lock themselves in a bathroom together and watch dirty movies. They're both the type."

Paul's laugh was strained. "Maybe you aren't being quite fair to her."

"As fair as she's been with me!" Cleo retorted. "You weren't around when the monokini campaign was being organized, so it could be you haven't heard the whole story. Marni had first crack at that assignment, but she didn't have the guts to let the world see her boobs. She not only turned down the assignment and criticized me for accepting it, but she had the damn nerve to be jealous when the campaign clicked and brought me more personal publicity than anybody ever dreamed I'd get. You'd think it didn't take courage on my part to stand half-naked in front of the camera."

"I'm sure Marni is enough of a pro to realize there's a difference between exhibiting yourself as a model and giving up your personal standards of decency."

"Don't you believe it, baby! If only a tenth of the snarky remarks she's supposedly made about me are true, she's been a bitch. Why, even today, when we said our hellos at the party, she kept staring at my neckline until I wanted to shout at her that I wasn't wearing a bra, and what of it?"

"Marni's interest wasn't unique. Look around you right now. Everybody at the bar is playing the same guessing game, and that fellow directly across from us is going to fall into his drink if he leans any farther."

A haughty, remote expression appeared on Cleo's face and hardened as she struck a modeling pose; then suddenly she slumped for an instant, affording some of the bar's other customers a brief half-glimpse of her breasts. Straightening again, she pretended to be unaware of the stir she had caused, but under her breath she murmured, "They're all alike, and sometimes I just can't resist."

Not asking whether she wanted more to drink, Paul ordered another round.

"Some of them either recognize me or they'll realize later who I am." Cleo tried to sound matter-of-fact but could not conceal her pride.

"That's just what I want to discuss with you. The time will soon be ripe to change your image."

For a moment she thought he was joking and laughed; but a glance at his face told her he meant what he said, and she was stunned. "You've got to be kidding."

"Not unless you want to be stereotyped. You and the monokini have done each other a great deal of good, but you've used it for all the mileage it's worth. A girl needs many qualities to reach your standing, and I'm not decrying what you've done. Far from it. But if you want to hold at your present level—"

"I want to hit one-fifty an hour. I want to be way beyond everybody else!"

"All the more reason to change. You can't do it unless you break the mold and create a new one. Katya did it, remember. She went from pagan to little girl to the sophisticate."

"Well, that was Katya," Cleo said reluctantly, but listened with care.

"When a leader is lucky, she can hang onto an image for as long as two years. But sometimes the cycle moves faster. You've had dozens of monokini imitators—"

"But there's only one original. Brigitte Bardot was the first to wear the dish-mop hair, wasn't she? And she's still doing it, even though millions of others—"

"She's an actress, not a model, so the problem is different. And just for the record, it was Juliette Greco, the singer, who introduced the long, free-floating hair style. I might add that she had the good sense to change when the mob copied her. Stand outside any midtown subway station and look at the girls pouring in and out who try to look like Elizabeth Taylor. You couldn't count them. Which is why an Elizabeth Taylor changes her appearance every few years—and remember, an actress can keep her mold longer than a model because her kind of talent gives her beauty a different dimension. But any leader, any innovator must be prepared to change when the crowd starts treading on her heels."

Cleo took a large swallow of her drink, then stared thoughtfully at the white sapphire ring on the forefinger of her left hand, its size magnified by her black skin. "This would be a real gasser, after calling Marni a coward, but you don't suppose I'm one, too?"

"I'd be very much surprised if you were."

"I've used a technique that's worked; and maybe I'm in a comfortable rut now, but I hate the idea of changing."

"That's something only you can decide," Paul said. "You know the stakes. But I'll tell you one thing. I won't be able to get you one hundred and fifty an hour unless you keep yourself in the front ranks of the trend-setters. Nothing else will get you the personal exposure in the magazines and on television."

"I know." She studied the ring from different angles as she held her long hand up to the light. Then, abruptly, she turned to him.

Again their eyes met, and both were aware of the current they generated. Paul realized he still wanted her, that he had never rid himself of the feeling that their affair had been interrupted rather than terminated, and it was obvious that Cleo was still attracted to him too.

Both of them thoroughly aware of what they were doing, they allowed their hands to creep closer on the bar.

"What do you think I ought to do, baby?" she asked.

He covered her hand with his. "Let's make no snap judgments. We don't want to rush into this on impulse."

"Between us," Cleo said, "I imagine we know what we're doing."

Paul made an effort to keep his mind on business. "If we can, we'll work it out ourselves. But if we're in any doubt, we can consult some makeup and hair stylists and maybe a designer or two."

"You tell me, baby, and I'll do it."

"I won't let you down again." He tightened his grip on her hand.

She dismissed the possibility with a casual wave of her free hand. "Like I tried to tell you, nobody can ring the chimes every time."

Paul indicated with a glance that others at the bar were eavesdropping.

"Let's get out of here," Cleo responded, draining her glass.

He paid their bill, and again they enjoyed the attention they created as they departed. "I can think of a few fairly quiet restaurants," Paul said.

She shook her head. "There are some things that can't be settled in public. Unless you're especially hungry, I can fix us sandwiches."

Their knees touched in the taxi, and neither wanted to draw apart.

Cleo let her velvet skirt ride high on the perfectly formed, dark thighs that were accented by her sheer, gleaming stockings. "There's one change I won't make. I can't abide long skirts."

"Pants are fine on you, particularly the see-through kind, but you should never wear dresses or coats that hide the best legs I've ever seen."

"Do you really think they're that good?"

He rested a hand on her thigh. "You know damn well what I think."

"From way back, baby."

He removed his hand, and, their tension mounting, they did not speak again until they reached the apartment.

Paul looked around the living room as Cleo snapped on lights. "That painting, whatever it may be, is new."

"It's my portrait," she said, and laughed.

He stared at splotches of black paint on a stark white background. "It looks like something out of an ink-blot test."

"That's what I thought, but there was this artist who flipped for me, and the next thing I knew, he gave it to me. I would have thrown it away, but I found out that his paintings sell for thousands in the Fifty-seventh Street galleries. I hear he's hooked on a Chinese ballet dancer now, and I want to make sure of it before I take the painting down to the galleries and sell it."

"I guess it takes all kinds."

"Not men. There's only one kind. You want a drink?"

"I've had plenty, thanks," Paul said.

"More than plenty for me. If I hadn't had a little too much, I wouldn't say what I'm going to. You want to know something, baby? That nutty artist painted me—or what I must have looked like to him—for the same reason I made such a smash hit in the monokini. The segregationists have it all wrong when they say that black men go for white women. A white girl doesn't fit a black standard of beauty, and a black man couldn't care less about her. But the white man is something else. He really digs the black girl."

"He may find her attractive for herself, not because she's black," Paul said.

"Don't you believe it, baby. I don't. My freaky artist is honest. A black model or a yellow ballerina? Any day, any night. But a white ballerina or model, forget it."

"What got you on this antimiscegenation kick, Cleo?" He thought it possible that she had consumed far too much.

"I'm all for it. Mix the races!" She jumped onto a footstool in a parody of a soapbox speaker, looking incongruous in her rich, daring white velvet. "Races of the world unite! You have nothing to lose but your color. And you're making Cleo wealthy and famous." Tilting her head to one side, she glanced at Paul. "You won't buy that, I suppose."

"I'm willing to be convinced," he said.

Cleo stepped down from the footstool and, standing with her feet planted far apart, cupped her hands under her breasts so they were in danger of popping out through the low-cut slit. "Right now, today—not tomorrow, maybe, and certainly not next year— these are the best publicized boobs in what we occasionally call Christendom. Their shape is okay, but they wouldn't make Elsie the cow jealous. They aren't the biggest, they don't sit on a shelf by themselves and they don't bounce more than moderately when I walk. A half-dozen of your own girls at the agency have better, including that slinky ex-bra model you were so chummy with at the party tonight."

It pleased him that she had noticed him with Fran Black, so he concluded that her interest in him had been consistent.

"How come I get all the glory? That's simple. Because my boobs are black, which gives every white man who sees them in print or in person an extra charge."

"Apparently you think you've found a secret black power weapon," Paul told her, "but you go too far."

"Like hell I do. The monokini wouldn't have gotten off the ground if Marni had modeled it, or even Katya."

"I'll grant you the brotherhood of man isn't around the corner," Paul said, wondering why she had raised the issue. "But your insistence on the erotic importance of skin color puts you in the camp of the old-time southerner."

363 :

"Everybody is in that camp, whether he admits it or not. Including you, and I'll prove it. You thought I was great until my color stopped being a novelty, and then I bored you."

Until now he had been fairly dispassionate, but her accusation angered him. "I was worried about my drunken wife, my job with a power-crazy crook, all kinds of things. You kept me potent longer than any other woman could have done—"

"Because I'm black."

"Because there's something in the shape of your body that I find sexually beautiful. The shape, not the color. Just as you've always wanted me because of the way I'm put together, not because of the shade of my skin."

"What makes you so sure?" Cleo demanded.

Paul stared at her in exasperation for a moment and started to reply but checked himself. Instead he went to her and, reaching inside her neckline, brought her bare breasts into the open.

Cleo stood with her hands at her sides, neither protesting nor making any attempt to halt him.

"This," he said, "is why I'm positive." Bending his head, he slowly kissed one breast, then the other, caressing the nipple with his tongue.

Cleo clasped his head, her fingers becoming entwined in his hair. "I kept wondering," she murmured, "how long it was going to take you."

Not until later, after they had made love and fallen asleep, awakened because they were hungry and prepared something to eat in the kitchen, did they return to the subject of Cleo's career. She was wearing a tiny, elasticized version of the monokini she had made famous, and as Paul watched her moving around the kitchen, his mind gained the upper hand from his already satiated desires. "I dislike changing your image as much as you hate it," he said. "Are you quite sure you want all the bother?"

"I want to be a footnote in history. The most beautiful woman of her time, even by white standards."

"I'm beginning to formulate some definite ideas," Paul told her, "but you may need time to fit yourself into your new image and start enjoying it."

She interrupted her activity at the counter and, coming to him, rubbed her bare body against his face. "That's skin, baby. Feel it?"

"You bet," he replied enthusiastically.

"That's the only thing I've got that I can't change and wouldn't if I could. As for the rest of me, inside and out, I'm a chameleon."

Chic ran a series of provocative advertisements in more than four hundred newspapers, announcing the inauguration of a new feature. The unisex look was anything but new, the editors declared, but out of the deliberate similarity in dress and appearance cultivated by the modern man and woman had come something unique. Some couples grew closer in spirit and intellectual approach as well as in looks, and this blend was creating a new breed, that of "the most handsome couples in the world." *Chic* intended to run a series on the couples who best exemplified these traits, the advertisement said, and would explore their lives and personalities in depth.

No one in the know was surprised when a photograph of Paul Howell and Cleo appeared on the cover of the next issue of *Chic*, accompanied by a sixteen-page feature of both photographs and text. Even the most jealous of their enemies had to admit they made a strikingly handsome couple. Paul's hair was a little longer than he had worn it previously, and the cut of Cleo's was precisely the same, line for line. He wore a single, small hoop in one ear, and in her ears were larger versions of the same earring. Their twin wristwatches had been made to order for them, as had their carved signet rings of green jade.

Casually dressed in what *Chic* called sports attire, they wore identical, transparent shirts, belts that were four and a half inches wide and a new type of footgear that looked like a cross between high-heeled cowboy boots and sandals. Their elephant-bottomed pants were alike, too, but in them was a subtle difference: Paul's trousers were made of a solid, opaque material, while Cleo's were transparent.

The article about them, written by Didi Martin, was exceptionally frank, as were the photographs. Chic's readers were told that "these candidates for the title of the most handsome couple on earth," as Didi called them, were living together openly, in accordance with "the new morality." Although Paul dressed conventionally for his work as "the most successful of models' agents," and Cleo, "the highest paid model in history," wore what was neccesary for her assignments, they took great care to present an identical appearance at all other times and spent all of their leisure in each other's company.

Their intimacy, Didi wrote, had caused a few small flurries of jealousy at the Howell Agency, but most of the models had accepted the association with good grace, "realizing that no one could compete with Cleo, the greatest beauty of her era."

Some of Paul's old friends were dismayed by a photograph showing the couple, attired in identical pajamas, eating breakfast in a king-sized bed. Although the article made no mention of Barbara, it was common knowledge that Paul was still married to her and that she continued to languish in a sanitarium.

The Chic cover and spread increased the intensity of the spotlight in which the couple bathed. They were besieged for autographs in restaurants and at theatrical openings, and police had to extricate them from an enthusiastic crowd when they attended a football game at Yankee Stadium. Several clothing manufacturers brought out items for both men and women that were copied from the originals seen in Chic, and a number of others quickly jumped on the bandwagon.

But there were disadvantages, too, that became apparent as the new way of life stretched into months. Returning to Cleo's apartment one evening after making a joint appearance at Schwartzman-Burns to help promote a "total look" line of garments in which they had been given a financial interest, they undressed wearily, stripping down to identical monokinis.

Paul went off to the kitchen to mix nightcaps, and when he returned to the bedroom he found Cleo stretched out on the white satin sheets that had been a gift of a household linen corporation. She was staring at the ceiling and, without turning, reached out a languid hand for her drink.

"Sometimes," she said, "I think I know how Adam and Eve must have felt."

Paul laughed as he sank into the double easy chair across the room. "I hate to say I told you so. But establishing the new image was simpler than keeping it up."

Cleo closed her eyes for a moment, and her false eyelashes fluttered on her face. "I'm not complaining, really."

"You shouldn't, and the same goes for me. We're cleaning up on the licensing of our names."

"Oh, I'm duly grateful for all that money in the bank, baby."

"You've moved so far ahead of every other model in the business that no one will ever catch up. And what astonishes me is the shot in the arm that all this idiocy had given the agency. I knew we'd do better, but our bookings have almost doubled." Paul's laugh was a trifle forced. "Obviously, beauty is its own reward, to coin a phrase."

"I've been doing a lot of thinking this past month or so." Cleo propped herself on the pillows, sipped her drink and regarded him thoughtfully over the rim.

He immediately raised his guard. "Oh?"

"Where do we go from here?"

"The twins routine is good for another six months, I believe," he said.

"And then what?"

"I've been thinking, too. The image is paying off so well that even my mother-in-law has become reconciled to our living in sin.

She was actually cordial to me last night when I picked up the children for dinner. But we can't go on like this indefinitely."

"That's what I mean, baby." Cleo inserted a cigarette in a long ivory holder and reached for her new lighter of white gold.

"I can't do anything until Barbara is released from the sanitarium. That hasn't changed."

"You still haven't told me what the doctors said to you the other night."

"Her therapy has reached a crossroads," Paul replied, "and if she keeps improving, they'll turn her loose in another year, more or less."

"What do they mean by crossroads?"

"I'm coming to that. Barbara will never be able to make it alone, emotionally. She's reached the point where they'll either have to start orienting her toward me. Or if not me, toward her mother. I wanted to pick the right time to take all this up with you, but you've brought up the subject, so we'll make it now. I believe they should guide her toward her mother."

"What a life for both of them."

"I know, and I'm sorry, but I'm thinking of you and me."

Cleo inhaled deeply. "What about us, baby?"

Paul grinned at her. "A formal proposal will sound a little foolish as well as superfluous, but if that's what you want—"

"It's the one thing I don't want," she said.

His smile vanished. "Something seems to have gone wrong with my hearing."

Cleo slid down the bed, sat on the edge and reached out to him, putting a hand on his bare thigh. "There's nothing wrong with your hearing, baby, any more than there is with you, or with us. We started this his-and-hers act as a sort of huge, cynical joke—"

"Knowing it would pay off."

"Which it has, in more ways than we realized it could. Just look at us, baby." She climbed onto his lap so they could see themselves in the large mirror over her dressing table.

"I've got to admit we look pretty snappy together." He regarded their reflection with satisfaction, then began to fondle her.

"Don't start anything. Not yet." Cleo made an unsuccessful attempt to free herself. "We've actually become all the things that Didi wrote about us, which is freaky. We're not only an honest-to-God beautiful couple, but I sometimes begin to wonder which of us is which."

"I always know," Paul said, "and any time you're in doubt I'll be glad to set you straight—"

"Stop." She caught his hands. "I'm not talking about our sex together. I don't know what makes us click, and it doesn't matter. I *do* know I'll never find better with anyone else, and neither will you." She squirmed out of his reach and retreated to the bed.

Paul was startled by the tears he saw in her eyes. "If everything is so great, and it is, what's the problem?"

"Thank you for wanting to marry me. Maybe you really don't care about color, or if you do, it's caring in a good way. But I won't marry you. It isn't that I don't want to. I can't."

"Because of Barbara?"

"I could make a good case for her. She's the mother of your kids, and she needs you more than I do—"

"What about my needs? And yours?"

"But she isn't the real reason. You and I could make out fine all by ourselves. The beautiful couple live happily ever after. Except that I want children when I marry."

"Naturally."

"A baby that's half coffee and half cream wouldn't be beautiful to anyone except us. The world would say he was ugly." Cleo shivered and briskly rubbed her bare arms. "The blacks wouldn't accept him, and neither would the whites."

"You're exaggerating. Tolerance and understanding are growing—"

"Not fast enough, and I won't subject any child of mine to an even worse hell than I've known. Look at me—"

"I am," Paul said.

"Not like that, and don't try to humor me. I've made it big in the white world, all the way. But I'm the freak who is accepted because I can't be ignored. And the blacks hate my guts because I'm not up on the ramparts, fighting for the cause. When I've had enough of beauty and glamour and have stashed away enough bread to satisfy me for life, I'll rejoin them and they'll take me in. Which they'd never do for our child, any more than your people would. You and I just aren't *that* beautiful."

"You're being defeatist," Paul said. "Now, listen to reason—"

"No!" Cleo clamped her hands over her ears. "I won't listen to anything. I've been whirled around by false values, but I won't let it happen to my kids. One of these days you and I will have to accept reality, and separate. But not now, not tonight, so I don't want to listen or talk or even think about what's ahead."

Paul wanted to insist they make no arbitrary ruling, but he was afraid she was right.

Slowly Cleo extended her arms to him, unheeded tears streaking her face. "While we can, let's do our thing. Love me, baby!"

The scents of the world's most expensive and exotic perfumes blended, making the air heavy in the Designer Salon on the second floor of Schwartzman-Burns, which Clothco had just expanded and redecorated for the second time in two years. The crystal chandeliers and trim in 22-karat gold, the brocaded wallpaper and oriental carpeting provided an opulent background, and even the folding chairs that had been set up for the fashion show were padded with the best quality of genuine velvet plush. It was axiomatic that when Ian MacDonald was making money, he spared no expense.

The guests made the decor fade into insignificance, however. The ladies were dazzling in their furs, jewels and exorbitantly expensive designer original dresses, and the men, almost without exception, wore custom-made suits and shirts, neckties and shoes. Because of the subdued cocktail party preceding the fashion show, it was inevitable that everyone wanted to outshine all the rest.

Even the representatives of the press had made an effort, although it was suspected that Andrew Reilly's double-breasted Edwardian suit had been made for him at cost by a publicity-hungry tailor. Didi Martin was there in a working capacity, but instead of her customary little black dress, she was wearing a silk tunic and pants in fireman red. Her few friends claimed she was trying to impress her newest companion, a very young, very feminine model upon whom she pressed drinks.

The only woman in the salon wearing unrelieved black was Audrey Burns, who was spending the winter in New York after the sudden death of her husband. She took care not to make herself conspicuous, so she was forgiven her widow's weeds, and most of the guests made a point of paying their respect to her. No one was surprised to hear that she had grown tired of her Florida exile, and it was agreed that, as she had moved south strictly to accommodate her husband in his retirement, there was nothing to prevent her from following her own desires and moving back to her cherished apartment in the city, where she entertained in such charming style.

Already seated on the center aisle in the first row, accepting no drinks and ignoring the hubbub around him, was an exceptionally handsome, well-groomed foreigner who, it was rumored, was a Chilean millionaire. The cognoscente were uncertain whether cattle or copper was the source of his wealth, but everybody who was anybody knew he was the latest suitor and constant escort of the show's star model, Cleo. It was rumored on the best authority that he had not only bought her the new emerald solitaire she was wearing, but had surprised her with a birthday gift of a small mansion in an old, wealthy Long Island community that was trying hard to pretend its newest citizen was not black.

Ian MacDonald was everywhere, the jovial host incarnate, and

371 :

the sharp-eyed were certain he had gained considerable weight since his marriage. He looked and acted like a man who had found contentment in life, and a small minority argued that his features had softened somewhat, making him less ugly. Those who did business with him, however, swore that he was unchanged.

His former assistant, Carlo Bennett, now employed by a real estate tycoon with a weakness for models, took care to avoid MacDonald. Bennett was allegedly the author of a scurrilous remark about the host's sex proclivities, and the comment quickly made the rounds, even though everyone protested that it couldn't be true.

MacDonald's wife, the former Marni Kendall, appeared to be living proof that the story of his weakness was a lie. She looked lovelier than ever in the new sable coat thrown carelessly over the shoulders of a suit made for her by a leading designer, and she exchanged smiles of genuine affection with her husband whenever he hurried past her.

Marni gave the same answer to everyone who asked her whether she missed modeling: her new life kept her too busy, and when Ian traveled, visiting Clothco's out-of-town stores, she usually went with him. If she was vague about her activities when in the city, it was only because she had nothing to tell. There was so little to say about a life in which she slept late, met a friend at a fashionable restaurant for lunch and then went shopping before returning home to change for her evening with her husband. Ian was the least demanding of men, and made no protest when she spent most of her nights alone in her own bedroom, but she felt the least she owed him was fresh makeup and a dress he admired when he came home from work.

One person, overlooked by most of the guests, was concerned about Marni, but kept her own counsel. Barbara Howell, who stood by herself in a corner of the salon, sipping unadulterated tomato juice, watched Marni take her third martini in a half hour but knew that a warning word would be a waste of breath.

Of all the guests in attendance, Barbara herself had undergone the greatest change. Although the new mink her husband had bought to celebrate their anniversary was luxurious and her dress was appropriate enough, even according to the demanding standards of the fashion editors present, Barbara was no longer beautiful, probably because she had stopped caring. Her hair was an unashamed gray, and she made no attempt to hide the wrinkles in her forehead, around her mouth and at the corners of her eyes.

Life, she had learned, was a series of compromises, and it was enough that she look presentable in public, that she not let down her dashing, successful husband. The cattiest of her old acquaintances said they weren't in the least surprised that she had returned to him after his notorious affair with Cleo had ended; where else, they asked rhetorically, could a woman just released from a sanitarium find refuge?

None of them knew how Barbara felt, and they would have been surprised to learn that she literally didn't care. What Paul had done during her incarceration was of no concern to her. All that mattered was the present, and she cast frequent, surreptitious glances at the entrance to the models' dressing room as she waited for him. Not that she was impatient. After all, she understood the demands of his business. But she wouldn't feel like mingling with the crowd until he joined her.

Paul, meanwhile, was going through his usual preshow routine backstage. Still handsome and youthful in appearance, he nevertheless was dressed and groomed with the conservatism befitting a man who owned his own thriving cosmetics company and had become a partner in a major Seventh Avenue dress house. But the Howell Agency was still his keystone, and he took care to say precisely the right word to each of the models preparing for the show.

He smiled steadily, his manner bland, and only his eyes betrayed his total lack of personal interest in beauty. His approach was completely professional, and he was quick to spot the slightest flaw. Some of the younger models exchanged significant glances when he paused for a somewhat longer chat with Fran Black, whom he was allegedly grooming for stardom. But the veterans quickly disabused the newcomers: Paul Howell, they said, wouldn't bother with any woman, and besides, Fran was his wife's best friend.

The veterans were right. Paul felt literally nothing when he hugged Fran, even though she was wearing only a half-bra and bikini panties. "You look great, honey," he said automatically.

Fran thanked him, then asked, "Would you and Barb like to join us for dinner tonight? My new boyfriend says he knows you. Dave Bernstein."

Paul smiled faintly. "Sure, I remember him. I'll ask Barb."

Fran giggled. "Imagine me going out with a professor."

"I can imagine anything," Paul told her, and headed toward a cubicle at the rear of the dressing room, half separated from the rest by a curtain.

There Cleo, wearing only her model's smock, was making up before a large mirror, and although she did not turn, she knew who had joined her.

Paul watched her dispassionately. Their emotions drained, he and Cleo could converse or remain silent when together, and he still didn't know whether their present relationship was a mere void held together only by fading memories.

"I hear the dress Rosalie designed for your spread is a knockout."

"*Life* spent an hour photographing me in it yesterday for their cover," Cleo replied, affixing a long, curled strip of false eyelashes.

"Tell them I'd appreciate a set of color proofs."

"I already did." Cleo sighed deeply.

"Are you tired?"

"Out on my feet. But Ramon insists that we fly to Vegas tonight for the weekend."

"I don't want you showing up with smudges under your eyes Monday," Paul warned.

"Have I ever?" she replied. "Don't worry, baby. The job comes first."

"That," he said, "is why you're still number one."

Making his way back through the dressing room, he went out

: 374

into the salon, and after accepting a bourbon and water from a passing waiter, he went to the corner where he had left Barbara.

Her relief was obvious, and taking his arm, she clung to him. "I've been waiting to speak to Marni, because Ian is with her," she said.

"Would you rather skip the hellos, Barb?" Paul asked solicitously, finding it comforting that any human being could lean on him so heavily.

"It really doesn't matter. Whatever is important to you."

"Then we'll wait. There's a very intricate deal cooking, and it's better that Ian comes to me."

A famous, fading motion picture star who had been hired as the commentator went to her microphone, and the guests hurried to their seats, many elbowing their way to places of vantage.

Loudspeakers began to play a soft, insidious number, the lights were lowered and Cleo appeared in the glow of a spotlight on the runway. Her long hair fell to her waist in thick waves, and the soft, clinging chiffon of her evening gown showed off every line of her sinuous body, although she managed to make everyone present conscious of the gown itself.

There was a sharp burst of applause, led by the Chilean, as she started up the runway, and photographers' flashbulbs flared. Buyers and wealthy customers bent to make notations on their programs, and Rosalie James, the designer, smiled contentedly in the darkness.

"Beautiful, isn't she?" Barbara Howell asked her husband.

Paul made a mental note to tell Cleo to wait a half-beat longer before she started her walk. "Very feminine," he said, and automatically looked for the next model at the head of the runway.

A Note About The Author

Noel B. Gerson was born in Chicago in 1914.
Educated at the University of Chicago, he has
been a newspaper reporter, was a captain in U.S.
Army Military Intelligence during World War II,
and has for a number of years devoted his full
time to the writing of books, one hundred of
which have preceded *Mirror, Mirror*.

withdrawn

Mirror   Mirror

Gerson, Noel B.